SEDUCTIVE INNOCENCE

"You would help us?"

She sounded as if he'd asked her to eat a live toad. "Aye, fair Giselle. For a price."

She crossed her arms and narrowed her eyes. "I should have known. What price? What do I have you could possibly want?"

He pulled her close and lowered his head toward hers. She offered no resistance. Her hands went around his waist and her hips rocked against his. Her lips were soft and sweet beneath his and he was gentle, savoring her. He played her expertly and with an awkward innocence she followed his lead.

With a groan, he crushed her to him and his kisses deepened, became more demanding. She responded with growing passion, clutching him to her, until he was dizzy with her.

He kissed her neck and she arched her head back, seeking his caress. "Woman, have mercy."

She opened her eyes and looked at him, like someone dreaming coming awake. "Nay, m'lord. You are the one without mercy."

QUEEN OF THE MAY

Denée Cody

Zebra Books
Kensington Publishing Corp.
http://www.zebrabooks.com

ZEBRA BOOKS are published by

Kensington Publishing Corp.
850 Third Avenue
New York, NY 10022

Zebra and the Z logo Reg. U.S. Pat. & TM Off.

First Printing: June, 1997
10 9 8 7 6 5 4 3 2 1

Printed in the United States of America

This book is for Fred and Betty Runkewich.
Thank you for your unwavering support and encouragement.
I love you both.
As always I would like to thank my fellow Word Wenches,
who help keep me sane (most of the time):
Margaret Conlan, Barbara Kidneigh, Anne Avery,
Mary Gilgannon,
and Jessica Wulf.

Chapter One

The child had been wolf-killed, gnawed until there was raw flesh with nothing in it of yearning humanity. Where her face was unmolested Alexander saw a nascent loveliness. He caressed the pale gold of the girl's hair with shaking fingers.

"Sweet Jesu," Geoffrey whispered, and turned from the sight.

The child's mother, her face leaden with shock, was wrapped in inflexible sympathy by the village women, who joined their grieving to hers. Those thankful it was not their child laid out for view were careful in their consolation, knowing the next accident, illness, or famine could claim their own.

An old man, toothless and stooped, shuffled over to Alexander. "Never hear of no wolf doin' so ugsome a thing. 'Tis devils' work, like ravens crying the moon at midnight.'' Those near enough to hear crossed themselves, nodding agreement.

"It's a wolf, no more than that," Alexander said. "It can be hunted and killed."

Muttering to himself, the man retreated to spread his belief to a more receptive audience.

"Patience, Cousin, he but speaks in fear," Geoffrey said.

"And will make others fear his phantoms. The reality is serious enough without giving it shadows as well."

The tiny cottage, with a thatched roof that rained down mouse droppings and other filth, was windowless and dark, the dimness broken only by bleached light beyond the open door. A wolf killing in the village was cause for fear and Alexander had come immediately from the castle on the hill. The entire village of Wolfhurst, one hundred and thirty souls, frightened and fascinated by the violent death of the child so close to their dwellings, gathered to hear what he would do. Word spread quickly when the new lord appeared, the baron himself, whom most had caught no more than a quick glimpse of in the week since his arrival. What sort of man was he? What would he do to protect them from a wolf so bold it took one of their children in the fields?

The villagers were plain men, accustomed to the heft of a hoe or plow in their callused hands; men who caught an occasional hare or a deer taken surreptitiously from the king's vast forest surrounding Wolfhurst. They never hunted wolf. In their eyes prowled dread, and in their fear they looked to Alexander for their deliverance. They gathered in the shelter of the door and whispered their distress into his ears. The cottage grew warm with the press of bodies. Alexander shouldered his way through them to the muddy yard, where they followed.

The earlier rain had diminished to a cold drizzle, turning the November morning gray with a sky full of bruised clouds. The weather had been wet all last year and again this year, until the few crops rotted in the fields. The grain harvest was as low as anyone could remember. In spring men kept their fear to themselves. By summer they whispered it to each other. By autumn it was spoken aloud as the horror teased the edges of their brains. Famine.

Alexander feared with them that the winter would prove a hard one, especially at Wolfhurst, where no surplus had been stored against lean years. The steward in charge in his absence had sold all for profit, greedy for the coin in his hand, giving little thought to the empty bellies of the folk who plowed the land and planted the seed and gathered the crops, year after year.

They looked to Alexander to rescue them from the predator who killed the child, and from the hunger that stalked their minds and would soon lay claim to their bodies. Somehow he must find enough to sustain them through the coming months, until a new crop could be planted and better husbanding of resources put into practice. All of his careful plans would come to naught if the weather played havoc again next year. There was coin to buy grain enough to see them through this winter, if there was grain to be had. Another year as bad as this and no amount of silver would buy rye or wheat that did not exist.

He took a deep breath and then another. The day smelled of wet fields and apples laid out in orderly rows under the eaves; of sharp autumn-ale and onions braided and hung for later use; of brambles in the hedgerows ponderous with sweet berries. Harvest smells, full of promise, but he knew the apple crop was light, the cider and perry and ale would be gone before Lent, half the onions were rotten at the core. Only the pastures had flourished under the relentless rains, and so the herds of sheep were fat and prosperous. But peasants did not eat mutton. The wealth of the sheep was in their wool, which clothed his household and his villeins. Any surplus was sold for a tidy profit. From the tattered garments he saw on most of his serfs, Alexander guessed his steward sold the wool, reserving little for use at Wolfhurst.

"What will you do?" Geoffrey asked.

"Kill a wolf, before it kills again."

"Do you need my help?"

Alex studied his cousin, so newly knighted he fairly shone with the honor, young and tall and angular, with the dark hair that marked most of the de Mandeville family. Alex, bastard born, with hair so fair it was almost white, little resembled any of his kin. Geoffrey was the hope for the future, the de Mandeville pride, heir to the great earldom of Essex. He could not risk injury to his kinsman in so routine a task as this. "Nay, you return to Wolfhurst. Someone with authority needs be there, now that I've rid myself of my steward." He slapped his thigh with his leather gloves and prowled an area beneath the oak tree where their horses were tethered. "Damn, this is untimely. I meant to leave for Blyth Abbey in the morning, to see if they have grain for purchase. This can't wait. I'll be gone a day or two, no more. Do you think you can handle the duty?" He watched with hidden amusement as his cousin struggled with an answer. Any man of mettle would rather be hunting, but he'd just offered Geoffrey the chance to play lord of the manor, and that was more tempting still.

"I'll prove worthy of your trust, Coz."

"I've no doubt of that."

They stood in companionable silence, the tall, fair warrior and the dark youth, solemn with the occasion. They didn't make light of death in this unpredictable land, where it was often sudden and seldom easy. There was no stray laughter about the village this day. The villeins came as a group from the cottage, the dead child's father in the vanguard. The motley entourage came to a standstill near Alexander. They would want to know what he planned to do to keep them safe. The child's father stepped forward, those gathered behind him murmuring their encouragement, relief they were not expected to talk to the baron making them enthusiastic with their suggestions.

"M'lord, we are afeared of this beast."

Alex said, "Show me where the child was found, then I will track down this wolf and kill him. This I swear to you."

There was relief in their faces, but doubt as well. He was unknown to them, having arrived at Wolfhurst so recently. Though he'd been their baron for over a decade this was the first time he'd been to England since leaving with King Richard on crusade twelve years earlier. Richard was three years dead and his brother, John, now ruled.

Upon his arrival Alexander found a castle fallen into disrepair, fields and meadows producing far below capacity, and a village full of poor and near desperate folk, in far worse condition than one poor year could do, all for lack of a strong arm to guide the daily life of village and castle. He despaired of making sense of the accounts left by his steward.

Swinging into the saddle, as much to put some distance between himself and the others as to signal his departure, Alexander settled the horse beneath him with soft sounds. "My cousin Geoffrey will be in charge in my absence. You will obey him as you would me and take him your problems and concerns."

They nodded their understanding, accustomed as they were to having men over them. A wiry boy ran ahead of their horses, leading the way across the harvested strip-fields to the edge of the tenacious forest. The others followed, a solemn mass of humanity relieved to have passed this burden to their baron. They found the site in a recently scythed barley field where the child died, near where scarlet-hawed thorn trees edged the oaks. It was quiet, with a few geese fattening on fallen grain and a small stream chuckling over stones nearby. Alexander crouched in the sandy loam, his long fingers sifting through the barley stubble, looking for a clue that would tell him in which direction the wolf disappeared. Wolves were not solitary killers and usually avoided men's steadings. Only in winter, when deep snow made hunting difficult, or in summer famine did wolves take human prey near settled areas.

The land around Wolfhurst was unfamiliar to Alexander. In the week since his arrival he'd ridden twice into the oak weald, taking a hunting hawk as companion. It was the solitude Alexander craved, as some men coveted wine or women. There was something haunted about the vast wood that stretched between Wolfhurst and Nottingham, fifteen miles south. Dark and primal, it was a world he visited uneasily, knowing he did not belong. Here dwelt wolves and other dangers, known and unknown, seen and only felt with uncanny sureness. Here dwelt fairy folk and demons, here witches chanted under moonlight and outlaws ran. The wood was a mysterious, wild, unredeemed place and it called to him seductively. He was a warrior, a man accustomed to danger. His dread of the forest was as old as mankind, and he was determined to master it. Whenever he rode into the depths of the wildwood he felt he was being watched and the conviction increased the farther he ventured from the castle. It was the very mystery of the place that drew him in, though he'd not had the nerve to spend a night alone there.

The fear was foolish since he knew what dangers to expect and was well able to defend himself. It was the fear of being lost in the dark, the remnant of a childhood experience, that made his skin crawl and his eyes keep track of the light of day, to be sure he returned safe to the familiarity of stone walls before the sun set. Now he was about to go alone into the wildwood, to follow where the wolf led, and hope his skills were great enough to find his way back to his castle.

He'd never before killed a wolf nor been close enough to one of those elegant hunters to lay ax or spear to it. Nor had the need. The few times he saw a wolf or two in the distance he watched them watching him, and envied their freedom. He found the wolf's track and stood, hands on hips, studying the footprints just visible in the soft soil. It was a large animal, but there was something peculiar about the track.

"Is that the beast?" Geoffrey asked.

The village boy whistled low. "Look't the size of the brute."

"See the mark of this rear foot," Alex said, pointing. "It doesn't run in a line with the others, nor is it set as deeply."

"Crippled?" Geoffrey asked.

"It would explain why it takes such easy prey."

"It has a two-hour lead on you," Geoffrey said. "Even with a track to follow, after this much time how will you catch up to it?"

"I won't." Alexander looked into the thick of the woods, where the trail disappeared into the autumn-stained forest. Somewhere in that darkness the wolf lurked. "Never track an enemy into his own realm, where he has the advantage of knowing where to hide. I'll make him come to me. A hungry wolf will eat carrion. I'll set out a sheep carcass. Then I wait."

"What if, while you're waiting, it finds another child?" Geoffrey spoke quietly, but Alexander heard the worry in his voice.

*   *   *

When the earth grows autumn-dark and folk huddle near
their hearths, then wolves loom their echoing voices into
the fabric of the night. Men hear that feral chorus and
rise to shutter windows, and hang wolfbane at their doors.
Women bundle small children onto their laps and croon
lullabies, to ease their own fears as much as those of the
wide-eyed bairns. Folk avoid the woods of a night when
wolves are running.

Wolf crouched in the dimness under a mossy rock that
formed a shelter in the forest. The pain in his hip kept
him from sleep, as it had often since Boar laid it open.
The pack leader, that proud old bitch, stayed with him the
first day. She brought him a hare she caught, but he lay
too close to where man lived and the hunters moved on
to their secluded den far in the hills. It would be hard
enough to survive the winter without his help. They could
not feed him too.

He had been weak before, in long winters of deep snow
when hunting was exhausting. He'd survived. The leg
would heal. He would hunt again, and lie in the summer
sun with pups crawling over him, pulling at his ears, pounc-
ing on his tail in mock attack.

He had been run off his last kill just as he began to feed.
Now, in the night, he snuffled in the dark. Good hearing
and sight and a sharp nose had Wolf. He saw the sheep.
The hot smell of blood tempted him. He knew the man
was there, recognized his fetid scent. The man didn't move.
Asleep? Or waiting for Wolf?

The night was filled with the scent of danger, but Alexander
dared not light his lantern. The moon, just past full, cast
pale light at the deep shadows among the trees. There was

no sign of the wolf and he began to fear his plan would fail. He resisted the urge to shift the weight where his legs had cramped. Damp oak leaves littering the forest floor smelled melancholy with the scent of the earth stooping down to rest, the ephemeral sweetness of a declining autumn clinging to the moist air. A late bloom on a rose gave its faint breath to the night. His woolen cloak kept the damp from his shoulders and back, and beneath its folds he tightened his grasp on the handle of his hunting-ax. It was keen-edged and the weight of it was familiar in his hand. He heard the hush of an owl on whispering wings and the nervous scurrying of small creatures in the dark. The wind tickled brittle leaves clinging to branches, raising a sound like the silk of women's feast-day gowns when they glided down the aisle of a church. He huddled deeper into his cloak.

He saw the glint of reflected light from an animal's eyes, but could not tell how far away or what the creature was. Then the wolf came into full view, its head lowered, massive shoulders bunched, mouth pulled back from hard, white teeth. A low growl escaped the wolf's throat as it gathered itself to leap. The animal was a dark mass of fury and slashing teeth.

Terror wove Alexander's belly into a hard knot. He whispered an *Ave* and tamped the fear down to a secret place. With a shout he braced to meet the impact. At the last moment he turned aside, burying the ax deeply in the wolf's shoulder. Howling, the animal fell away.

Alexander sprawled on the ground, gasping for air. Frantically he pulled his sword from its scabbard. There was no time to gauge how best to attack or defend himself. He turned onto his back and heaved the weapon above his chest. The animal leapt, and impaled himself on the blade, wrenching the weapon from his hands. The wolf died with a bloody spasm.

Alexander knelt in the damp oak wood. Only the ragged sound of his breathing, the savage pounding of his heart, confused the silence. Slowly the fear twisted. He felt cold. Even watching for the wolf, he'd been taken by surprise. He cursed himself for a fool to think he could hunt the animal alone without risk. When he tried to rise, the arm he leaned upon gave way and he noticed the wound near his shoulder for the first time. He sat down heavily and flexed his fingers, gingerly moving the arm up and down. The gash didn't appear deep, nor was it bleeding badly. He'd had worse by far. A sword did ugly things to a man's body and twelve years a soldier in Richard's wars had dealt him a fair share of such wounds. It would need stitching, but if he rode to Wolfhurst at first light, tomorrow would be soon enough.

He tore his short linen tunic into strips and bound the wound to stop the bleeding. Then he sat for a half hour or more, alone with the dead animal. Finally he stood and retrieved his lantern, and with steady hands lighted it. He stared down at the old wolf. It was a dark animal, the fur grizzled with long gray hairs over a black undercoat. He looked near starved, with a half-healed wound on one hind leg, but the massive shoulders proved the wolf had once been powerful. He could see the animal in his prime, racing across Nottinghamshire with the arrogant grace of a warrior. He set to the task of skinning the carcass. It didn't pay to think too much what the wolf had been before it became his adversary.

He started east soon after daybreak, down through the dense oak woods toward the hills and vale of Wolfhurst. The rain held off, the clouds cleared, and for the first time in a week candescent sunlight flowed through the bare branches of trees. It felt good to be riding through the warm countryside, the sun beating down on him. It was a day throaty with glory just to be alive. He had the wolf pelt tied to the back of his saddle, which made his horse uncommonly nervous. It would make a warm cover for his bed, and a reminder of the adventure. A man was said to take on the qualities of the animals he killed, whether it be bear or boar or wolf. It seemed appropriate, since he was baron of Wolfhurst. He realized for the first time the appropriateness of the manor's name. *Wolfwood.*

The wound in his arm had kept him from sleep and he grew sandy-eyed and irritable as the morning wore on. He'd tracked the wolf farther into the forest than expected, and now knew he'd taken a wrong turn and spent a good two hours lost. Finally, he found the landmark he'd been searching for. Another hour would see him to his castle, where he could have the wound tended, eat something, and sleep. He stopped his horse, suddenly alert to— what?—in the forest. Something, someone, lurking, watching. A primal chill slithered down his spine and he nervously clutched the pommel of his sword. The sun was bright in the meadow he was about to cross. Why he should feel menace now he did not know, but he'd not survived those years fighting in the Holy Land without learning to trust his instincts. Everything spoke of danger. He dismounted and used the horse to hide one side of his body, his shield held high to cover his chest and side, and walked forward slowly. In an instant he could either draw his sword and fight, or mount his horse and flee.

He was not looking at his feet. He felt the taut rope and knew in that instant what had happened but could not defend himself from the arrow that came hurtling out of the brush to bury itself deep in his thigh.

"God's feet!" He threw his shield to the ground and used both hands to try to pull the arrow free. It would not budge. He'd been caught in a poacher's trap, meant for a deer. His anger grew with his frustration. The damned thing would need cutting out. He'd heard these woods were thick with outlaws. It seemed one of the things he'd need do, after rebuilding his castle and feeding the village, was rid his forest of its trespassers. He made his way painfully up into his saddle, and cursing loudly, set off once more for Wolfhurst.

She watched from her high perch in the oak tree. It was seldom she saw one such as he, and her curiosity was roused. She saw as he tripped the rope and the arrow found a mark in his flesh. Her own flesh jerked at the impact. He remounted his horse but she knew he'd not make it far. The arrow, one of hers, was poisoned.

Chapter Two

"I like this not." John tugged at his beard and scowled, his thick dark brows drawn down to half obscure his eyes.

"I have no choice," Giselle said. "The trap was not meant for a man."

"He's a nobleman." John stared down at the man she'd brought him to. Even passed out on the forest floor there was an unmistakable arrogance to the man's hard-planed face. He'd be recognized for what he was without the more obvious trappings: the horse, the well-made sword, the shield with his family colors of gold and scarlet, the good quality of his wool cloak.

"Will you help me?" she asked, chewing on her lower lip.

John sighed. He could deny her nothing.

"Hold him still while I cut the arrowshaft. We can't move him with it sticking out of his leg."

The big man knelt and pinned his prey. With a sharp knife, she quickly cut through the shaft and flung it aside.

The arrowhead, tipped with wormwood, rendered the nobleman deeply unconscious, the poison working on his heart to slow its beat. She chewed her lip more vigorously. The dose was meant to fell a deer, a smaller animal, but she did not know how much, or how little, would prove fatal to a man. Would he survive?

"Hold this beast steady," John said, handing her the reins of the knight's horse.

Giselle did not like to be too near a horse. They were large, unpredictable, and undoubtedly stupid and bad-tempered. Gathering her courage, she did as he asked, taking the reins into her hands. Every time the horse moved, even to swivel an ear or twitch its tail, she jumped, jerking the reins, until the animal lowered its head and blew hot, grassy breath on her in a discontented snort.

John stripped the narrow-seated saddle—with its high cantle and pommel, meant to hold a knight steady under attack of lance or sword and large enough for one rider only—from the nervous horse and laid it on the ground. With a great heave of muscle and determination, he slung the knight over the horse's back, belly down, then mounted behind him. "There's room for you pillion," he said, holding out his strong hand.

"Nay, I'll walk." She was careful with John, knowing the depth of his feelings and wishing to be no trap for him. She stooped to retrieve the saddle with its wolf pelt. If the noble did not survive, they'd not want to leave it for his men to find.

Walking through trackless forest, crossing open meadow now and then, they came to the hidden limestone caves deep within the greenwood. Heavy shrub, sentinels of oak, a swift stream with a hidden ford, and superstition born of generations of people living dangerously on the edge of wilderness made the place nearly impenetrable.

John turned toward the largest of the caves in the complex and she called him halt. "Nay, take him to my dwelling."

He scowled darkly at her. "What's wrong with here?"

"We know not who he is. I'd speak with Robyn first, before chancing the man seeing too much."

"You think he'll recover?"

"Not if we stand here gibbering."

John dismounted and slung the noble over his shoulder like a sack of grain. Several men came forward to take the horse and lead it to the corral where five others were hobbled. It was a fine, strong animal and would be a welcome addition to their meager collection.

"What have ye found?" Alan asked. He leaned against a great rock concealing the entrance to the main cave, playing idly on an Irish harp, his long-fingered hand delicate on the strings.

"A half-dead noble. Giselle is of a mind to mend him."

"What wealth has he?" Alan asked.

"Not much." John made a sound of disgust in his throat.

Giselle stepped forward, her voice bright with indignation. "He killed the wolf who killed the child of the villagers. More than either of you took upon yourselves to do."

Alan eyed the man with interest. "He was alone?"

"He was," she said.

"Then he's either a great bloody fool, or brave beyond foolishness."

"He'll like be a dead brave fool soon, if you keep me much longer from tending his wounds," she said.

"Lead on, fair maid." John made as courtly a bow as he could manage with his burden.

She left the saddle for the others to deal with and hurried the short distance to the tidy cavern she called her own. John had to duck far down to get through the low entrance, but then the space opened up and he stood.

"Where would you have him?"

She pointed to her straw-filled sleeping pallet against the far wall. "Don't look at me like that. There's noplace else."

"There's the floor."

She slipped out of her cloak and shook it absently, ignoring him, her mind busy on the herbs and potions she'd need for her work. With a grunt the big man laid the other onto the bed.

"Is there aught else you'll be needing?" he asked.

"Where's Odin?"

"I haven't seen the brute. I'll have him sent over if I find him." John stood for a moment, awkward, his face masked in shadow. "Be careful, Giselle. He's not one of us. Call for me or one of the men should he wake. I like it not, you being alone with him."

"He's in no condition to be of danger and Odin will keep me safe."

He left with a final grunt of displeasure.

The cave was never warm. She'd grown accustomed to it over the years and worked with her sleeves pushed up past her elbows. A mat of woven rushes kept the fine, gritty dirt of the floor from infiltrating everything, and the tiny hearth set near the entrance, to draw the air needed to keep the fire burning, lay cold with yesterday's ash. The man would need to be kept warm. His body had much to battle without fighting the cold as well. She took her tinder and flint from their place near the hearth and quickly lighted the fire, laying dry logs atop as the flames grew. There was always a supply of firewood, just as she never wanted for food or any of the other necessities of life. They were payment for her healing skills, which she shared freely with the men and few women of her strange woodland family.

Little natural light seeped into her home and she busied herself lighting candles, placing them on stone outcroppings marked with layers of wax drippings. It was an extravagance when she was accustomed to one candle or the hearth fire to light her way, but she'd need to see clearly what she did when she tended him. Soon the cave glowed with light and smelled of honey from the fat candles stolen from the abbey church. Next she went to the tiers of stone shelves gouged into the rock and with sure hands took down a jar of dark glass filled with vinegar. Then she found the cloth bag filled with dragon's blood, to keep the wound clean and reduce the swelling, and lion's ear to counteract the poison. From a wooden chest she took a pile of clean linen squares and strips, and from the leather purse at her girdle the gold case with its precious needles and the silk thread she used for sewing wounds. Robyn had stolen them for her and they were among her most prized possessions.

She poured a small amount of the vinegar into a wooden saucer and placed her needles and a sharp knife in it to soak. Robyn and the others thought her odd using vinegar to clean her instruments; another of her eccentricities they teased when they said it was a shame to use it so. They trusted her healing skills, so gave her what she needed, when they could.

The man moaned and moved restlessly. She knelt quickly by his side. She did not want him coming to before she had a chance to dig out the arrowhead and stitch his wounds closed. Yet it was a good sign that he did not lay as silent and pale as before. He wore no shirt, he'd used it to bind his arm, and she laid her hand on his hard, broad chest, feeling the beat of his heart. Slow, but strong. His skin was cool and felt clammy to her touch. She stuffed rolled blankets under his feet, to lift his legs, to keep the blood flowing to his heart and brain. She pulled the stout leather boots from his feet. He wore hose of a soft, closely woven wool dyed a light blue-green, a beautiful color, bright next to the dull greens and browns and grays favored by the forest folk; colors meant to blend into the trees and brush, to keep them hidden from prying eyes. His wool cloak of gold and scarlet would be welcome as bedding, but was too conspicuous to be worn. The boots were a great prize, one Robyn was sure to reserve as a reward for one of his men.

She removed his clothes until he lay naked save for his linen braies, but she'd seen naked men before and her mind was on his injuries. She washed her hands with the stinging vinegar then poured some into the wound where the arrowhead still hid. It was a small wooden head, but it was barbed to keep it from pulling free and she would need to dig it out. Taking the knife from its bowl, she firmly grasped the stump of the shaft with one hand and pulled, to see where the flesh needed to be cut away. Working swiftly and surely, her hands never wavered in their task. Beads of sweat broke out on her brow as she concentrated and she wiped them away. Soon the arrow was free. The wound was raw and ugly, but not deep and no important blood vessels had been severed. He'd not bleed to death. She cleaned it with more vinegar then began sewing together what she could. The man had scars crisscrossing his body. Most had seen the hands of a healer, others had not been sewn and left large, ugly scars. She wondered why they hadn't been tended to properly. She was proud of her neat, strong stitches. She left the best scars of all, Robyn's men often told her.

If a wound did not kill outright it was the infection that followed which most often proved fatal. Why some injuries festered and others did not was a mystery as vast as the heavens, and one she'd dearly love to know the secret of, for often as not a man died though the initial injury seemed trivial. She held a candle close and examined the area around the wound on his arm. There was little swelling, no red traces lancing off the wound, no smell of rot. It looked clean. Still she doused it with her vinegar, as the old woman had taught her, and stitched the jagged edges together. It was one of many strange ideas Maeve had, that dirt could make a wound sick. Giselle did what she'd been taught, without questioning the necessity of it. It never seemed to do any harm. Finally she was done, and bandaged him with clean linen.

She stretched, easing the ache out of her shoulders and back and hands. His color looked a little better. Once more she laid her hand to his chest, closing her eyes to concentrate on the beat. Strong, steady, but slow. He would sleep yet, for how long she could not guess. When he woke he'd be in some pain, but judging by older scars he was no stranger to that.

When she opened her eyes she was startled to see him watching her. His eyes were blue. As blue as a clear sky in June. She sat very still as the hand of his uninjured arm clasped her tightly by the wrist. He looked confused, and then the look cleared and a sort of joy seemed to wash over him. His eyes fluttered shut and he slept again, not so heavily as before, and with a smile carved on his lips. Carefully she pried his fingers from her wrist. He had not fully wakened, had not truly seen her. She wondered what made him smile.

He was beautiful, she knew then, seeing him for the first time as a man and not wounds to be tended. Broad at the shoulder and deep in the chest from years of wielding a sword; narrow at hip and waist; long and strong of leg. He was no longer a youth, but neither did he show much age, a few fine lines around his eyes where he squinted against the sun, or etched there by laughter. His face was well made and pleasing to look upon, with straight nose and high cheeks and a mouth that looked as though it could as easily laugh as shout. His hair was fair, like the tassels of ripe wheat under the sun, but dark brows and lashes, and those amazing eyes. She wished he'd open them again, just so she could be sure the color was as intense as she remembered.

Absently she ran her hand over his chest and down the muscled belly to his hip, then back again, stroking lightly, enjoying the warmth of his skin beneath her fingers. She brushed hair away from his eyes. His hair was soft and clean and the stubble of his beard rough. Her thumb traced the curve of his upper lip and his smile deepened. She skimmed the back of her fingers across his cheek and down the strong column of his neck to where the muscle met the bones of his shoulders. She would try to keep him alive.

With a sigh she parted from him, and careful not to disturb his injured limbs, she pulled a wool blanket over his near-naked body. The man's clasp had been so strong she knew a twinge of fear. John was right. This could be a dangerous man. She needed Odin near to feel safe. She pulled her cloak from its peg, and with one last glance over her shoulder, left to eat her supper in the large communal cave and find Odin.

Alexander expected a few centuries of purgatory. He was surprised to find himself in heaven, especially since he could not think what he'd died of. But there was the glow of soft light and scent of honey. Most of all there was the fiery-haired angel. Though they'd failed to win Jerusalem from the heathens, the misery he'd endured to fill his Crusader vows had earned him heaven after all. There were some questions he'd like answered and wondered if it was impertinent to expect God himself to answer. Perhaps he'd ask the angel, when she returned. Her touch on his body still lingered. A very sensual angel she'd been, and wondered if that were possible. Mayhap the Saracens with their idea of heaven filled with women to give men pleasure were right after all. He was confused. He was tired. He would sleep, and when he woke, he'd ask his questions of whomever happened to be waiting for him.

She found Odin half hidden under one of the tables, waiting for the odd scrap or bone to be tossed his way. "There you are, you traitor," she said.

The huge, black, one-eyed dog stood at her approach and wagged his tail vigorously, making happy whining noises in his throat.

"Who is the traitor?" Robyn asked, with laughter in his voice. "You leave before dawn, tying the dog down so he can't follow."

She squatted beside the animal, who licked her face joyously, and lifted his right front paw. "I don't want him running far until this is better." She turned his foot to look at the pad that had been torn open. It was healing well. "Another day or two should see him back to his mischievous self, and since I'm not going far for a few days, I'll keep him with me. I thank you for your care of him."

"He's easy enough, and well mannered, but 'tis plain for all to see he's your dog." Robyn tore a leg and thigh from a roast goose, and after tossing the dog a hunk, tore some off for himself and chewed loudly. "Sit and eat. John Little tells me you've had an adventuresome day."

She sat and quickly filled the wooden bowl at her place with pieces of venison. There was no bread, but there hadn't been all week. What the villagers didn't have, they couldn't share. Robyn and his followers had only what they hunted, or were given, or could steal. It was an unbendable rule of Robyn's that they stole only from those who could afford the loss, or those who oppressed the common folk. Of course, those robbed did not appreciate the distinction. She filled her cup with ale and settled to her food. She'd always had a healthy appetite, but then she was no small and dainty woman. She was tall, strong, and well able to care for herself, as she'd learned of necessity she had to be.

Though twenty-odd men shared their exile with Robyn, none were truly her family. None were bound by blood ties to protect or succor her. Yet many were as dear to her as any family could be, and she trusted them with her life, if not her happiness. It was a hard life for a man, harder still for a woman, to live half wild in the greenwood, never knowing when or from whom betrayal would come, living in fear of discovery, their safest place this echoing series of deep caves, and safe only so long as the law did not find them.

She did not complain. Maeve, knowing death would soon claim her, had brought Giselle here six years earlier, when she'd been no longer a child but just barely a woman, and left her under Robyn's guardianship. She'd known only Old Maeve before then, and at first the crowd of folk worried her. But she'd grown accustomed to them and had quickly won her place among them, for she'd brought with her all the skill in healing Maeve had taught her. It was the life she knew and she endured the hardships because there was nothing else to be done.

Most of the men had already eaten and the long, rough table was nearly deserted. The sounds of dice games and knives being sharpened at a whetstone wove into the night and the light of fires threw dancing strange shadows on the cave walls. She preferred her small, snug abode to this, but here she sought company when the loneliness threatened too heavily. Robyn waited patiently for her to ease her hunger and thirst, quietly picking food from between his teeth with a sliver of bone from the goose leg.

"Where's Marian?" she asked.

A puckish grin spread across Robyn's face.

Giselle rolled her eyes. "You two. You're insatiable."

"I left her warm and sleeping and happy."

"Is she holding her food better?"

"A little. How long will the sickness last?"

"A few weeks more, then she'll feel fine for a few months. It won't be difficult again until the babe grows large."

"I wish I could find a safer place than this, before the child is born."

"We'll keep them safe." She put more assurance into her voice than she felt. Babies died under the best of circumstances. Though their lives were comfortable enough, there were no luxuries, and the constant threat of discovery made everyone tense. Robyn seldom admitted to fear. But the safety of his wife and child worried him deeply.

Odin lay with his big square head in her lap, his eye watching each morsel of food as it traveled from her fingers to her mouth. John and Alan joined them.

"Our Giselle has fetched home a rare prize." Alan winked, his mischievous smile lighting his dark face.

"So I've heard. I've sent men out to see if they can discover your nobleman's identity." Robyn leaned back, his powerful shoulders stretching against the dull green of his wool shirt. "He wasn't carrying much of value, except the sword and tack. No purse, no silk tunic, not even the golden spurs I thought no knight left home without."

"Mayhap he's an absentminded nobleman," Alan suggested.

"Or a poor one," John said.

"Do you think he'll live?" Robyn asked.

Giselle nodded. "He's doing well, considering. I don't

think the dose of venom I used on my arrow will do permanent harm, though he will likely sleep heavy through the
night. I'll know better in the morning, if he has no fever.''

"I've been meaning to talk to you about those arrows
of yours," Robyn said. "Do you think you can make some
that will purposefully render men unconscious but not kill
them?"

The idea horrified her. The poison was to kill an animal
quickly rather than have it wander wounded and suffering
into the forest. "Nay, I cannot be so exact as that. It is
impossible."

"But a small bit of this poison renders a man insensible?"

"I do not know; I do not make a custom of trying it on
men." There was a sharpness to her voice she meant as
warning, and Robyn, no fool, heard it.

" 'Twas just a thought I had. It could prove useful."

She drank her ale and glared at him over the rim of her
cup. Robyn was not a bloodthirsty man, merely pragmatic.
Still, she wanted no part in any scheme that might kill a
person, whether intended or not.

"What will you do if the man dies?" John asked, his
attention on Robyn.

"If he dies we'll have no problem. A body is easy enough
to hide. His folk will never find him and never know his
fate. He'll become another of those unlucky enough to
wander into the wildwood and disappear. 'Tis if he lives
that has me worried."

Giselle nearly choked on her ale. "What mean you by
that?"

"He's a nobleman. He's not like to look kindly upon us
should he live."

She sat silent, twisting the cup between her fingers. While
it was true they often took from the rich, they did not
bring them home to visit. "He need see nothing more

than my small place, until he can be escorted away, blind-folded so he cannot find his way back."

Robyn studied her. "He's a danger to us all."

Her anger matched her fear. "Do you say I should have let him die where he lay?" She held her hands out toward him, palms up. "These hands have never brought harm to a living soul. Do you not understand? It was my arrow that injured him and 'tis my duty to see him well again. I would not have the guilt of his death upon me."

John heaved a huge sigh and stood. "She's right, Rob. Giselle has never been bound by the same oath you get from your men. Asking her to let the man die is the same as asking her to kill him, and that you cannot do without defiling yourself more deeply than you would the woman. You'd put your soul to danger."

Robyn stood. "If it's that clear to you, old friend, I'll not contest it. But we will be careful with this unknown noble. He will learn as little as possible about us and he will be returned to his world as soon as he can travel. Tomorrow would be to my liking."

John and Robyn wandered off and soon Giselle was alone at the table with only Odin and Alan as company. "Play me a song, friend."

Alan lifted his harp and began to play an Irish tune, melancholy as only the Irish could be, about lost love and loneliness. She sighed, drank more ale, and rubbed the big dog behind his ears, losing herself in the sadness of the song. When the last note quivered into nothingness she smiled her thanks. Of all of them only Alan could touch her soul so profoundly, his music reaching places nothing else could. Handsome, smiling Alan was in love with Alice of Barnsdale. Poor Alan. How he longed for his cherished Alice. Soon, if all went well, they would be reunited. She suspected that even Alan did not feel the same ache of aloneness she did; the helpless sense of being an alien among others, unknown, untouched. For all his melancholy, he would have his Alice with him and they would be happy together. Before she made a fool of herself she rose, and calling the dog, made her way back to where she most belonged, among her healing herbs and alone.

The roses that clambered near the entrance to her cave were in the last burst of their blooming. She breathed deep of the spice and sweet of the flowers' heart and was calmed by their beauty. Whatever the cause of the strange effect her wounded nobleman had upon her, she could not afford to let it cloud her judgment. If he became a danger to the others, she would need to submit to Robyn's dictate. It was the survival of the group that mattered. She was but one of many, all dependent on the other, and loyalty the most necessary of virtues. One person in a mood to betray could destroy them all. Clouds raced across the face of the moon and the wind picked up, bringing a chill to the air. She retreated to her cave, Odin fast on her heels.

The man was as she'd left him, the single candle she'd kept burning illuminating the calm beauty of his face. Odin sniffed at the stranger in his den, his brow bunching with worry, and looked to her for guidance. She reassured the dog there was naught amiss, and the animal settled to his usual resting place, across the entrance to the small cave. Her bed was more than wide enough to accommodate two and she was not of a mind to spend the night on the hard rock of the cave floor. She stripped off her cloak and removed her soft buckskin boots and wool hose. Hesitant, she decided not to discard her gown, then climbed in beside the man. He did not move. His breathing was deep and steady, and when she placed her ear to his chest, his heart beat strong and true. No doubt he'd be gone tomorrow. With a sigh she settled on her side, her back to him, and slept.

* * *

The woman fit to the curve of his body as though they'd been sculpted together. He buried his head near her shoulder, where her hair lay in silken clouds. She smelled of green meadows and cold, clear water and the musty clean odor of the earth. With one arm around her waist he pulled her closer, the hard ridge of his desire pressed up against her back. Her skin was so soft and smooth under his hand, her breast full, that he sighed with contentment and did not wake.

With great care she disengaged herself from the man. She would find no more sleep this night and though dawn was an hour or more away, she was not tempted to stay late abed. Or rather, she was tempted far too much. His embrace felt so natural and right she had at first not realized what happened. As she slowly came awake she'd been astonished. She'd thought him so deeply drugged he'd not move much in the night. That his touch excited her, she did not fight; it was only natural that it should. That they were from different worlds was what drew her from the bed. She'd not give herself to a man likely to be her enemy, no matter how appealing or exciting he might be. She smiled to herself as she dressed. It would also be more interesting if the man in question were conscious at the time.

Odin, unaccustomed to such early rising, grunted his complaint when she made him move to let her out. She moved as quietly as any forest creature through the woods, walking quickly away from the camp, until she came to her usual place for her morning ritual. She stripped off her clothing and stepped into the warm pool of water, letting her hair float around her shoulders. The heat

soaked into her muscles and she relaxed, laying back in
the water. She tried to clear her mind, to let the calm
peace of this place soak into her. The man intruded on
her thoughts, just as he had on her sleep. She moved to
where the water trickled out of the rocks, where it was the
hottest, knowing she could stay there for a short time only.
The temperature of the pool was moderate, but for this
spot. She knew she would not be disturbed. The hot spring
was reserved for the women of Robyn's band each morning. The men would come at noon or later. Couples had
the nights. She wondered what it would be like to share
this place with the man under a starlit sky. She swam to
the far side, the water moving over her body like his hand
upon her. She turned to her back and floated, the peaks
of her breasts exposed to the morning air and growing
hard and upright in the chill. The bird chorus began in
the oak forest. The sun would be up soon.

Climbing onto the grassy bank where violets bloomed,
she wrung the water from her hair. She dressed and padded
the way back to her place, to check once more on the man
before she went to her morning meal. She ducked through
the low opening, then stood. The man was awake. Wide
awake, sitting on the edge of the bed, pale, but hot with
anger. Odin, massive and snarling, kept him there.

"Who the hell are you? Where am I?"

She did not answer him. "Odin, stay," she commanded
sharply, and slipped back out the way she'd come.

Chapter Three

Alex cursed and tried to stand, but between the deadly-serious growl of the dog and the wave of intense nausea that swept through him, he was defeated and sat heavily. Damn, he felt weak as a babe. He shook his head, trying to clear it, but could not seem to order his thoughts. He ached all over, as though he'd been beaten, and his mouth tasted like a cesspit. All in all he was in a dangerous mood.

The woman who had flitted in and out so quickly could no doubt provide answers to his questions. He'd had an impression of red hair, height, and slenderness. There was something familiar about her he could not place. Moving more slowly this time he managed to stand. He was naked except for his braies, which did not unduly alarm him, but not seeing his sword anywhere near did. What had the woman done with his weapons and his horse? How long had he been here? Apparently she'd stitched his wounds. He remembered the wolf, and the arrow in his leg. After that it became unclear. He checked the wound in his leg, which was not sufficient to make him so weak, nor was he fighting a fever. Something else made him vulnerable. He heard the sound of men approaching and looked around frantically for a weapon, anything to defend himself with, but could see nothing. Besides, the ugly, one-eyed dog was not about to let him move. He stood as straight as illness would allow, scowled his most arrogant, and waited for his visitors.

Two men and the woman entered. There was barely room for all of them. The woman stood toward the entrance, behind the men, who were both impressively strong. A knot of unease churned in Alexander's stomach. He was at a definite disadvantage.

"Who are you?" the smaller of the two men asked.

"Who am I? Who the hell are you and what are you doing in my forest?"·

The men glanced at each other and shook their heads. The brown-haired man spoke again. "Mayhap you do not understand your position. I am the one who will ask questions and you will answer, if you want to live beyond this day."

The words were spoken firmly and Alexander knew the man meant every one. Anger roiled inside him, but he'd spent too many years surviving one battle after another to let unruly emotion overcome his sense. He was weak and weaponless. He'd need to use his wit. "Alexander de Mandeville, baron of Wolfhurst," he said, with an ironic tilt of his head. They did not look as surprised as he'd expected, though the woman's head came up and she stared at him.

"Can you travel?" the man asked.

"I can." He wondered if he could. He still felt as though he'd puke his guts up at any moment, but he'd take any chance to leave.

The man turned his attention toward the woman.

"There are those who counsel killing him and would be more adamant still if they knew his identity."

The words chilled Alexander. The man spoke as though killing him were no more disquieting a decision than what to wear that morning. Why the woman had a say in it he could not fathom.

"My arguments for his life are as valid now as they were last night, Robyn. Why do you hesitate?"

"Last night I did not know who he is."

The other man spoke for the first time. "Wolfhurst has need of a strong lord. The villagers have fallen to poverty, the keep to ruin. If the man be fair and just, it would be good to have him there."

Alexander felt as though he must be asleep and dreaming. These peasants discussed his merit and would decide if he deserved to live. He'd been in dangerous situations before, but this was by far the strangest. If it hadn't been so serious he'd give way to laughter at the absurdity. The man called Robyn eyed him long and hard and Alex did not doubt his life hung in the balance.

The woman stepped forward and laid a delicate hand on Robyn's arm. "What John says is true. You've never killed a man without cause and there is none here. He cannot betray us. He has seen nothing but this cave. He is recovered from the poison enough to travel. You have but to escort him out of the forest and it will be as though none of this happened. He cannot find us again."

Poison? His head cleared rapidly. Had the arrow been poisoned? The nausea was not so strong as before. Apparently the woman and the man called John were in favor of releasing him, but it was Robyn who would decide. No doubt the three were runaway villeins, or worse. The forests were full of such outlaws and they were justified in fearing retaliation from him. Except that Alexander was not a man to hound the poor and desperate, as so many of his kind were. It would be ironic indeed if he died to salve their fear when there was nothing much to fear from him. He wondered if offering a ransom would persuade them, then realized he had no coin to offer. "If I make a vow not to try to find you again, will it suffice?"

The three of them stared at him as though the rocks had spoken.

"Am I to take the word of a nobleman?" Robyn asked, but there was a smile in his hazel eyes.

"I do not break my vows." It was true and Alex saw no reason to try to prove it. He was not accustomed to a man, most assuredly not a man of humble birth, questioning his integrity.

"Then vow on this," John said, and drew a crucifix from under his tunic.

He handed the relic to Alexander. It was a fine ivory carving of Christ on dark wood, most likely stolen from a nearby church. No humble man could afford such a thing as this. He wondered if a vow was valid if said with a stolen crucifix. He looked from one to the other—the healing wench, the man of the wildwood, and the pious giant— and knew no one would believe him if he did tell his tale. He laughed then, startling them all. "I do swear by the name of Christ not to hunt you, as long as you do not step on my land, or poach my wildlife."

John snatched the crucifix back as though from a madman.

"Heed my words well, Wolfhurst," the man called Robyn said. "If we see you treat cruelly with your folk, or unjustly in your courts, we will avenge them."

Alex mustered what dignity he could. "Mark me, Robyn of the Wood. I do what I consider right according to my conscience, not by the order of any man."

Slowly Robyn smiled. "We understand each other, then."

* * *

He was given rags to wear, blindfolded before leaving the cave, mounted on a bony nag, and led through the forest for what seemed like hours. Whoever his escort was remained silent, but he knew there were several of them. He wished the knights he'd fought with in the Holy Land were as well disciplined as this troop of Robyn's men. They gave nothing away, of themselves or where they traveled. Alex knew it was fruitless trying to figure out where he was. The wood was so dense he could not differentiate sounds to mark a place, and he suspected they walked in circles for a time to confuse him further.

Finally they came to a halt. He waited but nothing happened. "Why have we stopped?" There was no answer. He ripped the blindfold from his eyes, but there was nothing to see. Whoever led him had disappeared back into the forest. He saw Wolfhurst Castle less than a mile off. Audacious fellows, Robyn's men, but he understood the message. They were familiar with his land and would not hesitate to come so close again. His hands were bound together, an indignity that burned more than all the others. He did not like feeling helpless. He kneed the tired nag to a walk and began the last leg of his journey home. Anger grew in him. He was lord of Wolfhurst. No man would threaten that, certainly not a band of lawless men. He would tolerate Robyn only so far. Where the line might be, he did not yet know. He'd know when it was crossed. For now he'd keep his vow not to hunt him down like the thief and outlaw he was. But if the man did not heed his warning to stay clear of the forest acres belonging to Wolfhurst, his pledge was void.

A time would come, when he was stronger, when Wolfhurst was more stable, to find Robyn and his men and clear the forest of their kind. He wondered about the

woman. Why was she with a band of ruffians? Why should
he care? They were a nuisance he'd need to be rid of, the
sooner the better. For now he wanted nothing more than
to sleep away his sickness.

As he rode the main street through the village, no more
than a dirt path winding between the cottages, people
came out of their yards or fields or houses to stare at him.
Some laughed, thinking it a sort of silliness on his part,
the lord dressed as one of them, riding a broken-down
nag. Such folk were few and either very young or not very
bright. Most showed concern and fear, unsure how they
would be affected by whatever strange circumstances had
led to their lord's disgrace. Alexander tried his best to
ignore them, but between the nausea and the exhaustion
it was difficult to maintain his composure.

A burly man stepped into the path and pulled his horse
to a stop. "M'lord, can we not help you?"

Alexander tried to focus his attention. It was Michael
Tuck, the village priest. A look of genuine concern twisted
the cleric's face.

"If you'd send a boy ahead to the castle, to let them
know I've arrived."

"There's naught at the castle but the women and children. All the men rode at dawn looking for you."

What women and children? What was the man going
on about?

A big man, one of the village plowmen, pulled a knife
from his belt and gestured toward Alex. "I'll cut ye free."

He hesitated for a moment. He was unarmed. Was it
wise to let the man near enough? It was not unheard-of
for a peasant to attack a lord. Slowly he nodded and the
man carefully cut through the rope. He rubbed his wrists
to ease the abrasions. "My thanks."

The big man nodded and resheathed his knife, knowing
an unspoken test had been met.

Alexander urged the horse forward again. The priest walked beside him, unobtrusively ready to keep his lord from falling. "What know you of a band of outlaws in yon wood?"

The priest's face became wary and he did not look directly at his lord. "There are always rumors. The villagers have no business in the forest, save to harvest wood at your command or feed your pigs on your mast. 'Tis not a world they know."

In other words, whatever he did know, he wasn't about to tell. Alex sighed. He couldn't expect much else. The priest, of all men, was privy to what went on in the village. Had he been a corrupt or venal man he would have been eager to tell all he knew of his flock's misdeeds to the baron, in hope of reward. Alex was frustrated and comforted to know his village priest was a man who cared for his flock. To admit any of the villagers roamed about the forest would bring suspicion about what they were doing there. Though the lord of Wolfhurst held the forest rights near the castle, the vast expanse of Sherwood was the king's own, a royal demesne, with harsh laws against poaching of the animals, trees, or other produce.

He wondered if an occasional hare or side of venison did not make its way to a villager in exchange for some provision the forest folk might need, such as cloth or candles or bread. He could probably whip information out of his serfs, but it would be a stupid thing to do. They were needed in the fields and at their looms weaving cloth, working the fish weirs in his river, harvesting crops and making cheese and all the myriad daily tasks that saw him and them fed and clothed and sheltered from one day to the next.

When they reached the gatehouse that guarded the entrance into the castle yard, they had to wait for a boy to draw back the iron bars and swing the massive oak barrier open. That was another problem Alex needed to see to. He had no household knights when he had need of a mesnie of several men. The tournament at Blyth, scheduled for early December, should provide the opportunity for hiring the knights and archers he needed for his personal guard.

Father Michael left him at the gate, turning back to the village and the life he knew. Alex would need to know the priest better. He was a vital link to the villagers. Besides, the man intrigued him. Of noble birth, far more educated than most village priests, with dark, intelligent eyes and a wary way about him, the priest was an enigma. Why would such a man be content in so humble a place as this?

The bailey was nearly deserted, with none of the household serfs in sight. Alex glowered at the stable-boy. "Where are my men?"

"Gone with Sir Geoffrey and your brother at first light. We've all been sore worried."

"Did you say my brother?"

"Yes, m'lord."

Stephan and Julianna were not expected for another two days. Apparently his brother's business in Lincoln had concluded sooner than anticipated. Alex slid awkwardly from the horse and pushed aside the boy's hand when he offered assistance. "I can stand on my own." Walking was another matter. He wasn't sure his knees would keep him upright all the way to the castle, which suddenly seemed an impossible distance away. The lad caught him just before he fell, and Alex reluctantly allowed him to help.

"When did my brother and his family arrive?"

"Yesternoon. When you did not return by dark he was all for setting out then to seek you, but his wife told him nay."

Alex smiled weakly. Only Julianna could convince his stubborn brother to change his mind. No doubt Stephan would spend all day crashing about in the forest, making so much noise in his quest that Robyn and his followers would have ample warning to be elsewhere.

As he climbed the stairs toward the hall, a woman appeared at the top. She stared at him for a moment, then came rushing toward him. "Sweet Christ, you look truly dreadful."

"Good day to you, Julianna."

She wrapped her arm about his waist and gave his cheek an affectionate kiss. "Don't tease. We've been so worried."

"So I've heard."

"I'll have your banner raised on the north tower. We took it down this morning. When Stephan sees it he'll know you've come home."

She smelled of lavender and her wool gown was a soft cream color, with not a single patched place upon it. He tried not to lean too heavily; after all, she was but a woman and could not support his weight.

"Alex, what happened? Why are you dressed like this? Where are your weapons?"

"I had an accident."

She looked at him as she would one of her young children had they given her so inadequate an answer.

"In truth, if I don't get to my chamber soon I shall disgrace myself further by either vomiting all over your gown, or fainting in front of the servants." He spoke quietly, but she understood the urgency. She led him toward the stairs.

"Should I send for a physician?"

"There is none closer than Blyth Abbey, but do not bother. I look worse than I am. I've been assured a day of rest will do me much good."

"Who told you such a thing? You're not making sense. Do you have a fever?"

"Nay. Just a mild madness." They were at the door to

his chamber and she was looking at him as though he were truly delusional. "My thanks, Julianna. I'd not have made it this far without you."

She pushed the door open. "I'm not leaving until I get you out of those filthy clothes—they'll need to be burned; no doubt they're full of fleas and lice—and see you safely into bed."

He knew better than to argue. He was not quite so weak that he could not undress himself, dropping the offensive garments to the floor.

Julianna gasped. "What happened to your thigh? And your arm? What sort of 'accident' did you have?" She came closer to inspect the wounds then straightened and glared at him. "That is an arrow wound if I've ever seen one. How did you come by it, and who tended it for you?—for don't try to tell me you stitched it yourself."

"Later, sweet lady." He collapsed onto the bed and tried to pull the woolen covers over his body. "For now I needs must sleep."

Julianna tucked him in as though he were a sick child, then left him to his misery. His head was pounding, his stomach still roiled, and he was too weak to do much about either. The woman of the wildwood had told him the poison would not kill him, that all he needed was rest. He wondered if she'd told him the truth. He wondered why he trusted her at all. Was he being a fool? Would the poison work on him even now? Somehow he believed she wished him no harm, that the arrow was not meant for him. Why he felt so, intrigued him. There was something about the woman, something in the depth of her green eyes that spoke to him of purity and kindness. She would not harm him. The memory of her teased at him, until he cursed himself for an utter fool. He fell asleep and dreamt of a red-haired, sensual angel.

* * *

"The woman's a devil." Alex sat on the edge of the bed and waited for his head to stop spinning. By the look of the pale light beyond the shutters of his tower room, it was not yet dawn. He'd slept the day and night through, and still felt weak, though the nausea seemed gone.

"What woman?"

"Medre, Stephan. Give a man warning you're there." Alex squinted across the room to where his brother sat near the hearth, the fire burning low.

"Sorry. I thought you saw me."

"How long have you been sitting vigil?"

His brother did not answer and Alex knew he'd been there all night. He was sore as hell, but his head was clearing rapidly. For the first time in days he was hungry.

"What woman?" Stephan asked again.

He told his brother of the healer in the wood, but didn't bother with certain details, such as the woman's uncommon beauty and the way she'd deviled his dreams with temptation.

Stephan listened with hands steepled under his chin until the tale was told. "What do you mean to do?"

"About what?" Alexander scratched absently and stumbled toward the privy, heaving the door open with his good arm.

"About the band of outlaws that appear to run free in your woodland, little brother. That is what you've just told me, is it not?"

Alex grunted, wishing he'd been more discreet. Stephan caught him unawares, still groggy from sleep and illness. In truth, he'd not told much. He didn't know much to tell. Where Robyn and his band made their abode he did not know. Somewhere in Sherwood. They might as well be on the other side of the world. He could not hope to retrace his route. No doubt Stephan would want to go on a foray to clear the forest, as he set about all things, methodically and logically. All Alex wanted was a hearty meal and enough ale to dull the throb in his leg and blot the disturbing memory of female hands upon his body. Robyn and his men could wait.

"There are other things more pressing." He emerged from the privy and went to the narrow window, pulling the wooden shutter aside. It was a dismal day, gray and wet, and as soon as the sun was fully up he'd rouse the cook.

Stephan stretched his long legs out in front of him and sighed. "It's worse than you feared." It was a statement, not a question.

"You were right, the steward was a thief and a liar. He's robbed me blind." He pulled awkwardly at the lid to his clothes-chest, finding it difficult to do everything one-handed. He struggled with the linen tunic until it hung crookedly over his shoulders.

"I have gold enough to see you through to spring," Stephan said.

Alex's irritation mounted as he tried to get into a pair of wool hose. Between the bad arm and the bad leg he felt like a bad acrobat, hopping about the room. "The gold does me little good if there's no grain to buy. I'll manage."

Stephan arched an eloquent brow and forbore to say the obvious. Without a word he crossed the room and tied his brother's hose to his braies and straightened his tunic.

"I can get the boots myself," Alex growled.

"You need a squire," Stephan said.

"He needs a wife."

They turned to see Julianna in the doorway, her youngest child, Isabel, in her arms. Stephan greeted his wife affectionately, closing his arms around her and the child. "You're up early," he said.

"This one would not sleep. I thought to find Alexander still abed." She watched her brother-in-law with calculating eyes. "Are you well enough to be up?"

"Don't fuss over me." He sounded gruffer than he'd meant, but his mood was sour. He did not like being sick. It was an inconvenience when there was so much to do.

"We can change our plans and not attend the tournament," Julianna said. She came into the room and placed the back of her hand against Alexander's forehead, checking for fever.

"Nay, I need to find knights for my household," Alex said. Her hand was cool and comforting. The baby smiled at him and drooled. He was still unused to the idea of being an uncle to his brother's brood, a boy and three girls. The eldest, Rose, was eleven, this youngest girl less than a year; in between were William and Jordana. The year before, Stephan and Julianna had lost a child, a little girl aged five, named Eleanor, after the queen, and though he'd never met his niece, Alex knew a sadness lingered in her parents at her death. An absence of twelve years had left him a stranger to his family. He meant to amend that situation, and the tournament at Blyth was to be the beginning. It was to be a family outing, the de Mandevilles en masse, out among the nobles to be seen, to mingle, to make those important contacts and connections without which their lives were dull and isolated and uninformed.

"I'm glad to hear it," Julianna said. "William would be sore disappointed were he to miss the tournament. 'Twill be his first."

Stephan chucked his wife under the chin. "And you'd sore miss the best chance of gossip you're like to see in a year."

She pretended affront. "I am not so petty as you think,

Husband. What you call gossip can be important work among women. Where do you think most marriage alliances begin?''

"I had thought it was among the fathers and guardians,'' Stephan said, with mock innocence.

"Ignorant man. Do you not know it is the wives who whisper in their husbands' ears, 'This baron's daughter for my son,' until they think the idea is their own?''

"I suspected as much.'' He gave his wife an affectionate pat on the rear. " 'Tis time, I suppose, to begin finding good families for our own to marry into, though, God's truth, I'm no hurry to see any of ours leave.''

"Nor I. There are others in our family more of an age to marry.'' She looked directly at Alexander and smiled.

He suspected Julianna, given the least excuse, would go on a bride-hunt, with him the intended groom. Perhaps he should let her. It was time he settled, and Wolfhurst Castle needed the hand of a woman. The few servants were slovenly, the keep dirty, the work disorganized or not done at all. The kitchens were old and cramped, and the food was dull and uninspired. He was a man of some wealth and position. No doubt there would be eligible maidens at Blyth with their families. Julianna would know what to look for. Someone solid and practical, quiet and obedient. A young woman pretty enough to give him play in bed and strong enough to bear his children. A goodly dowry would not be amiss. He had noble blood enough and no need to buy more. The idea suddenly appealed.

"I'd not be amiss to you making inquiries,'' Alex said. At Julianna's squeal of delight he raised his hand in warning. "Make no promises, lady. I'd have a say in the matter.''

"Then I am to pick maids for you to choose among?''

He liked the idea better by the moment. "See they are rich and beautiful and I'll be well pleased.''

"If I find one pious and sweet, rich as Midas, but cow-faced and stupid as dirt, what will you then?"

When he hesitated she laughed at him. "Alexander, you've forgotten a small thing necessary to find you a bride who will bring you happiness as well as wealth, and treasure far beyond beauty or gold."

"What may that be?"

"Love."

"Love? Of what use is love? I need a chatelaine, a chaste wife and good mother for my children. Love I can find elsewhere."

Stephan grunted his disgust. "You'll pay dearly for that remark, Brother. You've just challenged her to a favorite task. Do not think to turn for help to me. You're on your own with this one."

Alexander's stomach growled, reminding him of more immediate needs. "I'm off to find the cook." As he passed them he was not sure he liked the scheming look in his sister-in-law's pretty green eyes, nor the smirk playing about his brother's smug mouth. One would think after twelve years of marriage the two of them would have settled into more usual ways of married folk, but their love burned as splendid now as it had in the beginning, when they'd fought so hard to be together. He wondered if he would regret giving Julianna charge of finding his wife. His heart was a thing he was not sure he was willing to give.

Chapter Four

Her cloth bag bulged with the roots of dropberry she'd gathered, more than Giselle was like to need in a year, but it gave an excuse for her wandering. The day was bright with slanting mellow light and that faint musty order of the cusp of autumn. A few apples still clung to the trees, and oak mast littered the forest floor, where the village pigs foraged greedily, their tails sticking straight up in their bliss. She was high in a tree with a view over the hills and woods behind her, the village and castle before. She'd been perched here the past hour, slowly munching the apples she'd brought for her meal, watching the coming and going of people about their tasks. If any had thought to glance up, they'd have seen her, for she took no great effort to hide herself. It was not as though she were poaching the lord's game, at least not today. But people had eyes to see only what they were accustomed to, and did not look for the unexpected.

She scratched lazily in the sunny warmth and stretched

like a cat, slow and long and arching. She'd not seen him today, though yesterday he'd been about the bailey for some time, and walked down at noon to the village, talking to the plowmen. It was more than a week since she'd accidentally shot him, and he seemed recovered from her poison, though he limped slightly.

Something hard hit her thigh and she flinched, startled out of her drowsing. It hit again, this time on her leg, and she scrambled back against the tree trunk to search for her assailant. Looking down she saw an impish dark face smiling up at her.

"Marian, what do you here?"

"What do I?" The young woman climbed quickly up the tree to join Giselle on the broad branch, bending her legs beneath her and sitting as comfortably at that great height as she would planted firmly on the ground. They were dressed alike, in dull, parti-colored clothing to blend with the forest, though Marian dressed in a short tunic and leggings, like a man, while Giselle wore a loose gown. Marian's dark hair, cut short to her shoulders, bounced in curls around her small face. "What do you here, Giselle, two days in a row? Have you nothing better to do than spy upon your nobleman?"

"He's not *my* nobleman." It was useless to deny what she did. Marian knew her too well, and the teasing was good-natured. She passed the last of her apples to her friend, who ate it happily, the juices falling down her pointed chin. It was not hard to think of Marian as one of the fairy folk, so small and dark and delicate was she. Giselle always felt large and clumsy next to her.

"He's handsome as the devil, is he not?" Marian asked, wiping apple juice from her face with her sleeve.

"I've heard the devil is a dark gentleman."

"An angel, then."

Giselle smiled. The lord of Wolfhurst was no angel; she'd wager her soul on that.

"Have ye cast a spell over him yet?"

"What sort of spell had you in mind?"

Marian crossed her eyes and wrinkled her nose. "I thought mayhap you'd turn him into a toad. What sort do you think, you hinny?"

Giselle knew full well what Marian meant, but she did not share her friend's firm belief in the efficacy of such charms. Even with the strongest love chant she could conjure, it was futile to think of the baron as her lover. Their worlds did not meet. Still, a woman could dream away an idle day in pleasant thoughts, though were she honest with herself, and she invariably was, her thoughts had wandered into decidedly sensual paths. She was glad for the distraction Marian provided, at least for a while.

"I can hardly wait to get to Blyth," Marian said, changing the subject without notice, as she was wont to do, her ideas and attention jumping from one thing to the next like a sparrow after seed.

"Are you not afraid?"

"A little, but think of the adventure, and Rob will protect us. We've little to do but distract the others' attention. Think how happy Alice will be when we've rescued her."

"And how angry Guisborne will be."

Marian displayed her disgust with an obscene gesture. "The man deserves whatever he gets."

"I'll not argue that. But who will see justice done? Not Rob or our men. Kill a lord and every knight in Nottinghamshire will be crawling through Sherwood, looking to hang us all."

Marian scowled and picked at a scab on her elbow. " 'Tis not fair. Why is it the lords do as they please while we're treated no better than dogs? A man can lose his hand for stealing bread to feed his starving child, yet a lord can force a woman against her will to be his leman and the law does naught."

"There's no good answer, friend." Giselle placed her hand on the other woman's knee, and felt her trembling with the anger that she bore. "It has always been so. The poor suffer. If all goes well, Alice will soon be free of her tormentor. Perhaps that is justice enough, to see her with Alan, who loves her true."

Marian smiled, her moods mercurial as her wit. "If you won't mix a love potion for your handsome lord, then some curse to render Guisborne impotent?"

"A curse to make his member wither and dry?"

"That would do nicely. Have you such a one?"

Giselle smiled at her friend's eagerness to do the man harm. She couldn't blame her. Guy of Guisborne was as brutal and greedy a lord as any in England, and that said a lot. Stealing his mistress from under his nose was the best they could hope to bait Guisborne. Still, a strong potion and a curse to go with it would not be amiss. She'd have to give it more thought, to do the job well in the time before they journeyed to Blyth.

Just then the gate in the castle wall opened and a small group on horseback trotted out. He was easy to see among the others, his fair hair uncovered and glinting gold in the sun, the yellow silk of his tunic a splash of color against the dark horse. With him rode a man and a woman. Giselle squinted. Who could the woman be? She was a lady, that was plain even from this distance, from the fine horse she rode and the way she rode it, with an easy grace and confidence, to the vibrant blue and red of her gown and cloak, and her laughter in the still air of the afternoon. She was a woman at ease in the world, as only the rich and powerful are at ease. Jealousy pounded through her, and Giselle sat back hard against the trunk of the tree at the unexpected emotion. Was she fool enough to think riches brought happiness? For all she knew, the other woman's life was a bleak and unhappy burden to her, full of tragedy and loss, no matter how happy she might appear at the moment. Happiness was fleeting, and not to be grudged another human. Nay. It was her proximity to the golden-haired lord of Wolfhurst that set the green fire in Giselle's eyes. She ached to be that noblewoman, astride a prancing pretty mare, wearing silks, with a handsome lord on either side of her.

"Who's the big dark man with Wolfhurst?" Marian asked.

"I don't know. He's been here a few days."

"And the woman?" Marian glanced back at her with slitted eyes in her cat face.

Giselle shrugged, hoping to appear indifferent. "I've not seen her before."

Something like a growl escaped Marian's throat. "You're hopeless." She slithered from her perch and shinnied down the tree to the ground.

"Where are you going?"

"To find out who those people are."

"You can't do that." She knew it was the wrong thing to say as soon as the words passed her lips. With a toss of her head Marian was off across the forest toward the village fields. Giselle hesitated a moment, then hurried to follow. Marian was the bold one. Giselle might as well try catching the wind as stopping her.

Julianna laughed and the sound made Alexander smile in spite of his peevish mood. His leg still throbbed, but less so, and his arm ached, but not as much. He was glad now she'd talked him into riding out from the castle, though why she wanted to see the poor, run-down village of Wolf-hurst he could not fathom. Boredom, most like. To his other side rode his brother, quiet and observant. "Will you be joining the tournament?" Alex asked.

Stephan cut a quick glance to Julianna, whose laughter disappeared. "Mayhap. I've not decided. It's been a long time since I've ridden in a melee."

" 'Tis a foolish, dangerous sport." Julianna's eyes flashed.

" 'Tis good training for war," Alexander said.

"Another foolish sport of men." Julianna's mouth set in a hard, determined line.

Alexander wished he'd not broached the subject. He turned back to his brother. "What of the rumors the king will bring us to war in France?"

"Still rising and seems more like with each day. I swear John is incapable of reasoning. He'll goad the French king beyond endurance until Philip is given no choice but to yank hard on John's reins."

"What of your fealty?"

Stephan shook his head. "I'm as caught as most. Philip is my overlord for the lands in Normandy, but John is lord of my English holdings. I've sworn fealty to both. If it comes to war, my loyalty is torn."

"I'm luckier than you," Alex said. "I have but this one English manor. There are no Norman lands to bind me or tempt me."

"Where are the boundaries of Wolfhurst?" Julianna asked, her temper calmed.

Alexander stopped on the road down into the village and pointed to the north. "To the river and the ford there." His arm carved an arc around to the south. "Three miles into Sherwood on all sides." He turned back toward the castle. "To the great North Road four miles east of the keep. I hold the castle and the village. Small but not poor, if managed well. Which it has not been for at least a decade. I fear my absence did harm."

"You were in the Holy Land. Hardly convenient for you to oversee the daily tasks. The steward should have done that for you." Julianna kneed her horse forward, on toward the cluster of cottages lining the single road.

"I should at least have had you check more closely," Alex said to his brother. "In truth, I gave it little thought. It seemed remote to me, in more than distance, all those years I rode and warred with Richard. Most of the time I had little faith I'd live to see England again."

"You're home now," Stephan said.

More than anyone Alex knew, his brother understood. When he was ready, if that day ever came, he'd talk to Stephen about the horrors of war he'd seen and hoped never to live through again. There was no glory in war. He'd not known that twelve years ago, when he'd been so eager to follow Richard on Crusade. Stephan, who had been there several years earlier, tried to warn him. He'd not listened, any more than most young men listen to the voice of experience seeking to keep them safe. He'd had to see for himself, and having seen, he knew there would be nightmares that would chase him through his days until the end, without escape or solace. Such was the fate of any fighting man who yet had a heart within him at the end of his warring. He was doomed to remember in silence, lest others suspect there was no glory in war.

The rye had been harvested from the fields and the golden grass was used now to thatch cottage roofs, plugging holes against autumn rain and winter storm. Geese wandered about, fattening on whatever fallen bits of grain could be found. In a few weeks more they'd be slaughtered for Christmas. There were not as many geese as he'd like to see, and the number of sheep and pigs needed increasing. Only the dairy seemed thriving, producing surprisingly good cheeses, stored for winter in the cool stone basement of the castle. The routine of the year went round in its circle, but Alexander noticed a burned cottage, and others fallen into disrepair, abandoned and left to molder into sad heaps of leaning wattle, their roofs caved in, the roost of chickens and haven of other small creatures, where feral cats hunted and bred and fought.

The fields were neat and orderly, plowed in long strips, the earth dark and sweet. The millpond and wheel were in good repair. It seemed whatever was necessary to bring profit to the holding was well kept. It was the people and their needs that had been neglected. Pasture ran on the higher ground and beyond it all, as always, loomed the ubiquitous woods. His eyes swept the edge of that vast forest, and thought he saw a flash of red, bright in a ray of sun, within the depths. Without warning he spurred his horse forward, crashing through an untidy, abandoned yard, straight toward that flag he'd been half looking for.

The woman stood for a moment, eyes wide, like a doe caught under a hound's gaze, then she turned and fled, as swift and graceful as any wild creature. He pressed on, the red of her hair a beacon in the dark forest. Hunter and hunted, he knew she could not escape and he did not stop to question his pursuit. She'd haunted his dreams and he liked not phantoms.

She did not waste time or energy with a backward glance, but ran, dodging sharply now and then to try to throw him off her trail, but where she could go his horse could follow. The woods were not dense enough here for her to be lost among thickets. He snared her easily, leaning down from his tall stallion and pulling her up with his good arm, bringing the horse to a jolting stop. Her breath was harsh from exertion and fear. Her small hands clutched the front of his tunic, to keep from falling under the prancing horse. He wondered why she didn't scream or struggle, then did not care. She was beautiful beyond what he'd imagined, this woman he'd dreamt was an angel. Her eyes were liquid green fire, fear and defiance filling them in equal measure.

"I would have you," he said, his voice harsh with desire.

An answering desire, hot and quick, swept her eyes and her hands tightened upon him. He slid from the horse, still holding her, and when his feet touched the ground, he crushed her to him, the soft curves of her body pressed into the hard, hungry planes of his.

'Tis madness, Alex thought, even as he lowered his lips to her red, moist mouth. *Utter madness,* as he savored the sweet, warm taste of her, and felt her shudder against him, whether in desire or fear he could not say, but his own body trembled in answer.

The unmistakable sound of an arrow leaving its bow jerked his head back in time to see the shaft come to a quivering stop in a tree trunk inches from his shoulder.

"The next one goes through your back. Let the woman go."

Slowly he loosened his grip, reluctant even with the threat behind him.

"Move away," the voice said, a young but sure and steady voice.

He stepped aside and his arms felt as empty as the destitute sky. The red-haired woman, tall, and lithe and warm, turned and ran from him, farther into the woods, until he could not see or hear where she had gone. He turned to look at his captor.

It took him a moment to notice the person was not the lad he'd supposed. It was a maid with a head of dark curly hair and crisp, dark eyes, dressed in the patched and particolored clothing of the forest men. She looked at him steadily, another arrow nocked to its place, pointed straight toward his heart. He wondered at his foolishness, to be caught so unprepared that a mere woman held his life in her hands.

The woman squinted at him and cocked her head slightly. "Get on your horse and start riding."

He mounted the beast and turned its head toward Wolfhurst. He'd not gone far when he heard the familiar whistle and answered it, as he had since they'd been boys together, and Stephan came riding toward him.

"What the hell was that about? What were you doing?"

"Nothing, Brother. Chasing the wind." Alex did not think he could explain the compulsion. If it were simple lust, running after a pretty maid, he'd not hesitate to explain, laughing about the misadventure. But he'd been left shaken, and that he did not understand or wish to talk of.

She did not shorten her stride when Marian caught up to her, and kept her silence, confused and angry, as much at her friend as at the man, which made no sense, and so made her angrier still.

"God's feet, your gratitude does overwhelm me," Marian said.

Giselle glowered at her.

"I saved you from that vile man, or hadn't you noticed?"

"I didn't ask for your help."

That brought Marian's strong hand tight on her arm, and she was pulled to a stop, her friend, several inches shorter, glaring up at her, now as angry as she.

"Did you think the man meant to kiss you pretty and let you go?"

"I could have escaped him, crippled as he is."

"He looked healthy enough to me. God's feet, what's wrong with you?"

She shook herself free from the other's hand and shrugged. "I know not. Part of me wanted his touch. I was not afraid of him."

Marian appraised her more carefully. "Virgins. Why not take John—he wants you bad enough—and have done with it?"

Giselle blushed. Perhaps that was all that was wrong. Her blood was hot and it was time she found a man. She could do worse than John. But he did not make her soul sing. One touch from Alexander of Wolfhurst and she thought she'd ascended to the highest heavens. Doubtless Marian was right. The man would have proved as crude and greedy as others of his kind; would have raped her and left her, his lust satisfied, having used her with no more thought than he'd give to the horse he rode. But there had been something in the touch of his lips on hers, something in the trembling of his body that roused a longing deep and unquenchable. If their worlds were not so far apart, could he want her, honorably, as a woman loved and cherished?

She hurried on toward the cave in the hills within the woods, hidden and secret, where Alexander could not follow. She'd need to dose herself with a strong tisane of wild cherry to clear such ridiculous thoughts from her head. Marian walked beside her, muttering about ingratitude.

Chapter Five

It was eight miles from Wolfhurst to the castle of Guisborne, and another mile beyond that to Blyth where the Benedictine monks had an abbey. Alex rode with his brother and Julianna at the head of the wagons bearing the nurses and children, while Geoffrey rode with Stephan's knights at the rear. It was a small entourage but there was no mistaking the scarlet banner of Rosmar, with its black lion and gold rose, carried by one of the knights. They traveled the ancient highway running from Nottingham north to York. A branch of the road, just south of Wolfhurst, led east to Lincoln. Within that triangle of prosperous towns lay Alexander's demesne.

He'd been gone from England so long he'd almost forgotten the wild song she sang in his blood. He'd never grown accustomed to the heat of the Holy Land. It remained an alien land to him, as had the others he wandered while serving the king. The siren call of England played him through the years, but he had not known what

those vague feelings of longing meant. Now he knew. He'd
been homesick, deep in his soul. He'd felt uprooted, dis-
connected, a wanderer through life. He had missed this
land more than he'd realized, though the weather had
been miserable, wet and cold, since he returned almost
two months ago. Ah, England. He relaxed and enjoyed
the ride.

It was strange that the land looked so lush, when the
crops were such a disaster. But the appearance was deceiv-
ing. While the grasses flourished, nothing else did. Rivers
were high and would go higher before the winter was
through with them. If they were lucky the real cold would
be late in coming. Somehow he did not think it was a lucky
year. The autumn colors in the forest had been a brief
glory, mostly gone now under the onslaught of freezing
rain, to lie in sodden heaps among the dead grass and
ferns.

Stephan's two eldest children—Rose and William, proud
not to be consigned to the wagon with the maids and
babies—rode sleek ponies under their mother's watchful
eye. Rose nudged her mount closer to his. "Uncle Alex?"

He looked down into her upturned face. It was surprising
how quickly he'd grown accustomed to being addressed
as "Uncle," and how much he enjoyed it. "Yes, sweetling?"

"Mama said I may sit at the high table while we are at
Guisborne."

He saw the pride in her straight, small shoulders, but
also the uncertainty. She was eleven and this would be one
of her first forays into adult society. "You'll be the fairest
maid in Guisborne's hall. Would you do me the honor of
sharing my trencher the first night?" Her smile was dazzling and he felt his heart open wide to let her in, knowing
she'd never be gone from there again as long as he lived.

Nine-year-old William nudged his pony between his sister and Alex. "Will you show me again that scar you have from the Muslim swordsman?"

Alex cringed. William had seen him without his shirt one morning and was fascinated by the scars on his chest and arms, especially the one that almost kept him forever in the Holy Land. It was a grisly curiosity, but one shared by most boys William's age.

"You should see it, Rose," William said, then described in gory detail what he'd seen. Rose grew pale, her eyes huge in her oval face, until tears threatened.

"Enough, Will," Alex warned.

"Girls!" William put all his young disgust into the single word, but kept his tongue quiet.

"There's naught to cry about." Alex tried to keep his voice light, to reassure his niece.

"But Uncle Alex, who would want to hurt you?"

His breath caught at the innocent confusion in her voice. How did he explain that he was a knight, as were most of the men she would know in her life? Fighting was a part of their being. That it was so he could regret, but he could not change it. "Men ofttimes must do things they would rather not. Sometimes we are hurt." He'd not mention the dying.

"I shall be a knight," William said, the look on his face daring anyone to contradict him. No one did, for it was true. He was the eldest son. Whether he wanted it or not, it was his fate to be a fighting man. Rose looked newly aghast as the realization that her beloved little brother might grow up to bear scars of his own worked itself into her brain. So far William saw only the bragging rights his future scars would bring. Rose saw the suffering.

"What are you two badgering your uncle about?" Julianna asked, looking over her shoulder at her children.

"I'm enjoying the company," Alex said.

She looked at him skeptically. "If they grow tiresome send them up here."

But Alex found the time went quickly that day on the journey to Blyth. He'd not spent much time around children and thoroughly enjoyed himself.

The land between Blyth and Tickhill was one of five places where English knights were legally allowed to gather for a tournament. This autumn, in the third year of John's reign, they came from throughout the Midlands and farther south, from the hills of Kent to the Marches of Wales, driven by discontent. John, like his brother before him, taxed his barons heavily, finding new and ingenious ways of exacting money from them, until the grumbling grew in the halls and keeps and fortresses. Worse than the coin that drained away into the royal coffers was the threat that John, in his arrogance, would risk their lands in France. Most of the nobility of England were descendants of those Normans who came conquering more than a hundred years earlier. Most still held manors and castles in Normandy, or Anjou, or Poitou; manors subject to the French king as their overlord. They gathered at Blyth in the wet autumn to practice their skills at war, and to talk among themselves. So the seeds of revolution are sown, when men of a common grievance gather together.

By midafternoon Guisborne Castle came into view. Square, solid, and dismally gray, the castle squatted on its deforested hill overlooking the tournament grounds at Blyth. Originally built at the time of the Conquest, and held by the family of Guisborne since, each decade had seen additions and amenities accrue, until the castle and its complex of stables, barns, workshops, kennels and mews, was an impressive sprawl. The high stone walls had recently been expanded, adding a towered barbican and outer bailey to the north of the original enclosure. Guisborne Castle served not only as the family seat of the powerful baron, it was a formidable fortress, made more so by ambitious building in the last few years.

It was one of the few castles of any size near the tournament grounds, so an invitation to attend the baron at Guisborne was highly prized. It was much preferable to be housed within the castle, no matter how cramped the accommodations might be, to sleeping in tents near the tournament fields.

Geoffrey rode next to Alexander. "It appears your neighbor is prosperous. What do you know of him?"

"Not much," Alex said. "From the little I've heard, he can be a harsh man. He's high in the king's favor."

Geoffrey snorted, knowing the last was no compliment. The king had an affinity for men who were as corrupt, cruel, and dishonorable as himself. Having learned at an early age not to trust another soul, John surrounded himself with untrustworthy men, thus fulfilling his expectations.

"Will your father be here?" Alex asked.

Geoffrey shrugged. "I doubt it. My stepmother is very near her time, if she hasn't already had the babe. Her brother, Richard de Clare, was planning to attend when I saw him at Tunbridge last summer."

"I hadn't realized your stepmother was the earl of Hertford's sister."

"Doesn't every family in England have at least one Clare connection?"

Alex chuckled, knowing it was not far from true. The Clares were a prolific clan, and the most powerful in England. It was to a Clare cousin Julianna had been betrothed when Alexander first met her. He had kidnapped her and brought her to Stephan, knowing the two were meant to be together. He wondered now at the audacity of youth, to have done such a thing without real fear of royal retaliation.

Alexander had spent years in close service to King Richard, and so was accustomed to the stir the arrival of an important man made on an establishment. He was a bit surprised nonetheless at the amount of fuss made when his brother arrived. It seemed the earl of Rosmar had become a man to be reckoned with.

Grooms came scurrying for their horses as a man-at-arms rushed to the castle to announce their arrival. Alexander was curious about the lord of Guisborne, who was his nearest neighbor yet had not traveled the eight miles to Wolfhurst to offer a greeting. The man was quick enough now to play host to the great earl who came to visit. The lord of Guisborne, a man of middle years, but hard and lean, with red hair beginning to turn white, stood within the shelter of the stone porch of his castle. Apparently he was reluctant to muddy his shoes by descending into the bailey. With a look of irritation on his rugged face, he came down the stairs and across the wet yard. Alex felt his mouth quirk in a smile. The battle the man waged between the need to offer an obsequious greeting, and the desire to stay out of the rain and muck, was obvious.

"My lord Rosmar," Guisborne said, in a booming voice. "Welcome. We have been waiting your arrival."

Stephan smiled politely at the man. "My thanks, Sir Guy."

"This lovely lady must be your wife."

"Aye," Stephan said. "This is my son, William, and my eldest daughter, Rose."

The children nodded politely and murmured a greeting. Alex narrowed his eyes. Was it his imagination or did the man take an inordinate interest when introduced to Rose?

Stephan continued his introductions. "My nephew, Geoffrey de Mandeville. My brother Alexander, Baron Wolfhurst."

That caught Guisborne's attention, as though he hadn't

realized Alexander's connection to the earl of Rosmar. There was something hostile in the man's gaze.

Alex dismounted and handed his reins to a waiting groom. The nurse-maids descended from the wagon, and carried tiny Isabel and five-year-old Jordana toward the keep. Stephan dismounted and was helping Julianna step down from her horse. Rose and William stared at the confusion around them, trying to make sense of this new place, but their attention soon wandered toward the stable, where the grooms were leading the horses. Alex called them back before they could follow. "There's time to see the baron's horses and dogs later."

They looked disappointed, but stayed near him. They hurried toward the shelter of the hall, careful to avoid the deeper puddles.

The exterior of the castle was deceptively plain. Within was every comfort and luxury known. The whitewashed walls were covered with murals of bright colors; hunting scenes and religious allegories competed with geometric and curvilinear designs. Huge tapestries hung throughout the hall, which was well lighted by many narrow windows high up. Two hearths, one in the center and the other along a wall, warmed the room and gave light, as did torches blazing in wall brackets. The hall was crowded with knights and nobles and their ladies, gathered in clusters, talking, drinking, eating, or playing games of chance. The noise of so much humanity in one place was resounding.

"Alice!" Sir Guy shouted. Servants scattered as he plowed his way toward the hearth. "God's blood, where is the stupid woman?"

Those nobles gathered near the roaring fire in the hearth either ignored Guy's eruption, or smirked and shook their heads. Whoever Alice was, Alexander felt sorry for the woman. Guy's anger grew by the moment.

"Had I known our host was such an unpleasant sort, I'd

have declined the invitation," Stephan whispered to his brother.

"It's but a few days. With luck we'll spend little time with Guisborne."

Sir Guy was once more approaching them, this time with a young woman in tow. She was small and very blonde, with gray eyes huge in her pale face, and she carried a double-handled welcoming cup in her hands. Guy had her by the upper arm, and apparently his grip was tight enough to hurt, for the woman's mouth was set and her eyes teared. Alexander marked one more thing against Guisborne. He did not care for men who treated those weaker than themselves with cruelty. The woman, forced to keep up with Guisborne's longer stride, tripped on something in the rushes, and the wine in the cup sloshed onto her gown.

"You clumsy fool." Guisborne raised a hand to slap the woman, who cringed away from him.

Alexander cursed angrily and strode forward. He grabbed the man's upraised arm and pulled it back, hard.

"God's blood!" Guisborne turned his anger on his attacker.

"Let the lady go."

A cold smile played across Guisborne's mouth. "Alice is no lady, and this is no business of yours."

"Let her go." Alexander kept his voice low, but the huge hall had quieted to near silence, everyone staring, waiting to see who would back down first. Guisborne noticed the quiet and looked around. His eyes narrowed. Alexander had him backed into a corner. If he gave in he'd appear weak. If he did not, he'd appear foolish.

Julianna laid her gloved hand on Guisborne's arm. "My lord, if the lady will show me to the chamber you've set aside for us, I really must see my children settled. They are weary and hungry."

Guy could hardly refuse such a request, even if it hadn't come from the countess of Rosmar. Alexander glanced at Julianna and saw that her smile was tight, her eyes hot with anger. His sister-in-law disliked Guy. Stephan was silent, but by the look on his face he was also ill pleased.

Guy frowned, but seemed unwilling to argue. "Alice, show the countess to the guest chamber and see her attended to."

"Yes, m'lord."

"And change your clothes. Do you think me made of money, that you can ruin your gowns?" Guy took the cup of wine from the woman and shoved her in the direction of the stairs. She seemed only too glad to leave. He turned his attention back to Stephan and Geoffrey. "We'll share a welcoming cup, then I'll show you to your rooms."

Alexander wanted nothing less than to share a winecup with the man, but it would be insufferably rude of him to refuse this ritual of hospitality. The man was disagreeable, but he was also the nearest neighbor to Wolfhurst.

With an unctuous smile, Guy handed the ornate silver cup to Stephan. "I'm honored you have chosen to stay at Guisborne, Lord Rosmar. I do hope your visit will be a pleasant one."

Stephan took a sip and handed the cup back. "I do thank you for your hospitality."

Next, Guy handed the cup to Geoffrey. "I was sorry to learn your father, Lord Essex, would not be attending."

"My stepmother is too near her time for him to travel."

"A devoted husband, I see. Does that not worry you?"

Geoffrey passed the cup back to the man. "Worry me? How could it possibly?"

"If he dotes so on the woman, no doubt he will also favor whatever children she bears him."

Alexander understood clearly the implication, that Lord Essex would slight his older children by his first wife, in favor of those by the younger. Why would Guisborne want to plant such a suspicion in Geoffrey's mind?

"My father is an honorable man," Geoffrey said. "He'll provide for all his children in the usual manner."

"Of course," Guy said. "I never meant to suggest otherwise. And you, as the eldest son, will of course inherit the bulk of the estates and titles."

"In due time. I'm in no hurry for such responsibilities, and wish my father many more years of health and happiness. With luck he will sire a dozen more children."

Guy nodded, a slight movement Alexander wasn't sure anyone else noticed. The man might be shrewder than he appeared. By playing at being crude, he'd just had more information from Geoff than an hour of cautious prying would elicit. He knew Geoffrey to be a loyal son, who would one day inherit great wealth and power but who was in no hurry to do so. As such, he would prove a valuable ally in the future, and could be used now to carry messages back to his father, who, as the king's justiciar, was one of the most powerful men in England. Alexander wondered if Guy didn't underestimate Geoffrey. For all his cousin was young, he had enough experience with people who tried to get close to him because of who his father was, who he would one day be, to be cautious. Sir Guy, a simple baron with the single holding of Guisborne his only wealth, seemed intent on ingratiating himself with Stephan and Geoffrey. He had no such need to cultivate Alexander's goodwill.

"Wolfhurst," he said in greeting, handing Alexander the cup. "I thought to have seen you before this."

Alex glanced over the rim of the cup. The wine was terrible and he took only a small sip. Did the man really think he should have ridden to Guisborne to introduce himself? It was usually the newcomer who was visited. Alexander handed the cup back. "I've been busy."

"Yes, I can imagine you have. Wolfhurst has been sadly mismanaged since the late king took it from me and gave it to you."

"I didn't know you held Wolfhurst." Alex saw now where the animosity came from. Guy no doubt felt Wolfhurst had been stolen from him when Richard granted it to Alexander. Guisborne was by far the richer and larger of the two holdings. Still, few men, once they believe themselves to be wronged, can be made to change their opinion. Alexander was not likely to be held dearly by his neighbor, and in a strange way he was relieved. He'd be glad to have as little to do with the lord of Guisborne as he could manage.

"Have you had trouble with the outlaw band living in Sherwood?" Guisborne asked, taking a deep drink from the winecup.

"No," Alex lied. "Have you?"

"Not lately." Guy laughed. "Last winter I caught three of the bastards with their hands still bloody with the king's deer they'd killed. Strung them and the damned deer up in the nearest tree. The cowards haven't dared come near Guisborne since then, but there's been no one at Wolfhurst to keep them under control. I'd take a careful count of my sheep were I you."

"Yes. I'll do that." Alexander pointedly ignored the quizzical glance from Stephan. He wasn't about to tell Guisborne he'd met the leader of one such band. Why he was reluctant to do so, he wasn't sure, except that he knew he disliked Guy.

"Tell me, who is the lovely Alice?" Stephan asked.

"A real beauty, isn't she? And hot between a man's legs."

Alexander tried not to cringe at the man's crudity. Was Alice his wife? More likely his mistress. She was indeed a beautiful woman. She was also very young, probably not more than fourteen, and obviously miserable. "Who is her father?"

"An orphan. Sir John of Barnsdale, a poor knight, no real family, no wealth to speak of. I took pity on the girl. Of course, there's no dowry so I can't marry her, but she'll do nicely until I find the right noble-born maid to wed. She's biddable enough, most of the time."

"I see." Stephan's voice was as cold as winter shade, but Guisborne did not notice. "If you will excuse us, Sir Guy, we would refresh ourselves after our journey."

Even Guy knew when he'd been dismissed. "Of course. I've given you the best chamber, after my own, of course. Up the stairs and to the right, the first door on the left. I'll send servants with hot water."

Alexander followed Stephan and Geoffrey up the stairs. The chamber set aside for them was not overly large, but it was private, and Alex made sure the heavy door was closed firmly behind him after he entered. A large bed dominated the windowless chamber. There was no hearth and the rushes on the floor were old. Torches set into wall brackets had been lighted and the flames sent shadows and light skittering across the stone walls. The smoke rose to the high, blackened ceiling. If this was the second-best chamber at Guisborne Castle, the place was in need of improvement. Apparently all Guy's efforts went into the appearance of the great hall, the public part of the castle, meant to impress his betters and intimidate his serfs. He wondered if the lord's private chamber was as Spartan as this. Still, because of Stephan's rank, they had been given this private place. They would not have to sleep in the hall with the other guests.

Julianna sat on the edge of the bed, comforting a weeping Alice. William sat sullenly in a corner, his skinny legs pulled up under him. He looked as though he'd been scolded. Rose approached them from where she had been standing beside the bed.

"Papa, why is the pretty lady so sad?"

Stephan crouched down to his daughter's level. "Your mother will help her. Do not worry yourself, sweetling."

"I do not like Sir Guy." Her mouth set in a stubborn line.

Stephan sighed. "He is our host and will be treated politely."

"Yes, Papa."

William came striding across the room, a frown deep on his face. "This room is dark and it stinks of smoke."

Stephan straightened to his full, impressive height and stared down at his son. "I have not raised you to be a complainer. Be grateful for what you have. Most people have far less."

Knowing he'd find no more sympathy with his male parent than he apparently had with his mother, William turned his attention to Alex. "Can we go see the dogs now? You promised."

Alexander wasn't sure he had promised any such thing, but he had no more desire to be in the dark, stuffy room than the boy. "Get your cloak. You too, Rose."

"I'll come with you," Geoffrey said.

They maneuvered quickly through the crowd of guests and servants in the great hall and were soon out into the bailey and headed for the stables. It was raining again, but the air was fresh and the barns would be dry. Alex rubbed at the nearly healed wound on his leg. The wet weather seemed to make it ache, but otherwise it gave him little trouble. He thought of the woman who had tended his wounds. She was never far from his thoughts, and usually he indulged in pleasant fantasy about being with her again.

The memories brought frustration. How was he to find her? He couldn't spend his time scouring the wildwood like a madman, seeking that hidden cave she lived in. But that was exactly what he wanted to do.

Chapter Six

Giselle and Marian walked through the barbican and into the castle yard. "Now what?" Marian asked, tugging nervously at the neck of the rough gown she wore. She was never comfortable in women's clothes and felt half naked without her bow slung across her back and a quiver of arrows at her hip.

Beside her, Giselle quietly surveyed their surroundings. She pointed at a large stone building set very near the castle. "By the smells coming from it, that must be the kitchen. I'll find work there. You try to get into the castle. We need to know where he keeps Alice, what her routine is. And we need to let her know we are here."

"I don't know how people live like this." Marian wrinkled her nose. "It stinks."

She was right. The line of privies behind the castle gave off a potent stench in the damp. This combined with the myriad smells of many animals kept in close quarters, the pall of wood smoke hanging low, and the general smell of rot induced by the unremitting rain, made it far from pleasant, especially for someone accustomed to the clean smell of the forest. "Cities are even worse from what I've heard. Get on with you, and meet me at the kitchen door near sundown."

Marian squared her shoulders, tugged her skirts and marched toward the huge castle. She looked very small and vulnerable and not for the first time Giselle wondered if their plan were not foolhardy. Yet they must accomplish this rescue by stealth and wits alone. It would be impossible for Robyn and the men, even if they were successful in infiltrating the castle in sufficient number, to force their way back out once they captured Alice. Two women, inconspicuously working as servants, had a better chance of sneaking her out. Or so they hoped. Robyn and John and Alan waited with the others, just beyond the edge of the wood surrounding Guisborne Castle. If all went well Alice would be with them soon. It would go as planned. It must. She swallowed her fear and made her way to the kitchen.

Because the castle was crowded with noble visitors, knights eager to participate in the spectacle of melee and joust, and their ladies come to observe them, as well as squires and servants, the work of the castle folk was increased beyond durance. So it was that extra servants were hired for the fortnight the guests were expected to make Guisborne their home.

A great feast was planned for tonight, and the kitchen was in a tumult of preparation. Giselle stood just within the doorway, careful to keep out of the path of cursing servants. Sweating cooks shouted at each other across tables laden with food. Fires roared in huge hearths where whole sides of beef and mutton and wild boar roasted, while slave boys turned the iron spits to keep the meat from burning. Cauldrons of soup simmered, with fragrant steam adding to the heat and comfort of the rooms. Bread, hot from the outside ovens, were piled on a table. Bowls of eggs, dyed yellow with saffron, waited their final decoration. Sweet berry pies filled a tray and Giselle was mightily tempted to snatch one, so delicious was the sight and smell. Never had she seen so much food, such abundance, such variety in one place. She was assaulted with wonderful smells until her stomach lurched. If naught else she'd have her fill of good food from Guisborne's kitchens before she returned to the wood.

"Don't just stand there gawkin', ye senseless twit. Pluck these."

Giselle stared at the wooden bowl full of tiny birds a man thrust into her arms. Before she could question him, he had disappeared back into the bowels of the kitchens. So much for finding someone to hire her. Apparently all she had to do was be there. She smiled as she moved to a quieter place where she could sit with the bowl on her lap and pluck the tiny feathers out of several dozen sparrows. She held a naked bird up by its feet. There wasn't more than a bite or two of meat on each bird. That she would spend hours cleaning the things so that nobles might devour them in seconds seemed a monumental waste of time. But she'd never claimed to understand the way noble minds worked.

"Be there room beside ye, lass?"

She glanced up to see a large woman, red-faced and grinning, standing near her. She moved over on the bench, making room for the woman's ample behind.

"God bless ye. Me feets are about sore enough to make a saint cry. Never saw so much food and confusion in one place in me life. What be that ye'r doin'?"

Giselle held up a sparrow and the woman puckered her lips and squinted at the bird, then shook her head.

"That tyrant, Will Baker, had me cutting up apples for hours. Blessed Mary, and I won't even get a bite of the pies he'll make of them. They be full of sugar and cinnamon and cloves.''

"Have you ever tasted such things?" Giselle asked. She'd heard of the exotic spices the rich used in their food and wondered if they tasted as wonderful as the names sounded. She knew sugar was sweet, like honey, but couldn't imagine what the others tasted like.

The large woman looked over her shoulder, to see if anyone were near enough to overhear, then leaned closer and whispered. "I took a piece once, when it was all mixed together, afore it be cooked. Never tasted nothin' so good in me life. Like eating a bit of heaven."

Giselle sighed, as did the woman beside her. "I'm Hawyse from Finningley. Be you from these parts?"

"Nay, from south of here. I heard there was extra work at Guisborne, for the tournament." Giselle hoped the woman would be satisfied with her answer. She could not very well tell her the truth, that she lived with a band of outlaws in Sherwood, and that those men waited just beyond the walls of Guisborne Castle. But the woman might be a source of useful gossip.

" 'Tis why I'm here. The baron be stingy as the devil with a penny, so don't count on being paid fair. But you'll eat well while you're here, and these days they's much to say for that. Are the harvests as bad in the south as they are here?"

"They're bad enough. Folk will be hungry come winter."

"Give me some of them birds to clean, or that old harpy what hired me will find something else for me to do."

Giselle handed her several birds and the other woman set about gutting and cleaning them. She was surprised that the woman's huge hands were so quick, even graceful, in their work. She could strip two birds for every one Giselle plucked.

"Have you worked here before?" Giselle tried to keep

her voice light, and didn't look at the woman, concentrating on her birds.

"A few times. The baron entertains regular. He lives well, even if his people suffer."

"He's a hard man, then?"

The woman snorted and slammed a bird onto the platter full of naked little sparrows.

"Careful, you'll break them."

"Aye, you be right." Hawyse patted the birds gently, as though to compensate for her roughness. "Sir Guy be as bad as they come."

"What has he done?"

Hawyse looked about her again, then decided it would be better not to say more. "Just you keep your distance. You be a pretty young maid. You keep away from the man."

Giselle shrugged her shoulders and plopped another bird onto the growing mound. "I've no reason to be near the lords. But my thanks for the warning."

It was raining, again, and Alexander pulled the hood of his cloak over his hair. From the parapet of Guisborne Castle he could see the abbey and village of Blyth just to the east. Though the year had been as hard here as it was at Wolfhurst, the people had not the same hungry look, the keep was not run down. Though none prospered when crops failed, Guisborne would not starve. There was to be a feast tonight in the great hall. As the rain continued he wondered if the tournament would take place. The fields would be a wallow of treacherous mud. Luckily, most of the harvest had been gathered, so damage to the crops would be kept to a minimum, though the churning hooves of warhorses would leave the neatly plowed fields a morass.

Stephan found him at his brooding. "What do you out here in the rain? The hall is warm and dry."

"I needed some quiet."

"You've found that." His tone implied only a fool would be out in such weather.

"Mayhap the games will be canceled."

"We'll wait a day. The rain may ease."

"A day won't give the ground time to dry."

Stephan clamped a big hand on his brother's shoulder. "Come within the stairwell at least. You may enjoy the rain, but I'd rather stay dry."

Alex let himself be led to the sheltered doorway. He shook the wet from his cloak. Stephan stared down at his shoes, now soaked, and sighed.

"You've been in a sour mood since before we left Wolf-hurst," Stephan said.

"Forgive me."

Stephan grunted. "I'm not criticizing your manners, Brother. What's wrong?"

Alex gestured toward the rain. "The wet fields for one. All England has suffered a poor year in her crops. Now we'll trample the peasants' fields when we play at war."

"The fields will recover."

Alex crossed his arms and glared at his brother. "They will, but do you think they'll plow themselves? The work will be heavier, having to break up the clods we leave. There will be fences to repair, once we've been through them. A melee is no pretty thing for those left to clean up the mess."

"Everything you've said is true. Those of us who have seen war have little need to play at it."

"Then why do we do it?"

"Because we have the right." Stephan raised his hand to forestall more argument. "I understand your anger. It seems careless, and it is. They are naught but peasants, and accustomed to labor, or so men say. I care not for the abuses some men indulge in all too easily. It's a waste of time, resources, and men, all of which are precious. At least tournaments are now restricted to a few places in the kingdom, and so the damage is contained. There's not much you can do about it."

Alexander knew the truth in what was said, but he still fumed against it. "I can see my lands and people are not misused."

"That you can. I'd expect no less from you."

"Why do you smile?"

"To see you transformed. When you left England you were a warrior, with naught but thoughts of crusading on your mind. You're becoming a landowner before my eyes."

"I've *been* a landowner."

"You've been a man who owned land. Now you're learning to husband that land, to see it as a part of yourself that needs nurturing and protecting. It's a good thing, when the land wraps itself around your soul. The land endures. It is the true wealth."

"Mayhap you're right. I'm tired of war. I want nothing more than to settle peacefully at Wolfhurst and watch it prosper."

"If not for the men I hope to see and the news they carry, I'd not bother with this tournament."

"William is exited beyond measure." Alex smiled at thought of his nephew.

Stephan grunted. "He's been training for two years now, though still with wooden sword. He'll make a fine knight in his time."

"There's sadness in your voice."

Stephan sighed and gazed out over the hills, then shrugged a shoulder. "He has no more choice than we did. You may have noticed he's not made to be a monk. There are worse lives for certes than the one of power and privilege he'll inherit. I just hope he has the sense to know the real treasures to be found, and that he'll be lucky enough to find them.''

"Which treasures are those?''

Stephan turned and smiled at him. "The love of a good woman, above all else. And children. Wait until you have your own, little Brother. They have a way of crawling into your heart and soul. It's unlike any other love I've ever known.''

The reason for the sorrow was not mentioned. Stephan's daughter, Eleanor, had died less than a year before. Alex wondered if his brother would ever recover if it were Julianna he lost.

"Julianna is with child again,'' Stephan said, softly.

"Congratulations. Mayhap it will be another son.''

Stephan looked at him and shook his head. "I care not, son or daughter, as long as Julianna is safe.'' He looked away again. "That is one of the hardest things, watching her labor to bring our children into the world, and knowing my loving has put her in danger.''

They stood silently. What could he say? It was one of the ironies of life, that love could hold such peril.

Alex scratched at the newest scar on his arm. Julianna had pulled the stitches and he was glad to be rid of them. The wound had healed well, the scarring minimal. The woman of Sherwood did fine work. Why did he think of her now? She was of another world, alien to him. Perhaps that is what intrigued him, as much as her beauty. She was a mystery to him. Who was she? He did not even know her name, this woman who visited his dreams and intruded on his thoughts. Why did she live so strange a life? What could she possibly have done to warrant living as an outcast? If he found her again, he would not let her go so easily.

Stephan was right about the other. Wolfhurst beguiled him. Was that where the new restlessness came from? There was much to do, so much to worry over. Where would he get the grain to see the village and castle through the winter? The abbey at Blyth would be the most likely of any nearby holdings to have surplus grain to sell. He'd go over in a day or two and have a visit with the abbot, to see if anything could be done. How could he repair what needed repair and build what needed building if he could not feed his people? His ambitious plans to expand castle and fields would need to wait until more urgent matters were taken care of. For now he'd come to Guisborne to enjoy a few days' respite and to find knights for his household mesnie. If naught else he owed it to his host to take part in the festivities he planned.

Alex glanced again at the wet hills and noticed movement on the road leading to the castle gate. Riders, nearly a dozen, made their slow way through the rain and mud. Banners lifted above their heads to identify them were sodden and could not be clearly seen, so limp did they hang about their poles. "More company is on the way. Who is expected?"

"The countess of Gloucester."

Alexander's head snapped around to stare at his brother. "Elizabeth? Here?"

"It was Julianna's idea. She thought her aunt could use the diversion, and I agree with her. It'll be crowded, but there'll be room in our chamber for a few more bodies. Elizabeth hasn't been far from Gloucester Castle since her divorce. It's time she was about again."

Alexander frowned as he stared at the slow progress of the train of people and horses. Elizabeth had been ill-used by her husband John, now king of England. After eleven years of marriage he'd divorced her because of barrenness and married the twelve-year-old heiress to the count of Angoulême within weeks of the divorce decree being finalized. Elizabeth FitzWilliam should have been queen of

England. Alex could not blame her for hiding on her estate rather than facing the gossip or pity of others. John, busy in France, would not be in attendance at Blyth. Elizabeth would be spared the embarrassment of running into her husband and his child-bride at a public event.

Elizabeth. Memories of her filled Alexander's heart with a quiet joy. Sweet, gentle, and shy, with the voice of an angel and laughter to lift a man's weary soul, she was a lady in the truest meaning of that honor. Charity flowed from her hands, with genuine care and concern for those she ministered to with her alms or her soothing words. Elizabeth.

The gate to Guisborne Castle opened to admit the company. Alexander turned, ran down four flights of stairs and through the hall, where people who had gathered out of the rain stopped whatever they were doing to stare at him. The sound of horses echoed through the bailey, moved toward the stable, and grooms ran to meet the riders.

There was a young man and an even younger woman riding with Elizabeth, as well as a guard of her household knights. Alexander, taking note of the others, was interested only in the woman riding the small bay palfrey, the hood of her dark woolen cloak pulled up around her head to protect her from the rain. He pushed aside a startled groom and lifted his hand to help her down from her saddle. She lifted her face to glance at him and puzzlement was quickly replaced by recognition. "Alexander?" It was no more than a whisper.

"Elizabeth." He could think of nothing else to say.

"Are we going to sit here and listen to this witty conversation, or are we allowed to dismount and find a dry seat, preferably near a fire, preferably in yon hall, before we freeze our wet arses out here in the bailey?" The voice was young, masculine and teasing.

Alexander glared, but the youth was grinning at him.

"Come, Alexander, surely you remember me?"

There was something very familiar about him.

"I was to marry Julianna, remember? Before she told the bishop and the king she'd rather not."

"Gilbert de Clare?"

"More scathing wit, I see."

"I'll scathe you, you rascal. What do you here?"

"I've escorted my lady aunt, who was of a mind to visit my cousin, Julianna, who is rumored to be sheltering here."

"Gilbert, for pity's sake, shut up." The young woman beside him, cold and obviously at the end of her patience, slid gracefully from her saddle and found her red leather shoes buried in mud. "God's blood, they're ruined."

"Maud, do not blaspheme," Elizabeth said, but there was a note of indulgence in her voice.

"I'm going inside," the girl said. "It seems to me this is a ridiculous place for a conversation."

"You are being very rude," Gilbert said.

"I didn't ask to go riding across country in the rain, Brother dear. Why couldn't you leave me at Tunbridge?"

"You know why, Maud," Elizabeth said. "The incident with the carving knife is much too fresh in everyone's memory."

"I wouldn't have used it on the sap-wit," Maud said.

"Lady Isabeau did not believe that." Gilbert slid from his horse. Wearing boots that covered his knees, the mud did not bother him.

"Elizabeth, come down from that beast," Alexander said. He had no desire to listen to the bickering of her niece and nephew. What he wanted was to be alone with this lady. She slid into his arms and when she would stand he restrained her, instead sweeping her into his arms and carrying her across the bailey to the castle.

Maud and Gilbert followed. "If you weren't such a shrew

mayhap a man would carry you through the muck," Gilbert said.

"If you weren't such a weakling, mayhap you'd be capable of carrying me."

"Careful, little girl. Your tongue draws blood."

Alexander marched into the hall with his burden. Elizabeth had always been small and delicate. He carried her easily.

"Alex, you may put me down," she said.

He stopped where he was and let her stand, but was reluctant to allow her to leave his arms. "It is good to see you again, Beth."

She smiled up at him, but it was not the same shy, uncertain smile he'd known. There was confidence and maturity in this woman who stood before him now. He found the change appealing.

"Alex, you have been gone so long. Much has happened, to both of us."

"There is time enough to catch up." He led her toward a quiet table where several serving women, working on the constant sewing and mending necessary in any household, large or small, moved down the long benches to make room.

"I did not know you were at Guisborne," Elizabeth said. "Will you stay long?"

"My plans are not set. I've a mind to spend some time with Stephan and his family. In truth, it's the first family life I've had in over a decade."

"That sounds like regret."

"Nay, I'd not trade the adventures I shared with Richard. I'll never regret seeing the Holy Land, and while it lasted there was reward in the friendships I made. Now I feel it's time for other things. I've returned to Wolfhurst and mean to see the *honour* prosper. It's been somewhat neglected. It needs a lord's guidance."

"Mayhap this impulse has been fed by the happy family Stephan and Julianna have?"

"It has. I'd never thought much on marriage and children. They were always something in the future, unreal . . . something I'd get to eventually."

Elizabeth unclasped the brooch at the throat of her cloak, and one of the women was quick to take the fur-lined garment from her. "Tell Lady Rosmar I've arrived."

"Yes, m'lady."

The servant hurried to do her bidding and Elizabeth turned her attention back to him. "If you are ready for marriage, my friend, it will not take you long to find a wife."

He looked at her quizzically. He was in the market for a wife. Why hadn't he thought of Elizabeth? He'd been half in love with her before she married John. He turned to the seamstresses. "I wish to speak privately with the lady."

The women did not question the authority in his voice, gathering their work and hurrying to other parts of the castle. Soon the only two within hearing were Gilbert and Maud, but they were still bickering with each other and not likely to pay much attention.

Alex took Elizabeth's gloved hand in his own. "You are free now, lady. I thought mayhap—"

She put the fingers of her free hand to his mouth. "Hush, Alex my dear, before you say more and break my heart. It is true I am divorced from the king, but I am not free to remarry."

He was stunned. "What do you mean? John has married again, what could possibly be the impediment for you?"

"The marriage fee the king has set."

"How much?" He waited with gritted teeth, dreading the answer.

"Twenty thousand marks."

Even John could not be so greedy. The king set the price for the marriage fees of his nobles. It was one of the ways he had of collecting revenue. Under John's rule the rates tended to be high, but Elizabeth's was exorbitant. Alexander could not begin to dream of gathering such an amount. All he owned was not worth that. He doubted even his brother was worth as much.

"Is there nothing—"

"Alexander, please. It is not just the fee. In truth I am not unhappy at my fate. I have no desire to remarry. Eleven years as John's wife was more than any woman should have to endure."

He felt sick in the pit of his stomach. "I am not John."

Elizabeth leaned her hand against his chest. "You, Alex, are a dear and beloved friend. I am blessed in that. Please, I beg you, if you care for me at all, do no seek to make it more."

He held her close, his arms tight around her slight body. Something deep in him knew what she said was true, not just for her, but for him. God rot John for his cruelty to her. She could not have made it plainer than claiming she wanted nothing more to do with marriage. "If that be your wish, Elizabeth, I'll honor it." Alex glanced up, over her head, and saw Gilbert and Maud staring at them, silent as the carved angels in a chapel. At least something was capable of shutting them up.

Julianna came rushing into the hall and soon all was a flurry of feminine greeting and fussing. Alex retreated to where Gilbert stood, Maud standing beside him with a smirk on her impish face. "Why don't you join the women," Alex suggested.

"I'd rather not," Maud said.

"I'd rather you did." He glared at her to little effect. She glared back. How old was the nit? Thirteen, fourteen?

She must be the youngest of Richard de Clare's children, and spoiled enough to prove it. What a dreadful girl.

"Go on," Gilbert said. "Before Aunt Elizabeth notices your lack of enthusiasm."

"You're right. She'll nag at me for certes."

Alex watched her march across the large room, more like a boy with a sword at his hip than a young woman. "Is she always like that?"

"Like what?" Gilbert absently scraped the mud from his boots, leaving great clouts to dry in the rushes.

"Argumentative, bad-tempered, sarcastic."

Gilbert glanced up to where his sister and aunt were gathered around Julianna. "She's a good-enough sort. All my sisters are independent-minded and high-spirited."

"Is that what you call it?"

"They're not much like Aunt Elizabeth, if that's what you mean."

Alex tried to ignore the boy's impertinence. Were all the Clare family so forward with their opinions? With a grunt of impatience, he turned and left the hall to wander once again around the rainy courtyard.

Later that day, Alexander escorted Elizabeth to the second-floor solar, with its windows looking out over the wet fields. A light rain was falling but the breeze was slight, so the shutters were open. There was no hearth here and they sat on a stone bench carved into the wall with a heavy fur rug over their laps.

"That poor young woman, Alice, is in such pain. I would help her, but I've no wish to pry," Elizabeth said. "Her eyes are haunted and I hate to see it."

Alexander wondered how accurate Elizabeth's assessment could be. How much of the other woman's trouble had Elizabeth guessed at, and how much of it echoed her own?

"John was nasty to me in many ways," Elizabeth said. "But he never struck me, as Guisborne does Alice. John's cruelty was far more subtle than that. In the end he ignored me, and in truth I was glad of it. I was lonely, but no longer tormented. The greatest gift he ever gave me was the divorce, for I am with my family and free."

"You need not tell me these things."

"I wish you to know. You of all people. I cherish my freedom, Alex. It's as though I've been a prisoner, locked away from sunlight and laughter. I have the freedom to come or go as I choose. I have my dower estates and can live quietly there with contentment. I have a large, boisterous, and loving family to keep me entertained, worried, and busy. My life is full and I would not have you pity me."

"I do not. I never have."

She studied him for a moment. "I'm tempted to believe you."

In the light near the windows he could see her clearly. There were faint lines around her blue eyes, yet she was as slim and delicate as the girl he'd known those few weeks before she married; a few weeks over ten years ago. He'd known more women than he could remember in the intervening years and he realized now it was his image of Elizabeth, pure and clean and unattainable, that he'd held before him. No wonder he'd not found more than physical pleasure with those others. Who could compare to such a paragon? He felt a bit of a fool, and suddenly much older than he'd been a few minutes before. "God's truth, Beth, you keep me honest."

She did not question his strange reply. "Enough of me. What are we going to do to help young Alice?"

"We?"

She smiled at him and he was charmed. "Sir Guy has her terrified, and the poor thing has nowhere to go, no family or friends. Perhaps I shall offer to make her a lady-in-waiting of my household."

"I don't see how Guisborne can refuse to let her go, should the lady be willing. He is not married to her."

"No. He's bedded an innocent maid of good but poor family with no intention of marrying her. I despise men such as that."

"As do I, lady. But are you quite sure Alice wants to be rescued?"

Elizabeth nodded. "Julianna was very angry when I saw her earlier. She told me what Alice said to her. I won't go into the horrible details, but the woman is near despair. She needs to get away from that man and to a safe place."

"Then we shall see that she does."

"Alex!" The shout was loud and impatient and footsteps accompanied it, hurrying toward the solar.

"Are you not going to answer?" Elizabeth asked.

"Not if I don't have to. It's my cousin, Geoffrey de Mandeville."

"I don't believe I've met the man."

"His father is the justiciar, Geoffrey FitzPiers, earl of Essex."

"I know Lord Essex. He recently wed Gilbert and Maud's aunt, Avelina de Clare."

"That makes Geoffrey your cousin of some sort."

"I suppose. I've never been able to keep the more distant relations clear. I'd no doubt be safe in saying every noble family in England is cousin to the Clares."

"And most will descend like locusts on Blyth for the tournament."

"I've heard talk dozens are expected."

Alex wondered if he should tell her the true reason so many barons would gather at Blyth in the week to come.

The discontent in England since John became king had grown rapidly. The king's greed, his new means of taxing his nobles, his endless demands for more money, both angered and worried his barons. His stumbling in France, where he seemed likely to go to war with the French king, worried those barons who held fiefs there. Under Richard at least the continental possessions had been safe. What better excuse could they have to gather openly than a tournament? What better chance to speak together privately? At Blyth men would begin to know whose loyalty was shaky, who had been unjustly deprived of land or coin, who the king had mistreated or humiliated. It would be a time for men to confirm or deny the rumors they'd heard; to weigh what options there might be against a king who threatened their ancient freedoms and privileges. Who, more than Elizabeth, knew the man they all served as their liege lord?

He leaned back against the wall and scowled. He was enjoying her company far too much to welcome an interruption, but since the door to the room was open Geoffrey soon found them. Gilbert trailed behind. The two knights were almost of an age, Geoff a few years older, and both young enough to find a cloudy, rain-washed day a goad to their tempers. Though Geoff was dark-haired and Gilbert fair, they had eyes of the same pale blue, more striking in the older man's darker face. They were both tall, lean and powerful, young men who were healthy and strong and had far too much energy to stay within castle walls unless absolutely necessary.

"There you are, Coz," Geoffrey said. He smiled as he came toward them, rather openly inspecting Elizabeth, who ducked her head to hide her embarrassment. Alexander's scowl deepened.

"Who is your fair lady friend?" Geoffrey asked.

Alexander's voice rumbled his displeasure. "Lady Elizabeth FitzWilliam, the countess of Gloucester."

Geoffrey's face immediately lost its hint of bawdiness. Gilbert passed him by and lifted Elizabeth's hand, placing a courtly kiss on the back of it. "Aunt, it is good to see you again. This uncivilized brute and I have come to try to steal your escort." He turned his attention to Alexander. "We've heard the lists have been finished at Blyth and thought to ride over for a few hours' practice. Care to join us?"

"I think not." Alexander looked pointedly out the window, where the rain still fell. The idea of mock battle in full armor under those conditions did not appeal, not with the warmth of the castle and the enjoyable company he'd be forfeiting for the dubious pleasure.

"Ah, of course, 'tis a young man's game," Gilbert said.

"Try again with someone else, Gil. You'll not spur me with such taunts. I've been a Crusader, remember? I've seen enough of the real thing to make me more able to wait the pleasures of a test of skills. Next week will be soon enough for me to think of lists and lances and the bruises that come with them."

Gilbert relinquished his aunt's hand and turned to slap his companion on the back. "I warned you he'd not go for it. Come, Geoff, 'tis you and I it seems."

It was then Alex noticed how uncommonly quiet Geoffrey was.

"I do most humbly apologize, lady," Geoffrey said, "for not knowing who you were."

Elizabeth cocked her head to one side and her smile was warm and gentle. "There is no need, sir. Indeed, it is refreshing not to be caught in tedious protocol with all I meet." She elegantly extended her hand to him, and with a bow he placed a kiss there. When he lifted his head their gaze held for a long moment.

"Well met indeed, lady." His voice was a caress and Elizabeth did naught to break the stare between them. Both seemed reluctant to part. Her hand lingered in his for long moments. Finally Gilbert roughly cleared his throat and said, "Are you coming, Geoff?"

It broke whatever spell there had been and Geoffrey straightened and gave the lady a most dazzling bright smile, full of youth and happiness. "I'm coming."

The silence when the two young men left was complete and awkward. Alexander studied Elizabeth, who was acting like a shy and untried maid, tongue-tied and blushing. She rose and brushed the folds from her heavy wool skirts. "I promised Julianna a visit. She's worried about Alice."

He stood and offered his arm. "You sound worried as well."

"I am. That poor girl. How can anyone be so cruel?"

They left the solar. "Some men are brutes. We've all known them."

"This is a sweet young woman. Forgive me, it is that I am worried. I do not see that she has many options."

Alexander tightened his hold on her hand. "I share your outrage, Beth." He escorted her to the guest-chamber, which was filled with women, all talking at once. He watched as Elizabeth waded into the crowd. He felt like a bull among geese. Inwardly he cursed the man responsible for robbing Alice of her youth and hopefulness. Guy of Guisborne would need be wary of his step if he ever came within range of Alexander's arm. If he hurried he could probably catch Geoffrey and Gilbert before they left the stables. He felt a sudden need to use his anger in the lists at Blyth.

Chapter Seven

"I don't know how we're going to do this." Marian spoke as she ate, stuffing her mouth with roast duck and good wheat bread. They had stolen their dinner from the groaning platters and bowls crowding the kitchen, waiting to be taken to the hall for the feast. They sat now, well hidden behind stores of grain, in a shed beyond the bake ovens.

"You couldn't get close enough to Alice to speak to her?"

"I couldn't find a good enough reason to go up the stairs and I didn't see her come back down. What are we going to do?"

"I don't know," Giselle said. She washed her stewed beef down with a draught of ale. "We need some sort of diversion, something to draw Guisborne's attention away from Alice long enough for us to get to her."

"Then what?"

"Then we take her out of here."

Marian looked at her as though she thought Giselle

simpleminded. "We just walk her through the gate, past the guards, and no one will notice?"

"We'll cover her up with a cloak. It'll be three serving women leaving the bailey, nothing to draw attention." When Marian looked no less uncertain, she asked, "Have you a better idea?"

"No."

Their original plan had presumed they'd be able to talk to Alice and coordinate an escape. It appeared that wouldn't be possible. Everything would have to be done quickly, and Alice would have little or no forewarning. "Now what can we use to cause enough of a diversion to sneak Alice out of a hall full of people?"

Marian groaned, and concentrated on eating.

Alexander watched as a seemingly endless array of squires and pages brought platters of food into the hall. By the generosity of Guisborne's larder it would be hard to guess there was famine threatening. Of course, famine rarely touched the wealthy. If there was no grain, there was always meat from the forests, which the common folk were not allowed to hunt, and fish from the streams and weirs the lords owned.

He sat at the high table, but far to one end. Beside him sat Rose and on the other side, Alice. His niece was stiff with careful dignity and curious as a cat in a dairy. The table they sat at was covered with a white cloth of linen and the plate they ate from was silver, as were the cups filled with a hearty wine. The lower tables were uncovered, and the plates and bowls of wood, and here the simple knights and their ladies sat. Only the great lords, the earls and other barons, sat at the high table with Guisborne. Alex was the least important of these, and so was the most removed from Guisborne himself.

"Have you lived here long?" he asked Alice.

She looked at him with a startled expression, as though she did not expect him to speak to her. "Nay, sir. A little more than a month. Since just before my father died."

"I did not know his death had been so recent. You have my sympathy."

Tears filled her eyes but she wiped them away and smiled tremulously. "I thank you for your kindness. His death was sudden and unexpected. It has been a shock."

Julianna had told him how Alice came to be here. Guisborne had offered her father five pounds of silver. He stared at the baron and wondered if those five pounds had been paid before Alice's father met his conveniently untimely death. Julianna had also told him the woman was terrified of Guisborne and was desperate to leave, but had nowhere to go. She loved a man named Alan, but he had no means of rescuing her, being but a simple man, not even a knight.

A young page presented them with a pheasant for his approval. Alex nodded and the boy began the ritual carving of the bird. The pheasant had been stuffed with a smaller bird, and within that bird had been stuffed a sparrow. Rose smiled with delight as each layer was revealed, and clapped with pleasure when the page laid choice pieces of roasted fowl on her plate. Alex had never much cared for elaborate ritual. He much preferred simple fare and good company to sumptuous dining in luxurious surroundings. He found the lord of Guisborne most unpleasant. How was he to spend a fortnight here without throttling the man for his treatment of Alice, who was only a few years older than Rose?

"Uncle Alex, why is that woman staring at you?"

"What woman?"

"There." Rose pointed to the far end of the hall.

He saw her standing beside the screen that separated the hall from the food preparation area. Her presence hit him like a fist in his gut. She stood with her hand to her throat, her eyes large in her beautiful, pale face, her red hair in wild disarray around her head and shoulders. *What the hell was she doing here?* Next to him Alice gasped and choked on the wine she was drinking. He tore his attention away from the red-haired woman and pounded gently on Alice's back.

When he glanced up, she was gone. "Did you see where she went?"

Rose nodded. "Back toward the bailey."

Alex left the table, ignoring the various inquiries and comments as he moved quickly through the hall. Outside, he caught a glimpse of her just as she turned a corner and was hidden behind the kitchen building. He ran after her. By the time he rounded the corner she was nowhere in sight. He plunged into the kitchen. Cooks screamed and shouted at him.

"Where is the red-haired wench?" he asked, grabbing the nearest man by his tunic.

He pointed over his shoulder. There she was. She looked frantically around her, but there was no escape. Finally, she squared her shoulders and looked at him defiantly. He walked over to where she stood. "We meet again," he said.

"So we do."

She sounded frightened. That puzzled him, until he realized he was scowling and hulking over her. He moved back a step and smiled. "I did not know you belonged at Guisborne."

"I'm working just through the tournament. The food is good."

She was lying. Why? What was she doing here? She looked nervously past him, but he crossed his arms, signaling he would not let her go. "Tell me your name."

"What?"

"Your name."

"Giselle."

"Only Giselle?"

"Yes."

She most assuredly did not want to be here, talking to him. Her green eyes were filled with worry and anger and her impatience was obvious. "Where are your friends? Robyn and John?"

"Hush," she hissed, and looked around nervously to see if anyone had heard him.

He'd meant it as a jest. Now he wondered if there was reason to worry. Was she the only one of Robyn's outlaw band to have infiltrated Guisborne, or were there others? He placed a hand firmly around her upper arm and leaned toward her. "What are you doing here, Giselle?"

She tried to pull away. "I've come to do a fair day's work and that is all."

"You do not lie well. Mayhap if I bring you to the hall and have Sir Guy question you, you'd be more forthcoming." He had no intention of taking her anywhere near Guy, but the woman didn't know that. Would the threat work? It did. She chewed her lower lip and stopped struggling against his hold.

"We truly mean no harm," she said.

"We?"

" 'Tis only Marian and me."

"Who is Marian?"

"You've met."

"Ah, the lovely young lady with the bow and arrow who threatened to shoot me through the heart if I moved. Yes, I can see there is naught to be worried about. Who is her intended target tonight?"

"It's nothing like that."

"Then what is it?"

"Why should I trust you? You're a nobleman."

Her reasoning confused him. To his mind a man of his station was more likely to be a man of honor than those she kept company with. "You've no need to trust me, Giselle. Just tell me what you're doing, and if I think it harmless I'll not interfere."

"I saved your life, noble. What if I ask payment for that?"

He drew back, startled. The woman was bargaining with him. Didn't she realize she had no position of influence to bargain from? "My life would not have been in danger if you didn't show a penchant for poison. Good God. Between you and your friend Marian, you can kill an entire hall full of people."

"Would you stop saying such dreadful things? I don't kill people. We're just here to . . . help . . . a friend."

"Who do you know here? Who is in need of your help?"

"You're infuriating. If we don't get this done before sundown, they'll close the gates and we can't leave."

She wasn't going to tell him, at least not without more forceful persuasion, and he wasn't about to use force. He believed her when she said their intent was not deadly. "All right. Let's say, for argument's sake, I owe you a debt for saving my life. Tell me what you're doing here and I'll do nothing to interfere."

She eyed him suspiciously. "Do you swear?"

"On all I hold holy."

She still hesitated. He released her arm. "I do not make vows lightly, Giselle. As long as no one is in danger, I'll not betray you."

"The baron here, Guisborne, he is keeping a woman against her will."

"Do you mean Alice?" He noted that she said Guisborne's name with particular loathing.

"Yes. Do you know her?"

"We've met."

"Marian and I are trying to rescue Alice."

"The two of you? No one else is with you inside Guisborne's walls?"

"Nay. This place is crawling with knights. He's not stupid, m'lord."

"But he waits near, he and his men?"

She nodded. "Near enough. All we need do is get Alice beyond the walls and into the forest. She'll be safe."

"Does Alan wait for her there?" If she was surprised he knew about Alan of Barnsdale, she did not show it. He brought one finger to his pursed lips and studied her. "Just how did you and Marian plan on getting Alice out the gate? Guisborne watches her like a mongrel on a bone."

"I know. Marian is planning a diversion during the feast and in the confusion, we'll lead Alice to safety. But now you've kept me from letting Alice know we're here, so she can be prepared."

Alex remembered Alice's sudden coughing spell. "I think she saw you, when I first did. She'll not be taken completely by surprise. Your plan has merit, but you can use some help. What say you if I keep Guisborne distracted while you work your rescue?" He had to admire their spirit, though this was no game. If they were caught, Guisborne was not likely to be lenient.

"You would help us?"

She sounded like he'd asked her to eat a live toad. "Aye, fair Giselle. For a price."

She crossed her arms and narrowed her eyes. "I should have known. What price? What do I have you could possibly want?"

His smile widened and the realization of what he might want played across her face, until she was looking at him with a smoldering glare. Was that passionate look one of anger, or desire? He did not bother to ask. He took a step closer, until they stood so close her breasts rubbed against him when she breathed. He was a tall man, but he did not have to stoop. He pulled her close as he lowered his head toward hers. She offered no resistance. Her hands went around his waist, pulling him closer. Her hips rocked against his, inflaming his desire until he was hard against her. Her lips were soft and sweet beneath his and he was gentle, savoring her. When his tongue played against her lips, she gasped. Her lips parted. He played her expertly and with an awkward innocence she followed his lead. With a groan he crushed her to him and his kisses deepened, became more demanding. She responded with growing passion, clutching him to her, until he was dizzy with her. Giselle. Sweet and hot, innocence and passion, and all soft, wonderful woman.

He kissed her neck and she arched her head back, seeking his caress. "Woman, have mercy."

She opened her eyes and looked at him, like someone dreaming coming awake. "Nay, m'lord. You are the one without mercy." Her voice was sultry and warm and low.

"My name is Alexander."

"Yes," she whispered. "I know."

He wanted her to say his name, to say it with passion and wanting and need. "Giselle," he said, and buried his face in the fragrant gift of her hair. "Giselle. I must have you."

"Fire!"

He jerked away from her.

"Fire! In the castle!"

The kitchens burst into chaos as people stumbled over each other, grabbing whatever could be used to hold water and rushing out the door. Something twisted in his gut and he held her at arm's length. "Is this what you call a diversion? God's blood, there are women and children inside the keep." With a sneer of disgust, he left her and rushed out into the bailey.

* * *

Giselle stood for a moment, stunned by his sudden departure, his accusation at first not penetrating her confused emotions. She gasped as his meaning became clear. Surely he could not believe she or Marian would deliberately set a fire? She plunged out into the bailey. She'd never been inside a castle before today, and then had gone no farther than the screen in the great hall. She stared up at the hulk of stone that made up the body of the castle. The stone would not burn. But inside were wooden floors and ceilings, tapestries along the walls, and rushes on the floor, all tinder. A line had formed from the well to the castle entrance and people handed water in buckets and bowls and anything else that could be lifted along the line. It was an agonizingly slow process. Nobles worked alongside slaves and serfs to try to prevent the castle from burning. She saw Alexander near the entrance. He was talking to the same woman she'd seen him riding with at Wolfhurst. A young boy and girl clutched the woman's skirts. The woman was screaming something, and a man and a woman held her from fleeing back into the burning hall. The wind shifted and her words came to Giselle.

"My babies!"

Her heart clenched at the anguished cry. There were children within the castle. He'd told her that. She'd seen a few of them. Alexander and another man ran into the building. Quickly Giselle crossed the bailey and climbed the stairs to the entrance. She was jostled and pushed by men carrying water, cursed at but unhindered. No one thought she would actually go into that inferno, so no one thought to stay her.

A moment of overwhelming fear assaulted her at sight of the fire, its brutal flames confined against one side of the hall. The smoke was thick and choking. Alexander thought she'd set the fire. How could he think that of her? Her eyes teared. She pulled the hem of her gown up to cover her mouth and nose, to filter some of the smoke, then hurried across the hall to the stone stairs leading to the upper floors. Alexander was fast disappearing up those stairs and she followed him to a chamber where another man and two serving-women stood, one holding an infant.

"What do you mean, you can't find Jordana?" the other man shouted at the women.

"My lord, she was here but a moment ago."

"Stephan," Alexander said. "We'll find her. You must stay calm."

"Have you checked the small room in the north tower?" Giselle asked.

They turned to stare at her.

"What room?" Alexander asked.

"It would be quicker if you followed me," she said.

"Take the women outside," Stephan said. "I'll go with her."

"No." Giselle was surprised by the authority in her voice. "The smoke is too thick. They will be safer if they go up to the roof. The tower stair will take them there."

"She's right," Alexander said.

Giselle led them into the hall, where smoke from below was beginning to billow in waves toward them. She turned in the opposite direction, down the dark hall, turning left and then right. They followed, one of the women weeping softly, the baby crying.

The stairs were where she knew they'd be. "There is a door halfway up. That is where the small chamber is found."

Alexander bounded up the stairs ahead of her. The others followed more slowly. Soon a sharp whistle came from above them.

"Thanks be to God," Stephan said. "He's found her."

By the time they reached the top of the stairs and emerged onto the roof, Alexander was there with a girl of about five years in his arms. The child was crying, and when she saw her father she lifted her arms to him. Stephan ran forward and took his daughter from Alexander, crushing her to his chest. The serving-women, both stout and unaccustomed to running, were busy trying to catch their breath from rushing up the stairs. Giselle took the infant from her nurse and held the baby gently against her shoulder.

"Hush, little one. Hush." The baby quieted, now that the people around her were not shouting and rushing about. Looking up, she saw Alexander staring at her. He leaned against the stone wall of the battlement, his shoulders slumped.

"Bring my niece here," he said.

His niece. Then that woman, the child's mother, would be his sister or sister-in-law. Why did that thought comfort her? She closed the space between them and handed him the child. He held the baby close for a moment, his eyes tight shut. When he looked at her again, there were tears in his eyes. "My thanks, Giselle."

"Her lady mother will be most worried."

"Aye." He turned and peered over the wall, down to the green fields that stretched away from Guisborne's foundations. "We're not near the bailey."

"No. It's there." She pointed to her left, and followed as he walked over to the other wall. Stephan came also, holding his daughter.

Stephan and Alexander looked at each other, then nodded. Together they let out a piercing whistle that carried far. Giselle watched as the people below looked up, Stephan's wife among them. She saw her husband and daughters and knew her family was safe.

Giselle wondered if a noblewoman had the same fear

and joy and sorrow in her heart as any other woman. That she was rich and powerful did not diminish her mother love. Could it be that not all nobles were evil? She'd suspected that, in a secret, inarticulate way. Now she knew, beyond doubt, that she had as much in common with that elegant woman who waited below as there were differences between them. They both loved and hurt and laughed, and for the same reasons.

Alex cradled tiny Isabella against his chest. High upon the ramparts of Guisborne Castle he could see for miles and watched as the stars came out in a clear sky. It was not raining and he thought of the irony of it; the land so wet it was a curse, and the fire raging below, with no easy way to get water to it. They were safe here, as long as the fire did not burst beyond control, as long as it did not devour all of the castle. It would have to be a great fire indeed to do so. He prayed, as he had seldom prayed in his life, that it would not be his day to die. Not for himself so much, but for the little ones, for his nieces, who were so young and fragile and did not know yet the great joys of life. He glanced at his brother, who sat with his back against a gray stone wall, Jordana pulled close to him. The little girl slept, trusting what she had been told, that once the fire was out, they'd go down. He saw his own worry reflected in Stephan's eyes. What was taking them so long to put out that damned fire?

Giselle stood apart, her hands braced against stone as she gazed out over the wall. She had been brave and clear headed. And foolish beyond belief. He walked over to her, and saw her stiffen at his approach, but she did not turn. "Why did you follow me into the castle?"

"You do not know?"

He kept his voice soft, so the baby would not be frightened. "Should I? You make no sense. Why did you risk yourself?"

"Why did you?"

"Do you always answer a question with a question? No, don't bother. My family was in danger. I couldn't not help."

"Why do you think I am different than you? My motives are the same. There were children in danger. Or perhaps I simply don't know enough about fires in castles to be afraid."

"But you know the castle very well. You led us up here without hesitation. Why did you tell me you'd never been to Guisborne before?"

She turned then, a puzzled look on her face. "I haven't. Today is the first time I've been inside a castle in my life."

Why would she lie about such a thing? It was obvious she knew the castle, knew where the rooms were, where the quickest way to safety lay, where the small chamber a child would find fascinating and sneak off to was located. When he'd opened that door and found Jordana, he'd known a moment of profound relief that Giselle had guessed where the girl would be. If they'd had to go back to look for her, God knows what would have happened. Yet the woman claimed ignorance of the castle's design. What else did she lie about? The fire. His anger rekindled. Had she had a hand in setting this fire? Was it the diversion she'd mentioned?

"Do you think Alice has got away?" His voice was angry.

"I don't know. I haven't given it a thought."

"It's certainly confused enough down there. An army could march through the gates and no one would notice."

She looked at him strangely, then turned again to gaze over the hills. "You believe the fire was deliberately set."

"I have reason to think so, do I not?"

"No. You do not. I've told you I had nothing to do with

it, and that I swear. Do you truly think I'd endanger these sweet children?''

He heard the tightness in her voice, as though she fought against tears. Why did he want to believe her? She had risked herself for the children, but she could have been motivated by guilt. Or horror, if she thought her friend Marian responsible. Alexander realized suddenly how tired he was. ''I do not know what you are capable of, woman. Nor does your vow mean aught to me. If I find evidence you had anything to do with this, do not think any debt of gratitude I may have owed you in the past will keep you safe from my vengeance.''

She whirled about. The look of stark terror on her face did not temper his anger. She had reason to be afraid of him, for he did not lie. No matter how beautiful or tempting, if she'd had a hand in endangering his family, he'd not hesitate to hand her over for punishment. He'd see her hang.

Chapter Eight

The fire was out. A shout went up from those gathered in the bailey. The castle was saved. Giselle felt the hard knot of tension that had gripped her belly loosen. They were safe now. Truly safe. She glanced at Alexander where he stood with the other man, the one named Stephan. At least *they* were safe. She wasn't sure about herself. Earlier she'd claimed Marian could not possibly have had anything to do with the fire. Now doubt nagged at her. Marian was impulsive, sometimes acting first and regretting later. Never would she purposely endanger so many, but she had as little experience with castles as Giselle. What if she had meant only to cause a small fire, a diversion, and it had grown beyond control? And how had she known where the room Jordana hid in could be found, or that these stairs led up to safety? She could see in Alexander's eyes that he had not believed her when she claimed she'd never been here before. In truth, she wouldn't have believed her either, under the circumstances. It made no sense, but then the entire day had been one of misadventure and surprise. Beginning with that kiss in the kitchen. She would not think of that. She was confused, and exhausted. All she wanted was to be gone from here. Had Marian and Alice made it out of the enclosure? Had they left her here, alone?

The others began to descend the stairs, but she held back. She'd be the last down and hoped she could slip away without notice once they reached the ground.

"You go ahead of me," Alexander said, pointing at her.

He waited, the look on his face hard, the command in his voice clear. He was not going to give her a choice. He still thought she had something to do with this fire, but he did not know her, did not know how incapable she was of any cruelty or malice. She was a healer, and it was a sacred trust. She cherished life, and tried to preserve it, to ease pain and suffering, not create more. He did not know her at all.

The hall was dark and smoke hazed the air. Across the immense room, on the side opposite from the door a great hole had burned through the wooden floor and down into the basement. Giselle coughed as she inhaled soot and quickly covered her mouth against it. While not ruined, the hall needed extensive repairs and the smoke would take days if not weeks to clear. She shuddered at the thought of what a disaster it could have been, with so many people crowded inside when the conflagration started. A man holding a torch stood at the door to show them the way out. The night air was clean and fresh compared to that within and she breathed deeply, for the first time in hours without the quivering fear in the pit of her belly. Alexander had a hand clamped around her upper arm but for the moment she had no intention of trying to slip away from him and into the crowd.

The people gathered in the bailey were dirty and

exhausted from fighting the fire, but now they were exultant to see Julianna and her family reunited. Women wiped tears from their eyes, and men smiled and pounded each other on the back. Alexander stood quietly to one side as his nieces were given to their mother, and Giselle was content to watch as well. The woman was lovelier than she had imagined, and Stephan held her in his embrace in such a way none could doubt the loving devotion they shared. What was it like to know such a love? To know there was another in this world who held your life more precious than their own? Someone to cling to, to believe in, to trust with all your soul. Someone who would not betray or deceive or abandon you. Would there ever be a man who would look at her the way Stephan looked at his wife? And the light in Julianna's eyes, would there be a man in Giselle's life she loved in that all-consuming way?

Something brushed against her leg. Giselle glanced down to see Odin next to her, his big head pushing into her hand. She scratched behind his ears, then realized he shouldn't be here. Her actions drew Alexander's attention.

"What's he doing here?" Alexander asked.

"I know not. The gate must be open, in all this confusion, and he wandered in looking for me."

He eyed her suspiciously, but before he could ask another question, a woman's terrified scream split the quiet. The cries came from near the stables. Something in them seemed familiar. Fear exploded in Giselle. "That's Marian!"

Alexander's hand shifted to the pommel of his sword. The air was full of danger, but where it came from he wasn't yet sure. Across the yard, near the stables, lights flared and he saw Guy dragging a woman by a rope tied around her hands. Giselle was right. The woman was Marian and her screams pierced the night. The gates were open and it was doubtful there was a guard at them, every man needed to fight the fire. He scanned the crowd, searching, but carefully, so not to attract attention to himself.

He saw the big man, John, first. Near him stood Robyn. How many more men of the outlaw band had slipped into the bailey? How many even now had hands at bows, ready to rescue Marian and Giselle and Alice? It would be a bloodbath should anything happen in this crowd. Robyn's attention was riveted on Marian and he started toward her but John held him back. Guy was dragging the woman toward the hall. She was quieter now, trying to keep pace with her captor's long stride. Behind them came Alice, fear plain in her face. She was pleading with Guy, but he roughly pushed her away.

"God's feet, what is he doing?" Geoffrey asked.

Alexander glanced at his cousin, soot-grimed and weary. It was good Geoff was near. Stephan still stood beside Julianna. Where was Elizabeth? He found her, near Julianna, and saw Gilbert and Maud beside her. "There may be trouble. Protect Elizabeth."

Geoffrey looked at him quizzically, but did not question him. He moved swiftly but unobtrusively to Elizabeth's side. Giselle squirmed and he tightened his grip. "You're not going anywhere."

"You don't understand," she hissed at him.

"I've seen your Robyn. How many of his men are with him?" When she did not answer he shook her. "I understand only too well, it seems. What is your next diversion? An arrow in the back? Do you really think any of you will leave this place alive? Look around you. There is a score of knights, all armed. How many, Giselle?"

"About ten or a few less. They aren't supposed to be inside the walls."

"But they are." His family was in danger, again, and

this woman was at fault. He'd thought to tolerate Robyn's presence in Sherwood, thinking the band did little more than steal one of the king's deer now and again. He saw now he'd been a fool. One of his first tasks when he returned to Wolfhurst would be to clear the forest of outlaws. He'd begin tonight. He whistled, hard and sharp.

Giselle stared up at him but he ignored her. Julianna and Stephan turned to look and when he nodded they moved closer together. Rose and William quieted and pressed closer to their parents. Geoffrey and Gilbert moved to put Maud and Elizabeth between them, shielding them with their bodies. The knights of Stephan's household gathered around their lord and lady, until the women and children and maids were barricaded inside the protection of their wary, watchful presence.

Alexander was gratified to see how well Stephan had trained his children and retainers to respond to that warning. For the moment he was satisfied as to their safety and turned his attention once more to Guy. The man had stopped his determined progress across the crowded bailey and now stood beside a large stump of an old tree, the top of which was scarred with generations of ax and sword wounds. He pulled hard on the rope until Marian was forced to her knees, then jerked until her hands and forearms lay on top of the stump. Alexander did not wait to see what would happen next. He rushed toward Guy, slipping his sword from his scabbard as he went. He prayed Robyn and his men would control their urge to help Marian long enough for him to prevent what Guy intended.

The crowd grew quiet, their faces in the flare of torches curious, horrified, or excited, depending upon their natures. Guy raised his sword high in one hand. Marian screamed then with all the fierce terror of knowing that with the fall of that blade she would lose her hands. Alexander wasn't sure he'd be in time. He roughly pushed people out of his path, cursing, expecting an arrow to be shot through Guy's heart at any moment. Still Robyn held back. Something in the back of Alexander's brain wondered at the man's constraint, but he hadn't time to ponder it. With a final push he was upon Guy, and swung his sword up in a desperate arc even as the other sliced down. The blades collided. Guy, unprepared for the parry, nearly stumbled, his sword glancing off the side of the tree stump harmlessly.

"Who dares!"

"What has the woman done?" Alexander forced himself to speak in a calm, clear voice. Guy had every right to be sorely provoked by his interference. Whatever Marian had done, the baron no doubt felt justified in his punishment. That Guy would be a dead man should he execute such discipline was the only reason Alex interfered; not that he cared much for Guisborne, but others might come to harm.

"What business is it of yours?" Guy asked.

Alexander glanced at Marian, who was staring wide-eyed, Alice and Giselle standing just behind her. He saw the pleading in Giselle's eyes and wondered that she did not take the opportunity to escape. No one would notice if she slipped away. "It seems whatever she has done, the punishment is quick and perhaps too harsh."

"Too harsh? By God! I've a mind to hang the wench. The woman set the fire. I saw her do it."

There was a collective intake of breath at his words, followed by a vehement outburst of rage.

"Hanging's too good for the bitch!"

"Burn her!"

The cries for blood rose like a rogue wave out of a calm sea, ready to smash everything in its path. He knew such bloodlust, once roused, was hard to quench. If Marian had indeed done as Guy claimed, he could not see how he could prevent her maiming, or her death. There was something that made him hesitate in moving away and giving Guisborne a free hand with his prisoner. He knew Guy to be cruel, that was part of it. But it was Giselle and her conviction Marian could not be involved, her adamant denial of her own involvement in the fire, that stayed him. Her words rang true to him, for all he had little reason to believe her.

The cries of the crowd grew louder and nastier. Alex noticed something moving quickly toward him from one side and turned to see his niece, Rose, as she raced toward him. Stephan was in close pursuit of his daughter, but she dodged him, a look of determined purpose on her face. She stood beside him and Alex placed a hand on her thin shoulder. She was trembling. Stephan caught up with her, but didn't say a word, standing to her other side, grim of visage and with his hand ready on his sword.

"This woman did not set the fire." Rose spoke clearly and those close enough to hear, quieted, hushing those behind them. "I saw how the fire started. This woman was nowhere near."

"What did you see, Rose?" Alex asked. He thought Guy would have cuffed the girl, had she not been the earl of Rosmar's daughter. His hand tightened slightly and she was calmer, the shaking less noticeable.

"A squire knocked over a candle and it set the rushes afire. He poured wine on it and stomped the embers out."

"Then you saw different than I," Guisborne said.

Rose hesitated, then spoke again, louder, so the quieter crowd could hear. "I know not what you saw, m'lord. The squire thought he'd put the blaze out, and so did I. I was sitting beside the lady Alice, and this woman"—she pointed at Marian—"was serving us and nowhere near the place the squire had been. A few minutes later, a tapestry near where the fire had been burst into flame. This woman helped Lady Alice and me escape."

Alexander believed his niece. He had no reason not to. What she said made sense. "The fire must have run through the rushes and behind the tapestry, where the squire did not see it."

The crowd was quiet now, though some looked disappointed that there would be no hanging to add to the day's excitement.

"There has obviously been some sort of misunderstanding," Stephan said. "I would suggest you release the woman."

Alexander knew, as did Guisborne, that it was not a request. He watched as Guisborne worried through his options. Choosing not to be stupid, with a grunt and a curse, Guy resheathed his weapon. He stared down at Marian, who lay weeping, her arms still pulled tight across the chopping block. He gave one last, vicious tug on the rope, then released it. "I know not who you are, woman, but I know your face. I ban you from my lands and declare for all to hear, if you be caught within my demesne I'll hang you yet."

"The woman has my protection." Alexander wasn't sure what prompted him to make such a declaration. It was obvious to him association with Robyn and any of his band was bound to be troublesome, but he'd never been tolerant of men who abused their power.

"You know her?" Guisborne asked.

"She lives in the village at Wolfhurst." The lie came easily enough, and it was half true. He thought Robyn and the others probably did live on Wolfhurst land, though in the forest, not the village, but Guisborne did not need to know that.

Guy narrowed his gaze and gestured toward Marian. "I'm familiar with the villagers there, and I've not seen this woman in the twenty years I've been lord of Guisborne

Castle. I suppose the red-haired wench is yours as well?"
Guisborne asked.

Alex glanced to where Giselle and Marian stood, comforting each other. He sighed. He'd never been good at
lying. Even now his brother was standing, arms crossed,
with that familiar smug look on his face, waiting to see
how he would get himself out of this mess. "She's one of
the serfs as well."

"At Wolfhurst?" Guy asked.

"At Wolfhurst." He let irritation color his answer.

"You there," Guy shouted, pointing at Giselle. "Come
here, wench."

She hesitated, then reassured Marian, and stepped forward. Alex saw her square her shoulders and admired her
composure, even as he wondered what Guy would do next.

"Are you an inhabitant of Wolfhurst village?" Guisborne
demanded.

She glanced quickly at Alex, then away. "Aye, m'lord."

Guy moved closer to her, until he reached out and took
her face in his hand. He slowly turned her head from side
to side, then looked her up and down. With his other hand
he picked up a strand of her bright hair and twisted it
around his fingers. "Do you truly think I would not have
noticed you?"

Alex itched to strike the man for touching her. Stephan
must have seen how tense he was, because he laid a warning
hand on his arm.

"This maid and the other have only recently come to
Wolfhurst," Stephan said. "Before that they were in service
to me, at Rosmar."

Guisborne untangled his hand from her hair. "It would
seem your serfs are troublemakers, Wolfhurst. Keep them
away from my land."

Stephan put his arm companionably around Guisborne's shoulders and steered the man toward the dam-

aged castle. "We really cannot impose any further on your hospitality, under the circumstances. I will take my family and my folk to Blyth Abbey for the night."

"What of the tournament?" Guy asked.

Stephan gestured toward the stone keep. "You'll no doubt be busy with repairs. Winter will be here soon. There are other seasons for play."

Alex knew that if Stephan left, others would as well. Guy's carefully orchestrated effort to ingratiate himself with his betters would fail, if men left before he could ply them with the week of hospitality he'd planned. But the keep was uninhabitable and Stephan the most important man in attendance. A few minor knights, young and adventurous, would linger, eating Guy's food and enjoying the melees and fighting in the lists, before wandering back to where they came from. Alex had hoped to find a few such men for his mesnie for Wolfhurst was woefully undermanned. With a neighbor like Guisborne, he'd feel safer with a full guard at his own castle.

Guy looked as though he'd been sucking vinegar, but he could not force the earl to stay. "My men will escort you to the abbey."

"No," Alexander said, too quickly, and both men turned to look at him.

"We have more than enough as a guard," Stephan said, frowning at his brother before turning his attention back to Guisborne.

Stephan managed to calm the man's anger, talking to him in the confidential tones of an intimate, laughing at something Guisborne said. Alex relaxed. It appeared they'd dodged disaster after all.

"Uncle Alex."

He glanced at Rose, standing beside him. She looked worried. "You, my dear, were disobedient. You know better than to move away from your protectors until the danger is past and the signal given.''

She looked confused then, and a little angry. ''I couldn't let him cut off her hands. Not when I knew what he said wasn't true.''

He pursed his lips and looked down at her, with what he hoped was appropriate sterness. Damn the maid, but she was right, and he was proud of her for having the courage to speak up. Still, she'd put herself in harm's way after being warned. He shook his head, not sure what to say. ''You did right. But you were still disobedient.''

She smiled then and hugged him. ''I love you, Uncle Alex. You're sweet.''

Sweet? He supposed there were worse epithets than that. ''Then why do you still look so worried?''

''We can't leave Lady Alice with that man.''

He'd forgotten about Alice. She was standing with Giselle and Marian, the three of them clinging to each other for support. If Rose hadn't been there he would have said a very foul word. Instead, he went after his brother and Guisborne. By the time he reached them he knew he was too late. Elizabeth was there first.

''I'm sure you will agree it is much more appropriate for Lady Alice to become a member of my household,'' Elizabeth said.

''You do her far too great an honor,'' Guisborne said. ''She is but a simple knight's daughter. She is content here.''

''Nay, she is not,'' Alexander said. ''She will be leaving with us.'' He deliberately tried to provoke the man, and knew it was foolish even as he did it. He'd like an excuse to pound his fist into Guisborne's face.

Stephan spoke before the confrontation became physical. ''Lady Elizabeth has assured me Alice is indeed willing to join her household. Since you are neither her husband nor her guardian, I see no reason why the lady cannot do as she pleases. I would most strongly advise you acquiesce to Lady Gloucester's wishes.''

Guisborne's face mirrored the anger he fought. Eventually prudence won out. He could not very well insult the earl of Rosmar and the countess of Gloucester over so trivial a matter as a troublesome bed partner. Their patronage was worth far more to a baron of Guisborne's modest standing than any woman could be. ''Take her, then, and be gone.''

Alexander took Elizabeth by the arm to escort her back to where the others waited. He was glad to put some distance between himself and Guisborne.

''Thank you for your help,'' Elizabeth said. ''Sir Guy is a most unpleasant man. I was afraid he'd not let Alice go without strong persuasion.''

''Which is exactly what he got,'' Alex said. ''Guisborne is pragmatic enough to know Stephan is not a man to defy over small things.''

''Power has its privileges,'' Stephan said. He walked on the other side of Elizabeth, and Rose took his hand to walk with them. ''It's perhaps unwise for you to antagonize so near a neighbor.''

Alexander smiled at his brother's diplomatic understatement. ''It is decidedly unwise and you know it. The man rubs me wrong. I'll be happy to have little to do with him. Do you think we'll have trouble finding shelter at the abbey for the night?''

''I know the abbot. There'll be no problem,'' Stephan said.

''Elizabeth, will you take Rose to her mother?'' Alexander watched as they moved away, then turned to face Stephan. ''We're like to have a problem on the way to the abbey.''

Stephan merely raised an eloquent eyebrow and waited for him to continue.

"There are those here who have an interest in Alice, and the woman, Marian, Guisborne was intent on punishing."

"Odd that, accusing her of setting the fire if she didn't do it. Do you know what was behind Guisborne's behavior?"

"I can guess. Marian and the other woman, Giselle, were here to help Alice escape. Guisborne may have seen them trying to leave and sought to frighten Alice into submission. I can only imagine his anger when told Alice would be leaving with us."

Stephan frowned. "Don't underestimate Guisborne. His pride has been hurt and that can goad a man into doing unconscionable things. But why would we have trouble on the road?"

"Do you remember the band of outlaws I told you of?"

"I'm not like to forget."

"The women are part of that group."

Stephan's eyebrows rose to new heights. "And the men will not take kindly to our having the women?"

Alexander nodded. "The men are here. I had to intervene with Guisborne before the fool had an arrow planted in his back. If he'd hurt Marian, he'd not be alive now."

"You'll need to do something about it. You can't allow a group of outlaws to roam the king's forest with impunity."

"What would you have me do? Hunt them down and kill them? So far I've seen no evidence of any brigandage. If they'd killed Guisborne tonight, however, they'd have given us little choice."

"It would seem you have a strange situation to deal with, little brother. You may tolerate this band of men for now, but mark my words, eventually they must be dealt with. Do you truly trust them to keep the peace?"

"I don't know. But I don't intend to keep Marian or Alice with us should they decide to return to the outlaws."

Stephan cocked his head and stared hard at his brother. "What of the other woman? You didn't mention her."

Alexander hesitated. Stephan knew him too well. He'd never been able to lie to his brother. "She stays with me."

Chapter Nine

The night was cold with a black dome of sky pierced by stars. Pale moonlight silvered the trees and rocks and tumbling streams in the woods. Strong arms held Giselle in place on the back of the large horse, and in her exhaustion she was tempted to let herself fall back against Alexander, to share his warmth. He had wrapped his cloak around her and the heavy folds kept out the cold. She felt protected and secure, but knew it to be illusory. Robyn and the others would be waiting, somewhere along the road. So she sat tense and watchful. Marian and Alice rode beside them, doubled up on a gentle mare, a lead rein firmly in Alexander's hand. Her friends were as watchful as she, searching the darkness for the first sign of men, straining to hear the rustle of underbrush or slap of boot on road that would give away their presence. Alexander reined his horse to a stop. The mare stopped as well and dropped her head to graze in the grass by the roadside. Odin, trotting beside them, sat and waited, his long tongue hanging from his mouth. The rest of the entourage continued on into the darkness, toward Blyth Abbey.

"Why do we stop?" Giselle asked.

"To wait for Robyn."

She was surprised, then realized she shouldn't have been. "What will you do?"

"I'm but one man, what could I do?"

She turned to stare at him. His blue eyes were unreadable. She saw neither humor nor anger there, but a cautious veiling. She was sure he was capable of destructive power should he choose to fight, even outnumbered ten to one. Apparently he'd told his brother of his plan since no one questioned it when he fell away from the rest of the group. She turned back around to wait. Whatever the baron of Wolfhurst had in mind she could not begin to guess. "Will you let us go?"

"Do you want to leave me?"

The words were soft, his mouth close to her ear. A shiver of longing coursed through her at the words, at his nearness, a yearning so strong she found it hard to breathe properly. What could she answer to such a question? Stay with him?

Odin barked, and suddenly where the road had been empty except for shadow and moonlight, Robyn stood with several other men. Alice gave a squeal of recognition and slid from her mount. She ran toward Alan, who caught her up against him and held her hard, his face buried in her shoulder.

"I take it she prefers yon woodsman to Guisborne."

She heard the sarcasm in his voice and did not answer him. Her opinion of Guy was no better than his. She turned her attention to Alice and Alan, their obvious happiness a balm to her weariness. Everything had worked out as planned after all. The two young lovers were reunited.

Robyn walked toward them, betraying no trace of hesitation or humility, approaching Alexander as he would an equal. "I owe you a debt of gratitude. You brought them safe to me." He held the mare's bridle in his hand and when Marian slipped from the horse he gathered her to his side, his arm around her in an unmistakable gesture of protection.

"Do not be too quick in your thanks," Alexander said.

She liked the way his voice rumbled through her body. It took a moment to notice what he'd said. She glanced at Robyn, but he gave a small shake of his head, signaling her to wait.

"What would you have?" Robyn asked.

"Your word."

"Why would you believe a pledge from me?"

"Because of the hostage I hold."

Giselle tensed in his arms. He was holding her in such a way she could not be free of him, yet he did not hurt her. She had no doubt if she tried to move, his hands would clamp down more tightly on her arm and waist.

Robyn's eyes narrowed and he hesitated before speaking. His words were careful. "There is no need to keep her. I will abide by my vow, whatever you ask."

"I cannot be sure of that."

"Nor can I be sure Giselle will come to no harm while in your care."

"Still, I will keep her."

She heard the possession in his voice, felt the determination in his body. What exactly was he bargaining for? She squirmed, trying to look around at him, to see his face, to puzzle out what lay behind the words. His hands tightened on her. Only she was aware of his quickened breathing.

"Stop moving like that."

It was whispered, his mouth again next to her ear. She felt his warm breath against her skin and shivered. "My home is with Robyn and the others."

"Nay, Giselle. My need is greater."

The hunger in his voice gave birth to an answering wave of longing that began in her belly and warmed her limbs. She could not mistake his meaning, but she felt no fear. The night grew colder under the clear sky and still they stood in the midst of the road, the stubborn knight daring her menfolk to make a move toward her rescue. She loved Robyn and John and the others. They were all the family she knew, and she would not see them come to harm because of her.

"What is it you want?" Robyn asked.

Alexander shifted in the saddle, pulling her closer against his broad chest. "Your word you will cause no harm to any man within the protection of my lands, nor lay a hand to any of my family or kin."

"What do we get in return?" Robyn asked.

"I will not hunt you down to hang."

The silence was long. The challenge hung between them. She would be held hostage to Robyn's good behavior. Robyn and the others would be safe from the baron's justice as long as the bargain held. Robyn was outlawed, as were most of the others. They could be hung by any man who caught them and with complete impunity. They were outside the law, hunted men, living dangerously, hiding in the woods for safety.

"What of the hunting?" Robyn asked.

"Stay within Wolfhurst land and you can hunt freely. Stray outside its bounds and I cannot protect you."

There was a murmur of incredulity among the men gathered around Robyn, but he quieted them with a lift of his hand. "Why would you give us hunting rights?"

"The coming winter is like to be a hard one. If a deer or two found its way to the village or the castle each week I'd not question how it got there. I'm but one man. I can't put meat on everyone's table."

"You'd feed your serfs venison from the king's forest?"

"Careful, Robyn. From *my* forest. I do not want trouble from the king's foresters."

"Nor do I."

"Are we agreed, then?"

Giselle glanced from one man to the other. Alexander, big and bold and proud as the devil, so sure of himself he had not even kept a guard with him; and Robyn, looking for all the world like he was bartering for some trivial thing at a fair, his long, lean body relaxed, his eyes bright with merriment.

Alexander leaned down to her once more and spoke so only she could hear. "If you wish to leave me at the end of a month, you are free to do so."

A month. What could happen in a month? A few short weeks, gone by so quickly she would hardly notice, then home again to her cave in the hills. What could happen in a month? She had no doubt that at the end of the month she would no longer be a virgin. She could get with child in a month. Worse, in those weeks she was very much afraid she would lose her heart to the man who held her so close she could feel his heat through her clothes. She wanted the man, damn him. What frightened her was the time when she would be forced to let him go.

She felt vulnerable in a way she'd never known before and it frightened her. Who was this man who could affect her so strongly with his touch? His voice echoed in her and she knew she would recognize it among all others. He was becoming important to her, a thing she had not sought and now could not deny. It could well be disastrous, if she gave her heart to the man, for he would not offer her permanence. Once he tired of her she would be gone, and another would take her place in his bed. Once he took a wife she would not be tolerated in his household. She knew all this, yet she did not fight him. If she could have him for only a short time, she would make it enough to last her a life. She would treasure the memories. If she were lucky, he would not tire of her for a long time. If she were lucky there would be a child of his to love, when she no longer interested him. He offered her a life of luxury such as she had never known and only vaguely imagined. What would it be like to live within the stone walls of a castle? To be dry and warm and safe, with enough to eat, not fearing that any moment you would be discovered and hauled away to a rough justice?

The thought suddenly came to her that she could be very useful to Robyn as the baron's bedmate, and wondered if the outlaw had realized the same. There would be little she couldn't find out about Wolfhurst, and relay to Robyn. Was that why he made no protest to her going? It must be so, or something like it. And perhaps even Alexander knew the same. Surely, had Robyn been of a mind to do so, Alexander would be dead by now and she free. She shuddered at the thought, grateful that for whatever reasons of their own the men had come to a wary truce, even if she were the token they used.

Alexander urged his stallion forward, until they were within arm's reach of Robyn and Marian. "I strongly suggest you quit this area. Guisborne is none too happy at losing Alice. Should he discover she is with you—"

"I know well enough what that bastard is capable of." Robyn glanced back over his shoulder, in the direction of Guisborne Castle, and his face was set in hard anger. "There will come a day when it is me and that man." He turned back to look at them, his face once more the pleasant mask of reasonableness he normally wore. "I was sore tempted to put an arrow through his black heart tonight, once I saw he had Marian. If you hadn't been standing in my line of fire I might not have stayed my hand."

"You wouldn't have escaped."

"Mayhap not. Guisborne assuredly would not have."

"I'll turn my back on some poaching, but be warned, I'll not tolerate murder. Even of Guisborne."

"You may well regret those words."

"It wouldn't be the first time," Alexander said, with a hint of laughter in his voice. "As to the woman, I'll keep her safe."

Marian stepped forward, small and defiant. "Do you think that is enough? What of her happiness? I'll not stand here and let you make a prisoner of Giselle."

Exactly what Marian thought she might do, Giselle wasn't sure, but she did believe her friend capable of anything, no matter how ill-conceived, if she thought a loved one was threatened.

"Happiness?" Alexander asked. "I cannot give or take such a thing. We each create or destroy our own happiness."

Marian shook her head, her dark curls bouncing around her shoulders. "You've much to learn of life if you believe such a thing as that."

"Enough, Marian," Giselle said. "I am no prisoner. I go willingly enough."

Robyn put a hand on his wife's arm and pulled her away from the horse. "Godspeed, then, Wolfhurst. Know I will keep an eye on Giselle. Should she be misused or ill-treated, our bargain is void."

"Fair enough. Keep yourself and your men quiet and hidden this winter and I'll ignore your presence. Come spring we'll see where we stand with each other."

Robyn nodded once and with uplifted hand, signaled the others, who silently slipped into the cover of the forest and were soon lost to sight.

They were alone on the road.

"You need not fear me, Giselle. I will not hurt you."

She wanted to believe him, but knew it was not true. He

could hurt her more profoundly than anyone else in her life, if she allowed herself to be vulnerable to his charms. "You have made your bargain, m'lord. I hope neither of us comes to regret it."

He chuckled and reined his horse toward the abbey. "Lady, I fear I will regret this before the night is out."

He was not going to be able to explain his actions to Stephan because they were not logical. That his brother would bombard him with uncomfortable questions Alexander had no doubt. If he were lucky he'd be able to avoid them until morning. For now he intended to enjoy the short ride to Blyth. Giselle rode before him in his saddle, and it was a tight fit. The way her bottom was rubbing against him made him hard and aching. He should stop now and take her into the woods and be done with it, but he did not trust Guisborne not to follow. That she would prove a lusty bedmate he had no doubt. It was well-known peasant women were more robust than the delicately bred ladies of his acquaintance. And he'd not have to deal with a virgin's fears and inexperience. No doubt Giselle knew well how to pleasure a man. He wondered which of Robyn's followers had been her lovers, and felt an odd twinge of jealousy at the thought. It mattered not. For now she was his.

When in need of a woman he'd used whores and paid them well. The virgin maids who were eager to be his bride he kept a careful distance from, as was proper. A lusty widow or two had been generous to him in the past, and he'd enjoyed their company, but somehow Giselle was different. That she was beautiful was obvious, but other women were beautiful. She set his blood on fire and the only way he knew to put out that blaze was in her body.

He'd never taken a leman before, though most men of

his station and age had done so. It made sense. Whores could carry disease, and were not always pleasant to be near. Unlike many he knew, he would not use the women of his estate to slack his lust. The last thing he wanted were his bastards running around the place and him not knowing it. If he fathered a child he wanted to take care of it, not leave it to some unlettered peasant woman to raise. Until he married he'd do as others did, and keep a mistress. No doubt Giselle would be grateful for the comforts he could provide. She could not have had an easy life, living among outlaws in Sherwood.

He let the horse walk at a leisurely pace. With one hand he brushed the hair away from her shoulder and neck, then leaned down to place a kiss just behind her ear. He felt her tremble at the touch and he smiled. There was passion in her and he meant to have it. "Soon, Giselle, you'll be mine."

"Aye, m'lord."

He frowned. "My name is Alexander."

"Aye, m'lord."

He rubbed his thumb along the line of her jaw, from ear to chin, then down the delicate arch of her neck. "Say my name, Giselle."

"Alexander."

She said it softly and it was like a caress, gentle and shy. It sounded right to him, her low, quiet voice saying his name. He was surprised at himself. Why should he care for aught but the sport she'd be in his bed? He suspected he knew the reason. He'd never been a hard or cruel man. He wanted her to care for him. As ludicrous as that was, it was nonetheless true. He saw flickering torches ahead and knew they were fast approaching the abbey. They would be separated for the night, Giselle going to the women's dormer, he to the men's. The good monks did not allow even married folk to sleep together within their sacred, chastity-bound walls. They would be horrified at the idea of him keeping his mistress with him through the night. He was sore tempted to offend the brothers.

"I was about ready to come looking for you." Stephan greeted them from just outside the monastery gatehouse. Behind him the brother guestmaster anxiously wrung his pudgy hands, rising on the balls of his feet to see over Stephan's shoulder.

"Is this the last of the lot?" the monk asked.

"We're all here," Stephan said. "I thank you for your patience, Brother Theobald."

"We are most pleased to be of service, Lord Rosmar."

Stephan took the reins of Alex's horse and held the animal steady. Alex dismounted then held up his arms to help Giselle down. She was awkward, apparently unaccustomed to riding, but he caught her and gently lifted her down, keeping her as close to him as he could without offending Brother Theobald, who looked quite put out at being roused from his bed in the middle of the night, no matter his words to the earl. Even a man of God, perhaps especially such a man, knew better than to show irritation in front of an earl wealthy enough to pay handsomely for a night's hospitality.

A young monk, sleepy-eyed and shy, took the horse from Stephan and led it toward the stable. "See he's rubbed down and given a bag of oats," Alex called.

The young monk glanced over his shoulder and smiled. "Aye, m'lord. I'll see he's well cared for."

"Giselle, go with Brother Theobald. He'll show you where you'll be sleeping." Alex smiled at her, but she did not relax. Her eyes were large and she appeared nervous, though why she should be, he didn't know. He gave her a gentle push in the monk's direction and she reluctantly followed his lead. Odin trailed her like a shadow.

"Our bower is this way," Stephan said.

They walked in silence, the bulk of the monastery church to their left. Through the high, narrow windows the faint glow of candles lighted the walls. It was near midnight and the monks were gathering in the choir for the night office of Vigils.

"Well?" Alexander blurted, when he could stand the silence no longer.

"What?"

"Have you naught to say about the woman?"

Stephan shrugged. "You've taken a mistress. There's nothing so unusual about that, little brother."

"You don't approve."

"You're long past the age where you need my approval, or anyone else's. I don't necessarily disapprove. I'd caution you to be careful."

"You think she is dangerous?"

"Not in the way you mean. I know you better than you may think. You're not one to dally in a casual liaison. It's your heart I'm concerned about."

"My heart is safe enough. Other men have fallen in love with women they could not marry. Our father for one, with your mother and again with mine. There's no dishonor in it."

"Unlike Father, I do not think you are a man capable of dividing your loyalty. I do not think you can have both mistress and wife, and as you said, you cannot marry this woman. I would see you wed, with legitimate children. You know what being bastard-born means."

Alexander laughed. "You worry overmuch. I've no intention of falling in love with Giselle. A few months' pleasure is all I expect. There's no reason for Julianna not to continue her hunt for my bride."

Stephan glanced at him, but did not speak.

* * *

Giselle hurried after the monk, who moved at a surprising pace for his bulk. Odin trotted beside them. She was glad for his familiar presence in this strange place. She'd been reluctant to leave Alexander, but apparently she'd not see him again before morning. The silent monk led her to a large timber bower with a thatched roof. She could hear mice running through the thatching. Brother Theobald knocked once on the door and left her standing on the porch, leaving without saying a word. She stood for a moment, uncertain. There was no one to stop her. She could turn and run, find her way back to Robyn and the others. Glancing over her shoulder she saw no one near in the darkness. Would Alexander come looking for her? Once in the wood she would be lost to him, he could not find her. The door to the bower opened and she recognized one of the maids from earlier in the day, when they'd made that mad dash up the stairs to safety in the burning castle.

"Who is it, Gertrude?" a voice called from within the room.

"It be the wench what helped save the babes." The maid beamed, her round cheeks red with sun, her smile revealing crooked teeth. "Come in, child. Lady Rosmar be most eager to meet ye."

Giselle let herself be led into the bright, warm room. There was a large bed against one wall, and a fire burned in the stone hearth in the center of the room, the smoke curling up to the vent in the roof. Candles lighted the darkness. The room was crowded with females of all ages, from the infant daughters of the earl and countess to the elderly maid who sat rocking one of the children. Near the bed stood two women who appeared of an age, and a young maid. All were beautiful and regal and Giselle felt suddenly very shy. Surely Alexander did not expect her to spend the night with his sister-in-law and these other ladies?

"Giselle, is it?"

One of the gorgeous creatures was walking toward her, smiling, her hands held out in greeting.

"Yes, m'lady."

"I am Julianna. I have been eager to meet the woman who showed such bravery. From what I've been told, you saved the lives of my youngest daughters. For that I owe you a debt that cannot be repaid."

There were tears in the woman's green eyes and Giselle quickly took her hands in her own. "I did little enough, lady. I am happy the babies are safe."

Julianna leaned forward and kissed her on the cheek. "Do not make light of your bravery. Courage is a rare enough thing; it is to be honored."

Giselle felt comforted by the woman's words, and put at ease by her friendly manner. This woman, Alexander's sister-in-law, was a countess, yet she treated Giselle with respect. She'd never been near ladies before, but expected them to be haughty and disdainful. The other woman and the pretty maid now approached.

"You are the woman Alexander spoke of?" the girl asked. "Weren't you terribly frightened?"

"I was too busy to be frightened," Giselle said. She wondered just what Alexander had told them about her. Surely not that he'd decided to make her his mistress. They'd not be so polite to her if they knew that.

"Maud, you are rude," the other woman said. "My niece often forgets the proprieties. May I present to you my niece, Maud de Clare, daughter of the earl of Hertford. I am Elizabeth FitzWilliam, countess of Gloucester."

Giselle stared at the woman. The lady Elizabeth was King John's wife, or had been, before he divorced her. Giselle's life had taken a very odd turn today, because of Alexander.

She'd never met anyone more important than the village priest at Wolfhurst. Now she stood in a room before a countess, a woman who should have been queen of England, and an earl's daughter.

"My dear," Elizabeth said, "you look ill. Come, sit. They day has been exhausting and here we keep you chattering. Have you eaten?"

Giselle was led to a leather chair near the fire. Odin settled with a grunt at her feet, forcing the others to step around him, but they didn't seem to think his presence there odd. A trencher of bread filled with cheese and mutton was placed on a small table beside her. A cup was put in her hand and she took a long drink. She expected ale and found wine, another new experience. She was not the sort of woman who drank wine. It was far beyond the reach of the average peasant, a thing which must be purchased, while ale and cider, mead and perry, could be made by any farmer who grew the right crops of wheat or apples, honey or pears.

Maud sat at Giselle's feet, contentedly scratching Odin's head. The girl wore a gown of pale yellow wool, the cloth so finely woven it was lustrous. Surreptitiously Giselle fingered the coarse gray gown of undyed wool she wore. It was her best gown, but it was soiled with grease from Guisborne's kitchens and soot from the fire. These women, elegant and refined in their dress as well as their manner, must think her crude. She felt a sudden surge of anger. The idea that she belonged anywhere in Alexander's world was ridiculous, even humiliating. She could not hope to fit in, any more than he could become a man of the wildwood, without the trappings of civilization, the comforts of wealth he was so familiar with.

"Is it true you are to be Sir Alexander's leman?" Maud asked.

"Maud," Elizabeth said, sharply.

"What? Oh fool! Don't tell me I've found another subject that mustn't be discussed. I've never met a leman before."

"It's all right," Giselle said. "She only speaks the truth. It is what I am, or rather what I am expected to become."

There was an awkward silence. "It is late," Julianna said. "Maud, go to bed and leave Giselle to eat her meal in peace."

The girl reluctantly rose to do as she was bid and Giselle was relieved to have her go. She needed quiet and time to think. So much had happened so quickly, she wasn't sure how she felt about any of it. Except that Alexander excited and intrigued her as no man had. She wanted to be with him, of that she was sure.

Julianna placed a hand gently on her shoulder. "Alexander is a good man. He will be kind to you." With a reassuring squeeze, the countess was gone.

Giselle stared at the food beside her but had no appetite. A kind, good man? She knew him to be proud, strong, and forceful. There had been moments of tenderness, when he'd touched her, or whispered reassurances in her ear. There had been flashes of passion, when he'd kissed her and held her close against him as they rode. With a sigh she rose and went to find a place on the sleeping pallet with the nursemaids. She was tired. Tomorrow she'd be able to think more clearly.

She did not sleep well for he charmed her dreams. When dawn came she was awake. The woman sleeping next to her snored softly. None of the others stirred. Quietly she pulled back the blanket, found her shoes, and tiptoed to the door. The morning was cold and clear and achingly sweet. Trees, bereft of their leaves, held choruses of birds. Dark sloes drooped from the branches of blackthorn bushes. Odin yawned mightily and sat to scratch behind his ear. She patted the big head and he licked her hand, his tail thumping against the ground. There were a few black-robed monks already about the business of the day, moving in silent, shadowlike calm through the chill morning. She hugged herself against the cold, wishing she had a cloak. Hers had been left behind at Guisborne, forgotten in the excitement of the night before. How was she going to retrieve it? She could not go through the winter without her cloak.

She walked to relieve the tension, not paying much heed where she went, until she found herself beside the monastery herb garden, with its low stone wall. An elderly monk squatted at his work, pruning an overgrown clump of sage, but he must have heard her for he looked up. His gentle face was at first bemused, then he broke into a delighted grin, and with surprising agility for one his age, he unfolded his thin body, wiped his hands on his habit, and strode toward her.

"My lady, you've returned. It has been so long, I'd near given up hope. But you're back now, thanks be to God."

Giselle shook her head. "You have mistaken me for someone else, brother."

He tilted his head, and his merry brown eyes squinted. "You be Giselle of Guisborne?"

"I am called Giselle, but I am not of Guisborne."

The monk seemed to ponder this, but the confusion did not leave his face. He began to mutter to himself, as though presenting both sides of some profound argument. Apparently he'd forgotten she was there, for he turned and began pacing. Now it seemed he was talking to someone else, who appeared to hover somewhere just above his head. Giselle smiled. The old monk, for all his spryness, was senile. No doubt he was talking to angels. She wondered, though, how he'd known her name.

"You're about early."

She turned, startled at his voice, and irritated Odin had not warned her of his approach. She looked for the dog and saw that he had wandered over to the monk, who was absently scratching behind the big dog's ears as he continued his heavenly conversation. Alexander looked as tired as she felt and she wondered if he had spent a restless night, tossing and turning. Surely he was not as uneasy about the situation as she.

"I've come to see Father Bernard," Alexander said, nodding toward the monk in the herb garden. "He was priest at Wolfhurst for more than thirty years, from what the abbot tells me. He'll no doubt be able to fill me in on much of the history of my estate."

"I don't know how much he'll be able to help." She pointed a finger at her head and made a circular motion. "He seems a bit off."

The monk in question wandered back toward them, Odin walking patiently beside him. When the old man saw Alexander that beatific smile once more lighted his face. "Ah, my lord, you've returned from Crusade. Safe and whole, I see, God be praised. Guisborne will prosper again, now that you and Lady Giselle are reunited. The land has been poor since you left."

"See what I mean?" Giselle said.

Alexander frowned. "Father Bernard?"

"Of course, who else? Don't tell me your mind has been affected by the sun in Palestine?" There was genuine concern in the man's voice. "A tisane of sweet woodruff will help unaddle you. Lady Giselle will make it for you. She is skilled in healing, as well you know."

"Why does he call you 'lady'?" Alexander asked, in a low voice so the monk could not overhear.

"He thinks I'm someone else, from Guisborne Castle."

"But he calls you by name?"

"I can't explain that. Perhaps he heard it mentioned when we arrived."

Alexander turned his attention back to the monk. "Good father, I am lord of Wolfhurst—"

"So ye are, lad, I know that well enough. I was there when you were baptized and when you wed. I heard your Crusader vows. Just as your lady be chatelaine of Guisborne, so you are born lord of Wolfhurst. You must take care of your wife, Sir John. There are those who are greedy and wish her harm. It is good you have returned."

"My wife?"

"He means me," Giselle said. Why was Alexander trying to make sense of anything the monk said? "You'll get no useful information, I fear."

"Mayhap you're right. He does seem confused." Alexander stepped forward and placed a hand on the monk's frail shoulder. "Good morrow to you, father. I'll heed your advice."

The priest traced a cross on Alexander's forehead. "Go with God." Then the monk winked. "And bring me your firstborn son for his baptism."

Chapter Ten

Giselle shivered and rubbed her arms with her hands. The day was growing colder.

"Where is your cloak?" Alexander asked.

"At Guisborne Castle. Can we retrieve it?"

He shook his head. "I think not. I'll have Julianna or Elizabeth loan you one for the ride home."

"You think a countess will give me her cloak?"

He looked at her oddly. "Neither of those ladies would allow you to go cold, any more than I would."

He removed his mantle and wrapped it around her shoulders. His warmth lingered in the folds of heavy wool, and his scent, heady and masculine, surrounded her. There was reproach in his voice and she blushed. What did she know of how ladies acted? She lived her life in hiding, in constant fear of discovery, of being handed over to those who enforced the laws of the nobles. She had little experience with those born above her, and less reason to trust any of them. "Why are you doing this?"

"Doing what?"

He walked toward the church, and she followed. "Why do you want me at Wolfhurst?"

He glanced down at her and smiled. He was beautiful when he smiled, and looked younger than his years. She felt a flutter of excitement when he looked at her like that.

"Mayhap it's because you are beautiful."

"Now you tease. I'm serious. I was content with my life and you have disrupted it, for no reason that I can see."

He stopped then and turned toward her, his hands on her shoulders. "You are beautiful, Giselle. Never doubt that." One hand caressed her cheek, his fingers skimming down to her neck, then lifting a strand of her hair. "Aye, you're a rare beauty." His voice was husky and low and she shivered anew, but it was not from the cold.

"You do not know me," she said.

"No, I do not. But I shall."

"I am doing this only to protect Robyn and the others." It was a lie, but she didn't want him knowing the truth, that she wanted him. If he knew, she would be too much in his power.

His mouth quirked into a half-smile. "Then that must be enough, for now." His thumb drew a slow circle on her cheek, then lightly traced the outline of her lips. His head descended toward her and she raised her face, eager for his kiss. It was soft, gentle, his mouth warm. His arms went around her back and gathered her to him. She reached up and wrapped her arms around his neck. His kiss became more insistent, his tongue probing, until she opened her mouth slightly. Sensation flooded her, threatening to subsume her will in the web of desire he wove around her. When he pulled away, she longed for more. When she looked into his eyes she saw there surprise and confusion, but it was quickly masked.

"I do look forward to bedding you, my red-haired wood

sprite. But now is not the time or place. We wouldn't want to scandalize the good brothers.''

He was smiling again, and with a courtly little bow, offered his arm to her. She placed her hand on it, a little embarrassed by the gesture. She was unaccustomed to men with gentle manners. In truth she was a stranger to his way of life, and wondered that he did not see the truth of it. But he'd made it plain enough. He lusted for her, and wanted her in his bed. If she told him she would not have him, would he let her go unharmed? She slanted a glance at him. She didn't know him well enough to predict his response. It would be easier if she were willing, and truth be told, her body was all but begging for his attention. It was the fear in her heart at the hurt he could cause her, and the doubt in her thoughts that he could ever be as much to her as she might want that made her unsure what she did was wise.

"I was going to hear Mass," Alexander said. "Do you wish to come with me, or would you rather return to your bower?"

"I will go to church, m'lord." Perhaps if she spent a quiet hour the ritual would calm her. Perhaps in the cold church with the monks chanting their ancient prayers she would find an answer to her questions.

Alexander found his brother in the stable, overseeing the tacking of the horses. "You do not intend to stay for the tournament?"

Stephan absently rubbed the velvet soft muzzle of his stallion. "Nay. I've had more of Guisborne's company than I can stomach. We'll ride with you to Wolfhurst and stay a week or two, if you're willing."

"More than willing. You're welcome for as long as you wish."

"How did your talk with the abbot go?"

"Not well. He's already promised his surplus grain to Guisborne. All that's left is to pray we'll have a mild winter. Even so, there is bound to be hunger and sickness at Wolfhurst."

"I can send what surplus I have."

"All the way from Kent? That hardly seems expedient."

"I have other estates, here in Nottinghamshire, and in Lincolnshire. Should you need it, the grain is there. You can pay me when you're able."

"My thanks." Alexander busied himself brushing his horse with a switch of braided straw. A monk had already seen to the animal, whose dark coat was shiny with health and attention. "You've never taken a mistress, have you?"

"No. I was younger than you when I married. And once I'd seen Julianna there was no other woman for me. There never will be."

"I'd like that sort of love." He hauled his saddle down from the peg it hung on and lifted it onto the back of his stallion. The animal twitched irritably at the weight and Alexander crooned nonsense to calm him.

"You think you'll find it with some half-wild peasant from the woods?"

He looked over the horse's back to see his brother was no longer smiling. "Nay, Brother. Giselle is for pleasure, and temporary. She knows that, as I do. But why do you ask it as though such a love would be impossible between us?"

"You know why. It's the same reason you assume her to be a plaything rather than a life-mate. She's a peasant and you're noble-born. She's unsuitable to be your wife."

Alexander tightened the saddle girth, then pulled the stirrup irons down their leather straps. What Stephan said was true enough, but hearing it badly was disconcerting.

It made him sound callous. "You say that as though I mean to use Giselle and discard her when I no longer want her."

"Which, of course, is exactly what you intend. Not that you'll be cruel. You'll see she's well rewarded."

"Damn it, Stephan, you make me sound some sort of beast. Other men take mistresses."

"Our father among them. Are you willing to see your children bastard-born?"

Alex recognized the bitter tone in his brother's words. It had always bothered Stephan to be a bastard far more than it did Alexander. But then Stephan was the eldest. If he'd been legitimate he would have inherited their father's vast fortune, estates, and title as earl of Essex. As it was, all would go to their cousin Geoffrey instead. By his marriage Stephan had become a rich and powerful man, and Alex knew it was not the loss of an earldom that embittered his brother. "Father would have married your mother, if he'd been able."

"But he wasn't, and she died shamed."

"She died knowing he loved her. She had no regrets."

"What of your mother?"

"What of her? She was lowborn, no more than a pleasant bedmate. Father used her for his pleasure. He was saddened when she died, but he was married by the time he met her. Even had he been willing, he could not wed her. That he accepted me as his son and saw to my knight's training proved he was a decent man. He was always a good father to me, as he was to you."

"So, you intend to follow in Father's footsteps? You'll use Giselle, but she'll not keep you from marrying a noblewoman? And you'll raise any child she bears you?"

"Yes. I see nothing wrong with any of that."

Stephan grunted. "Then you're a damned fool. We were raised openly as the earl of Essex's sons. Do you think that would have happened if he'd had legitimate heirs? We would have been fostered out, or gone unacknowledged. You condemn your own children to a harsh existence if you let them be bastard-born.''

Alexander was beginning to grow angry. Stephan had an irritating way of lecturing him, as though he were still young and in need of guidance. "God's feet, I haven't even bedded the woman yet and you've condemned my unborn children. Any child of mine will be loved and acknowledged.''

Stephan leaned back against the wooden rails of his horse's stall, his arms crossed over his broad chest, his silvery eyes tight. "Then you mean to wed a wellborn lady who will not only tolerate your mistress, should you form an attachment to Giselle and find yourself reluctant to repudiate her, but will also raise your bastards with her own children?''

"Others have done so.''

"I thought you said you wanted the sort of love Julianna and I share. You'll not find it in that sort of domestic arrangement.''

Alexander slipped the bridle onto his stallion's head, deliberately avoiding looking at his brother. Why was Stephan hounding him about this? He forced himself to control his rising anger, and didn't turn until he'd buckled the bridle and made sure the bit sat correctly in the horse's mouth. "I've never been cruel to a woman. All I seek is a little companionship.''

"Don't be an ass. What you want is your cock inside that very tempting body—''

Alexander's fist landed square on his brother's jaw. Stephan reeled back. Alexander stood, trembling. He seldom lost his temper, even under great provocation. He plowed his fingers through his hair. "I'm sorry.''

"Aye, well, no damage done.'' Stephan tenderly touched the spot on his jaw where a nasty bruise was beginning to show. Softly he said, "Let the woman go. Keeping her against her will dishonors you."

Dishonor? Damn. Stephan knew exactly which argument to use to make him squirm. "You're not my conscience, Brother."

"No, I'm not. I trust you to make the right decision."

Alexander gathered his horse's reins in his hands. "That I will." He led the horse from the stable into the cold, dreary day. He'd been in such a good mood, earlier, when he saw Giselle. Now he felt as stormy as the clouds racing across the sky. No doubt they'd be rained on before they reached Wolfhurst. He cursed the foul weather. He cursed his brother. He cursed his own weakness. Give up Giselle? That he would not do, no matter what Stephan might think. He joined the others gathered in the monastery yard, the knights mounted, the women in a wagon with the children. He could not find Giselle among the crowd.

Giselle lingered in the church after Mass ended. The solemn splendor of the ritual, the reverence of the monks, calmed and soothed her. It was usually the small, simple church in Wolfhurst village she visited. This was the first time she'd been in an abbey church, with its gold vessels and silk vestments. The walls were painted with bright scenes from saints' lives, or with the torments of hell that awaited the damned. Her favorite paintings were of the Madonna and Child. The tender love of Mary for her infant son was something Giselle could understand. God in majesty, or souls damned for eternity, were frightening to contemplate.

"My child, is there anything I can help you with?"

She started at the unexpected question, turning to see the monk standing near her. She'd not heard him approach, so absorbed had she been in her thoughts. "No. I'm sorry, I didn't mean to linger."

"There's no need to apologize. You are with Lord Rosmar's party?"

"Aye." She didn't know what else to say. She wasn't about to tell him her status as Baron Wolfhurst's leman. She felt herself blush. "I was talking to Father Bernard earlier, and something he said confused me."

The monk smiled, the skin around his brown eyes wrinkling. "That is normally the case when one talks to Bernard. Poor man. He makes little sense these days. Some of the brothers believe he talks to angels."

"Do you believe that?"

The smile deepened. "Who am I to question? No doubt he does. Whether they answer him or not, I cannot say. I am Father Edgar. Perhaps I can clear up your confusion."

He seemed friendly and she saw no reason not to ask. "Was there a Lady Giselle of Guisborne?"

The smile faded and the brown eyes rounded in surprise. "Why do you ask that?"

"Father Bernard mistook me for the lady."

He cocked his head and studied her. "You do have some of the same look about you. Her hair was red, like yours. But she's been dead more than twenty years. Bernard served as her tutor and household priest, until she died, then he came here."

"Was she married to a Crusader?"

"To Sir John de Clare of Wolfhurst. He took the cross and served in the Holy Land. It was tragic really, what happened. They married as soon as he returned. A few years later the lady died in childbirth."

"What happened to Sir John?"

The monk shook his head and sighed. "He was thrown from his horse while hunting. Broke his neck. That was less than a month before his lady's death. They say she died of a broken heart."

"What happened to the baby?"

"The child died with her mother."

"How did Sir Guy come to inherit Guisborne?"

"Lady Giselle was his sister. He was heir to her estates."

"But, isn't it usually the son who inherits?"

"Sir Guy is a bastard. He inherited only after the legitimate heir was dead."

There was something strange in the man's voice, but she could not place it. "You know a great deal about the family."

"They've been the main benefactors of the abbey for three generations. The story is well known, Giselle."

Something jumped to life in her. That mysterious note in his voice she now identified. He was lying to her. "How did you know my name?"

He looked startled, then smiled. "I heard the others call you. That is your name, is it not? That is why you were so curious about Lady Giselle?"

"Yes." His explanation was reasonable enough, and why would a man of God lie to her? She must be imagining it. "Thank you for explaining Father Bernard's confusion to me. It all makes sense now."

"I'm glad to put your mind at ease."

As she walked toward the doors she knew he stared at her. He seemed vastly relieved that she'd asked no more questions. For some reason he very much wanted her to leave Lady Giselle and Sir John undisturbed, which she would have been willing to do, had she not mistrusted him. What more there could be to the story, she'd have to find out some other way. Perhaps she'd talk to Father Bernard again. Much of what he'd said actually made sense, once she understood what had happened. No doubt he knew more about the tragic couple. Who was this woman who shared her name, and why did she feel such an over-whelming need to know more?

She didn't have a chance to search out Bernard. As she stepped from the church she saw Alexander striding toward her. She watched him, struck anew by the powerful beauty of the man. His handsome face was marred by a frown.

"There you are. We'll be leaving in a few minutes." He held out a hand and when she hesitated he gestured with his finger for her to come to him.

She put her hand into his. His hand was large, rough and warm. She felt an unfamiliar sense of safety, with him so near. Would he protect her from harm, or would he be the one to hurt her in a deep and irrevocable way?

"You're shivering," he said.

"It's cold." Why, then, did she feel so hot? His touch fed the blaze he'd started with that kiss in Guisborne's kitchen.

He glanced down at her, and his hand pressed hers reassuringly. "You have no need to fear me, Giselle."

"I am not afraid of you." It was a lie. He would not be unkind to her, of that she was sure. Except that if he won her heart and then abandoned her, she wasn't sure she'd be able to live with the pain. She headed toward the wagon, where the other women and children waited.

"Nay, you'll ride with me."

"I would rather not."

He did not break stride. "Why?"

"I do not like to ride."

He stopped then and looked down at her, clearly puzzled. "I'll need more reason than that to forgo the pleasure of your company."

She was embarrassed suddenly, realizing she might have to explain to him what her reason was.

"You're not afraid of horses?"

She nodded. She thought he would laugh at her, or scorn her for her weakness.

"I imagine it would be uncomfortable, if you're not accustomed to it." He placed a finger under her chin and lifted her face so she had to look at him. "Do not hesitate to tell me such things. I do not wish your discomfort, but I cannot know what troubles you if you do not say."

"Yes, m'lord."

"I wish you wouldn't call me that. You know my name."

She lowered her eyes so that he could not see the unease there. She could not call him by name. He was still a stranger to her, she did not know him, and did not know if she could trust him. The situation was awkward at best, and might prove dangerous to her if she misjudged the man.

"All right. I'll live with it for now. Go join the women."

He turned her toward the wagon and gave her a small push. Gratefully she scampered away from him. She could not think clearly when he touched her. He'd abducted her, no matter that he'd promised she could leave him at the end of a month. There was nothing to keep him from changing his mind and keeping her longer, just as there was nothing to prevent him from turning her out in the cold if she displeased him. Yet the safety of Robyn and the others apparently depended on her pleasing the lord of Wolfhurst. She did not know what he was capable of. Until she did, she'd need to be cautious when near him. She could not allow him to use her to learn too much about Robyn and the others, if that was his intention. Just what he did want from her, besides her body, she wasn't sure. Perhaps it was simple lust that drove him, and once satisfied he'd let her go. She shuddered at the thought. She'd hoped for love with the man she first gave herself to. In her heart she knew Alexander could not love her. He was a great lord and she was a simple, ignorant woman. She could not fit into his world and he certainly would not stoop to joining hers.

The rain began before they reached Wolfhurst. Alexander cursed and pulled the hood of his cloak over his head. It was a cold rain and it made the road treacherous. If it grew much colder it would begin to freeze. The trees and bushes lining both sides of the road were naked of their leaves, weeks earlier than normal. If winter set in this early it would be disastrous. The combination of hunger and cold would decimate the simple folk, and he needed every serf, alive and healthy, come spring when it was time to plant the crops.

The flock of sheep would suffer as well. Much of his wealth rested on the backs of those sheep. Their wool commanded good prices in the market towns of Nottingham and Lincoln. He could ill afford to lose men or sheep. If need be, he'd take up Stephan on his offer for grain. It would help this season, but if the weather next spring was inclement, if they could not plant a crop, there would be no grain to buy next winter. He'd lived through famines. Because of his high station he'd never gone hungry. Earl's sons do not starve. But he'd seen peasants and townspeople die. It was not a thing he wished to witness ever again. He would not allow his people to starve.

"You look as gloomy as the clouds," Geoffrey said.

Alex glanced at his cousin. He'd not seen much of Geoffrey the last few days. "Where have you been keeping yourself?"

"I've been getting to know the countess of Gloucester better."

"Elizabeth? Why?"

Geoffrey looked at him quizzically. "She's a beautiful, fascinating woman. Why wouldn't I wish to know her?"

"She's near ten years older than you, Geoff."

Geoffrey shrugged his broad shoulders and smiled. "She doesn't hold my youth against me. We enjoy each other's company. I seen nothing wrong with that. Though I rather like your idea of absconding with nubile peasant women."

"I haven't absconded with her," Alexander growled.

"Oh, aye, Coz. She's most willing, no doubt. What woman wouldn't love to share your roof and your bed, you're such an even-tempered, sweet-talking man."

"What the hell are you going on about?"

The smile faded from Geoffrey's face. "You're in a foul mood. What's eating at you?"

"Nothing."

Geoffrey grunted. "I'll leave you in peace, then."

Alex found himself once more alone on the muddy road. What Stephan said earlier gnawed at him. Was holding Giselle dishonorable? If she asked, he would let her go. Reluctantly, but he would do it. He did not like having his conscience pricking him so painfully. He did not need the confusion added to his worries about Wolfhurst. He should send the woman away, back to the savages she was accustomed to living with. He swore under his breath, knowing he'd do no such thing. He wanted Giselle, as he'd never before wanted a woman. It wasn't as though he planned to ravish her. He could offer her comforts, even luxuries, she'd never known. Why then did his brother think what he did was an offense?

He was relieved to see his castle come into view on its hill. Within minutes they passed through the village and into the walled bailey. A surprised groom came running from the stable.

"My lord, we did not think to see ye afore next week."

"We've decided to forgo the pleasures of a tournament." Alex looked around, but none of the other grooms appeared. "Where are your fellows?" The boy looked at the ground, reluctant to answer. Alexander stepped down from his horse and handed the reins over. "Get word out they're to return by noon tomorrow, or I'll have their hides."

The boy looked up with a mixture of relief and fear on his face. "Yes, m'lord."

Alexander had no intention of whipping any of the boys, but they didn't need to know that. His mood served to put real fear into the lad, which no doubt would make him more persuasive in convincing the others to return. Stephan's knights still sat their horses. Alexander walked over to the most senior of them. "It seems my grooms have taken an unexpected holiday. We'll each need to see to our own mount."

The man did not protest, though it was with obvious effort he kept his comment to himself. Alexander well understood his response. They were cold and wet. What they wanted was a hot meal and a dry hall, with a roaring fire to warm them. He stalked through the confusion of horses and men until he came to the wagon with the women and children. Julianna and Elizabeth were efficiently seeing to the disembarking. Giselle held Rose by one hand and William by the other. From the look on his face Will thought himself far too old to be hand-held by a woman. Rebellion was brewing.

"William, come here," Alexander said.

His nephew gladly withdrew his hand from Giselle's grip. "Aye, Uncle Alex?"

"The men will be busy with the horses for the next half hour or so. I want you to be sure your mother and sisters are safely settled in the castle." The boy looked disappointed to be given the task of overseeing women and babies. Alex squatted down to his nephew's level. " 'Tis a duty of all knights, to keep their womenfolk safe. I'd not trust such a task to just anyone, lad. Do you think you can do it? If not, I'll find another.''

William's eyes sparked at the insult. "I'll see to it, Uncle.''

He looked up to see Giselle smiling at him, but she quickly looked away.

She's beautiful when she smiles. I haven't seen her smile much. I'll need to do something about that.

Chapter Eleven

When Alexander walked into his hall an hour later, shaking
the rain from the folds of his cloak, his mood darkened.
There was no fire in the great hearth. No torches lighted
the gloomy interior. None of the long trestle tables had
been set up for a meal. He saw no servants. Except for
Giselle's black dog, the hall appeared uninhabited. He
could hear noise from upstairs. Julianna, Elizabeth, and
the children had found their chamber and would have
their own fire to keep them warm. He threw his wet cloak
onto a nearby bench. The one-eyed dog came to him,
unsure of his welcome until Alex spoke softly to him and
patted his thigh to call the animal closer. He scratched
behind the dog's ears. Except for the loss of the eye, he
was a handsome animal. Wherever the dog was, Giselle
was sure to be near. Alex looked around the hall again,
but saw no one. He didn't have time to go looking for her
now. Following his nose, he made his way to the kitchen,

to be sure the cook had meal preparations well under way. From the smells, something savory was cooking.

He stopped in the stone archway. The kitchen was warm, with a fire blazing in the huge cooking hearth. There the cook was busy turning the crank of the spit on which six fat geese roasted. But it was the sight of Giselle, with a large, sharp knife in her delicate hands, busily chopping onions, that caught his attention.

"What are you doing here?" Alex asked.

She backhanded her eyes, wiping away onion-induced tears. "I'm helping the cook, m'lord." Her tone held some irritation.

"I can see that," Alex said. He walked to the scarred oak table with vegetables scattered across it. "Why?"

Giselle resumed her chopping, with slightly more force than strictly necessary. "Because he needs help."

"Aye, m'lord, the wench be most useful," the cook said. He was a fat, dark man and sweat ran down his face. His muscular arm turned the crank in a smooth rhythm. He'd have no burnt spots on his geese. "Troth, I don't know what I'd have done without 'er."

"Where are your helpers?" Like the rest of the castle, the kitchen was deserted, except for these two.

"I sent them to their homes in the village when ye went to Guisborne. Ye said ye'd not be back till next week, m'lord."

There was reprimand in the man's voice. Alexander's irritation grew. "How soon will you be able to serve?"

The big man nodded at the birds. "It'll like be another hour afore these be done."

"An hour!"

"Aye, m'lord. Had ye sent word ahead that I'd be feeding nigh on twenty people tonight, ye'd not have to wait. As it is, they's not enough bread. I have the wench cutting stuff for a soup. It'll have to do."

Alexander saw the meager pile of round loaves. Not nearly enough. "Why isn't there more bread?"

Giselle set the knife down with a bang. "Why would your cook do so wasteful a thing as bake bread for people he had no reason to think he'd be feeding?"

The cook bristled with righteous indignation. "There's the gist of it."

Alexander closed his eyes and took a deep breath. They were right. It wasn't the cook's fault, but damn, the whole place lacked efficiency. He'd spent enough time in well-ordered households to know the difference. "Do the best you can. I'll send my nephew to the village to fetch the castle servants back."

"Have him see Father Michael. The priest be easy to find and he'll know who to send." The cook did not look up from his geese.

"Yes, I'll do that." Alexander's voice was full of sarcasm, but the servant seemed not to notice. That he'd just told his lord and master what to do, in as offhand a way as he might a kitchen worker, apparently didn't occur to the man. It didn't help that Giselle was struggling to control a smile. When she reached to pick up the knife to resume her work, he grabbed her hand. "You're coming with me."

"But what of the food? Your men and guests are hungry."

"The kitchen workers will be here soon enough." He pulled her after him. He came to an abrupt halt just after entering the hall, Giselle bumping into him. The dog, thinking his mistress was being mishandled, lowered his head and growled, baring sharp white teeth. "Call him down," Alex said softly.

"Odin. Down."

The dog obeyed, looking curiously from one to the other.

"Did you train him?" Alex asked.

" 'Tis necessary with a dog as large and powerful as Odin. Were he not obedient he'd be dangerous.''

"You've done a good job with him. Would he really tear my throat out if I hurt you?''

"Yes.''

Alex glanced at her and saw that she looked worried rather than boastful. He wondered if she worried for the dog or for him. "Then I must be careful not to hurt you. Come with me. We're going upstairs.''

"Can Odin come?''

He studied the dog. "He can come, as long as he behaves himself.''

She slapped her thigh and the dog bounded up to greet her, his tongue wiping across her hand. She patted his head and smiled. "Good dog.''

"That's a matter of opinion.'' Alex started up the stairs, knowing she followed. He opened the door to his bower and stood aside for her. "You stay here. I need to find William and send him down to the village. I'll be back soon.''

She and the dog entered the room and he closed the door. He stood for a moment, his heart pounding. What was it about the woman? He was so eager for her his body ached. If he did not have her soon he'd go mad.

The room was dark and cold. There was one narrow window, high in the stone wall, but it was shuttered. She stood until her eyes adjusted to the faint light. It was not an overly large room. Somehow she'd expected something more grand for the lord of the manor. There was a bed against one wall, a large chest, a small table with several candles in an iron holder, and a chair. No fire burned on the hearth for warmth. There were two doors at the far side of the room. She tried the first one, but it was locked.

What would be there? His treasure? She wondered if there were piles of gold and jewels. The other door opened easily. It was a tiny room, with a window and a stone shelf with a hole cut in it. It was the privy. She quickly closed the door. So, even in their most basic bodily functions lords were different from regular folk. No one she knew had such easy access to the place used for such purposes. It was certainly preferred to walking through the winter snow, or slogging through the mud to a communal out-house.

Odin had taken up residence on the bed, which was covered with a fur pelt. "Get down," she scolded. "He'll not want you on his bed, you flea-bitten beastie." Odin cocked his head at her and did not move. "Down," she said, more forcefully, pointing at the floor. With an indig-nant grunt the dog climbed down and settled on the bare stone of the chamber floor. Giselle sat on the one hard chair, her hands clasped tightly in her lap to keep them from shaking. He would be back soon. Then what? She was so nervous her stomach roiled.

The door opened and she jumped, her heart pounding.

"Giselle?"

"Yes, m'lord."

He did not enter. "What are you doing in the dark? Why didn't you light a candle."

"Candles are precious, m'lord. I did not know if I was allowed."

He muttered something and left, returning with a lighted torch from one of the wall brackets in the hallway. The light flared the room to brightness. He flung a pile of clothes onto the bed, then picked up one of the candles and lighted it. He handed it to her. "Light the others while I put this torch back."

With shaking hands she did as he told her. He seemed angry, but then he'd been short-tempered in the kitchen.

She wondered if he was a man who easily lost his temper, and if he became violent. By the time he returned, the room was washed in the warm glow of candlelight. He closed the door and stood, staring at her. Giselle did not know where to look. His eyes, so blue and clear, were dark with lust. His high, sharp cheeks were flushed. Absently he pushed a lock of golden hair off his forehead, then he smiled. She turned from him. The room seemed suddenly very small.

She heard him behind her. When his hands closed on her shoulders she gasped. She felt his breath, hot on her neck. He kissed her, his lips warm and firm, behind her ear, along the side of her jaw. His breath came as ragged as hers. His hands slipped down her arms, until he caught her trembling hands. He lifted one to his mouth, turning it to kiss the palm. It was as though all the heat of summer shimmered through her to center below her belly. He circled her waist with one arm and drew her close against his hard, strong body. She could feel his penis pressed against her back. With his other hand he cupped her breast. He found the nipple and rubbed it until it peaked. She moaned and pressed herself against him.

"Giselle." His voice was husky.

She could not speak. Not with these new, profound sensations chasing through her body.

"Touch me."

She raised her hand until her fingers touched the rough stubble on his face.

"Not there." He guided her hand down, behind her, to that hard shaft between his legs. She touched him gently. When he groaned she snatched her hand away. He pulled her harder against him. "Touch me like you do a lover." There was something desperate in his voice.

"I don't know what you want."

He turned her to face him. His face looked half wild. "Touch me as you do your lovers."

He thought she had known other men. "I haven't . . . I don't know how."

He held her at arm's length. "Are you telling me you are a virgin?" His voice was very low and soft.

"Yes, m'lord."

He looked as though she'd slapped him. His eyes raked her body and when he again looked into her eyes there was a frown of bewilderment on his face. He released her and, turning, stalked to the bed. She felt bereft. She wanted to be held in his strong arms. She longed for his kiss. She had not meant to disappoint him. He still did not look at her. Finally he turned.

"How old are you?" he asked.

"Twenty."

"Twenty. I thought so. Why are you still a virgin, if you are?"

She did not like the way he said that. "If I am? Why would I lie about such a thing? And why do you find it odd that an unmarried woman is a virgin?"

"You live in the wildwood with a band of outlaws. It's natural to assume you'd known other men."

"Nay, m'lord. What you mean to say 'tis a woman of low birth would not have the same morals as a lady."

He had the decency to look embarrassed. "I was mistaken, it seems." He picked up something from the bed and held it up. "I've brought you a gown to wear tonight. You're about the same size as Julianna, so it should fit well enough." He handed it to her.

The wool was dyed a dark red and was so fine and smooth she could not help but caress it. She'd never donned so grand a gown in her life. "I can't wear this," she said, softly.

"Why not?"

"It is too refined for me."

"Ah, Giselle, that it is not. It would give me pleasure if you wore it this night."

There was sadness in his voice and in his eyes. She held the gown against her chest, longing to feel the rich cloth on her body. "Tonight, then."

He reached out and touched her cheek in a gentle caress. "Why did you not tell me you're a maid?"

"You did not ask, m'lord."

He smiled. "I'll remember to do so next time."

She moved closer to him, her face lifted. She closed her eyes and waited.

"Do not tempt me, woman. If I kiss you now I'll not be able to stop at that." He stepped away.

She opened her eyes. He was staring at her with a strange, melancholy expression.

"It seems I've done myself more dishonor than I realized, and you as well. Wear the pretty gown. We'll dine tonight with the others. Tomorrow I'll return you to Robyn."

He left her standing in the middle of the cold room. The door closed. She stared at it, her throat tight with tears. "Alexander." She felt her heart breaking even as she cried his name, but he did not hear.

Alex stared into his empty alecup. A fire roared in the hall hearth, folk sat at the long tables, servants rushed platters and bowls of hot meat and soup, boiled eggs and cabbage, to the diners. He poured himself another cup of ale and drank it down. Everyone was gathered in the hall except Giselle. He was beginning to think she'd spend all night hiding in his chamber. Though he would send her away in the morning, for tonight he longed to have her near.

He ached to see her, to touch her. It was the ache he was trying to deaden with the drink. So far it wasn't working.

"Eat something before you make yourself sick," Stephan said. He dropped a mess of roast goose on Alex's trencher.

"You were right," Alex said.

"Was I? Is that why you overindulge?"

He was hungry. He ate the meat. "I'm sending Giselle away."

Julianna, sitting on the bench on the other side of him, placed a slender hand over his. "Are you sure that is wise? From what I've seen of the woman, she is unique and may be well worth fighting for."

He'd always liked Julianna, especially when she forgave him after he kidnapped her and brought her to his brother. At the time it seemed the only way to get the two of them together. That had worked. But he was older now. Running off with unwilling women was not a habit he wished to develop. "I'll not keep her against her will."

"Are you so sure she is unwilling?" Julianna asked.

"She's not what I thought." No. He'd thought her a woman well versed in lovemaking. He'd wanted to use her, as a plaything, as a pleasant bedmate to quench the hunger she'd roused in him. He found now he could not use a woman he cared for. He poured more ale. When had he started to care? When she'd risked her life in the burning castle to save his nieces? When he'd seen her humor and tenderness? There was a quiet dignity about Giselle that set her apart, a calmness and peace that drew him. And she was a virgin. He still could not believe it, except that he knew it to be true. Her responses to him, while passionate, had been unschooled. He knew some men would find the idea of bedding a virgin most appealing, and were she to be his wife he'd expect her to come to his bed untouched. Giselle was not to be his wife. But neither was she available to him like the whores he was accustomed to using. He would do the honorable thing and let her go.

He'd been raised by a strict, uncompromising code of honor. He was a knight and he took his vows seriously. Doing the right thing did not, however, mitigate the pain. It seldom did. That was why honor was so difficult, and why the vows and training and commitment were necessary. He'd always worn his honor like a bright mantle. Those who liked him thought him a bit odd and teased him. Others called him a fool. He felt every inch a fool tonight.

"Alex."

He turned to focus on Julianna.

"Have you asked her to stay?"

"Asked her?"

She smiled at him and shook her head. "I don't know what has happened between you two. Give her another chance. Give yourself a chance. This woman might be exactly what you need. You've been far too much alone for too many years."

"Nay, Julianna. What I need is a rich wife. Find me one, and soon."

"If that is truly what you want."

"It is." A wife and children would keep him busy, would cure the terrible loneliness that at times seemed to flay him raw. He was not a rich man. He needed a wife with a goodly dowry. Giselle might bring him pleasure, even a measure of happiness, but she would also bring great pain. He was hurting now at the thought of giving her up when he barely knew her. How much worse would it be after several months or years, when he finally wed and must turn her away? He would not keep a mistress once he was wed. He'd not do that to his wife. It would not be honorable. He growled a curse and drank more ale.

*   *   *

Giselle smoothed the fabric of the dark gown over her hips. It was so soft, and so warm. She'd never hoped to wear such a gown in her life. It was kind of Alex to think of her comfort and bring it. She wasn't sure she'd wear it, then decided since it was for one night only, that she would. It would be a memory to cherish when she was back in the woods, clad in her rough wool, cold in winter and hot in summer. She peeked down at the edge of the linen chemise that showed at the hem of the gown. It was so finely woven it did not scratch her skin, but lay upon it like a caress. She wished she could keep the undergarment, but knew she'd return it with the rest of the borrowed finery. He had not thought to bring a veil for her hair, but then she was not the sort of woman accustomed to wearing one. Instead, she ran an old wooden comb through her hair until it lay smooth and thick down her back to her thighs. It was her glory, this wealth of curling red hair, and she did not care to cover it. She had no jewels, not even a simple belt to girdle her waist, but she knew she looked pretty.

Still she hesitated to go downstairs. She'd have to leave the safety of this chamber soon, or he'd come looking for her. She dreaded going into that hall full of people, all of whom knew why she was here. No doubt they also knew of her dismissal. She did not understand what she'd done to displease him. He seemed reluctant to relieve her of her virginity, which she found slightly absurd. If so, he would be one of the first men she'd met to have such scruples. The irony of it was that he was the man she wished to give it to.

Odin pushed his big head against her hand and she obediently scratched him behind the ears. "What a coil. How do I let him know I want him?"

The dog looked up at her with his one bright eye, his brows scrunched together as though giving the question his full attention. It really did not matter that she wanted Alex, not if he decided to be rid of her. Their positions were inequitable. He was the lord, she was the commoner. He could order her to his bed, or command her gone. She did not want to leave. Not now. Not when her heart had opened to the man. She was a fool. She should be relieved to go. He would use her and abandon her if she stayed, and she did not think she could endure that. *Admit it. I want him to care, and that is the one thing that will not happen. It's better this way. Before he knows what is in my heart.*

She could no longer put off the inevitable. "Come, Odin. It will be over soon enough."

The dog followed her out of the quiet chamber and down the stone stairs to the noisy hall. The hearth fire and wall torches lighted the cavernous room, but did little to mitigate the cold. She was thankful for the warm wool of her gown. There were three tables set up, one at right angles to the other two. At this table Alex sat with his family. She hesitated at the foot of the stairs, unsure where to sit, then headed for an empty spot at one of the lower tables. If he wanted her gone he surely could not want her seated near him. Nor would she be comfortable with the noble ladies who shared his table. Though Julianna and Elizabeth had been nothing but gentle with her, she knew she did not belong there.

A young knight blushed furiously as he moved down the bench to let her sit. The men nearby stared at her, some with lust in their faces, others with mere curiosity or surprise. Odin settled under her, half hidden by the folds of her gown. She saw Alex rise from his place. He stood a bit unsteadily before marching in her direction. Panic threatened. Would he make a scene? Had she been wrong to come down after all? She forced herself to appear calm and sat quietly until he stood behind her.

"I would have you seated with me."

"Yes, m'lord." She carefully gathered her voluminous skirts and removed herself from the bench. Odin crawled out from his place to follow. A muscle in Alex's jaw clenched tight but he said nothing, merely offered his arm. She placed her hand on it and let herself be led to the high table, knowing everyone stared. She forced herself to hold her head up. She'd done nothing to be ashamed of; she would not allow them to make her feel small.

"I am so glad you have joined us," Julianna said, making room for her on the bench. "You look lovely in that gown. The color flatters you."

"Thank you, m'lady." She wished she could express all her thanks, especially for Julianna's kindness.

"You must call me Julianna."

She was shocked at the idea, but said nothing. Alex sat on her other side. His hard thigh rested against hers and she moved to put some space between them. She would not be able to get through this if he touched her. Fearful she would do something to embarrass him, she watched as Julianna ate and drank, then followed the countess's example, using her fingers less than she was accustomed to and her eating knife more. She kept her ale well-watered, knowing she must keep a clear head. She felt something bumping against her legs. Odin was squirming his way under the bench, as was his custom. His big head appeared between her and Alex, waiting for her to drop him his share of her meal. To keep him from whining she slipped down a piece of goose to him. He ate it noisily. Julianna looked in her direction. Perhaps nobles did not feed dogs at the table. Giselle blushed and hoped Odin would behave.

He did not behave. When no more meat came his way he grew insistent, pushing her knees with his head.

Julianna finally saw the animal and smiled. "I believe someone wants your attention."

"I'm sorry, m'lady. I should have locked him upstairs."

"He's doing no harm. I suggest you feed him before he grows desperate."

She dropped more meat and the dog quieted. She had yet to glance at Alex, who sat silent beside her. His hand reached toward her and she sat very still. He touched her hair, and lifted a strand. She looked at him then. He let her hair fall through his fingers, watching the firelight play in the bright gold and red strands. When he looked at her his face was full of sadness that clawed at her heart. She wanted desperately to touch him, to hear his deep voice.

"I had nothing to cover it with," she said.

"Such beauty should not be covered." He spoke softly. "Thank you for coming down."

"It was what you told me to do, m'lord."

The muscle in his jaw clenched again. "Yes. So it is. No doubt if given a choice you'd stay far from me. After tonight you're free to do so."

I do not want to go from you. You are sending me away. She did not have the courage to say the words. He did not speak to her again. Tears were thick in the back of her throat and she ate very little of her meal. Odin received most of it, and grunted with pleasure at the unexpected feast.

People were beginning to leave the lower tables. Soon she would be able to hide in his chamber. Or would he tell her to spend the night in the hall? If so, she'd slip out during the night and be gone. It would not be difficult. She knew where the postern gate was and she was expert at moving through the forest in the dark. She could be back with Robyn's band in a few hours. It was better than waiting until morning and having to say farewell.

Farther down the high table Alex's eldest niece and his nephew scampered from their seats with the exuberance of childhood. They disappeared to explore the hall and Odin joined them. He was a friendly animal and seldom had the opportunity to join in children's mischief. The younger girls were bundled away by their nurses. Elizabeth and Geoffrey departed together, to sit near the hearth and talk quietly over their ale. Gilbert was arguing with his sister Maud and the girl finally grew tired of the bickering and left in a huff of indignation. Giselle, Alex, Julianna, and Stephan remained at the table.

"I know I said we'd stay, but I think we should be on our way tomorrow," Stephan said. "I don't trust the weather to hold much longer. It's damned cold already and it's early in the year."

"Tomorrow? I had hoped we could stay through Christmas. It's been so long since we've had a chance to visit with Alex." Julianna sighed.

"Indeed, I'd planned on it," Alex said. "I'll be in sore need of your company, I think. It will be too empty here come the morrow."

Stephan raised his hands to ward off further argument. "You win. We'll stay. In truth I will be glad to spend the holiday with my little brother. It's been far too many years."

Was that the ache of loneliness Giselle heard in Alexander's voice? It echoed through her. She knew the pain of lonesomeness that broke a person's heart and then their spirit. It was her constant companion. Could it be Alex knew somewhat of the same affliction? At least he had his family. She was alone in the world. She wondered, not for the first time, if that was her destiny, to be alone. She wondered if she could endure it.

The children came running through the hall, Odin in

their wake. Their faces were full of excitement. William ran to his father. "It's snowing!"

"God's blood," Alex growled. "That's the last thing we need."

They pushed away from the table and gathered at the door, staring into the night. It was indeed snowing. Great swirling masses of white fell from a bitter sky to cover the ground and limn the bare branches of trees and shrubs. Each blade of grass was jeweled with frost. What delighted the children brought dread to their elders. With winter would come famine.

Chapter Twelve

Giselle watched as white flakes swirled out of the gray sky. It was beautiful, and deadly. She turned away from the door where the others stood, and wandered back into the hall, toward the hearth and its warmth. Odin padded quietly beside her.

She'd never lived within a castle, with its immense rooms and soaring ceilings. Her homes had been small and snug and simple; some would say primitive. Yet for all its size, the walls seemed to close in on her. She was unused to being inside. The forest and wild were her place. It was there she was comfortable. It was there she belonged. Except that she was beginning to think she belonged with the imposing baron of Wolfhurst.

"What are you musing on so hard?" Alexander asked. His voice was soft and held a note of teasing.

She felt warmed by his nearness. "The snow will make travel difficult."

"The roads will be a mess. My family will be staying longer whether they are happy to or not."

"What of me?" she asked.

"I've said I'll see you safely to Robyn. I keep my promises."

She gathered what courage she could. If she didn't say it now, she never would, and what life was worth living if you didn't take a chance once in a while? Happiness did not throw itself in one's path so often that it could be ignored or taken for granted. "What if I do not wish to leave?"

He looked at her strangely then, and a small smile quirked the corner of his mouth. "Then I would have you stay."

"As your mistress?" She wanted to be sure she understood her position.

He touched her gently, his thumb rubbing along the line of her jaw. "I doubt I can keep my hands from you if you are near. I would not have you stay just to torture me. Neither will I force you. It is up to you, Giselle."

He was giving her a choice, this man who could, if he desired, force what he wanted from her. What sort of man was he, that he cared what she wanted? A rare one, no matter his rank, no matter that he came from a world that was strange and frightening to her. If she was wrong about this it was her heart and soul she would lose. If she was right, it was her fate to love this man and no other. Giselle took the risk of her life. "If you will have me, I would stay."

He stood unmoving and said not a word. Just when she was beginning to think he would refuse her, Gilbert said, "Tell her yea, you damned fool."

"I'd thank you to stay out of this," Alexander said.

Gilbert quirked a brow and smiled. "Oh, aye, I can see you've got it well in hand by yourself." He punched

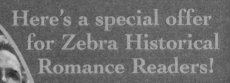

HERE'S A SPECIAL INVITATION TO ENJOY TODAY'S FINEST HISTORICAL ROMANCES— ABSOLUTELY FREE! *(a $19.96 value)*

Now you can enjoy the latest Zebra Lovegram Historical Romances without even leaving your home with our convenient Zebra Home Subscription Service. Zebra Home Subscription Service offers you the following benefits that you don't want to miss:

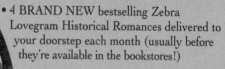

- 4 BRAND NEW bestselling Zebra Lovegram Historical Romances delivered to your doorstep each month (usually before they're available in the bookstores!)

- 20% off each title or a savings of almost $4.00 each month

- FREE home delivery

- A FREE monthly newsletter, *Zebra/Pinnacle Romance News* that features author profiles, contests, special member benefits, book previews and more

- No risks or obligations...in other words you can cancel whenever you wish with no questions asked

So join hundreds of thousands of readers who already belong to Zebra Home Subscription Service and enjoy the very best Historical Romances That Burn With The Fire of History!

And remember....there is no minimum purchase required. After you've enjoyed your initial FREE package of 4 books, you'll begin to receive monthly shipments of new Zebra titles. Each shipment will be yours to examine for 10 days and then if you decide to keep the books, you'll pay the preferred subscriber's price of just $4.00 per title. That's $16 for all 4 books with FREE home delivery! And if you want us to stop sending books, just say the word....it's that simple.

It's a no-lose proposition, so send for your 4 FREE books today!

4 FREE BOOKS

These books worth almost \$20, are yours without cost or obligation when you fill out and mail this certificate.

(If the certificate is missing below, write to: Zebra Home Subscription Service, Inc., 120 Brighton Road, P.O. Box 5214, Clifton, New Jersey 07015-5214)

Complete and mail this card to receive 4 Free books!

YES! Please send me 4 Zebra Lovegram Historical Romances without cost or obligation. I understand that each month thereafter I will be able to preview 4 new Zebra Lovegram Historical Romances FREE for 10 days. Then if I decide to keep them, I will pay the money-saving preferred publisher's price of just \$4.00 each...a total of \$16. That's almost \$4 less than the regular publisher's price, and there is never any additional charge for shipping and handling. I may return any shipment within 10 days and owe nothing, and I may cancel this subscription at any time. The 4 FREE books will be mine to keep in any case.

Name _____

Address _____ Apt. _____

City _____ State _____ Zip _____

Telephone ( ) _____

Signature _____ LF0697
(If under 18, parent or guardian must sign.)

Terms, offer and prices subject to change without notice. Subscription subject to acceptance by Zebra Home Subscription Service, Inc.. Zebra Home Subscription Service, Inc. reserves the right to reject any order or cancel any subscription.

A $19.96 value.... absolutely FREE with no obligation to buy anything, ever!

ZEBRA HOME SUBSCRIPTION SERVICE, INC.

120 BRIGHTON ROAD

P.O. BOX 5214

CLIFTON, NEW JERSEY 07015-5214

Alexander lightly in the shoulder and strolled away, whistling.

"He's right, you know," Alexander said. "I'd be a fool to do anything but take you up to my chamber before you had a chance to change your mind and flee."

She blushed but did not look away from him. "I won't run away from you." He took her hand in his and started toward the stairs.

"Sleep well," Gilbert called loudly from across the hall.

She glanced over her shoulder in time to see Elizabeth give her nephew a sharp poke in his ribs. The grinning knight ducked out of his aunt's reach. Elizabeth shook her head and smiled, then made little waving motions with her hands, signaling Giselle to go with Alexander.

"If we ignore him, he'll eventually go away," Alexander said. He did not look back but tucked her arm more securely under his own.

The chamber was as she left it, dark. He sighed. "You need not put out the candles when you leave the room. There are plenty more." He left her standing just within the doorway while he trotted down the hallway to fetch a torch. He soon had a fat night-candle lighted. Odin headed straight for the fur cover on the bed and busily made himself a nest, settling down to sleep.

"Off the bed," Alexander said sharply.

The dog eyed him mournfully, his brows scrunched together, his nose quivering. "None of that. Get down."

With a grunt, as though he were ancient and arthritic, the dog lumbered down to the floor and lay, staring up at Alex.

"He's accustomed to sleeping with me." Giselle did not add she enjoyed the dog's company. It was preferable to sleeping alone.

"He'll get used to the floor." Alexander looked from her to the dog and back again. "I'll find an old blanket for him to bed down on."

"Thank you, m'lord."

He paused in unbuckling his sword belt, his hands dark against the cream wool of his surcote. "I do not wish you to address me so. If you will not call me Alexander I'd prefer you not call me anything at all." He removed the belt with its scabbard and sword and laid them carefully on a table near the bed. Then he sat on the edge of the bed and stared at her for a long minute. "Come here." He held out his hand.

She was trembling, but she went to him and put her hand in his. He covered it with his other hand. He was warm and gentle and she calmed under his touch.

"You must not fear me, Giselle. I promise I will not hurt you."

She wanted to believe him, but knew he spoke only of her body. It was her heart she feared for. He pulled her closer, until she stood between his wide-spread thighs, and placed his hands on her waist, his warmth spreading through the wool of her gown and the linen of her undergarment. What would it feel like when he touched her skin? She trembled anew, but not from fright.

"In truth I did not think to find you a virgin."

"Do I disappoint you?"

His eyes opened wide and he smiled. "Nay. 'Tis just that my approach must need be different. I'd have you loved in such a way as to give and receive pleasure. There are men who think it great sport to take a virgin roughly. I am not one of those."

"I know that. You have been gentle with me."

"Have I? I've taken you from everyone you know, brought you to a strange place, expect things of you that others have not. I would be gentle with you, though God knows if I'll have the patience for it.''

She was confused by his last words and he saw it in her face.

"You are beautiful and innocent and good. You have no idea the powerful allure of that combination to a man as lonely as I've been. I've seen things that haunt me. If you can make me forget, even for a few minutes, I'll be grateful.''

She had never thought of herself as beautiful. She was too tall, too thin, her hair was too red, her skin too pale. Nor innocent. Her healing skills brought her into contact with suffering, bleeding, despairing humanity at its most desperate. That she had not yet experienced the secrets between a man and woman was not enough to make her innocent. She tried to be good, to be kind and compassionate, but she was selfish and lazy and too quick with her tongue for her own comfort at times. But then perhaps she was as good as most, for most people struggle to do right.

What had he seen that was so terrible he wanted to forget it in her arms? He'd been a Crusader, she'd seen his scars. War was an evil thing. If she could give him some ease from his pain, she was glad to do so. Slowly, she reached out and touched him. His face was hard and smooth and beautiful, with wide cheeks, sensual lips, and those incredible eyes. He sat very still, his gaze fixed on her. His hair glinted gold and silver in the candlelight. He let her stroke him, exploring his face and neck. A day's growth of beard was rough, but beneath it his skin was warm and soft. His lips parted slightly and she stared at his mouth. She knew the feel of his lips on hers. She lowered her head until their mouths met. It was as she remembered. At the touch of his lips a fire sprang to life deep inside her and began to spread.

He opened his mouth, his tongue slipping across her lips. She imitated what he did, and he moaned as her tongue found his mouth. They played this game gently, until he pulled her closer and his mouth became more insistent. She followed his lead and the fire grew hotter. She leaned into him, until her breasts were crushed against his broad chest and his arms enclosed her. He lowered his head to trail kisses down her neck and she trembled at the feel of his warm mouth on her hot skin.

"You are exquisite torture," he said, his voice rough.

She understood now what he meant. She was impatient for more. She wanted to feel his skin against hers. Her body ached for his touch. His hands cupped her breasts and he rubbed her nipples with his thumbs until she wanted to rip away her gown, to free herself of the barrier between them. He unlaced her gown and she helped him ease it down her shoulders and off her body. The linen chemise followed, then the soft leather shoes. She stood naked before him but was not shy.

"You'll get cold," he said.

She didn't think she'd be cold again as long as she lived, so hotly did she burn for him. "I want to see you."

He tore off his surcote, boots and leggings. Last, he slipped out of his braies. She watched with mounting excitement. He was tall and lean, with long, strong legs and a broad, muscled chest. Gold hair matted on his chest and narrowed in a line down his belly, until it flared again between his legs. He was golden in the light of the candles, lithe and graceful as a cat. His eyes glittered with a hunger that matched hers. He closed the distance between them and gathered her against his body. He was hot under her hand, his skin scorching hers, and she pressed closer, until she felt him along the length of her. It was as though they were made to fit together, so easily did her curves join the hard planes of his body, so naturally did their bodies meet at that place where the fire burned hardest.

He growled something she could not understand and carried her to the bed, laying her down on the fur. He moved on top of her, bracing himself above her.

"I thought to take more care, this first time," he said. "I don't think I can."

"I want you."

He moved against her until she matched his rhythm and grew wet with need and anticipation. The fire grew until she thought it would consume her, until she thought surely the world was ablaze all around them. The rhythm of his movements changed and she felt him at the entrance to her body.

"I want you," she said again, in a voice so low she did not recognize it as her own.

He slipped into her. The sensation was startling at first. This was what she had longed for, the feel of him inside her. He filled an emptiness that went beyond the longing he roused in her body. He was moving again, no longer as gentle as he had been, and she matched this new dance, enthralled by the flames they created.

Clutching the fur tightly to keep herself from spiraling up off the bed, the world contracted to the sensations arching through her and she matched his urgency with her own. The fire built to a molten flow. When she thought she would go mad, all the tension released in crashing waves. She felt the pulsing rhythm of his body inside her and it matched perfectly with the waves moving through her flesh. Their bodies were molded in that most intimate embrace and she lifted her legs to circle his hips, to keep him inside her. She lay in a special torpor of blissful content and never wanted to leave that place.

He caressed her cheek, her neck, her shoulder, then

pulled her closer to him and kissed the top of her head. "You're not going anywhere," he whispered.

She smiled and snuggled into the warmth and safety of his embrace.

Alexander lay awake far into the night. He was intoxicated, but it was not from the ale he'd had with his supper. Giselle slept with her head cradled on his shoulder, her warm body half covering him. He had lusted to have her in his bed, but lust could not describe what he felt now. She was more than a lovely body for his enjoyment. Much more. That this surprised him as much as it did, also made him feel a twinge of guilt. She was lowborn, not to be compared to the refined and delicate ladies of the nobility. He must look for a wife among those ladies. But he had found his heart with this woman, who was so strange a mixture of gentleness and wildness, of calm and passion. He knew he would not give her up, no matter whom he decided to marry. He stroked the incredibly soft skin of her neck and shoulder and she murmured in her sleep and moved closer. With a sigh he closed his eyes, happier than he could remember being in a very long time.

When he woke she was no longer next to him. He reached his hand across the bed, until he touched a warm body. Something wet slid across his hand several times. He opened an eye. Odin smiled back at him, his head on Giselle's pillow, his tail thumping lazily. Alexander withdrew his hand and wiped it clean on the bedcovers. "Where is she?"

The dog cocked his ears. Alexander knew she couldn't be far, not if the dog was here. "You're not allowed on the bed."

Odin yawned, smacked his lips several times, and lay his head down.

"Don't you know who I am?" Alexander said, yawning and stretching. "You show far too little respect, Sir Odin. I'll not have insubordination from one of my men."

He heard a giggle from within the privy closet.

"I am a serious man and must be feared." He deepened his voice to a dramatic tone. "I eat small children when the moon is full. And I have developed quite a taste for bad dogs."

Odin's head whipped up and he barked once. Alexander barked back. The dog bounded to his feet, barking, his tail snapping back and forth. Alex crouched on knees and elbows, then lowered his shoulders and butted the dog in the chest. Soon they were wrestling across the bed, and with a thud fell to the floor, where they continued the rough game.

Giselle came naked from the privy to watch. "Careful, you'll hurt him."

"I'm glad . . . to know . . . you care."

"I meant you'll hurt the dog."

He lay on his back, the dog straddling him, and tried to avoid the animal's marauding tongue. When he looked up Giselle was laughing.

"You think this is funny?"

"Aye."

Odin barked, as if in agreement. Alex pushed the dog away and sprang to his feet. Before she could run he picked up Giselle and carried her squealing to the bed. "We'll see how funny you think it when you're my wrestling mate." He tossed her into the middle of the bed and leered. When he launched himself toward her she screamed and rolled off the far side of the bed.

"You don't have me yet."

Alexander growled as the dog joined him in the bed, eager to renew their bout. Alex bounded from the bed. The dog stayed in the center of the bed and barked.

"That beast makes a great deal of noise." Alex began to stalk her.

"What? I cannot hear you."

He watched as she ran across the room to stand behind the one chair. The smile faded from his face. She was beautiful, her naked body firm and strong, with high, proud breasts. The sight of that firm little rear running away from him made him tight, his erection strong and demanding. She noticed the change in him immediately and her smile softened.

"What would be my fate if you caught me?"

He moved slowly toward her. "I would make love to you, slowly and carefully, for a very long time. Perhaps all day."

"A fate that holds some appeal." Her breasts topped the chair, the pink nipples hard in the cool air.

When he reached for her she did not run. He drew her into his arms, the feel of her body against his more thrilling than he expected.

"Alas, I am caught." She wound her arms around his neck and lifted her head.

He kissed her, suspecting he'd been the one caught in a golden snare.

Chapter Thirteen

By the time Giselle and Alexander emerged from the chamber it was well past noon and the last remnants of the midday meal had long since been cleared away. Gathered around the hearth were Stephan and Julianna with their children and nurses, Elizabeth in conversation with Geoffrey, and Gilbert bickering with his sister Maud.

"I don't think they missed us," Alexander said.

She glanced up at him, wondering if he could be that unaware, then straightened her back and tried to look her most dignified as she walked ahead of him down the stairs and into the hall.

"Ah, there you are," Gilbert said, with a grin on his face. "I thought we might have to send in a rescue party. With all the noise emanating from your chamber we weren't sure what sort of mayhem we'd find."

"That dog makes a bloody awful noise," Geoffrey said. "What were you doing to the beast?"

"I told him to get off the bed," Alexander said, without

so much as a twitch of his lips. He sat beside Julianna on a low bench and signaled Giselle to sit on his other side.

"Who won?" Julianna asked.

Alexander stretched his long legs out in front of him. "You'll notice only two of us have come down. The dog is abed."

Giselle tucked her feet under the hem of her gown and tried to remember not to wave her hands about when she talked. Apparently ladies did not express their emotions as adamantly as she was accustomed to and she did not want Alexander to think her uncouth.

"Do you find Wolfhurst to your liking?" Julianna asked, smiling at Giselle.

"Very much so. 'Tis wonderful having a privy so near." The others laughed and Giselle felt herself blush. She knew they were not being callous, none of them had shown any sign of it before, but she felt she'd said something unmentionable in polite society.

"Yes, 'tis a great advantage," Geoffrey said. "Though mayhap my cousin would have preferred you say you find *him* to your liking."

Unsure what to say, she remained silent. Alexander touched her cheek and she leaned into his hand, comforted by the gentle gesture.

"Do you find me to your liking?" he asked.

Tears threatened but she blinked them away. "Yes."

He smiled and his blue eyes were brilliant with pleasure. "As I do you, Giselle. The rest does not matter."

But it does. I don't belong in your world, Alexander. Don't you see?

"I take it you will not be escorting the lady back to her home?" Stephan asked, grabbing for his daughter Jordana as she tottered toward the fire. He lifted the child into his lap, where she settled to play with the bright silver buckle of his sword belt.

"Not anytime soon," Alexander said.

Julianna rose from her seat, her youngest daughter asleep in her arms. "Would you walk with me, Giselle?"

Alexander nodded in reassurance. She was glad for the excuse to escape the group, but she found the elegant countess of Rosmar nearly as intimidating as all the others combined.

"I need to put this little one to her rest," Julianna said. She cradled her daughter's head in one hand, the other supporting the tiny rump, and held her against her shoulder and breast. "It never ceases to amaze me how beautiful sleeping babies are."

Giselle saw little more than a plump pink cheek and rosy pouting mouth, a tiny nose and a whisper of blond lashes and brow, but she had to agree. They looked positively angelic when asleep. "All of your children are beautiful, m'lady."

"Don't let my William hear you say that. He'd be mortified. Anything but beautiful."

"Handsome, then." Giselle picked up the long skirts of her borrowed red gown to keep up with Julianna's long stride. Though she was tall for a woman, the countess was taller.

"He's a rogue, like his father. And his uncle Alex." Julianna shifted her hold on the baby so she could use one hand to lift her skirts clear as she climbed the stairs. "Will you go ahead and open the door? 'Tis the second chamber down the hall."

Giselle hurried to do as she was bid and stepped aside to allow Julianna entry. The countess swept into the grand chamber and carefully laid the baby in the midst of the huge bed, piling pillows around the infant to form a blockade so she could not roll too far if she woke.

"Close the door, Giselle, and come sit by me."

Julianna sat on the edge of the bed, where she could

still reach her child, and she was focused on the little girl, her hand stroking the child's tiny back.

"How old is this little one?"

"Isabel is seven months."

It seemed she would say more, and for a moment she looked sad and tired, but it passed so quickly Giselle wasn't sure she'd seen correctly. The lady had lost one child to illness, Giselle remembered, and wondered if memory of that daughter had caused the fleeting melancholy. Or perhaps not so fleeting. People were adept at masking their pain when around others. She felt a surprising empathy for this woman, with whom she had so little in common.

"Sit here." Julianna patted the bed beside her. "So I don't have to crane my neck to look up at you."

"I'm sorry, m'lady."

"Don't apologize. And please, call me Julianna."

Giselle did not answer. She couldn't possibly call this woman by her given name. For that matter, what reason could the countess of Rosmar have in talking to her privately? Most probably it was to tell her how inappropriate she was for Alexander, and to be sure her ambition did not aim at becoming his wife and baroness. Of course, Giselle would have no trouble assuring the lady that she fully agreed with her assessment and had no intention of seeking to become Alexander's wife. The idea was too ridiculous to seriously consider. He was a great lord, scion of one of the most powerful families in England. He had royal ancestors, for goodness' sake, while she could not say for sure who her parents were. She had not a thing in the world to give, except herself, and that she'd give him freely, with no expectations.

Julianna nervously twisted a ruby ring she wore, as though unsure what to say. "I've seldom seen Alexander so happy."

"He doesn't seem a sad man to me."

"No, not ill-tempered or melancholy. He has ever been of a kind nature, though impetuous at times. He's much better now than when he was younger. He's more responsible. I meant that he has been lonely and you seem to relieve him of that."

"I am happy to do so, m'lady."

Julianna glanced at her sharply, but did not reprimand her. "You are a lovely young woman. I think perhaps you are exactly what Alexander needs in his life."

Giselle stared at her hands folded demurely in her lap. She understood the unspoken words. She was a meet plaything for now, but a wife would one day supplant her. That was as it should be. Alexander would need to marry and have heirs to inherit Wolfhurst. She wondered how long he would want to have her near him.

"Are you always so withdrawn and quiet, or is it that you are uncomfortable with me?"

Giselle was surprised by the question. Wouldn't Robyn and the others think it funny to hear her called shy? "I'm not accustomed to lords and ladies. Truly, I don't know what to say to you."

Julianna tilted her head slightly and a small smile teased her full lips. "You are a rare one, I think. Do not let us awe you. We're only human, the same as you in every way that truly counts. There is a wonderful innocence about you, Giselle. It would be a privilege, I think, if I could name you as a friend. For what it is worth, you have my blessing. I hope you and Alex will have many years together."

"You cannot mean that." Surely she misunderstood.

Julianna smiled. "But I do. Alex is a good man. You could do far worse."

"I could—what of Alexander? Surely you do not approve of him being with a commoner with no family, no wealth?

I do not even know how to dress or eat or talk properly. I'm an embarrassment to him.''

The countess was no longer smiling. ''Do you truly believe that?''

Giselle felt miserable. She'd said too much, revealed too much, but it wasn't fair to have hope held out to her when it was false. She had her pride and she was not stupid. She knew her situation. ''He is happy to have me in his bed. He has no use for me in any other aspect of his life.''

''You do not know my brother-in-law as well as I. If he wants you with him it is because of more than you can give him in the privacy of his bedchamber, I assure you. Relax, sweet child. Do not try so hard to be what you think he might want you to be. It is you he wants, as you are.''

''But I'm not good enough as I am.''

Julianna studied her carefully. ''Do you lie?''

''No.''

''Are you a thief?''

''No.''

''A murderer perhaps?''

There was the accident with the arrow, when Alexander had been hurt, but she hadn't meant to harm anyone. ''No.''

''Are you a woman of loose morals, promiscuous, drunken, slovenly, deceitful?''

She shook her head.

''I didn't think so. You are kind, gentle and beautiful. Alex would be a damned fool not to do all he could to make you happy. Do not make the mistake of thinking because he is a lord he is not human and does not have a heart. He can be hurt, as readily and as intensely as you. Alex is an easy man to love, he has many friends. He is not as easy to know. Take time to befriend him, and if you find you truly love him, have the courage to tell him so.''

"Why do you say these things? Surely you want him to find a wife, to have a family of his own."

"Of course I do. Nothing I've said to you contradicts that. I've learned that love sometimes does not happen when and where we would think to look for it. When it does come into our lives we must grasp it hard and not let go, no matter what others might think or say."

She had the distinct impression the countess spoke from personal experience. What story lay behind Julianna and Stephan's love? One day perhaps she would feel confident enough to ask. For now she was comforted by this generous woman, though she wasn't sure she agreed with everything the countess said. Other than Marian she'd never been close to other women. Had her years of isolation, first with Maeve, who raised her, then with Robyn's band, been more unusual than she dreamed? She'd missed the companionship of women and wasn't sure now how to reach out for the friendship Julianna seemed to offer, no matter how unlikely such a gesture might seem.

Before she could speculate further on the implications of their conversation, someone knocked on the door.

Alexander stepped into the room. He looked worried. "Giselle, I need your help."

"What is amiss?" Julianna asked, rising from the bed.

Giselle crossed the room quickly. He wrapped a heavy cloak around her shoulders. He wore one also. "Nothing serious, I hope. Father Michael said there was sickness in the village."

Julianna glanced back at her sleeping child. When she looked at them, Giselle saw plainly the fear in her eyes. *Curse the man for being so blunt.* "Do not worry, m'lady. Such things are seldom serious."

"Yes, of course. Go, do what you must." Julianna tried to smile, but was not entirely successful.

Giselle hurried along beside Alexander. "You could have lied in front of her."

"Lied? But you said there was naught to worry about."

"*I* lied."

He gripped her arm and propelled her more quickly through the dark hall and out into the cold, gray afternoon. "Just how serious do you think it could be?"

"I've no way of judging until I see those who are ill. Your sister-in-law will spend her time worrying and it may or may not be necessary. You should learn to guard your tongue, m'lord."

"Indeed."

She noted the irritation in his voice, but her own anger kept her from trying to soften her words. The reprimand was warranted. Just because men dealt with crises head-on, charging into a situation with brute force and determination, did not mean such tactics were always the best. She'd learned long ago to dissemble with her patients. The worse thing she could do was rob them of all hope, even when the case was incurable. Half her time tending the sick was spent helping them as peacefully as possible into eternity. She'd become a master diplomat in dealing with death.

She trudged through the snow of the bailey and out the gates, onto the frozen mud of the path leading to the village. The priest waited for them at the edge of the small settlement, where the tiny church stood. He looked at her with surprise.

"I don't know what you're doing here, child, but glad I am to see you. When Sir Alexander said he'd go for a healer I didn't expect him to produce one from his own castle."

"What illness is there?" she asked. Father Michael would weasel an explanation out of her eventually. For now there were more important matters to concentrate on.

"The miller's mother is sore afflicted with a lung fever, but then the woman's well beyond sixty."

At that advanced age it was not uncommon for a fever younger, healthier folk fought off in a week or two, to prove fatal. Giselle frowned, thinking what she might need. A fever and cough, aches. Nettle for fever, holly for the cough, perhaps hareburr if the dame could tolerate so drastic a cure. Then she realized she had none of her remedies with her. They were in her cave, far from Wolfhurst. She said a quick prayer asking for strength. She'd have to make do with what she could find for now, and retrieve her cures as soon as she could.

The miller's house was larger and kept in better order than most of the others, since he was one of the more prosperous villeins. He collected a fee for every bag of flour ground in the lord's mill, a larger fee going to the baron. Every bit of grain raised on Wolfhurst land was by law mandated to be ground in the baron's mill and no other. To be found with a hand-mill in one's possession could lead to the loss of a hand, or worse if the lord so willed it. So the miller, like the baron, was respected or despised, more or less according to how each man dealt with his fellows. A lenient lord was well liked; an evil lord hated. An unprincipled miller often did not live to see his grandchildren gathered at his knee. It was surprising how many millers drowned caught in their own millwheels. An occupational hazard, men would say, with a knowing gleam in their eyes. Giselle had never heard that Wolfhurst's miller was dishonest, but neither had she known the man to be praised for his compassion.

Even before they entered the cottage Giselle heard the harsh rales in the sick woman's chest, sign of a serious infection. The only light in the crowded room came from the fire in the hearth along one wall. The miller, a round-faced, balding man with a beard more gray than brown, sat at the only table. His wife, a child on her hip and two others clinging to her skirts, stood behind him. Several more children were crowded together on a pile of straw-filled pallets and blankets, huddled together against the cold. The miller stood when he recognized Alexander.

"M'lord, 'tis good of you to come. You do me honor."

Giselle made her way to where an old woman lay on a pallet on the floor, several heavy blankets covering her stout form. Fear gleamed in the woman's fevered eyes as she dragged each breath painfully into her lungs. Though her face was flushed and red, there was a blue tinge to her mouth and when Giselle picked up one of her hands, the fingers were cold. It was not good when the fever settled so deeply in a person's lungs, especially one who was old, but this woman appeared healthy enough otherwise. She was certainly not underfed, but a miller's family seldom was. They rarely lacked for bread.

"Who's the wench?" the miller asked, his voice surly with suspicion.

"Giselle is a skilled healer," Alexander said.

"The baron tells true," Father Michael said. "Leave the woman be. She'll know what must be done to help your mother."

Giselle made a careful examination of the woman's symptoms and her heart sank. "Has she been coughing much?"

"Aye, all night, it seemed," the miller's wife said. "Kept us awake, it did."

"Was there blood in what she coughed up?"

"Only the last two days. Not before."

"How long has she been ill?"

The woman pursed her lips. "She hasn't been to Sunday Mass two times now, is that right, Father?"

Giselle rose from where she crouched and approached the other woman. She reached out to touch the child in his mother's arms, and as she feared, the little one was hot. Several of the children were coughing. "How many of your children are ill?"

"All seven of them," the miller said, more than a little irritation edging his voice. "Can ye give them some sort of potion? There's work needs doing and it ain't getting done with them hacking all day in bed."

"I will have a tisane sent tomorrow."

The miller's brows drew together in a scowl. "That's it? We're to feed them some foul brew? What of me, mam?"

Giselle glanced at the man and guessed that he did care for his mother, inasmuch as the woman intruded on his consciousness. "Keep her warm, try to get her to eat and drink. If she's in pain give her as much ale as she'll take."

"Ye want us to get the old woman conked?" the miller asked.

"It's medicinal, to relieve her pain." She did not think the man understood what she was not saying. "Your mother is very ill. There is not much that can be done for her now. With God's grace and good care she might recover."

For the first time the miller looked worried. "She's dying?"

Giselle wasn't sure what to say. If the woman didn't recover, and soon, she'd die, slowly drowning as her lungs filled with fluid. But there was a chance she would get well again. "I'll know better in a day or two. I'll come back tomorrow, with the medicinals."

"Aye, see that ye do." The miller turned his attention to Alexander and the priest. "I've not much to offer, but I'd be pleased should ye share a cup with me."

"Another time," Alexander said. "I'll not have Giselle

run about tending everyone who comes down with this. You'll come to the castle for what you need."

"Aye, m'lord."

Giselle wondered why Alexander seemed angry. She followed as he marched out the door into the cold day. The priest trailed after them.

Alexander wanted to wring the miller's fat neck for the disrespect he'd shown Giselle. Instead he walked away from the cottage, toward the small church. The man hadn't bothered to acknowledge her help in any way, as though she were some sort of servant. The day was dismal, cold and gray. Smoke clung low around the cottage roofs and the only people not in their houses were those outside of necessity. Even the dogs hid under the eaves and porches. The air smelled moist with unshed snow.

Giselle caught up to him and pulled at his sleeve. "You go too fast."

He slowed, and Michael came puffing up beside them. "You'd think the devil was at your arse. What's the hurry?"

"Sorry. We need to talk and I thought the church a good place for it."

"My house would be better," Michael said. "There's always the chance of a pious parishioner in the church itself. I take it you don't want this conversation overheard?"

The priest was perceptive. He'd meant to get to know the man better and had not yet made the time to do so. It appeared now was as good a time as any. "There are things I need to know."

The cottage the priest called home was tiny but neat, with a small bed, a table and bench, and surprisingly, a shelf holding several books. Alexander absently ran his hands over the book bindings, none of which were adorned, but all of soft, good-quality leather. He picked one up and opened it at random. "You read *The Consolations?*"

"Some think because Aurelius was a pagan there's no worth in his writing."

"You disagree?"

"I look for wisdom wherever I might detect it. There's little enough to be found, even when searching. The book was a gift from Father Bernard, when I first came to Wolfhurst to take his place. He's told me often enough over the years that I'll find truth hidden in *The Consolations.* He was right."

Alexander carefully replaced the treasure with the other books. He hadn't expected an obscure country priest to be literate. Many priests were villein-born and little more educated than their parishioners. They memorized the words of the Mass and other rites, but often did not know the meaning of the Latin they spoke so brokenly. But then, so few people, even among the nobility, knew any more that the lack often went unnoticed. His father had been unusual in insisting his sons learn to read, but then his father had been acquainted with Queen Eleanor, and that lady put a very high regard on learning.

"Would you have some ale?" Michael asked.

"Aye, I would." Alex sat on the bench and motioned Giselle down beside him. The priest set three unmatched wooden cups on the table, and an earthenware pitcher. Alex poured the dark liquid into the cups and they drank in silence. "How many other villagers are sick?"

Michael sat on the edge of the bed, there being no other place for him. He was a big man and the one room seemed diminished with him occupying it. "A dozen or so that I know of. Mostly children so far. Only the old woman seems likely to die of it."

"I can visit through the village to check on the others," Giselle said. "But I need to retrieve my herbs if I'm to be of any use to these people. Most will need simple nursing care to recover. A few may become very ill."

"Will many die?" Alex asked.

"I cannot say." Giselle held her cup in both hands and peered into the amber liquid as though seeking an answer there. "Lung fever comes every autumn and winter but that is the only predictable thing about it. Some years many are ill and die, other years few sicken and then only slightly. There are years most of the children are sick but few of the adults. I cannot know until this attack begins to run its course how serious it may be. It is not good that the miller's mother is so gravely ill. She is elderly but otherwise hale. Nor is it good that all the miller's children have sickened. I'm afraid this may be a very contagious fever, especially among the young."

Alexander thought of his nephew and nieces and fear pierced him. "I'll tell Stephan to take the children away from here."

"Yes, that is best." Giselle glanced at him, then away. "See that they leave immediately, no matter how bad the roads may seem."

Fear wrenched his gut. He was beginning to understand how her mind worked. She was careful not to exaggerate a situation. If she was concerned about the children's safety, there was good cause.

"As always the old, the very young, the weak, and pregnant women, will be most likely to take ill." Giselle pushed her hair back from her face.

"Hunger will make the villagers weaker," Alex said.

"Yes."

"Then I must be sure the village does not lack for food." Alex finished what was left of the ale in his cup. "You said you'd need to get your medicinals. I'll go with you."

Giselle and the priest both stared at him as though he were a madman. "I can't take you there," Giselle said. "I will not chance putting Robyn and the others in danger by showing you where they hide."

He didn't like the stubborn look of her mouth. "I won't allow you to roam the forest alone. God knows what could happen to you."

"You won't allow? I am not your chattel, nor am I bound by law to this place. I am a free woman and will come and go as I please."

He was startled by her vehemence. What she said was true, but he thought what had happened between them gave him the right to think possessively of her. He only wanted to ensure her safety. Or was it that he was afraid if she left without him she'd not come back? "You won't go alone."

He'd never seen her so angry.

"You arrogant . . . *lord!*" She unfurled the word as though it were the nastiest epithet she could think of. Perhaps for her it was.

"You can rail at me all you want, I will still see to your safety. You are my responsibility now."

"I never asked for your protection."

"Alas, you have it. Get used to the idea, Giselle. I've put my mark on you. I take care of what is mine."

"May I make a suggestion?" Michael asked.

Giselle glared at the priest.

"Please do," Alexander said.

"I shall escort her to Robyn, if you feel it necessary, though I tend to think it isn't. The woman has lived all her life in the wood, m'lord. She's much less like to come to harm in it than you or I."

Alexander studied the priest. When he'd ridden back into Wolfhurst wounded and sick, Michael had denied knowing anything about Robyn and his men. Now he spoke the name with a casual familiarity. "Is that acceptable to you?"

"Yes," Giselle said.

"Why is it you will trust Michael with Robyn's whereabouts but not me?"

"Father Michael has been to see Robyn many times," Giselle said. "And he did promise to perform Alan and Alice's wedding."

Alexander saw the priest vainly try to shut her up, but she didn't notice. He raised a questioning eyebrow at the priest, who shrugged his big shoulders and looked embarrassed. "I see. How long will it take you to go there and back?"

"If we leave now we can return by tomorrow afternoon," she said.

"You'll travel faster on horseback. I'll have two animals made ready for you."

She looked ill at ease, and he remembered she didn't have much experience with riding. "Time is of the essence, I think. The snow will hamper you if you try to walk, but the horses can clear it easily. Can you manage?"

"I'll do what's necessary."

He liked the determination in her voice, all the more so knowing she was uncomfortable around horses. There were those who would call her cowardly because she feared the big animals, but then she'd never been trained the way noble ladies were, from childhood, to be comfortable on the beasts. It was one of the clearest distinctions between nobles and commoners. Nobles went mounted, commoners on foot. He thought her brave, to swallow her fear for the sake of helping others.

"You will keep her safe?" Alex asked.

"Aye, m'lord," the priest answered. "I promise you that."

He wanted to ask if she would vow to come back to him. He almost did. He decided instead to trust her to keep her word, no matter how difficult it was for him. He didn't want her out of his sight. For now he must let her go.

Chapter Fourteen

Snow piled in drifts between barren trees. Low clouds turned the sky to opalescent gray. It was bitter cold; colder than Giselle could remember in years. She concentrated on keeping her hands gripped on the reins. Even with wool gloves her fingers were numb. The mare she rode was surefooted, and an hour into the journey Giselle relaxed, realizing she had to do little but sit in the saddle and the horse would manage the rest. Michael rode ahead, the big hulk of him scrunched down into his cloak, a cowl of snow covering his head and shoulders and trailing over the rump of his horse. Odin followed patiently behind them. Giselle was grateful for the warmth of the fur-lined cloak Alex had insisted she wear, and the warm boots on her feet.

Thinking of Alex took her mind off the discomfort of the trip. Memory of his large, warm hand on her arm, the intensity of his gaze, the question that lingered in his eyes as she left him, played in her mind for miles. He had not wanted to let her go. She had not wanted to leave, but the situation was urgent and left her no choice. She knew she would return to him. It was as though she no longer had a choice about that either. Her heart belonged in his hands. Absently she shook the snow from her cloak, causing her horse to toss its head. Giselle tensed, wondering what the animal would do next, then relaxed as the mare continued her steady progress through the deepening snow. Perhaps horses were not to be feared after all. She had to admit they made their way more quickly mounted than they would afoot.

She was intimate with the wildwood in all its moods. Now the world was quiet and cold and brittle. Beneath the mantling snow was that throbbing, fertile green of summer and the ripe fruitiness of autumn and harvest. Silence held sway in the winter world as it did no other time of the year. The cry of a bird was seldom and plaintive. But it was not a stagnant world. Scattered in the snow were prints of forest creatures. So far she had seen no wolf tracks, for which she was grateful.

Eventually she noticed the priest had slowed and was riding beside her. She glanced at him and saw the stubborn set of his jaw.

"Well," Michael said. "Would you care to explain to me just what you're doing at Wolfhurst?"

Michael knew her well, she'd confessed to him enough and been absolved; her penances, she suspected, no heavier than she deserved and not as severe as many people won from the man. "I am what you think."

"And how do you know what I think? Are you with the baron of your free will or has he forced you to it?"

"If I were forced, would I be here now?"

"Depends on what he was using to keep you obedient. Fear is a powerful incentive to do what another demands."

Alexander hadn't exactly asked how she felt about it before claiming she was his. Had she been more unwilling, would he have let her go that first night on the road to the abbey? Would he let her go now, if she asked? "I do not stay because I fear him."

Michael grunted and looked away. "Be careful, child. The man's not likely to make an honest woman of you, even if he cares for you."

It was the same nagging doubt that deviled her brain. While he might dally with her, Alex was not likely to marry her. "I am not with him because I think to become baroness of Wolfhurst. I am not so näive as that."

"I've never said you were. I'm your priest. It's my duty to worry over your soul. I'm also your friend, and it's your heart I do not want to see battered. Can you not settle for John Little? He'd protect you and provide for you."

"And he's more my kind."

"Yes. The lords are different from us, Giselle. No matter how just or decent your baron may be, he's still lord of this land. He expects certain things, believes certain things. He can't help it, it's how they all think."

She frowned but kept silent. Something about what the priest said didn't ring true. She'd thought the same as he until a few days ago. But she'd seen Alexander and his family at close quarters and she was surprised to find they were not much different than others she knew. They were rich and so had comforts and trappings she was not accustomed to. They had a certain way of moving and speaking, full of confidence, that came from the power they were accustomed to wielding, the position they were born to. But she'd also seen the worry Alex had for his land and people. With his privileges came responsibility. Most of all, she'd seen the love and caring so evident in his family. Julianna had gone out of her way to be kind to her. Still she did not feel comfortable with them. She was too aware of the chasm that separated them. Like Michael she doubted the differences in their stations could be bridged.

She felt certain they could never be forgotten. "I will be happy for now just to be with him. If that be a sin, so be it."

"You'll not repent and separate yourself from the man?"

Michael had never talked to her so sternly before, but then she'd never done so reckless a thing as give herself to a man who could not be her husband. "No," she said, wearily.

"I thought not."

She eyed him suspiciously but he seemed absorbed in thought. "That's it? No lecture? No threats?"

He sighed, and his breath hung in a cloud before him. There was ice in his beard. "You must live your own life, child. My advice to you, as your priest, is run from temptation as far and as fast as you can. My hope, as your friend, is that you find happiness."

What he said astonished her. He would not berate her for her sin, nor judge her for her weakness. Neither could he rejoice for her, but she couldn't blame him for that. She wasn't sure there would be much joy in her life. Still, she would not leave Alexander. She would take what he could give. How long she could live like that, she wasn't sure. For now what he offered was enough. It would have to be.

The hall at Wolfstone was dark except for the glow of embers in the stone hearth. Alexander stood in the depth of the night shadows, staring unseeing at the dying fire. Fear twisted tight in his belly and he cursed its too-familiar presence. It was quiet now, in the small hours before dawn. His servants and the knights of his brother's household slept on pallets scattered about the hall. There was the soft sounds of sleep: a grunt, a snore, a sigh. Whatever they dreamed, they did so undisturbed by the phantoms that twirled through his imagination and left him awake and shaken.

His ears strained to hear the faintest sound from upstairs. Soon he would go back up to see for himself that all was well. His nephew, William, was sick with the lung fever. Suddenly, in the afternoon, no more than an hour after Giselle rode away, the boy had complained of illness. Within hours he was laid low with fever and pain. During the night he began to cough, that hard, echoing cough that Alex knew too well from other years when the fever raged. Walking carefully in the near-dark so he would not step on anyone, Alex made his way to the door and out into the brilliant night of cold and snow.

He cursed the snow for its disguise of purity and calm. Had it not been for the storm his family might have got away safe. He did not wear a cloak and the cold bit through his tunic. He welcomed the icy jolt. It reassured him that he was alive. Even as he cursed the heavens he knew it was foolish. It was God's will, or so the priests insisted, though why a loving God visited sickness on children, was a mystery of faith Alexander had never been able to penetrate. Trembling now with cold, his rage cooled, he slumped against the stone wall of his castle and he prayed. It was a desperate, disjointed prayer, prodded by fear more than faith. He begged God to let William live. He begged that all his loved ones would escape the death that had come to Wolfhurst. At last, with eyes tight-closed, with head bowed, with desperate need, he prayed Giselle would return to him.

"You do not need to return," Robyn said. He sprawled near the fire, his large hands stretched out toward the warmth. Marian sat beside him.

Giselle huddled into her cloak. Even with the fire near

she was cold. It would be dawn soon and they could begin their journey back to Wolfhurst. She had carefully packed all her simples and other herbs into the leather saddlebags Alex had given to her. Then she had slept a few hours, but not well. She woke stiff, cold and gritty-eyed. "I thought you did not want me here."

Robyn slanted a glance at her, then studied the fire. "I was not willing to fight Wolfhurst that night on the road, but I would have, had I thought you were in danger. The man intrigues me. He's not like the lords I've known."

"You thought I could spy for you, tell you what he plans?"

He quirked a smile at her and nodded, somewhat sheepishly. "It crossed my mind. But I'd not have you stay with him if you do not care to. He asks a great deal of you, to go back to where there is sickness."

"Still, I will go."

Marian poked vigorously at the fire with a long stick, sending sparks dancing upward in the cold cave. Robyn stilled her hand before she could send embers flying in her agitation. "I don't want you to go back there," Marian said.

Giselle heard the hurt and fear in her friend's voice. She also knew it was justified. As likely as anyone to come down with the fever, she risked her health, perhaps her life, by returning to Wolfhurst. But then so did Alexander, and the thought of him ill frightened her more than concern for her own safety. "I must return. I promised."

"What of your promise to me?" Marian asked.

"What are you talking of?" Giselle rubbed her hands together beneath her cloak but it did little to warm them.

"You said you'd be here when my baby is born."

"And I shall. The babe is not due until summer. I will help you with the birthing, I swear it. Do not fear for me, my friend. I do what I must. Surely you can understand?"

Marian wiped at her eyes and turned her head away. "That's how it is, then. God's mercy on you, I hope that devil doesn't break your heart."

So do I, Giselle thought. "I'll need to wake Michael soon. It grows light enough to travel."

"It's been snowing all night," Robyn said. "I'm glad you have the horses, though in truth I'm mightily tempted to keep them myself."

"You're a greedy man," she said, teasing him.

"Nay, just practical. The baron can afford to buy more horses; I cannot."

A month ago she would have accepted what he said without question. The lords had more than they needed and would not be hurt if some of it was taken to be used by those with an equal need but fewer resources. The redistribution of wealth Robyn was so talented at, did not enrich him or his men much. He gave most of it away to those with greater need, but she suspected he robbed the wealthy more for the sport of humiliating them than any other motive. Alexander was generous with his wealth. He'd sworn to keep the villagers fed, and many lords would not do as much, leaving their folk to live or die by their own means. A peasant, after all, was easy to replace. It was not as though there was a dearth of them.

Robyn stood and placed a hand on her shoulder. "Promise you'll send word through Michael if you need help."

"I will."

"I'll wake the priest." He walked away from them.

Marian sighed and resumed poking at the fire, but in a calmer way. "Do you love the man?"

Giselle had asked herself little else the last few days. Was it possible to love someone in so short a time? She was strongly lured by Alexander's strength and masculine beauty, but she was also enchanted by his kindness, the gentleness that colored so much of what he did. She believed him to be a good and decent man, and they were few enough. When he smiled or laughed, when he teased her, she felt as light and carefree as children are supposed to feel when they are loved and safe. When he touched her she came alive with desire. What their bodies shared she found exciting and frightening and miraculous. But was all, or any, of this love? Did she not have to know the man better before she could declare such a thing? "I do not know. I think it would be easy to love him."

Marian's bright eyes widened. "Does he love you?"

Giselle was quick to answer. "No. He does not misuse me. He is kind, but I am no more than a plaything to him."

"Is that enough?"

"For now. He may care for me, with time. It will have to be enough."

Marian shook her head sadly. "Don't give yourself to a man who cannot return your feelings. You will know only pain if you stay with him."

She did not argue, fearing what her friend said was true. Now, just getting to know him, the joy outweighed fear. He had not yet brought her pain, and so there was hope, weak as a butterfly, but tenacious nonetheless. Only time would show if she were foolish or wise, and she must give herself, and him, the time to know one way or the other. If he married another, she did know she could not share him. "I am content for now, Marian. Perhaps for the first time in my life I have a chance at real happiness. I must risk heartbreak or never know if his love can be mine."

Michael joined them, bleary-eyed and rumpled, with cheese in one hand and a cup of warm ale in the other. He ate quickly, sharing the cheese with Odin. "We'd better be on our way. The wind is picking up and that means the snow will drift."

The horses were saddled and waiting, Robyn and the

others gathered at the mouth of the secret cave to send them off.

"Godspeed and may He keep you safe," Marian said, giving Giselle a warm hug. "May you find happiness."

"Be careful," Robyn said. "I'm sending two of the men with you, as a guard. There are outlaws running about wild in these woods." His eyes twinkled, though he was serious enough. His men were disciplined. Others were not. There were desperate, vicious men at loose, and anyone caught was fair game. Many an unlucky or foolish person disappeared without trace. Only the strong moved openly through Sherwood.

They began the return journey just as the sun came up behind heavy clouds. The gray that had been the night sky became a paler gray, with the incessant white flakes falling, heaved by the shifting wind. In places the wind scoured the ground bare and icy, in others snow piled in treacherous drifts. It soon became apparent their trip would be longer than anticipated, picking a circuitous way around the barriers of snow. By midday the wind was howling into their faces. Giselle could see little beyond her mare's head and concentrated on following the rump of the horse in front of her. As familiar as she was with the woods, she felt disoriented and was glad for the men who led them.

She had seldom been so cold. Never had she been out in a storm of this intensity for hours at a time. Any sane person sought shelter and a fire and waited for the fury to pass. Even the animals hid in their secret places when the world grew as inhospitable as this. Still they rode resolutely on. By the time they came to the edge of the wood, where the fields of Wolfhurst lay buried in their cold shroud, she was beyond feeling, numb with the biting wind, her fingers gripped tightly around the reins. Slowly the village came into view. Robyn's men made their way to

Michael's house, where they would stay hidden until the snow and wind let up. The priest continued beside her, up the hill, through the gate and into the castle bailey. Their horses' hooves made no noise in the yard, muffled by snow, but they had been seen coming toward the gate, which had been opened for them. A groom came from the stable, making his way slowly through the drifts. Odin did not bark. He was too exhausted from his journey. He sat, head down against the wind, and waited.

Painfully she forced her fingers to release the stiff leather of the reins. When she tried to dismount, her limbs did not obey as they should, moving in graceless jerks, feeling heavy as lead. Slipping off the saddle she could not stand, but sank into the snow. Odin moved to her side and licked her face. She tried to stand, to get farther away from the mare, whose legs and feet loomed less than an arm's span from her, but her muscles did not respond, she could not feel her feet, her hands were numb.

Beside her, Michael dismounted and came around his horse to her. "Sweet Mary, you should not have pushed yourself so hard. Why did you not ask us to stop?"

She could not answer him, merely lifting her arms so he could help her stand. As soon as she warmed herself by a fire she would feel better. Michael struggled to support her and they made slow, labored progress toward the castle.

Suddenly she was lifted into strong arms. Alex carried her quickly and surely through the ice and snow, up the stairs, into the hall, up another flight of stairs, and into the blessed warmth of his chamber. She clung to him, sinking into his warmth. Michael and Odin followed more slowly, the priest carrying the bags with her herbs.

Alexander turned furiously on the priest. "Have you no more sense than to push beyond her endurance? You promised to keep her safe."

"I should have been more careful. She made no complaint, but I should have known. It was hard enough on the men. I should have known.''

'' 'Tis not Michael's fault,'' she whispered. Alex still held her in his lap, sitting on the great bed. "I'm so cold."

"Put more wood on the fire," Alex ordered. The priest obeyed.

Sure, quick hands removed her wet gloves and boots and the heavy cloak with its layer of ice and snow. She was vaguely aware of a woman's voice and of her gown and wet woolen stockings being removed. She was placed, shivering, into the large bed and blankets piled on top. Odin lay next to her, sharing his warmth. Slowly the shaking stopped and warmth began to penetrate the bone-deep cold. She closed her eyes. A warm hand gently stroked her head, over and over.

"Let her sleep," Elizabeth said.

Alex continued to stroke Giselle's bright hair. She was so pale, and so cold. Her eyes were circled by dark shadows like bruises. She'd pushed herself too hard, and for what? To come back to a plague, to nurse folk who were not her kin, to whom she owed no service. She had come back, and for that he was grateful and surprised. It would be so easy for her to stay with Robyn. It was hazardous for her to return, yet she was here, in his bed, safe for now. "I apologize, Father, for my unseemly outburst."

The priest stood quietly at his side. "Nay, you had reason enough. She's a brave woman. See you deserve her. Treat her ill and you'll have me to answer to."

"And me," Elizabeth said.

Alexander looked at them both, fierce as any parent protecting a beloved child. He turned his attention back to the woman in his bed. He'd lusted to see her there, naked and hot with passion, eager to quench his desire in her body. Now a flood of protective tenderness consumed him at the sight of her frail from so deeply asleep, and knew his lust had been transformed into something deeper and more frightening. He cared for the woman, more than he'd admitted even to himself. He'd do anything to protect her and to keep her. "She's safe with me."

Elizabeth sat beside him on the bed. "She is lucky indeed to have you as her protector. I'll stay with her in case she wakes. You go with Father Michael. There are things you need to discuss."

He did not want to leave but knew Elizabeth spoke the truth. Things had happened in the day since Michael and Giselle left that the priest would need to know. And he had a few questions of his own.

He escorted the priest from the room, down the stairs and into the cold, nearly deserted hall. He'd sent most of the servants to their homes in the village, where they could help care for their kin who were sick. The knights of Stephan's guard sat near the hearth and worked at mundane things: stitching harness leather or cleaning chain mail. Their grumbling had grown considerably as the sickness became more widespread. One of the men had the fever, which made the others nervous. He lay on a pallet, coughing and cursing while the others brought him broth and wine, saw that he was warm, and carried his slops away regularly. It was a rough sort of care, but they expected no more and they were as loyal to each other as they were to their lord. They'd look after their own.

Alex steered the priest away from the knights to a more private enclave formed by a stone pillar that supported the roof. "The miller's mother has died," he said. "At least half a dozen others have sickened in a day. Among them are my brother and my nephew."

"How ill are the earl and his son?"

"Both seem like to recover. Stephan is miserable and

sees to it that anyone who comes near shares in his misery. William seems to be getting better, thanks be to God, though he gave us all a good scare last night. I wasn't sure if Giselle would return, so I've sent my cousin Geoffrey to Blyth Abbey for help. I've asked the abbot to send as many brothers as he can spare to help with the sick. Do you think he'll send them?"

"If the sickness is widespread and has affected the monks he may have none to offer. And there is always Guisborne to consider."

Alex frowned. "What has Guisborne to do with it?"

"The abbot does nothing without first consulting the baron, who is his main benefactor."

"Then Guy owns the abbey?"

"Nay, but he owns the abbot."

"Is there a difference?"

"There is not. I do not see what purpose it would serve Guisborne to allow this fever to spread, so he is like to offer no protest. When do you expect your cousin to return?"

Alexander's frustration made his voice sharp. "Depends on the damned weather. Later today, if possible; he doesn't have far to travel."

"I'll go down to the village and get a better idea who is ill and how severely. Giselle will want to know, when she's recovered enough to begin working."

Alexander did not like the idea of Giselle among the villagers, where the fever raged so strongly. If he could, he'd have the monks attend to most of the folk, keeping Giselle's involvement to a minimum. He had the uneasy conviction she wouldn't acquiesce quietly to his demand. It was one thing for him to pledge to succor the folk of his barony, it was altogether different to allow Giselle to endanger herself to help them. As the priest moved to leave, Alex restrained him. "What did you mean earlier when you said the ride here had been difficult on the men? What men?''

Michael avoided looking at him, then squared his shoulders. "Two of Robyn's men accompanied us, as a guard. I've put them in my cottage until the storm passes."

There was no apology in the man's stance or voice and Alex admired him for it, even as it exasperated him. Outlaws sheltering in his village was not something he'd want known. "Keep them out of trouble and see they leave as soon as possible."

Michael nodded and turned to leave, but not before Alex saw the circumspect smile on the priest's face.

Chapter Fifteen

When Giselle woke it took a moment to remember where she was. The chamber was warm and bright, the bed soft, and Odin lay beside her. She snuggled deeper into the covers and closed her eyes. She would sleep awhile yet. Then she noticed the voices of women talking. She listened more carefully and recognized Julianna and Maud. The small sounds of a baby nursing also penetrated the fog of sleepiness that would no doubt claim her in a minute or two. The women spoke in low, murmuring voices. It was comforting to know someone else was near.

"Do you think Aunt Elizabeth will marry Sir Alexander?" Maud asked.

Giselle's eyes flew open at the unexpected question. They were sitting with their backs to her, Julianna with her youngest daughter at her breast. She saw that Rose sat on a low stool beside her mother, though the girl did not join in the conversation.

"Why do you ask?" Julianna shifted the baby to her other breast.

"Does he want to marry Aunt Elizabeth?"

"Whatever gave you that idea?" Julianna asked.

"Haven't you noticed how he looks at her?"

"As a matter of fact, no. I've other things on my mind."

"He's very handsome, though why he'd want someone old like Elizabeth I don't understand. Wouldn't he have to be immensely rich to meet her bride-price? Do you think he can?"

Giselle wondered how high a price Elizabeth's marriage-right was set at. She hoped it was very expensive indeed, then felt a twinge of guilt at the thought. No doubt it was costly because she held great wealth, which would become her husband's if she married. A man like Alexander would naturally look for a wife who could enrich him.

Julianna said, "Elizabeth isn't that old."

Maud shrugged a bony shoulder and brushed strands of gold hair off her face. "Could he meet the bride-price the king has set?"

"Good lord, I don't know. Why are you so interested in who Elizabeth might marry? I would think the poor woman would be happy to be without a husband for as long as possible after her disastrous union with the king."

Maud studied her cousin for a moment, then laughed. "Why are you so certain it's Elizabeth I'm asking about? I'm old enough for Father to begin looking seriously for a husband for me. I like what I see in Alexander de Mandeville."

"The man's far too old for you."

The very idea! Maud was little more than a child. An earl's daughter, an heiress, but still so young. Surely too young to interest a man like Alexander.

"In case you hadn't noticed, Julianna, I'm no longer a little girl."

Giselle looked more carefully and saw that it was true. Though she still acted like a rough-and-tumble child, Maud de Clare had the body and face of a woman, young, healthy and beautiful. Alexander could do worse. Maud would come with a substantial dowry. The idea of the Crusader and the attractive heiress was disconcerting. In fact, she felt an odd sort of panic growing in her belly.

"Well, what do you think?" Maud asked. "Should I ask Father to get me Alexander for my husband?"

"You make it sound as though you're asking for a new palfrey." There was humor in Julianna's voice.

"Is there much difference? I must marry some man, why not one I fancy?"

"And who will you fancy next week?"

"You're impossible to talk to." Maud stood and sighed dramatically. "I'm hungry. Will you be all right while I steal food from the kitchen?"

"Bring me something while you're at it."

"I'll see if there be honey to sweeten your tongue." Maud made a hasty retreat.

The babe had finished nursing and Julianna laid her over a shoulder to burp. The fuzz of hair looked reddish in the light of the fire and candles and Giselle felt a sudden bittersweet longing to hold a child of her own. Alexander's child. She squeezed her eyes shut, trying to forget the scene of domestic love, but it did not fade. It wrapped around her heart and the longing grew painful. What would it be like to have a man such as Alex as her protector? He would love his children, of that she was sure. He could provide for his children, and protect them as well. The baby belched heartily, then quieted and settled in a drowsy way, nearing sleep.

"Mama," Rose said.

"Yes?" Julianna spoke more softly than before.

"I don't think Uncle Alex will marry Lady Elizabeth."

"Neither do I, but why do you say so?"

"Have you not seen how Sir Geoffrey and Cousin Elizabeth look at each other? It's as if they don't always notice what is happening around them."

There was surprise in Julianna's voice. "No, I hadn't noticed."

Giselle thought the girl might be right, and smiled to herself. Elizabeth at least was not likely to be a candidate as Alex's wife. The smile faded. Maud was another matter.

She heard the door open, and expecting Maud to return, was startled to hear Alexander. Her heart beat faster at the sound of his voice, but she closed her eyes, pretending to sleep. She didn't want them to know she'd been listening.

"How is she?" he asked quietly.

"Still sleeping," Julianna said. "She'll no doubt be hungry when she wakes. I've told the cook to keep a hearty stew warm and to have fresh bread handy. You look tired."

"So do you. How is William?"

"Much better. The cough sounds worse than it is and his fever is nearly gone."

Giselle frowned. Alex's nephew was ill? She shouldn't be sleeping when others needed her help. She heard Alex move farther into the room.

"And Stephan?" he asked.

Julianna snorted, a most unladylike sound. "Foul-tempered and miserable. I've come here seeking some peace and quiet."

Just then Maud came trotting back into the chamber. Giselle cracked her eyes open to watch. The earl of Clare's daughter carried a bag of purloined food and a leather flask of wine. "Sir Alexander, we were speaking of you just moments ago."

Giselle could not believe the girl's audacity. Maud sat near the big knight. She dug through the bag and came up with a prize of bread and cheese. "Care for bread or wine, Alexander?"

He accepted both and Giselle watched as he tilted his head back to drink from the leather flask. His blond hair, worn longer than was strictly fashionable, was bright in the firelight and his dark skin looked warm. She had the sudden urge to touch him.

"Do you not wish to know what we were saying about you?" Maud asked.

Alexander sighed and squinted at the youngest Clare. "No doubt you're about to tell me."

Maud plunged on. "Do you fancy my aunt Elizabeth?"

"Maud, hold your tongue," Julianna said. " 'Tis not a question a maid may ask."

"Whyever not?" Maud asked. "It seems to me many of the problems between men and women would not exist if they merely talked honestly with one another. Why should I try to guess at Sir Alexander's feelings when I may ask?"

Giselle was startled by the girl's insight, and grudgingly admitted she agreed with her.

"Mayhap because the man has a right to his privacy," Julianna said sharply.

"Mayhap the man can answer for himself." Maud turned her attention back to Alexander. "Well?"

"What?" Alexander asked.

"Is there anyone you've a mind to marry?"

Giselle held her breath.

He scowled at Maud. "No." His tone left no doubt he wished no further discussion on the matter.

Maud smiled broadly and jumped to her feet. "Good day, sir. It was a pleasure talking to you."

Alexander stared after her as she left the room. "What was that all about?"

"My foolish niece has decided you'd make a good husband."

"For Elizabeth?"

Giselle could almost pity the man.

"Nay," Julianna said. "For herself."

"Good Lord. You can't be serious?"

"It's not as far-fetched as that. Not many men would turn down a chance to align themselves so closely to her father. My niece is young, wealthy and very pretty. You'd do well not to dismiss the idea too quickly."

"You sound as though you approve."

All her arguments were true, Giselle thought, with dismay. It was, in fact, insulting that he would dismiss the alliance so out of hand.

Julianna placed a hand on his arm. "Maud is wont to change her mind before the sun sets. I doubt you need fear hearing from her father on her account."

He was quiet, as though thinking the proposal through. Giselle's belly clenched at the thought he might take Maud seriously. What could the feeling be? It was jealousy, strong and miserable. The idea the heiress might have this man, who was brave and true, and damn him, gentle, made her want to cry.

"Maud is but a child," Alex said.

"So I thought, until she reminded me otherwise."

"Nay, Julianna. She may no longer look like a child, but she is, in her mind and heart. Some men are attracted to girls her age, thinking them malleable. I've always had a preference for women with some maturity in their souls."

"Like Elizabeth?"

He was quiet for a long moment. "It is easy to love Elizabeth. There was a time when I would have entertained the idea of making her my wife."

"But not now?" Julianna laid the sleeping baby in a wicker basket and carefully covered her with a blue blanket of soft lambs wool. "Have you changed your mind about my finding you a wife among the eligible young maids of the nobility?"

Giselle waited for his answer, appalled that Julianna had actually been commissioned with such a task. Was Alex actively seeking to find a wife? Giselle berated herself for her foolishness. She knew he would marry. She'd hoped it would not be soon.

"I no longer feel so urgent a need to wed," Alex said.

Relief mingled with sadness washed through Giselle. He would not marry her . . . she was foolish to even imagine it . . . but neither was he eager for any other woman.

"But Uncle Alex, aren't you going to marry Giselle?" Rose asked.

There was an awkward silence. "Your uncle is a bit confused at the moment, Rose, so don't torment the man. Take the baby back to our chamber and be sure her nurse is there to look over her."

"Yes, Mama. I'm sorry, Uncle Alex, I didn't mean to confuse you."

He didn't answer. Rose left with the basket held carefully on her hip.

Julianna stood and stretched. "Would you be a good man and go keep your brother company before he drives all the servants to desertion?"

Alex eyed her suspiciously. "I know when I'm being dismissed." He held up his hands and smiled. "Very well, you win. I'll be back in an hour, sooner if Stephan proves truly intolerable. Then I will sit until she wakes. You need to sleep as well. You were up all night with William and if you become ill I'd never forgive myself."

"You are hardly to blame for the fever, Alex dear. But I will do as you say. Now go."

He kissed her on the cheek and left. Giselle wished Julianna would leave as well. She felt close to tears and would like time alone to yield to them, but knew self-pity to be a vicious and useless indulgence. Instead she turned over so her back was toward the countess.

"Would you care for some food now, or do you want to wait?" Julianna asked.

How long has she known I'm awake? She turned onto her back and absently scratched Odin's head. "Now, I think. It sounds as though there is work to be done."

It was early evening, with darkness spreading rapidly across the sky. Giselle came from another of the villagers' houses and rubbed her aching back. She'd been going without a rest from the moment she stepped from the castle several hours ago, and did not see an end in sight to her work. Everywhere she went there were sick folk who needed tending. Some families were hard pressed to find anyone well enough to care for the others. While few seemed likely to die, many were miserable enough to do little more than lay abed and wait for the agony to pass. She left willow bark to be boiled into a tisane for the aches and pain, and instructed them on how best to care for each other. It was all she could do. The fever would run its course, taking an old person, or a baby, or someone weakened by disease or accident, but most would survive.

Alexander walked beside her, the look of determination on his face growing more intense with each cottage they visited. She suspected this was the first he'd seen of exactly how his villeins lived, and what he saw did not entirely please him.

"You are worried?" she asked.

"I believe you when you say the fever is not as serious as in some years, but there is less food than I thought. What are they living on?"

"There is still grain for bread and some meat from the autumn slaughter."

"For how long? How many of them owned a hog to butcher? Less than half, I would venture. The few chickens will not last long, and once eaten, there will be no eggs. If desperate enough they'll slaughter the brood sows and so have no pigs next year. Their quarterly rents are due at Christmas and I fear I will need to remit many of them."

She was startled. Most lords demanded their rents, in kind and coin, no matter how desperate the people were. "You would do that?"

"I need these people. Without them my land cannot be worked."

"I see. You are husbanding your possessions. It must be much less costly to take care of what you have than to replace it."

He looked at her oddly. "I am not as cold-hearted as you make me sound. I do not wish to see people suffer. A man would be foolish not to take care of what is his."

"But you do not think the life of a villager is as important as those of your family?"

He caught her arm as she slipped on an icy spot, and steadied her before replying. "It's natural that I love my family, and yes, in my heart I count them more important than other folk. That does not make me a brutal or dishonorable man. Why is it you wish to judge me so harshly?"

She wasn't sure how to answer him. "I am a peasant; freeborn, but common. You are a great lord. We are of different worlds, no matter how you pretend to ignore it."

"I do not ignore it. I simply do not give it much significance. You are much more to me than some peasant woman I'm eager to take advantage of. I'd have thought you realized that by now."

"What do I mean to you? What am I to you?" She stopped in the middle of the icy path, waiting for his answer, sure her life depended on his next words.

He turned to face her and held her chin in one hand,

gazing long into her eyes. "You are a delight and a temptation. Were it not so bloody cold I'd take you into the nearest copse of trees and show you just what I feel. For now, this must suffice." He bent down to kiss her.

She warmed at his touch, at the feel of his lips on hers, yet her heart felt icy. She was no more to him than a bedmate. What had she expected him to say? She pulled away and resumed walking.

He grabbed her by the arm and pulled her to a halt. "What is wrong, Giselle? First you pounce on me for my lack of compassion toward my villeins, then you turn away from my affection."

She would not look at him, fearing he would see the tears in her eyes. "I am being foolish, m'lord. I'm tired and worried and my tongue does not always keep silent when it should."

He gathered her into his arms, holding her against the broad, warm breadth of his chest. She leaned her head against him and closed her eyes. The comfort of his embrace weakened her resolve and tears fell on her icy cheeks.

"Sweetling, why do you cry?"

"I am so lonely." It was no more than an anguished whisper, but she wished she had not said it. She did not want him to think her pathetic. He was quiet for so long she began to hope he had not heard.

"It is I who have been a fool. Forgive me. I did not realize your being with me would cause you such pain. If you miss your friends I will make it possible for you to visit them. Mayhap Marian can come here, when the storm passes."

She nearly laughed at the absurdity. He'd not understood. She was lonely for him, ached for his love. "It is not that."

"Then what? I never wanted to hurt you, Giselle. I'd

hoped you might come to care for me, but if you cannot I will not force you to stay. I know what it is like to be alone in the world, separated from everyone I love."

"I do care, that is what hurts."

He held her a little away from him so he could see her face, then once more held her close. "Sweet woman, you have just made me a very happy man. To hear that you do not find me an ogre is more than I'd thought to have from you. Surely you did not think that I care nothing for you?"

"You've never said otherwise, m'lord."

"Then damn me doubly a fool. I say it now. I care deeply. You are more than I thought possible to find. I am beginning to think you are the best thing to happen to me. I would have to be a stupid man not to treasure what I've found."

A warm happiness tentatively took hold of Giselle's heart. "It is a good place to start, is it not? That we care for each other?"

He smiled at her. "It is indeed, my lady."

"I am no lady."

"And my name is Alexander, not 'm'lord'."

"Alexander." She said it softly and lifted her face for his kiss.

It was the jingle and squeak of harness and leather that parted them. Giselle looked up to see three men on horseback riding toward the castle gate. At least, she assumed them to be men, but they were so bundled against the cold and there was so little light left to the day, she could not be certain. They did not see her or Alex standing in the snow-packed road.

"Geoffrey has returned," Alex said.

"You do not sound happy."

"I had hoped he'd bring more of Blyth's monks with

him. I will not have you exhausting yourself caring for others.''

She did not argue with him, knowing it would be pointless, but also knowing that she could not maintain the pace she'd kept for long. She could do only so much, no matter if the need be greater than she could manage. She needed help and was grateful for it. Alexander had proved a quick learner as he went the rounds with her today, and she'd grown accustomed to his unobtrusive help and calming presence. He had a special way with children, she'd discovered, and could entertain or comfort them, as need dictated, while she worked with others in each family. His presence was at first shocking to his people, but they soon grew easier with him. A few even had the confidence to tease him over small things, and his warm laughter would bring a smile to all who heard it. He asked what each family needed, whether it be food, blankets, firewood, or help with livestock, and arranged to have the need met.

"You've done enough for now," Alex said, steering her toward the castle. "Michael will let us know if there is urgent need among the villagers."

Tired and hungry, she went with him willingly. Tomorrow would be another long day and there were likely to be several more weeks before the illness ran its course. By then, she realized, they'd be into Christmastide, then the cold, austere months of winter. Spring seemed unimaginably far away.

Chapter Sixteen

Alexander saw that Giselle was settled in his chamber, and ordered food to be brought to her, then went in search of Geoffrey and the monks. What he found did not please him. One of the men was the addle-pated Father Bernard. Why had the abbot sent such a man? The other monk he did not recognize. They were gathered in a dark clump near the fire, steam rising from Geoffrey's wet cloak as it dried.

"Alexander, there you are." Geoffrey's tone implied he was more than ready to hand his charges over to another.

"Don't go anywhere just yet," Alex said. "Father Bernard, it's good to see you again."

The monk looked perplexed, his head tilted slightly as he stared at Alex. "You are not Sir John of Wolfhurst."

"No. I am Alexander de Mandeville, lord of Wolfhurst." He would have to send the man back. Damn the abbot for a fool. He needed strong hands and backs and clear minds to deal with this crisis. He turned his attention to the other black-robed Benedictine.

"I am Father Edgar. I've come to help Bernard."

"Help Bernard? Surely he is your assistant."

"Nay. Bernard is most knowledgeable in leechcraft. He's been the abbey herbalist since he returned to us, nigh on twenty years now."

Alexander struggled to keep a grip on his irritation. As confused as the old monk appeared to be, how could he trust him to do what was needed? What if he gave the wrong herb, or the wrong dose to someone who was ill? What if he did more harm than good? What choice did he have? Everyone not already sick was busy nursing those who were. Julianna and Elizabeth were run ragged tending those within the castle. He did what he could to help Giselle and Michael, but he didn't know enough to be left on his own. He needed skilled healers, not old men who saw angels and thought he and Giselle were people long dead. Father Edgar smiled at him expectantly.

"I will escort you to Michael's house. He can better explain the situation to you and he'll know where you are most needed."

The smile slipped from the monk's face. Alex perceived it had never lighted his dark eyes.

"I had thought we'd be put in a chamber here, in the castle," Edgar said.

Alexander understood well what was left unsaid. Edgar felt himself far too important to bed down in a simple country-priest's hovel. He probably did not yet realize it was the peasants of Wolfhurst he would be tending, and that the baron would be sure he did it without giving offense. "If you wish, you may sleep in the hall, with the knights and servants. I thought you'd be more comfortable in a private house. There are but two chambers at Wolfhurst and both are occupied."

Edgar's thin lips pressed together and his eyes narrowed slightly. The smile, when it reappeared, was less effusive and even more false than before. "Do you not know who your priest is?"

Bernard was looking more confused by the minute. Poor man. He was probably too simple a soul to recognize maliciousness when he saw and heard it. Geoffrey had stiffened, his boredom at bay. He liked innuendo as little as Alex.

"I know my priest as well as I need to." He made his voice dry and hard. If Edgar had any sense at all he would heed the warning.

The priest looked warily from one man to the next. "I will sleep in the hall, Sir Alexander, if it does not inconvenience you."

"As you wish. Father Bernard, where would you care to sleep?"

The man's smile was dazzling. "Oh, I'd be delighted to see Michael again. He was always my favorite novice, you know. He was by far the best of the lot, though most were good boys, mind you. It's that Michael knew what was important, which questions to ask. I wonder if he's learned yet how to wait for the answers."

As his estimation of the old man rose several notches, Alexander saw the flicker of contempt in Edgar's eyes. If he didn't need the man's help he'd heave him into the nearest snowdrift and leave him there until spring.

Geoffrey danced impatiently from one foot to the other, searching the hall for someone. Alex finally had pity on him. "Elizabeth is upstairs." The younger man looked surprised for a moment, then smiled and walked quickly away. Whatever was between Geoff and the countess was their affair, though what good could come of it Alex did not see. Eventually Geoffrey would inherit the earldom of Essex and become a very wealthy man, but when that might be, no one could know. Someday, though, the young earl might be able to afford Elizabeth's bride-price, if that's what he had in mind. Though he would never have thought to put the two of them together, for Geoff was all wild, impatient youth to Elizabeth's calm and dignified gentility, he wished them well. Elizabeth deserved whatever happiness she could find, even if it be in the most unlikely place.

Alex felt old. Not so many years ago he'd been very much like Geoffrey, impetuous to the point of recklessness, too often acting without thinking through what the consequences would be. Mostly his misadventures turned out well in the end. Fighting all those years in Richard's wars had scoured the youth from him. Too much death, too much betrayal and fear and dishonor, haunted him to recapture the insouciance of his earlier years. Since returning from Crusade, only Giselle had touched his heart in such a way that a glimpse of that former innocent joy was granted him. He'd begun to think his life might not after all be one of long and bitter loneliness. He ached to be with her, not just with his body, but with something abundant and truer. She had taken up residence in his heart and soul and he found that he welcomed her there, wanted her in the intimate way of a soul-mate as well as lover.

She was not what he thought he'd needed. She was not noble-born and trained in the gentle manners of a chatelaine, but those were deficits he did not count as important. He'd learned long ago that the purity of a man's pedigree was of far less importance than the content of his character. His own brother, whose mother had been a Jew, had been nearly destroyed by the bigotry some used as an excuse to hate and destroy. Yet Stephan was as good and honorable a man as any he'd known. No, he'd not judge Giselle harshly because of her lowly birth, and the skills of a chatelaine could be learned. That she was a loving, kind, and generous woman mattered far more than any dowry or family connection. That she was exciting and filled with the passion of life was a treasure he intended to keep if he had to grab on with both hands.

Staring into the flames of the hearth-fire, lost in thought, it took a hard tug on his sleeve before Alex noticed Bernard waiting patiently beside him. "Forgive me, Father. If you come with me, I'll show you to Michael."

"I know where he lives, there's no need for you to be out in the cold. I'm concerned about you, m'lord." The old priest patted Alex's hand in reassurance. "Let that fine wife of yours ease your worries for the night. Tomorrow's cares will come soon enough and we shall deal with them then."

Alex did not bother to correct the man. The priest obviously still confused him and Giselle with the old master and mistress of Guisborne and Wolfhurst, but the bewilderment was harmless enough. The old priest hurried away with unexpected speed for one his age.

"I did not realize you have a wife, Sir Alexander," Edgar said.

"Bernard is confused."

"He normally is. I think the abbot sent him here more in hope that the familiar surroundings might jog his memory than any help poor Bernard might afford you. He's not in the best of health lately."

"He appears quite hearty to me, despite his age," Alex said. He knew he was being contrary—the man was only trying to engage him in polite conversation—but he was impatient now to be with Giselle. "If you will excuse me, it has been a long day and I would seek my bed."

The monk nodded politely and continued warming himself. Alex made a swift departure, before anyone could waylay him with questions or problems. Sanctuary waited for him up the stone stairs, in the wide bed of his chamber. He opened the door quietly and slipped inside. The room was lighted by a single candle set on the low table. In the shadows of the bed he saw the small form asleep, curled tightly against the cold. Beside her, on the fur cover, was Odin. The dog raised his head in lazy greeting, his tail thumping a few times, before yawning and settling back to sleep. Slipping out of his clothes, Alex hurried to the bed, snuffing the candle on the way. The room was near as cold as outside. He climbed into the bed and bundled the thick wool and fur over himself, in the process dislodging the dog, who, with a grunt of disapproval, rearranged himself nearer the foot of the bed. Seeking warmth, Alex wriggled across the bed until he found Giselle, then pulled her close into the curve of his body. She stirred slightly and snuggled closer. Her backside fit perfectly into the front of his body. He tried to ignore his arousal. They were both exhausted. He'd not wake her now to take care of a selfish need. Gritting his teeth, he forced himself to relax and prayed sleep would overtake him soon.

Giselle woke slowly, drifting up out of the warm comfort of dreams full of sunshine and laughter. She was not surprised to find herself entwined with Alexander, his big limbs holding her close to his body. It felt so natural to be lying in his arms. Carefully, she poked her head out from under the covers to survey the frigid room. The darkness was only beginning to gray toward dawn, but she knew she'd need to be up soon. There were many sick to tend, and she'd need to coordinate her efforts with the monks of Blyth so they would neither duplicate her work, nor neglect anyone in need. For now she indulged herself in the haven of Alex's arms.

She turned so she faced him. When asleep he seemed younger, the tense worry gone from his expression. Running the tips of her fingers lightly across his lower lip, she watched enthralled as he smiled. Next she lifted his hair away from his forehead and brushed it back. The smile deepened. She played with his ear, circling it with a feathery touch. His eyes opened.

"Did I wake you?" she asked in mock dismay.

"Would that I woke every morning to so lovely a sight." He pulled her up against the long length of him, his hands on her back and thighs.

She settled into his caress, savoring the feel of his strong hands stroking up and down her body. Pulling one leg up to wrap around his waist, the fire exploded within, spreading instantly throughout her body. She wanted him with a desperate hunger. "Alexander," she whispered.

With a groan he crushed her to him, his lips tracing hot kisses down her neck, to her shoulder, to her breasts. He seared a nipple with his tongue, rousing it to a hard bud, then took it into his mouth and suckled. When he rubbed the tip against his teeth the desire blossoming in her grew hotter still, until she was begging him for more.

He gave her more. With hands and mouth and tongue he claimed her body. Her hands sought him, raking her nails across his broad shoulders, down his back, seeking that closer union her body ached for.

"Alexander," she cried, her voice hoarse with desire.

He entered her, hard and big, filling her with himself. She caught his cadence, that seamless dance lovers know. An exquisite completeness flowed through her. She felt she could dance this dance forever, the intensity flooding her senses. She was surrounded by him: by the firm, hard body which loved her with such tender passion; by the bosky scent of him; by the sound of his rapid, uncivilized breathing; by the heat they shared. Shattered and made whole by him, she knew, in that tormenting moment when her desire found expression and she lost control, that she loved this man with a pure and steadfast love, and that she always would.

In the next two weeks the days and nights fell into a routine. During the day all those who were able cared for the ill and saw that the necessary work was done. Each evening, which came earlier, the sun setting long before the hour of Vespers, they ate in silence and went gratefully to their beds. Most sought only sleep. Christmas came and went with none of the usual festivities, celebrated solemnly by those able to hear Michael's quiet Mass in the cold, nearly deserted church. Alexander held his first manorial court, and the disconsolate group of sick serfs gathered in his hall made him call the business of the day to a quick close. He remitted most of their tithes and rents, which they at first did not believe. As realization hit them that he meant the relief to be permanent, that they would not be held accountable for the dues at a later time, smiles broke out among them. It was the best Christmas they'd had in years.

Chapter Seventeen

"Are you sure you know where we are?"

Alexander scowled at his cousin. It was the third time in less than an hour Geoffrey had asked that annoying question. "Wolfhurst Castle is east of here."

"Yes, but where is 'here'?" Geoffrey leaned down along his horse's neck as the animal passed beneath the low limb of an oak. He cursed as the wet branches unloaded their snow down his neck. "We've not been on a trail in hours. Do you mean to keep wandering through the forest much longer? I've no desire to spend a night in the woods with the wolves."

The idea of leaving his cousin to his fate in the wildwood grew more appealing by the minute. If Alexander had not been thoroughly lost, the nagging would not be nearly so irksome. What had promised to be an uneventful day at its dawning was beginning to be one of the more miserable in recent memory. It was the second week of February, and no new cases of illness had come to light in almost a fortnight. Stephan had suggested the hunt, to fill the castle larder before the earl and his men returned to Kent. It had been cold and clear in the early morning, the breath of the horses and hounds and men hanging white in the air. A perfect day for hunting stag.

First they'd been unable to find any deer for their spears, then the damned dog had run off. Alex and Geoff had gone looking for the errant animal. It took hours to track him down, but Giselle would never forgive him if he didn't return with Odin. Then it started to snow. It had snowed for nigh on three hours with no sign of letting up, and grown appreciably colder. Their wet tunics and cloaks would not offer adequate protection if they were caught without shelter after dark. Alex cursed himself for a fool. He was not about to admit that they were lost.

"What's that?" Geoff asked. "There, do you see? To the left, beside that great oak. It's a hut of some sort."

Alexander slowed his horse and squinted toward where Geoffrey pointed. The cold, wet, and itch of his clothing was suddenly intolerable. A roof over their heads for the night, and a fire to warm his hands, would be most welcome. The building was a small but solid looking hunting lodge, probably belonging to Guisborne or some other local lord.

"I don't know about you, Coz, but I'd be glad to be out of the snow," Geoffrey said. "Since we'll not make Wolfhurst before dark, we may as well bed down for the night here."

Odin ran ahead of them, his energy undimmed by the cold, but as the dog came to the door he stopped and barked, his stance alert and menacing. Alexander's hand reached for his sword hilt. The door to the hut stood ajar. "It appears we have company."

"A poacher, do you think?"

"Mayhap. Or it may only be the door has come un-latched."

The sound of Geoffrey's sword leaving its scabbard whispered against the louder sound of the wind-whipped trees. "If so, yon dog is stupider than we thought."

How could Alex argue with that sort of logic? "You stay horsed. I'll go afoot." He dismounted, drew his weapon, and cautiously approached the dark building. The dog still growled and barked, unsure of himself, and he sharply called Odin down. He obeyed quickly, sitting, but his whole body quivered with anticipation. If someone was within, they made no move to make themselves known. It could well be poachers, as Geoffrey thought, and if so, desperation could make them violent. To be caught hunting in a lord's park was a capital crime. Geoffrey sat his horse, weapon at ready, to intercept anyone who thought to flee. Slowly, with his back against the cabin wall for protection, Alexander opened the door wider. There was no light from within. It was then he heard it. The noise was animal-like, primitive, and it raised the hairs on the back of his neck, for Alexander knew the sounds were human.

With the door opened to its widest, pale gray light made it possible for him to see the one small room, with its packed-dirt floor, no window and no furnishings; primitive indeed, its sole purpose being shelter from storm for horse and man. Against the far wall lay someone curled on their side, the moans of pain the sound he'd first noticed. There was no one else. Alexander resheathed his weapon and turned toward his cousin. "No danger here. Just a sick peasant."

Geoffrey groaned and sheathed his sword, cursing angrily as he dismounted and walked over to join Alexander. "I'm not spending the night with some disgusting serf puking his guts into the corner. Let's drag the man out and be done with it."

Alex quickly crossed the small room and squatted beside the intruder. He leaned over to have a better look in the dim light. " 'Tis but a lad, and he's hurt. Bloody hell, it's too dark to see what we're doing." The boy's cries of pain intensified.

"There's wood in the fire pit. I'll get it lighted."

As the fire blazed he saw the boy more clearly. Huge blue eyes stared at him out of a face gone gray with fear, pain, and exhaustion. His mouth was bloody from where he'd bitten it and his breathing was shallow and fast. Alex reached out and gently brushed aside the hair plastered to the boy's cheek by sweat and tears. Then he saw the wounded arm, which the boy held tightly to his chest. Alex struggled to keep the gorge from rising in his throat.

"What's wrong with him? Who is he?" Geoffrey asked. "Why is he making that dreadful noise?"

"I don't know his name. As for what's wrong, he's had his hand cut off."

Geoffrey stared, speechless.

"I need your help," Alex said.

"We'll need to get him to Wolfhurst." Geoffrey looked ashen. "Who would do that? Why?"

Alex had seen enough battle wounds to know the lad would probably not survive. The bone of his arm was white in the dim light, the pulpy mess of flesh raw and bleeding. The child was in agony. There was nothing Alex could do to ease him.

They did not hear the men until they burst into the hut. Alex spun around, drawing his sword as he turned. Geoffrey did the same. Four men challenged them, arrows pointed with deadly accurate aim. At this close range he and Geoff were at a distinct disadvantage.

"Wolfhurst?" one of the men asked, lowering his bow slightly.

"Robyn?" Alex squinted, then held down his sword.

"Have you lost your mind?" Geoffrey hissed.

"Put your sword up, Coz," Alex said. He slipped his weapon back into its scabbard. Geoff lowered his weapon but did not resheath it.

Robyn ordered his men to unnock their arrows, then moved swiftly to the boy's side. The lad quieted slightly. The forest men muttered angrily among themselves. Alex knelt beside Robyn.

"Who did this to you, Alfred?" Robyn asked.

"Guisborne."

That single word made the hair on the back of Alex's neck stand on end.

"John, take the boy home," Robyn said.

Alex stood aside as the big man, with surprising tenderness, lifted the boy.

"You'll be all right, lad," John said. "We'll have you in a safe place soon."

The boy cried quietly, gritting his teeth against the pain, but made no protest as he was carried away.

"What is your part in this?" Robyn asked.

Alexander's anger flared at the question, and its implication, then cooled when he saw the look on the other man's face. "We found the lad minutes before you."

Robyn eyed him warily, but seemed to accept his explanation. "Why are you on Guisborne's land?"

"I didn't realize we'd wandered quite that far. Odin ran off. We were tracking him."

The big dog whined at mention of his name and swung his tail back and forth. Robyn absently scratched the dog's head. Of course, the animal had given no warning of his approach. He knew Robyn and the others and did not perceive them as a threat.

"Alex, who is this man?" Geoffrey asked. He still held his sword, in case of need, but lightly at his side.

"An acquaintance." Alex didn't think Geoff would understand, or favor, his tolerance of Robyn and his men. "Why are *you* on Guisborne's land?"

"Looking for the boy. We had word of what happened, Guisborne made sure of that. The bastard accused Alfred of poaching a hare."

"For that he cut off the boy's hand?" Geoffrey asked. "The punishment seems severe, considering the crime and the child's age."

Robyn eyed Geoffrey, then asked Alex, "Who is this man?"

"My cousin."

Robyn turned back to Geoff. "The charges are false. Guisborne uses the boy to lure me. I would not otherwise be so careless as to cross onto his lands."

"Why would Sir Guy want you?" Geoffrey asked.

"Mayhap because I'm an outlaw. Robyn of Sherwood, sometimes called Hood. Have ye not heard of me?"

Alex almost felt sorry for his cousin, so flustered did Geoffrey appear. The man proved a quick learner, however. He kept his mouth shut.

"It's not safe for you and the others to be here," Alexander said.

"No. Now is not the time to confront Guisborne. He no doubt has armed men with him. I'm a patient man, Wolfhurst. I can wait." Robyn turned to go, then turned back, a small grin on his face. "You do know how to get back to Wolfhurst from here?"

"We go east," Alex said, trying to sound more confident than he felt.

One of the men, standing in the doorway, snickered.

"Which direction is east?" Robyn asked.

Alex pointed, hoping he was right.

"East is that way." Robyn pointed in a different direction. "But it does ye little good to know. Wolfhurst lies south of here, that way."

Alex nodded, and avoided looking at Geoffrey, who still, wise man, kept quiet.

"What were you hunting?" Robyn asked.

"Stag. Boar if we could find it."

"Any luck?"

"No."

"Any starving at Wolfhurst?"

"Not yet. But we need the meat. The grain won't last the winter. What of your band?"

"We've had no bread for weeks, but the meat is plentiful. We'll not starve."

"You know the boy will die," Alex said.

"I know. But he'll be with family and he'll have a decent burial. Are you staying the night?"

"I'll be here when he comes."

Robyn waved a hand in farewell and silently slipped out of the hut with the other men. Alex followed, walking toward the two horses standing in the lean-to next to the shelter. He stripped his saddle from the back of his stallion and filled a leather bag with oats, putting it over the horse's head to feed. Geoffrey did the same with his animal. They worked in silence, carrying the saddles and blankets into the hut when they finished.

Geoffrey heaved his tack angrily to the floor. "Are you going to make me ask?"

"I'd rather you didn't."

"You're on apparently friendly terms with a notorious outlaw, who appears to have the freedom to roam Sherwood at will, but I'm not to ask any questions? Guisborne had the right, you know, if the boy truly poached his land. He has the law on his side."

"The law is exactly what the men in power say it is. That does not always make it right."

"You don't believe we should allow the peasants to run

free through the forests? They'd strip it of all game within weeks.''

"I said no such thing. The boy should not have lost his hand for so paltry a crime. Guisborne has the right of law to back up his actions, but he was in the wrong on this. Especially if what he wants is Robyn and the lad was merely a ploy.''

Alex arranged the saddle to serve as a pillow, spreading the horse blanket on the cold dirt floor. They hadn't planned on being away from the castle for the night and so were ill-prepared, with only their cloaks to keep them warm, and no food. He lay down, his arms under his head, and stared up at the low ceiling. Snow leaked in near one wall and drifted there, but it didn't look as though it would spread as far as their sleeping space. Geoffrey lay down on the other side of the fire.

"Don't get too comfortable," Alex said.

"As if that were possible. I'm going to be cold and hungry all night.''

"Keep the dog beside you. He's warm. Stay alert. I'm expecting a visitor.''

Geoffrey sat up and glared at him. "Who?''

"Guisborne.''

The fire burned low. Wind growled with somber resonance in the trees and thatch. Alex waited. He'd known men like Guisborne, who used their power cruelly, made wanton with the headiness of holding other people's lives at their will. The world was too full of such men. He wondered, too, what tales Geoffrey would spread of this night's events. His cousin was young and still looked at the world in the simple way of youth. Years would add subtlety to his judgment, if nothing happened to embitter or warp him between now and then. In many ways Geoff was an innocent, though he'd resent being told so. Alex hoped that as he inevitably lost that naïveté he would learn wisdom, even as Alex knew, from hard experience, insight came at a price and carried many sacrifices, small and large, in its wake. It was men like Guisborne who stayed ignorant all their lives, their hatreds binding them like rings of iron.

Give an ignorant man power, and death invariably heaved its bloody head, as surely as dawn followed night. Alex heard the sound of men and horses and glanced over at Odin. The dog was sleeping, but a sudden noise crashed against his unawareness and he bolted up, growling and barking. Alex called him down. With a muttered oath Geoffrey stood, his sword held ready. Alex did the same.

The door burst open. Guisborne and several knights rushed into the tiny hut, one man stumbling into the embers and cursing hotly before jumping back out.

"Wolfhurst! What the hell are you doing here?" Guisborne asked.

Alex leaned on his sword, hoping he looked far more relaxed than he felt. "Do you always barge in unannounced? You're lucky I didn't run you through before you made it past the door." He waved indolently at Geoffrey. "My cousin and I took shelter for the night. It's crowded, but if you and your men are in need, you're welcome."

Guisborne's eyes shifted from Alex to Geoff and back. "That's damned decent of you, inviting me to stay in my own hut. What are you doing on my land?"

"Tracking a dog that ran off during our hunt. As you see, we found the dog."

"You use a one-eyed dog for hunting?"

Alex let that rebuke pass without comment. As it turned out, Odin was useless, but not because of his poor sight. He'd simply never been trained to run deer.

Geoffrey slammed his sword into his scabbard. "Damn

you, Guisborne. You woke me from sleep thinking I was being attacked. Just what is it you want? I'm in a foul enough mood without adding lack of sleep to the list.''

Not bad, Coz. Alex was grateful for the diversion of Guy's attention away from him. That Geoff felt genuine frustration at the situation only helped make him more convincing.

"My apologies, Sir Geoffrey. We had reason to believe a certain outlaw could be found here.''

"As you see, there is my cousin and myself.'' Geoff's voice oozed sarcasm.

Guisborne hesitated, his small eyes darting angrily. With a look of triumph he pointed to a spot on the floor. "That looks like blood. Who has been here?''

Casually, Alex glanced over his shoulder to where the boy had been lying. The pale dirt was stained a darker color, unmistakably blood, and a great deal of it. "I hadn't noticed until now,'' Alex said. "Did you, Geoff?''

"No.''

Alex turned back to look at Guisborne, satisfied that the man knew they were lying, but could think of nothing to do to prove it. He refused to break his gaze from the other man's, and Guy was the first to look away.

"Watch yourself, Wolfhurst. These forests are dangerous, especially at night. Men have been known to disappear without trace.''

"I'll keep that in mind.''

Guisborne shouted and pushed his men out of the door ahead of him. Before leaving he turned back. "Tell Robyn of Sherwood his days are numbered.''

Alexander crossed the small room and slammed the door behind Guisborne.

"That man threatened you.'' Geoffrey spoke calmly, but anger edged his voice. "He knows you've been with the outlaw.''

"He's only guessing at that. I'm a more powerful enemy than Robyn. Guisborne has taken on more than he can handle if he thinks to challenge me."

"I'd say he'll discover the truth of that, given time. You've got yourself into quite a predicament, Cousin. Outlaws running amok in your forest. Your nearest neighbor eager to do you harm. Your peasants near starving. What do you mean to do, if I may ask?"

"Hell if I know."

"At least you have a plan." Geoffrey settled himself once more in his makeshift bed.

Alex lay down, staring again at the dark ceiling. Everything Geoff said was true. All of it needed to be taken care of, and none of it mattered as much as Giselle. Without her, none of the rest of it meant anything to him.

He finally slept, battered by dreams of running through a trackless forest, searching desperately, but for what he could not say.

Chapter Eighteen

"Must it be goose dung?" Julianna asked.

Giselle thought for a long moment. " 'Tis the only way I know of, though to tell true I've never been fond of the cures that include dung. I use herbs and vinegars whenever possible. But the dung is what Maeve taught me."

Julianna carefully wrote the liniment recipe in the book open before her, her quill scratching softly against the vellum. They had been closeted together for several hours, Giselle listing every cure she knew while the countess wrote it in the chatelaine book she kept of household lore. Giselle leaned over Julianna's shoulder to look at what she wrote. It was gibberish to her, ink strokes on a page. That Julianna could take her words, transform them into these symbols, and have others understand what was written there was a marvel to Giselle. She'd heard of books, had seen the ornate gospels the priests used at Mass, but had never before considered the magic of them.

"Does Alexander read?"

"Yes. It's a skill not many other than priests and a few nobles possess. Also Jews and some merchants. Why do you ask?"

"Is it difficult, learning to read and write?"

Julianna dipped the quill in her small dish of ink. "I learned as a child, but I don't remember it being painful. I'm sure Alex would be happy to teach you."

Giselle looked again at the meaningless black marks. Could she learn to decipher them? The idea excited and frightened her. It would be wonderful to learn. She would ask Alexander when he returned. When that would be she didn't know, and the worry gnawed at her all morning. The other men had returned yesterday evening from the hunt with two small deer, far less than had been hoped for, but Alex and his cousin Geoffrey had not been with them. No doubt they'd taken shelter for the night from the storm and would ride in today, unharmed. She kept telling herself that, over and over, trying to distract the worry with the work she did, knowing the countess did the same. Anytime there was noise from the hall, they both paused and listened, but each time it was something other than Alex's safe return, and with sighs, they would return to the herbal.

They were in the guest-chamber. The youngest girls were asleep together in the huge bed. Rose quietly watched her mother while Maud sat near the one window with its pale light and worked on her embroidery, a task she apparently loathed, from the furious frown on her face and groans of frustration. Beside her sat Elizabeth, serenely working on her own needlework. William was nowhere to be seen, being fully recovered from his illness. Most likely he was in the stable, bothering the lads there. He was never far from horse or hound, and the castleful of females made him ache for male companionship. He'd been sorely disappointed not to be included in yesterday's hunt, but his mother had declared him too recently risen from his sick-bed for such exertion.

"Bloody hell!" Maud sucked on her finger where the needle had once more pierced.

With great patience Elizabeth took the mangled cloth from her niece and examined the work. A puzzled frown marred her serenity. "You went wrong here." She pointed with her needle.

Maud leaned closer. "I suppose you mean I must pull it all out back to there and start over."

"Why, of course." Elizabeth handed the work back.

"I'd much rather throw it down the privy and be done with it."

"You must at least learn the stitches. When you are married you'll be expected to oversee the household sewing and so must know if the work is done correctly."

"When I am married," Maud said, "I'll spend my days with my husband, on horseback riding after roe, or hawking, or . . . anything . . . but being shut up inside, sewing."

Giselle felt some sympathy for the young woman. Though she stitched wounds with a special care, her sewing was serviceable at best. She'd had no training in the fancy stitches noblewomen were expected to know. She could well understand Maud's desire to be outside, in the forest and hills, rather than shut up in a dark, drafty castle. She was beginning to think women spent an inordinate amount of their lives waiting for men to return. If she had begged Alexander not to leave her yesterday he would have dismissed her fears as unreasoned, and he'd have been right, but his going then meant that she waited now.

There was the clatter of horses' shod hooves and shouting from the bailey. Maud rushed to the window, craning her neck to see.

"Who is it?" Julianna asked, rising from her seat, quill in hand.

"I can't see, they're around the other side."

Giselle didn't wait for more. She left the room, hiking her skirts high to run through the hallway and down the stairs, through the great hall and out the door to stand on the windswept stone porch. Julianna, Elizabeth, and Maud followed more sedately.

There was one man, swathed in a blue cloak, riding a horse she'd never seen. With a sinking feeling she knew it wasn't Alexander or Geoffrey, even before the man pushed back the hood of his cloak and dismounted. Julianna's husband greeted the man as though he were well known to him, and they started toward the castle.

"Who is that?" Maud asked, the astonishment in her voice unmistakable.

Giselle looked again. The young man was the most handsome she had ever seen, with black hair and a face made slightly exotic by the strange upward tilt of his pale eyes.

"William Braose, one of Stephan's knights," Julianna said. "I wonder what has brought him here."

"William Braose." Maud said the man's name like a benediction.

Giselle almost laughed. Apparently the young heiress's interest in Alexander had been supplanted by one glimpse of the man now walking toward them. She almost felt sorry for William, if Maud set her sights on him.

"Stephan does not look pleased by whatever his man has said," Elizabeth observed.

The earl of Rosmar was looking more and more angry as the men approached. Giselle had never seen him in such a cold fury. Unlike many men who raved and shouted when angry, Stephan expressed it in the tight line of his lips, the clenched jaw, the slight flaring of nostrils. She'd seen that look before, on Alexander. She wondered that the brothers could be so dissimilar in some ways, and so alike in others. It was then she noticed the two men riding slowly through the gate with the black dog trailing after, and knew Alexander was home.

Food was rushed from the kitchen and his family gathered around the table, eager to know what had happened to keep them away for a night. Alex did not tell them of the boy and Guisborne, saying only that they'd sought shelter for the night. He was relieved to see he was believed, and that Geoffrey did not contradict him.

Julianna and Elizabeth quietly fussed, seeing that he and Geoffrey had everything they could want. Gilbert sat beside Geoff, stealing bits off the other man's trencher until Geoff growled at him. Gilbert's sister Maud, usually loquacious, sat silent and stared at William Braose like some mystic in the midst of a vision. Beside Alex on the long bench sat Giselle. She smelled of sweet herbs. He longed to take her in his arms, to bury his face in her red curls. Odin pushed his head between them, his one eye trained on Alex, watching the food travel from table to mouth. Absently Alex dropped meat and bread into the rushes for the dog.

Stephan paced back and forth, a scowl on his face. Alex watched him, knowing his brother was raging mad about something. The others watched as well, all except William Braose, who should be in Kent but was here. Alex ate, waiting for his brother to calm enough to explain what had happened. Finally Stephan stood still and planted his fists on his hips, looking for all the world like a child ready to take on anyone who looked at him cross-eyed.

"The king of France has gone to war against John."

Alex paused with his spoon, full of thick pork and onion stew, in midair and stared at his brother. Slowly he returned the spoon to the bowl. "You can't be serious?"

"William brings news of John's summons. I'm to appear at Southampton in three weeks' time, with my knights, ready for war. We'll need to leave tomorrow."

"God rot the king." Alex pushed the food away, his appetite gone. Geoffrey did not stop eating, though his attention was riveted on Stephan and William Braose. Hungry and tired after their night in the forest, Alex had wanted nothing but a hot meal and a warm bed, preferably with Giselle in it. Instead he was greeted with this news of the king's latest folly. "He has called up the entire levy?"

"He has." Stephan's anger made his words short and sharp. "What have you been assessed at?"

"Three and a half knights fees. You?"

"One hundred eighty-three. Do you have coin enough to pay scutage?"

Anger built in Alex. "I do. I'd planned on using it to buy grain. Do you mean to go?"

"I'll not join the king in this folly." A grim smile twisted Stephan's mouth. "Nor does John expect me to. He knows most of the nobles do not support this madness. All those who can get out of going will pay scutage instead. With the money John will hire his usual mercenaries. Damn the man, why can't he see that the constant flow of coin into his treasury for misguided ventures such as this is bad policy for England? The land is on the verge of famine. Money is needed to buy grain. Yet John takes it for his fruitless wars."

"John is heavy-handed," Gilbert said. "He takes too much."

Stephan paced. "It's not just that his taxes grow more and more onerous, it's that we see no result. He's not the warrior his father and brother were. Henry and Richard won territory, kept an empire together with their constant vigilance. John loses ground whenever he thinks to go to war. Philip of France is a more clever man than John, and just as ruthless. He has a forty-year hatred built up against the Plantagenets. He means to wrest every bit of land on the Continent away from English hands, and he's like to succeed with John as king."

"What can be done about any of this?" Geoffrey asked, between bites.

Stephan shook his head. "I don't know. It's ridiculous that so much depends on the character of the man who happens to become king. There should be some sort of safeguard, some way of defining and protecting our rights from the capriciousness of royal rule."

"Then you do not believe the king to be divinely appointed?" William asked.

Alex studied the younger man. The question was asked without rancor. It would appear the young knight had done some thinking of his own along these lines, which was a bit surprising considering his father was so intimate with the king.

"I should think our Lord capable of finding a better man than John," Stephan said. "Who becomes king is a matter of power, ruthlessness, and opportunity."

William said, "The common folk believe the land is sick because the king is evil."

" 'Tis an old belief, that the king's rule is reflected in the land." Alexander shook his head. "I can only hope it's no more than superstition, for if it be true, God help us with John as king."

There were murmurs of agreement from the men and women gathered around the table. Only Giselle seemed uncertain. Alex reached out and took her hand in his. "What think you of all this?" She looked startled to be asked her opinion.

"I think you sound like the simple men I know when they gather of a night over their ale and speak of nobles. They, too, wish for some sort of protection from arbitrary laws and the harshness of their masters. Too often a lord who is evil causes great misery among his folk and there is no recourse to be had. The people are bound to the land and to the lord. Should they try to leave they are considered outlaws."

There was silence at the table. Never had Alex stopped to think of the plight of so many of the villeins as having anything in common with the troubles of the nobles. Though the scale and specifics differed, the problem appeared to be the same. Men in power could abuse that power at will, if there were no laws to check them, no recourse to use against them. If the king did not rule by divine right, then neither did a baron. There should be a means of being rid of a corrupt lord, no matter how minor or great.

He wondered how many of the others thought as he did, and how many dismissed Giselle as naïve for making such a comparison. It was the nature of man to seek to protect his own privileges and power over those below him, while trying to mitigate that of the men above. The nobles were powerful, the commoners were not. It would be the nobles who would win their rights first, and only by force. How much longer it would take for the people he could not guess. What if the villeins ever massed together in revolt? The idea was frightening. Their sheer numbers could threaten those in power. It would be a bloodbath. There had to be a better way than battle and revolution. The rule of law perhaps, though law tended largely to be what men in power decreed, prostituting higher ideals to their greed and fears.

"Do you think villeins somehow equal to their betters, that they should have such protection?" Geoffrey asked.

Giselle answered, "Do you think yourself an equal of the king?"

"She has you there, Geoff," Gilbert said. He snatched a piece of cheese and popped it into his mouth.

Geoffrey nodded and sat quiet, deep in thought.

Alex turned to Elizabeth. "You know John better than anyone here. Why does he do these things?"

"The king is not a man who thinks soberly when a problem presents itself. He reacts to a situation, usually with anger and bravado, then finds his honor will not allow him to back down. I think he truly believes whatever he proclaims, no matter who tries—or how often—to convince him of the folly of his ways. He wants the power and respect his father had, the glory of his brother, yet he is not their equal."

"He's a fool and ever has been," Stephan said.

That made Geoffrey pause in his feeding. Alex shot his brother a warning glance. While Stephan's hatred for John was justified, he sometimes was too free with his opinion of the man. Geoffrey did not know the history between the king and Stephan, and so must wonder at so heated a statement. John, learning that Stephan's mother had been a Jew, did all in his power to destroy him. The king had failed. Though there was an uneasy truce between them, John finding it expedient to use Stephan's influence with the other barons, it was unwise to risk rousing the formidable royal ire.

"If we are to leave tomorrow, we must start packing now," Julianna said.

With her usual tact she diffused the tension, distracting people with activity. Alex was grateful for her calm pragmatism. They could sit here all night, arguing about John and his foolishness. Julianna recognized the futility of it and set her mind to what needed doing. Giselle rose to follow the other women. Alex caught her hand and turned it palm up, placing a kiss on it. She smiled at him.

"Don't be long," he said.

"You need to sleep. When you wake, I'll be there."

He watched her leave, enjoying the unconsciously sensual sway of her hips. When he turned back Stephan was staring at him, one brow quirked high.

"What?"

"I was just thinking, Brother. You're a lucky bastard. When are you going to marry the woman?"

Geoffrey nearly choked on his ale, spewing it across the table. Alex wiped the mess from the front of his tunic. Damn Stephan for always probing in exactly the right spot. His brother knew him too well. "I thought you disapproved?"

"I've changed my mind. Giselle is exactly what you need. If you don't marry her I despair of you ever learning what you should know of women."

Geoffrey and Gilbert waited eagerly for his answer.

"I've been thinking along those lines."

"You can't marry her," Geoff said. "She's a peasant."

Alex was losing patience with his cousin. Perhaps he should have left him wandering about Sherwood for another day or two. "And I'm a bastard."

"That's different. You have noble blood, you're a baron. The king wouldn't allow it."

"The king has nothing to say about it," Alex said. "I am free to marry as I will, and Giselle, as you say, is a commoner. The king only bothers with women of wealth when he decides whom they marry. He could care less who I take to wife."

Geoffrey changed his tactic. "She's beautiful, none can deny that, but you need more than an exciting bedmate when you look for a wife."

A muscle in Alex's jaw twitched. Stephan's brow came down as he scowled at the younger man. Gilbert wisely put some distance between him and Geoffrey.

"Watch your tongue, boy. You're talking about the woman I love, the woman I intend to make my wife."

"Don't be too hard on him," Stephan said. "He's still young and ignorant. Someday he'll fall in love, most probably with a woman who is inappropriate in some way. Then he'll understand. Until then, try to ignore him."

"That won't be difficult. Was I ever as puerile as he?"

"Youth and stupidity are an inevitable combination. Fortunately yours tended toward romance. Still, I'm heartened to see you've grown more practical over the years."

Alex settled more comfortably on his seat. Stephan was teasing him, fully aware that choosing Giselle as his wife was anything but practical, and every bit as foolish as anything he had done as a callow youth. He was at heart a romantic. He liked to think good of people, and that all things were possible when two people loved each other. What cynicism he'd acquired over the years had to do with the folly of war and the ambition of men. Love still held for him the bright promise of happiness. "I'm glad to see you approve."

"When does this wedding take place?" Gilbert asked.

Alex squirmed. "As soon as I can convince the woman to have me."

Stephan and Gilbert laughed. Geoffrey only looked more confused than before.

Though it was not late when Giselle returned to Alex's empty chamber, the sun had gone down several hours earlier. It was the time of year when darkness came suddenly in what would be daylight hours in the summer. Odin padded quietly at her side as she entered the room. A candle burned on the stone ledge beside the hearth, shedding just enough light for her to see most of the room, though the periphery was shadowed. The chamber was cold, the wooden shutter at the window insufficient to keep the chill out. When the wind blew from the west, snow filtered in through the cracks in a fairy-shower of sparkling silver. She rolled her shoulders to ease the ache of her muscles. She'd spent hours helping Julianna and Elizabeth pack. It surprised her that the women did much of the work themselves, rather than giving the tasks to servants, but it seemed both held a strong aversion to idleness.

Giselle squatted at the hearth. The firecover, inverted over the banked embers to keep any spark from jumping the hearthstones, was warm, so she knew there were live embers within. She removed the cover and placed small kindling on the embers, blowing to bring the fire to life. When the kindling caught she lay a log atop and waited until that caught fire as well, holding her hands over the growing flames.

She had to admit that a castle was preferred to the open woods in the winter. It offered shelter and warmth hard to come by in the wilderness. By spring she would no doubt find the gray walls a tortuous prison and would be eager to roam the woods, where she was so much at home. Alexander's life was still strange to her in many ways. She was accustomed to being alone. Only recently had she discovered how harmful her isolation had been. She'd grown accustomed to the laughter and noise of children, saw again how wonderful the world was, as seen through a child's eyes. The women of Alexander's family, especially Julianna, had become dear to her. What she would have thought impossible before, she now claimed; these highborn women were her friends. She would miss them. She would miss the children.

Though she had delivered babies she'd never spent much time with infants. Growing fond of Julianna's youngest daughter, a powerful new longing had awakened in

Giselle. She ached for a child of her own. She had not known, until she was admitted to the circle of Alex's family, how very alone she'd been; no parents, no siblings, no cousins or aunts or uncles. Only Maeve, then Robyn and his troop. Marian was all the female companionship she'd known. She knew now she never wanted to go back to that lonely life. It would all be so empty without Alexander.

She was sitting on the edge of the bed, her feet dangling well above the floor, when Alex opened the door and walked in.

"There you are," he said. He closed the door and bent over to scratch the dog, who gave him an enthusiastic welcome. "Is everything ready for their departure?"

"I think so. I will be sorry to see them leave."

"Will you?" He crossed the room toward her. "So will I, truth be told. I rather like playing uncle."

"When will you see them again?"

"Mayhap next summer. I've promised to travel to Rosmar for an extended visit. You'll like it there. It's not nearly so primitive as Wolfhurst, and of course we'll be near London."

She thought Wolfhurst was anything but primitive, but did not contradict him. And London. It was a mythical place to her, as removed from her world as faraway Byzantium. Another difference between nobles and commoners, she realized, was the ability and need to travel. Peasants most often wandered no farther than the nearest market town, living and dying in the villages they were born in. Once in a while someone might move to the next village when they married. Nobles, on their horses, traveled throughout the land, at all seasons, from one castle to another. To them a trip to London was, if not common-place, at least wasn't the sort of journey that a person would recount the rest of their lives, telling the tale to an enthralled audience who looked upon the traveler as a phenomenon as strange as a two-headed calf. She'd never been farther than Nottingham, to the great fair held once a year. What would London be like? Would she see the king?

"Have you been to London? Would you truly take me there?" she asked.

"If you want to go. I've been there a few times. There are things to see like none other in England."

"Is it beautiful?"

"I'd not describe it quite in those terms. Parts of it are grand, other parts crowded and filthy beyond imagining. Like most cities it is a continual cacophony of noise, with church bells ringing and folk shouting. We'll pass through on the way into Kent."

"Rosmar is in Kent?"

He nodded. "We can go to St. Thomas's shrine at Canterbury, if you have a mind."

She liked the idea of that. She liked the way he spoke of taking her with him, as though he assumed it would be so. She allowed herself, for the moment, to think her time with him might be longer than she'd supposed. It was a dangerous belief, so unlikely was it to be true, but she was tired and in need of comfort, and so let herself believe. Tentatively she reached out and gently touched the back of his hand. He sat very still. They had grown more comfortable with each other in the past weeks, learning how to love each other, exploring their bodies, the exquisite feel of each other, the taste and smell and touch that was becoming intimately familiar, but never had she initiated their loving. He had always come to her first, and she had followed, eagerly but shyly.

"I want you," she said.

He brought her hand to his lips and kissed her, his blue gaze never breaking with hers. "I have waited for you to say that. Do you know how I want you? How I need you? Not just in my bed, but in my life. I love you, Giselle.''

She could not have heard correctly. She studied his face but saw no deception there, saw nothing but the truth, and was astounded. He loved her? How could it be possible?

"Have you nothing to say?" His smile was uncertain. "Do you care for me at all?"

"Such words do not come easily for me."

"Nor for me. Believe me when I say I do not lightly proclaim my love. You are the first woman I've felt this way about. I'm beginning to think there cannot be any other in my life, no matter how long I may live, who can capture my heart and soul as you have done."

"Alexander, ah my love." She placed her palm against his cheek, where two days' growth of beard shadowed his jaw. He was warm beneath her hand, vital and alive and most wonderfully masculine.

He pulled her close and kissed her, his lips soft against hers, gentle and probing. That radiance his touch ignited within her, grew in now familiar circles of desire.

His hands deftly unlaced the back of her gown. He stood before her. The bed was high enough their eyes were almost at a level, with her sitting and him standing. He gathered the hem of her gown and chemise in his hands and slowly raised them, uncovering her legs to her knees, then her thighs. She raised herself off the bed and he worked the clothes up around her waist, up over her breasts, then off. He flung the garments aside then knelt. One hand gently gripped her ankle, the other slipped her leather shoe off. The touch of his warm hand was comforting and exciting. The circles of desire spread from her center to all parts of her body, like water when a rock has been dropped into it, the calm surface rippling out in ever-widening circles until the whole body of water vibrates with a pulsing rhythm. He uncrossed the garters holding

up her stocking, then slid it off her leg, letting his hand
linger along the back of her thigh in a long, smooth caress.
He did the same with the other leg, until she sat naked
facing him.

"You are so beautiful."

Slowly, deliberately, mocking his actions, she undressed
him, each garment tossed unheeded to the floor, until he
was naked. She could not help but think that it was Alexander who was truly beautiful. His body was perfectly propor-
tioned, strong and graceful. The hair of his chest was a
pale gold, soft to the touch, his skin warm and smooth,
except for the scars which marred the perfection. He was
an intriguing mix of contradictions; strong and gentle,
utterly masculine and truly a creature of beauty, with a
natural, unthinking grace that reminded her of a stallion,
sleek and proud and full of the mysterious force of life
that made some people seem more alive than others. He
was a creature of castle and town, a warrior and a lord; he
was also primal. It was easy for her to imagine him at home
in the woods, as much a part of the natural world as any
other creature, free and easy and sure of himself.

She felt beautiful when he looked at her with approval
and urgent need. He said he loved her. Did she dare
believe him? Did she dare not? Did she love him? Without
doubt, without hesitation, without caution, she loved the
man and it scared her to the core of her being. Loving
him made her vulnerable in a way she had never been
before. He loved her. Whatever else happened, she had
that.

"You're cold," he said, seeing her shiver. He pulled
back the fur cover and the wool blankets and together
they slid into the bed, the linens cold against their skin.
They held each other close, sharing their warmth, heating
the private enclave of their retreat. Soon all awareness

of cold disappeared in the mounting passion they wove between them.

"I love you, sweet woman." All his love shone in his eyes, as well as all his hope and fear.

She cradled his head between her hands. "I love you, Alexander."

With a sigh and a smile he proceeded to demonstrate what he meant.

Chapter Nineteen

"What is this?" Giselle stood before the bed in the large guest-chamber, staring at the clothes scattered over the dark coverlet.

"Julianna bid me wait until they'd left before showing you, knowing you'd protest," Alexander said. "They're yours."

There were half a dozen gowns, all of fine, soft wool, in various colors. Most were serviceable, everyday clothing, but in Giselle's eyes they were fine indeed, better than anything she could have hoped to wear. One was a gown of blue embroidered at neck and hem and sleeves in bright silk, the colors gay, the design artful. Where would she wear such a thing as that? Mayhap when they visited London? "These are all for me?"

"They'll do for now. I should have thought of it sooner and I do apologize. The one gown you've been wearing is inadequate."

Giselle glanced at the beautiful red gown she wore, her

hands absently caressing the smooth, soft cloth. She thought herself very lucky to have it. What lay spread before her was unimaginable riches.

"As soon as I can get to Nottingham, I'll bring back a skilled seamstress," Alex said. "You'll need summer clothes as well. Unwrap the one in linen."

She hadn't noticed it at first, but something was carefully covered by a length of creamy linen cloth. Carefully she folded it back. Her breath caught in her throat. With trembling hands she pulled the rest of the linen away to reveal the gown it protected. She'd never in her life seen such a thing, nor imagined its existence. It was made of a gold cloth she thought must be silk. She reached out to touch the marvel, then snatched her hand back. There had to be some mistake; surely Julianna had not meant to leave this? "I cannot accept this. When would I wear it?"

Alexander lifted the gown from the bed and held it before her, assessing the size and fit. I believe my sister-in-law meant it to be your wedding gown."

"My what?"

He replaced the gown in its nest of linen. "The gown you will wear when you marry me."

"I'm not going to marry you."

He turned to look at her, that familiar stubborn look on his face. "Yes, you are."

"Alexander, do not tease about such a thing." She was beginning to feel the first wave of irritation.

"I am quite serious. I'll have you to wife and no other."

With a shock she realized he was serious. Anger flared in her, surprising in its intensity. "That is ridiculous. You know it cannot be."

"I know no such thing."

Anger set her pacing away from the bed, and back again. She stopped in front of him, hands planted on her hips. "You are a baron, a lord of the realm. You must marry a woman of your own rank, not some uncouth peasant who will be nothing but an embarrassment to you. Good Lord, Alex, think of the gossip. People will think you a fool. Think of our children. Would you shame your sons by having me as their mother?"

He was staring at her as though at a talking dog. His frown deepened and a muscle began to twitch in his jaw. He crossed his arms over his chest and glared at her until she finally stopped, having exhausted her arguments.

"I never want to hear such nonsense from you again," he said. "Do you think I care for a second what others might say? As for any children we might be blessed with, they will be as proud to call you mother as I will be to call you wife."

She sank, shaking, into the nearest chair, gripping the arms hard. "You don't know what you are saying."

"I love you." He knelt before her and pried her hands loose, holding them between his own. "I would marry you. Is it so terrible to you that you will not even consider it?"

"Terrible?" Tears stung but she blinked them away. "Oh, Alex, I want nothing more in the world than to be your wife. But I am not suitable, surely you can see that?"

"No. I cannot see it."

"And I cannot marry you."

His blue eyes filled with disbelief, then pain, and finally a shattering sadness. She almost relented when she saw it. "My love, marriage is not necessary. Why can't we continue as we are?"

"Is that truly what you want?"

She nodded, not trusting herself to speak. What she wanted and what she believed best for him could not be reconciled. She could not marry him.

"All right. For now. But you'll change your mind. I am going to see you in that golden gown on our wedding day."

He lurched to his feet and left the room. She wasn't sure, but she thought there had been a gleam of tears in his eyes. For a while she sat motionless in the chair. She was right. Eventually he would see it. Slowly she rose and walked to the bed. She picked up the silk gown. It was softer than she had imagined. It was like their love, golden and beautiful, but the gown was also delicate, easily ruined if attention wasn't given to it. She covered the gown in its linen shroud.

Alexander felt a fierce need to do something physical, like slam his fist against a wall. He did not notice the priest until Michael grabbed him by the sleeve. He came to an abrupt halt in the middle of the road leading down into the village.

"What troubles you?" Michael asked. "I've been calling your name since ye came tearing out of the castle gates."

"Women!"

The priest grunted. "By that I take it you mean one woman in particular?"

Alexander resumed his walk, though at a slower pace to accommodate the other man. "She confounds me, Father. I ask the woman to marry me and she says no."

"No?"

Alexander glanced at the man, wondering if that had been amusement in his voice, but Michael was not smiling. There was a suspect sparkle in his eyes, however. It did not soothe Alex's mood.

"Did she perhaps state her reasons?" Michael asked.

"Reason has naught to do with it. She thinks because she is lowborn she is unsuitable for me." He expected the priest to agree that Giselle's argument lacked merit. The man remained infuriatingly silent. "She's wrong, you know."

"Is she?"

"Surely she knows that I, of all people, am unlikely to judge a man—or a woman—by the accident of their birth."

The priest turned a skeptical face toward him. "I've not noticed an overabundance of tolerance toward your inferiors in the months I've known you. While you're not a tyrannical lord, and that says much in your favor, you have your class's scorn for peasants and others."

He could hardly believe what he was hearing, and from whom he heard it. He'd begun to think of Michael as a friend as well as confidant and spiritual adviser. "That's a bit harsh."

"But is it untrue?"

"I am lord of the manor. It is fitting that I maintain a distance from my people. Otherwise they will not respect me when I must rule over them in my court. But I do not despise them, as you think."

Michael's mouth worked in an odd way, as though words were pushing to get out that he held back by will.

"You know that my brother is half Jewish. I've learned not to judge a man by his birth but by his merit."

"Then you're an odd sort of lord indeed."

There was anger in the priest's words, which set a spark to Alex's irritation. "That's what I've been trying to tell you, and Giselle. You both seem to think because I'm the son of an earl, and brother to another, that I have nothing in common with either of you. You're wrong. I have responsibilities that come with my station, and I take them seriously."

"You have privileges as well. Privileges you've done nothing to earn. Your birth alone makes you worthy of them."

"Then you want me to apologize for my birth? I should perhaps have been more careful in my selection of parents.

Does it count for naught what I've done with those privileges? Do I abuse my people? Am I harsh or unjust?"

"Nay, you're a good lord, I'll not argue with that. What I mean is something else entirely. It seems men do not share equally in God's gifts. Some folk are beautiful of face; others have great intellect; still others, physical grace and strength. Some endure hardship bravely; some seem born cheerful and make folk happy by their presence. Then there are those born ugly, deformed, and twisted, in body or soul. There are enough of the deadly sins rampant in the world to ensure many folk live in great misery. Some men murder and rape and steal, thinking themselves immune to the laws of man and God. Surely you must agree that the good and the bad are to be found in all ranks?"

"A man would need be blind and deaf not to see the truth of that. Human stupidity and greed know no class barriers, nor does love and devotion. But have you not proved my own argument? Giselle, a commoner, is uncommon in her generous nature, her beauty, and intellect."

"In other words, why waste her on a peasant?"

Alexander increased his pace and Michael had no noticeable trouble keeping up with him. "Why are you being so damned contrary?"

"Think long on what you've proposed. Most folk, common and noble, will echo Giselle's thoughts if not her words. They firmly believe the place of a man's birth conveys not only status, but worth. Giselle will be scorned by many of your kind. I think you may have allowed your passion to outrun your thinking. What you've asked of the woman is difficult at best and mayhap impossible."

"You think we should not marry?"

"I said no such thing. I want you to seriously consider what Giselle tells you. There is much truth in it. Though her fears may be unfounded, you should not scorn them."

"What would you know about women?"

Michael laughed and slapped him on the shoulder. "God forbid being a priest makes me a stranger to the human heart. I'm still a man, I can assure you. Who do you think the women of the village tell their woes to if not their priest? You'd not believe the problems people are capable of getting themselves into, most often with no evil intent involved."

They walked without speaking. There was no plan in where they walked and Alex now noticed they were headed toward the forest, away from the castle and village. It seemed appropriate. Giselle had lived there most of her life and it could not have done other than form her thoughts and perceptions, just as the life he'd lived had formed his. He'd seen much of the world, and much of it he wished to forget. He'd had little choice, born noble and poor, but to pursue a life as a knight-errant. He'd been lucky in being favored by King Richard. He'd never been forced to the degrading existence of some impoverished knights, begging or turning to outlawry to survive. But he'd seen more of war than any man should. The cruelty men were capable of never ceased to shock him, though it no longer surprised.

While Michael's words troubled him, for he considered himself the most tolerant of men, he was impartial enough to wonder if there were some truth to what the priest said. Michael was not a foolish man, and he'd come to trust his judgment on most issues. The possibility that he was not the sort of man he believed himself to be, made Alex uncomfortable. "If what you say of me is true, does it not make sense to marry Giselle? How better to understand those born beneath me? What more valuable connection could I have to the people?"

"You may have a point. Still, if the woman is not willing—"

"We shall have to convince her."

"We?"

Alex glanced again at the priest and again saw the betraying spark of amusement in his eyes, and knew he had an ally. "Surely she cannot stand against both of us. If nothing else we'll wear her down with persistence."

"I see. You plan a campaign of conquest?"

"I'll settle for nothing less than total surrender."

"What part do I play in your strategy?"

"Convince Giselle of the good she can do as my wife."

Michael was thoughtful, his lips pursed, his brow furrowed. "I can make that argument in good faith. What else?"

"What else can she want?"

"Robyn and the others are all the family she knows. No doubt she'd like some guarantee you'd not move against them."

Alex hesitated. Robyn was outlawed. In the strictest observance of form, Alex had a duty to bring the man to justice. He had been far more lenient than most lords in not betraying the band of men living in his woodland. Could he promise to never turn his hand against them? No. If he had reason to believe Robyn or the others did something truly reprehensible, he'd hunt them down and see that justice was done. Yet he did not do so now, when the law said it was already justified. He would defy the law, when it suited him to do so, when it went against his conscience to see that the letter of the law was upheld, and risk the censure or punishment his lack of action might engender. Was he any better than Robyn, who flouted the laws of the land? It was a muddle, and one he could not see an easy answer to. In all the ways he measured honor, Robyn was an honorable man; true to his word, meeting his responsibilities with determination and courage. And damn, he liked the man.

"I can't promise to never lift my hand against Robyn. It will depend on what he does. But I won't go after him for anything he's done so far, no matter what the law says."

The priest grunted. "Good enough."

"Then you'll help me?"

"I will, lad. Giselle could do worse than you."

Alex ignored the deliberate provocation. They walked in companionable silence for several minutes, deeper into the winter-stripped woods. Patches of snow lay under the shade of shrubs and on the north side of large trees. Old leaves were sodden underfoot, their bright autumn colors bleached to paler winter tones. Clouds rolled across the sky, thickening into a gray mass in the east. More snow was likely before dawn, but for now the sun warmed them between cloud shadows. There was a melancholy serenity in a winter wood, everything bare to the essentials. The mass of the tree trunks contrasted with the tracery of branches. Here and there red branches marked the location of dogwood. A few wild berries still clung to gean, where birds chattered and fed greedily. Ahead Alex saw patches of old snow, scattered somewhat thickly, and thought it odd that so much lay unmelted. There was something not right about what he saw, and he squinted.

"What is that?" Michael asked.

He suddenly realized what he was seeing. Fury warred with disbelief as he marched into the slaughter, Michael trailing after.

"Sweet *Jesu,*" the priest whispered.

With the toe of his boot Alex nudged one of the carcasses, but the sheep was dead, as were the others. He stood in the midst of his flock, surveying the loss. All of them, from what he could see. More than fifty sheep, most of the ewes pregnant with lambs that should have started coming into the world soon.

Michael slowly turned a circle, his face slack with disbelief. "What did this? Wolves?"

Many of the animals were so covered in blood it was hard to know what the death blow had been. With a curse Alex knelt and pulled an arrow from one carcass. "Wolves do not hunt with bow and arrow." He pointed at the unmistakable tracks in the soft ground. "Nor do they ride horses."

Michael stared at the arrow. There were a few more, and Alex gathered several. But arrows had not killed most of the sheep. They'd been hacked to death in a ruthless frenzy.

The priest clasped his hands together, his voice was barely audible. "Where is Brede?"

It hit Alex like a fist to the gut. Where was the young shepherd? The sheep had not been dead more than a few hours, but that was more than enough time for the boy to raise the alarm in the village, if he had been able. With growing dread he and Michael began their grisly search. They found the boy and his dog, dead with all the flock, sprawled next to each other. Alex knelt beside the body, which looked so fragile in death. Michael heaved his bulk down on his knees, head bowed in prayer. Alex did not know what to pray for. The boy's eternal rest. He was beginning to know his villagers, by more than their faces. He knew most of their names now, what they did, though how they were related to each other would take more time to work out. He wasn't sure the villagers knew themselves. Brede had been a likable boy who talked continually. Had he talked to his sheep and his dog, or did the boy reserved his loquaciousness for his rare human company?

He should pray for guidance, but his heart was so full of anger, his mind so filled with the need for vengeance, prayer now would be more sacrilege than petition. God help the man responsible. He lurched to his feet, unable to look at the dead boy longer.

Michael finally joined him. Alex stared into the distance, working brutally to control his emotions. He must think. Someone had done this intentionally, but who, and why?

"Surely you do not think Robyn had aught to do with this?" Giselle stared at the three arrows Alex clutched in his white-knuckled hand.

"They are the sort woodsmen use, but I'm no expert. Are these his or nay?" Alex dropped the arrows into her lap.

She picked one up to examine more closely. Many an archer used special markings so he could identify his arrows. After a battle or a hunt the arrows were gathered up and reused. "These are unmarked."

"Then they could belong to anyone?"

"It makes no sense for him to do this."

"Men seldom use sense when doing an unfathomable thing."

"Why would Robyn leave all that meat to rot when he has men to feed? Why would he kill Brede?"

"You echo my doubts." With a sigh, Alex lowered himself onto the bench beside her. A fire roared in the huge hearth in the hall, but it did little to warm the immense room beyond its immediate boundaries. "I want you to take a message to Robyn. He may know something I don't. I want to talk to him. I want you to arrange a meeting."

"Where?"

"I don't care. Just make it soon."

She placed her hand over his and was surprised by the desperate grip he used, as though clinging to her for needed strength. He was more upset by what had happened than he allowed himself to show. "What will you do?"

"I've sent the village men out to gather the sheep. Whoever did this has devilish timing. Lent begins soon, with its fasts. There would be mutton enough for everyone for weeks, were meat not forbidden. I will find whoever is responsible for Brede's death. That I swear."

She did not want to know what he would do to those responsible once caught. Slow to anger, Alex was formidable when roused. He had the righteous fury of a patient and decent man. She could not blame him. The murder of the shepherd boy was barbaric. Whoever did that was capable of anything. The loss of the sheep was a severe blow, not just to his pride, but more importantly, to the welfare of Wolfhurst. Much of the estate's wealth rested in the wool produced. She had learned that Wolfhurst was a thing Alex would fight for until his last breath, if need be. He was passionate about his land in a way she would not have expected. It wasn't the wealth or prestige he cared for, it was the land itself. His heart seemed to pulse with the same steady beat that gave life to field and wood.

"I will take you to Robyn," she said.

"Are you sure?"

She leaned her head against his shoulder and he wrapped an arm around, drawing her closer. "It will save time." When he did not reply she was grateful that he understood what she left unspoken. She trusted him enough to take him to the secret place in the woods where Robyn and the others hid. It was the surest way she had of telling him how much a part of her life he'd become. She longed to see the others, especially Marian. She needed a woman to talk to, a woman who knew her, who understood why she could not marry the man who was more dear to her than life. She desperately wanted to hear Marian tell her she'd made the right decision.

* * *

Alex saw the suspicion in their eyes and could not blame them. Robyn sat directly across from him, the broad wooden table between them. Next to Alex stood Giselle. Arrayed around Robyn were nearly twenty men, silent for now, listening to what he proposed. When he finished, the silence lingered.

Finally, Robyn spoke. "What you ask is risky, for yourself as well as us."

"I cannot guarantee your safety, but I swear I will do all in my power to keep you and yours from harm." Alex left unsaid that his power was greater than might appear at first glance. While he did not have a force of knights at his command, powerful men were his allies and he would not hesitate to call upon them if need be. What he needed was immediate help, and that Robyn could provide, if he were willing. Shrewd hazel eyes studied Alex and gave nothing away of what the other man was thinking. Alexander was impressed by the show of solidarity Robyn's followers displayed. None sought to influence Robyn's opinion one way or the other. Apparently they would accept whatever he decided, so thoroughly did they trust his leadership. Alex had known few men who commanded such respect.

Robyn turned toward those gathered around him. "You've heard what the baron offers. I'll not impose my will on any of you, you're freemen. It's a chance to earn some silver. You'll not go hungry this winter. Some of you may even earn a pardon, find something near the lives you were forced to leave. Take tonight to think it through. Those who wish to go into de Mandeville's employ may leave in the morning."

"What will you do, Rob?" The big man, John, stood just

behind his leader, his huge arms firmly crossed over his chest.

"I'll go with the baron, for a few days, perhaps more. But I'll not take his silver or commit myself to his service."

"Why do you trust him?" John asked. "It could be a trap."

"Giselle trusts him. I trust Giselle."

Alexander was surprised by the reply. He'd wondered why they'd been permitted to come into Robyn's hidden camp, to the cave where they now gathered. He'd been surprised at first, to realize the band of outlaws made their home in these hidden caves, for it seemed a barbaric way to live. But as he looked around he saw that, with the few essential pieces of furniture, with several fires to warm the echoing enclave and light the eerie darkness, it was not much different from most castles he'd been in. Drafty and cold near the entrance, and smoky from the fires, only the roughness of the walls and the closeness of the ceiling made it distinctly different from Wolfhurst. The most significant difference was the complete lack of luxury. There were no tapestries, no cushions for the benches, no beds, no carpets on the floor. The people who lived here were poor. Most had a gaunt and hungry look, as though they never had quite enough to eat. It was a look he was accustomed to seeing, among peasants.

He'd never thought much of it before, half-consciously believing what he'd been told, that peasants tended to be thin by nature. He knew now that was ridiculous, and was abashed at his ignorance. But these people had never been much more than a peripheral part of his world. He noticed them no more than he did the farm animals or fields they tended. When he had need of them was the only time he thought of them. Until he'd met Giselle. Now he saw the world differently than he ever had and knew he'd never again be the callous and unseeing man he'd been before.

He had not hoped Robyn would come himself, but if he did there was a chance more of his men would follow. Alex needed as many well-trained archers as he could entice. Until he knew who was threatening Wolfhurst, he was in desperate need of armed men. He did not have time to recruit the knights he would normally look for to man his castle walls. Robyn's men, honed by necessity, were excellent archers. They would prove a strong defense if he could convince them to come. All he had to offer were some silver pennies, the promise of bread and ale, the shelter of his high walls, and that he would not betray them to the authorities. It was the last promise that had him worried.

He'd keep his word, but that did not guarantee the king's men, if they discovered he harbored outlaws, would not force their way into Wolfhurst to capture and punish them all. It was the risk he took, losing all he had if it became common knowledge. Robyn and his men understood that, though he doubted they believed he would not turn his back on them if the situation grew desperate. Nor did he know for certain that these rough men, accustomed to acting on their own, would not turn against him, rob him blind and gut him in his hall. They understood that as well, so it was with mutual mistrust they came to an arrangement. Robyn's men hoped for some silver—a rare thing to cross their palms honestly; shelter from the worst of the winter storms; and full bellies. Alexander hoped to buy time to find whoever was attacking him. He would use whatever means available to him to save Wolfhurst. If that meant allying himself with outlaws, so be it.

Chapter Twenty

She led him through the cold mystery of trees, their path lighted by moonlight and quicksilver stars. Badger tracks played across the snow, mingled with the dainty mark of mice. One spot gave silent testimony to the meeting of a fox and a hare, the snow tinted pink in the pale light. The oak overhanging the pool was old, the rough bark gray and black in the night, the branches spreading in arcs like strong men's arms, dividing into smaller limbs, ending in a tangle of softly swaying fingers. The steam from the pool of water rose, condensing on the branches of the oak, hoaring the tree with velvety white, so that the tracery of the white-fingered branches shone starkly against the darker night. The pool was shrouded in mist, and nearest the warm water, at the very edge of the pool, the grass was still green. Violets bloomed in sheltered spots, their blue-purple petals nearly hidden in the night, their scent as delicate as the first light of a winter morning.

Giselle moved quietly, the black dog trotting beside her.

When she reached the edge of the pool she turned to look at Alexander. The enchantment of the place was working in him, for there was a softness to his gaze she had not seen of late and a bemused smile tipped the corners of his mouth. This was her world, the forest and the caves and this deep, dark pool of warm water. It was a place as alien to him as his world of castles and knights and luxury was exotic to her. Here she was comfortable and sure of herself, confident of her abilities because she knew what to expect from this world, she knew the rules that governed her safety and she knew what brought her pleasure and pain, what to seek and what to avoid. It was the pleasure and beauty of her world she longed to share with him now. She knew they would not be disturbed, Marian would see to that.

He closed the space between them, his arms encircling her to draw her against him. She could feel the warmth and strength of him, and smell the clean, cold winter in his hair and on his skin.

"You are so beautiful," he whispered, like a man at prayer, awed and humbled.

She felt beautiful with him. She felt whole and vibrantly alive, like nothing else she'd known. This man, who had once been a stranger to her, was now more dear than any man on earth. Her soul cried for him, as much as her body longed for his touch. She leaned her cheek against his chest, standing quietly in the circle of his arms, content to stand and wait, to stand and allow the peaceful night to flow around them and into them.

"I wanted to show you this." She indicated the pond, the trees, the silvery night, and hoped he understood the gift it was.

He glanced around, his pale eyes shining with a quiet joy. "I will think of you in this place, when I must be away from you. You are my woodland maid. I begin to think I do not know you any better than I know this beautiful, dangerous world of yours."

"God willing, you will never be far from me."

He did not speak, but his answer was in his lips as he bent to kiss her. They began with a gentle touch of lip to lip, almost shyly, as though first discovering each other. Feathery kisses touched her eyelids, the tip of her nose, her chin, the delicate curve of her jaw near her ear. Every other part of her body was covered in layers of wool; even her hands were protected from the cold by fur-lined gloves.

"Let's find a warmer place." His voice was suddenly rough with desire.

She smiled and stepped back from him, removing the gloves from her hands. He frowned, unsure what she intended. She unclasped the enameled brooch at her throat and let the heavy cloak ripple to the ground to pile like a drift of snow around her feet. His frown deepened as she untied the leather girdle at her waist, then began unlacing her gown. She started to shiver, as much from anticipation as the cold, and her fingers were clumsy. By the time she slipped the gown and linen chemise from her shoulders, Alexander was smiling; a crooked, wicked smile that made him look like a blue-eyed angel with mischief on his mind. Her shoes and thick stockings joined the pile of clothing and she stood naked, with the moon and stars silvering her body, the cold air drawing her nipples to hard buds. She pulled the blue ribbon from her hair and unbraided the plait until her red curls flowed over her shoulders and down her back. Alexander was undressing as quickly as he could, cursing softly when his fingers fumbled at the buckle of his baldric. She stepped into the warm pool, until the water reached her knees, then dove in, letting the water cover her, swimming with strong arms to the center, where she surfaced and looked back at him.

He stood at the edge of the water, naked. It was as though she saw him for the first time and her breath caught at the masculine beauty of his body. Blond hair, silver-white in the moonlight, curled long at the back of his strong neck. Wide, muscular shoulders and chest contrasted with the narrow waist and hips. There was no fat on the man, only sinew and muscle. He stood on long legs and she thought, somewhat oddly, that his feet looked surprisingly delicate, giving a glimpse of the boy, small and fine-boned he had once been. She let her glance travel upward until she looked into his face. His smile was anything but boyish, and in his blue eyes was the fire of a man's desire. In the moonlight he was flawless, the battle scars hidden, the tension of the past weeks smoothed away. He walked into the water, coming surely toward her. The ripples he created preceded him and she felt them like his pulse against her body, powerful as life.

Submerged, sleek as an otter, he swam to her, swam beneath her, his hands gliding over her thighs in a long stroke. When he rose to the surface she was with him, her back against his chest, his hands cupping her breasts. Her hair floated in the water like a living thing, graceful in the slow, languid unfurling and curling of long tresses. She felt like a water creature, a silkie or a mermaid, free from the normal bonds of earth and weight and duty. In the uncanny half-light of the moonlit mist she let go of all inhibition, all worry. Tonight was for pleasure, for loving this magnificent man who held her, who trailed kisses across her wet neck and shoulder. Tonight they were alone in a world all their own.

Slowly they moved together, body rubbing against body with a silky whisper, flowing over and around each other, legs twining and coming apart, hands touching, lips touching. They smelled of secret wetness, of water heated deep in the earth, dark and clean as the night sky. The water could not match the heat of their hands, of their bodies coiled together, of their lips, searching, searing, seeking. They came eventually to a black rock, its massive shoulders lifted above the pool. On one side was a shelf, almost level, large enough to sit upon. With a groan, Alexander sat, and pulled her to him. Her breasts brushed lightly against his chest; his penis, defiantly stiff, moved with the gentle currents that eddied around them. She straddled him, slipping over him, onto him in one smooth wet motion. They found the rhythm the water allowed, a variation on the usual dance, and slowly, deeply, danced each other in circles of spiraling excitement.

She watched his face. His eyes squeezed shut, his nostrils flared, his lips parted. He threw his head back, the long column of his neck bare to her lips, the strong pulse beating hard. His shuddering release triggered hers and they climbed high on the aching waves of pleasure, coming slowly back to the womb of water and night.

A fierce, greedy love overcame her. This was her man. No matter what happened, until the day she died this man was her soul-mate, her destiny and all her desire.

He cupped her face in his hands. "I love you, lady. My God, I do think I love you more than life itself."

"Alexander." She said it softly, but all her love was in that one word. It was a whisper of hope, of hunger, and of joy.

When they left in the morning they were accompanied by Robyn and Marian and a dozen men, ranging from a youth of fourteen to men in their fifties, each of them an outlaw. They made a strange sight, seven of the men mounted on an odd assortment of horses, the rest walking. They were dressed in clothes that mimicked the colors of the earth: brown, drab green, dark yellow, gray. Several wore bright feathers stuck raffishly into their wool hats. All had quivers slung at their hips, bristling with arrows, and bows across their backs. They didn't talk or laugh but walked in silence, like the creatures of the forest they'd become. On silent, leather-shod feet they followed Alex. It made him nervous, the first few miles. He was accustomed to the clink of swords against mailed legs, the creak of saddles, the rough, boastful talk of armored, mounted knights riding together—not this sinister quiet. Any one of those men, should he be so inclined, could put an arrow through his back at any time. He refused to allow himself to look over his shoulder. On one side of Alex rode Giselle. On his other side rode Robyn with Marian pillion.

"I've been giving more thought to your problem," Robyn said. "I have some ideas, but more questions than aught else. Sometimes two brains rubbed together can generate insights either one alone would not."

"Aye," Alex answered. He was intrigued by this man, who lived his life as an outlaw but with a code of honor as strict as his own. He was curious to know what the man thought.

"Whoever killed the sheep wants something."

"Mayhap my sheep." Alex's tone was sarcastic, but he'd not expected Robyn to be so simple.

Robyn gave him a look of scolding disdain. "If he'd wanted the sheep he would have taken them. Nay, 'tis something else he's after. Who are your enemies?"

"The king would top that list. He's no friend of my family."

Robyn blinked twice, then he smiled. "We have something in common after all. He's at the top of my list as well. But I think we may safely, for now, dismiss John as our culprit. He's busy losing land in France and far too preoccupied to bother with the slaughter of a herd of sheep belonging to one of his lesser barons."

"Your comprehension of the situation is astute." Alexander was uncomfortably aware he'd badly underestimated the man who rode beside him. Uneducated and lowborn, Robyn was by no means a dull-witted or uninformed man. Why had Alex assumed he would be ignorant and self-serving? Because that was how peasants were supposed to act. At least, that was how the nobility supposed they acted, as if most nobles would have any way of knowing what went on in a poor man's head or heart.

"Do you have any enemies closer to home? What of Guisborne? He did not seem well pleased with you. You did publicly humiliate the man when you took Alice from him."

"I've thought the same, but why would he bother? There is mutual dislike, but not the sort of hatred that would lead to so intemperate an act."

Robyn shrugged his big shoulders. "Hate isn't the only thing to motivate a man to foul deeds. Revenge, greed, fear, anger, lust—all can prod a man to irrational acts. You no doubt have done so in the past and will again. I know I have."

"You're right. I have, much to my shame. I've always regretted it. Makes me look a damned fool when I don't stop and think before I act. My brother declares it my greatest fault."

Robyn laughed, startling his horse, which he deftly brought under control. "By God, I'd not thought to find an honest nobleman."

Alex was not insulted by the remark, though he suspected he should be. "Let's say, for argument's sake, it is Guisborne. He thinks himself ill-used because King Richard took Wolfhurst from him and gave it to me. But is that motive enough for this wanton destruction? For the murder of an innocent lad?"

"I've known Guisborne many years," Robyn said. "He

is capable of anything. If you have something he wants, he's ruthless."

"I'll not accuse him without evidence, and much as I dislike the man, I have only my suspicion to go on. I think it best if we display a show of strength with your men on the ramparts of Wolfhurst and wait to see if he makes another move."

"You've a reputation as one of King Richard's fiercest warriors. You're content to wait?"

"Do I disappoint you?"

Robyn studied him for a long moment. "You surprise me."

Apparently the man thought him a bloodthirsty, mindless fighting machine, without morals or honor. Not a flattering portrait. Nor could it be more wrong. He would try to remember to point out to Giselle that it was not only the nobles who held false beliefs. Her own people were equally capable of ignorance. "Then we're agreed? We'll keep an eye on Guisborne, but it may well be another who seeks my harm."

"I'll keep my word. My men will stay at Wolfhurst until spring, but only if you pay the silver you've promised."

"I keep my word as well."

Robyn nodded, seemingly satisfied.

They rode into the outskirts of the village an hour before sunset. People came to stand in the doorways of their cottages, or stopped their work where they stood, to stare silently at the cortege. Alex saw apprehension, even fear on their faces, which he could not understand. These people knew Robyn and the others, they'd dealt with them clandestinely for years. Surely it was not the forest men who inspired such suspicion. Giselle, riding beside him, had noticed the strange silence as well.

"What is wrong?" he asked.

"They are afraid."

"Of what?"

"That the presence of Rob and the others will bring the sheriff of Nottingham to Wolfhurst. He'd show no mercy if he knew there were outlaws here."

"He'd have to get into Wolfhurst, and that he won't do without my consent."

She glanced at him. "That is what they fear. Will a baron truly risk his life and property to keep his word to protect outcasts?"

"It won't come to that. There's no reason for the sheriff to know. Besides, I have no choice. I need protection now. As soon as I can hire knights for my mesnie my need for Robyn will no longer exist."

"Why is it so difficult to find the men you need?"

"The king's call to arms against France. Every able-bodied knight not already in service to a lord, has hired himself to the king's army. There are few men in need of a lord who don't already have one and I don't have sufficient money or reputation to win them away to me." He knew hiring Robyn and his men was risky, but so was having Wolfhurst, castle and village, unprotected.

He could only hope whoever was marauding against him would be discovered soon, and the need to have outlaws in his keep vanish. He could not ask his brother for help, for though Stephan would be willing to send knights until Alex could hire his own, the king's edict demanded those knights sail from Southampton to France, or the silver to buy their relief be paid, before Easter. Some of those men would no doubt wish to leave Stephan's service to join the king, as men invariably did when the prospect of plunder or adventure was dangled before them. Sending his men now would leave Stephan's own estates undermanned and it was likely England would be unruly with the king gone, so widespread was the dissatisfaction with John's rule.

Ironically, it was not the roving bands of outlaws that would cause the most damage to England while the king fought his futile war, but the great lords, who usually found the king's absence an excuse to settle personal grievances or grab for power. While the common folk blamed John's failures for the loss of crops and famine, for all men knew the land suffered if the lord was evil, greater men blamed John for usurping their ancient rights and privileges. Though men of all walks cursed John for his greed and cruelty, Alex feared for England with the king gone. Chaos needed little more fuel than anger and fear to ignite.

"He asked you to marry him?" Marian sat in the middle of the vast bed in the lord's chamber, wrapped warmly in the fur covering. Odin napped beside her. "When is the wedding?"

"I told him no." Giselle looked away from the incredulity on her friend's face.

"You said no?" Marian bounced up and down with agitation. "You said no! Have you lost your mind?"

"I thought, of all people, you would understand."

"Well, I don't. He's gorgeous, he must love you to offer marriage. You'd be rich and protected—even pampered. Pray explain to me what you find so disagreeable."

Giselle paced between the hearth and the bed. How could she explain her fears? "I don't belong in his world. I'm an embarrassment to him. Other nobles will mock him because of me."

Marian stared at her, a frown puckering her brow. "That's it?"

"It's enough." She was beginning to lose patience. Surely Marian could see her predicament.

"Alexander de Mandeville can likely have any woman in England he sets his mind on, and he has chosen you. Has he voiced the same fears you've just blathered?"

"I don't blather. Lord, what do I know about being a chatelaine? I'd be expected to tell people what to do. The servants would never respect me. I would be expected to mingle with nobility, even royalty. I can't do it."

Marian disentangled herself from the bedclothes and marched over to where Giselle stood. "I've never before known you to be a coward."

She was startled by the accusation. "That is not what is wrong with this."

"Do you love the man?"

"Yes, God help me."

Marian snorted. "I've never known you to be a fool, either. Where did you misplace your brain and your heart? You love him, he loves you. He wants to marry you. Don't you understand what that means? All that nonsense you've told yourself, none of it matters. That is, if you are the brave and wise woman I think you are. You can learn whatever a chatelaine does—no woman is born knowing such things.

"Think of the good you can do. You're a healer. The people of this village are in sore need of your help. You will be a rich woman. If you think yourself unworthy of comfort and wealth, by all means give it away as alms. Or do you want to leave your Alexander, return to the woods with Robyn and me? What waits there for you but loneliness?"

Giselle was surprised. Marian had never spoken to her so forcefully before, and she feared much of what the other woman said made sense. Had she been a coward, letting her fears overshadow her love? But that was what it really came down to. She knew she loved Alexander. Did he love her in the same way? He said he wanted to marry her, but a few years from now, when he knew her better, would he feel the same? She did not think she could survive if he sought out other women, as so many noblemen did.

Marian wrapped an arm around her shoulders and squeezed. "Don't look so downhearted, my friend. Think on what I've said. You risk losing so much by saying no."

But do I risk more if I tell him yes? There was no time for further discussion as loud footsteps and teasing masculine voices rapidly approached. The chamber door was thrust open to reveal Alexander and Robyn, grinning mischievously, for all the world looking as though they had been the best of friends since earliest boyhood.

"There they be," Robyn said, grinning wider.

"They're brim-full," Marian said.

"Nay, we've not had as much ale as that." Robyn staggered into the room, followed by Alexander, who steadied himself by grabbing the back of a chair, which was soon in danger of being overturned. With painful care, Alex sat in the crazily rocking chair.

"Come, wife." Robyn held out his hand, the crooked smile on his face belying the commanding tone.

Marian glided past him, throwing an enticing glance over her shoulder. Robyn followed, unsteadily but happy. Giselle closed the door after them, then turned and stood, her hands pressed against the wood.

"Never saw a man drink so much." Alexander slowly shook his head side to side.

"Did you try to keep up with him?"

He looked up sheepishly. "I did. Why didn't you warn me?"

"I would have, had I thought of it. Are you feeling sick?"

"Nay, I've sense enough to stop before I reach that point. I'll not be feeling well come morning, no doubt."

She sighed. There was no sense talking to him tonight about anything as serious as marriage. He'd either not remember what they said, come morning, or he'd feel she'd caught him at a weak moment, if he later regretted his decision. It wouldn't hurt to think a little longer on what Marian said. In fact, she should probably see Father Michael about it. He had a sensible head, he'd be able to see the problem clearly and tell her what to do. Or so she fervently hoped.

"Let's get you to bed."

He grinned wickedly. "Only if you come with me."

She doubted he was capable of bedplay, especially when he allowed her to support him, then undress him. When he was naked, sitting with his long legs hanging over the edge of the bed, she realized how wrong she was. Looking up she saw he was well prepared for loving, and her own desire soared at sight of him.

" 'Tis not fair." He reached for the neck of her gown and tugged gently. "You still have all your clothes on."

"Mayhap we can remedy that." She turned so he could unlace her gown. His fingers were slow and careful, leaving a trail of heat at his touch. By the time he was done with the laces she was ready to rip the gown and chemise from her body. Instead, she stood as he lifted the garments over her head, then pulled her down on top of him onto the bed.

"This is where I want you," he said. His hands combed through her hair and caressed her shoulders.

It seemed to her he was in a strange mood, and he wove a dreamlike web around them with his slow, deliberate loving, his husky, low, whispering voice, his searing kisses. She relaxed and let him take her where he would. Their bodies moved together now with a comfortable grace, unhurried, building the passion to a peak. No matter how familiar they became, there would always be the mystery that entranced her. The waves of powerful feeling washing through her at his touch went far beyond what he did to her body. He touched her soul with his loving. She knew then, laying in his arms, trusting him to keep her safe, believing in his love, that he was the only man she would ever want, and that she would marry him. "Alexander," she whispered. "Alexander, my love."

He lay her beneath him and his loving was slow and deliberate and tender.

Chapter Twenty-one

They were startled awake by pounding on the door and shouts, Odin adding his barking to the sudden noise. Giselle watched from the bed as Alexander marched across the room to unbar the door and throw it open.

"The grain barn, 'tis afire!"

With an oath Alexander grabbed a tunic and slipped it over his head as he rushed after the messenger. Giselle groped in the near dark for her own tunic and shoes, her mind racing, all thought of sleep gone. Wolfhurst's grain was stored in a large barn near the mill, where it was ground into flour for bread. Without the grain, there would be no bread, which was the mainstay of the villeins' diet, especially in winter when vegetables and fruit were not available. Only the nobles had the indulgence of meat year-round.

She locked Odin in the bedchamber, where he howled his protest, and hurried down the stairs and through the empty hall into the bailey. She could see the flames from there, roaring up into the night, crimson and gold against the black sky. The sound of burning wood, the roar of the updraft, the shouts of people, all mingled into a chorus of destruction and helplessness. The fire had already won. All that was left to do was put it out before it spread to the mill.

She found Alexander at the head of the line of people passing water from the millpond up the sloping ground to the barn. It seemed every villager was there, each with something grabbed on the way out the door of their houses to use as a bucket. They were accustomed to the dangers of fire and did not hesitate once the alarm was raised to fling themselves into the fight. Fire could leave an entire settlement, even large quarters of cities, ruined, the people homeless and destitute. Giselle joined the line, passing water up, while a twin queue rushed the empty containers back down to the pond to be refilled and hauled once more, from person to person, up the long row to the barn. It was tedious, numbing work. The muscles of her shoulders and back ached. Tomorrow she would be kept busy tending to injuries, with little time to worry about her own discomfort. For now she gritted her teeth and worked past the pain.

"Stand back!" Alexander shouted.

There was just enough time to abandon the line and rush away from the barn as it fell, scattering burning timbers and sparks in all directions, the fire flaring into long tails before falling back to earth. The lines reformed, but this time the people worked with less intensity, knowing the barn and all within was lost. It took two hours to put out the conflagration. Rosy color tinged the eastern horizon when they finally stopped. The villagers wandered back to their houses, covered with soot, weary and frightened. What would there be to eat?

Alexander stood near the ruins. He was as filthy as any

of his people. Robyn and the priest stood with him, surveying the catastrophe in silence. She touched him gently, to draw his attention, and was startled by the blaze of fury on his face when he turned to her. She knew he was not angry at her, and though the loss was great, his anger seemed too large.

"What is it?" she asked, her voice shaking from fatigue and apprehension.

"This was no accident. 'Twas deliberately set."

The idea was shocking. Who would do so disgusting a thing, knowing the hardship it would cause to innocent people?

"You're sure?" Michael asked. The priest looked diminished, weary beyond physical exhaustion. "Who?"

"I don't know." Alex's fists clenched tightly at his side as he stared at the smoldering heap. "I'm going to take my brother up on his offer of help. I'll leave within the hour for his nearest fief, near Lincoln. With luck I'll be back before dark tomorrow. The wagons of grain should arrive within the week." He turned toward the castle.

Giselle had trouble keeping up with Alex's long stride, but knew anger propelled him.

"Do you think it wise to leave?" Robyn asked.

"Do I have a choice? I trust you and your men to keep Wolfhurst safe until I return. I want men patrolling the village as well as stationed on the castle walls." Alex grabbed Giselle by the hand and pulled her closer to him.

She hated the thought of him leaving. She hated having to wait, but knew there was nothing for her to do, knew the last thing he needed now was to worry about her. She would wait, cursing every moment away from him. "Will you be safe, by yourself?"

"I'll be with him," Robyn said.

"I want you here," Alexander said, "in command of your men."

Robyn slanted him an angry look. "My men will do as they're told without my hovering over them. Don't argue with me, Wolfhurst. 'Tis dangerous for you to go alone, if someone is indeed determined to ruin you. Any man who would not think twice about starving a village will not stop short of murder."

Giselle tightened her grip on Alexander's arm at those ominous words, but she did not give voice to her fear. She would not ask him to stay, to keep himself safe, just to give her peace of mind. His people needed him and she must let him go. It was then, with the possibility of losing him suddenly real, that she knew she must marry him. Her heart was already given as fully as was possible, for she would mourn him as deeply as any wife. In all but name, he was her husband.

She said the words before she had a chance to change her mind, before her fear could dissuade her. "Return to me, my love, for I will wed you."

Alexander stopped, holding her at arm's length. A smile lightened his face. "Woman, you do continue to surprise me. When I return you shall be my bride."

"God be praised," Michael said.

"Amen to that." Robyn slugged Alex on the arm in manly congratulation.

After Alexander and Robyn left, Giselle found time dragging and so, bundled into a warm cloak, set off for the village church. Marian joined her. The small woman was all but engulfed in the fur-lined mantle she wore, which Alexander had pressed on her, insisting she needed to stay warm for the sake of the babe she carried. Marian happily agreed, reveling in the soft luxury, her impish face smiling out of the voluminous hood. She looked like a bouncing lump of wolf-trimmed wool walking beside Giselle.

The church was cold and deserted, with a lone candle giving light near the altar. Giselle knelt on the stone floor while Marian settled more comfortably on a step leading up to the altar, her elbow on her knees, her chin in her hand.

After a few minutes Marian asked, "What are you praying?"

Giselle ignored her. Marian was not as pious as one might hope. Nor would Giselle normally come to such a place as this, mostly because churches did not exist in her wildwood, but in her time at Wolfhurst she'd found the quiet, simple church to be a haven when her thoughts and emotions disquieted her.

"Be sure you ask that Rob and that lord of yours come back safe."

"Ask yourself."

"You're better at it."

Giselle opened her eyes at that, to see the worry on her friend's face.

"And ask that my babe be safely born and healthy." It was said in a whisper.

"I always do."

Marian was quiet for almost five minutes, by which time Giselle was sure she'd badgered God long enough.

" 'Tis nice here," Marian said. "Peaceful."

The church had that special quality generations of prayers gave a place. Giselle felt it as well.

"Do you suppose we'll stay long enough I might have my babe here, at Wolfhurst?"

Giselle knew the unasked questions, the unvoiced worry behind her friend's words. It would be safer here than out in the wood, where they were vulnerable to discovery. As long as no one happened to notice Wolfhurst was crawling with outlaws, as long as none of the villagers thought to make a few coins by going to the king's men with information, they were safe enough. "No matter what, I'll be with you. If you want the babe born here, we'll see it is so."

That huge smile that so often broke across Marian's face was there now. "You'll be lady of Wolfhurst by then. Think of it, Giselle. You, a baroness."

"I'd rather not. All I want is to be Alexander's wife, and I can hardly believe that will happen. The rest is too much for me to comprehend."

"You'll be in a position to help many people."

"That is what Alexander and Father Michael have told me, trying to persuade me. I will be happy to be able to help others, but I'm marrying Alexander because I love him, not for the position he can give me."

"I know that. But just think of all the nice things that come with it."

Giselle smiled at her friend's enthusiasm. Marian did not question the morality of having fine things. She used the cloak Alexander gave her gratefully, happy to have it, and did not moan that others had less and so she did not deserve to have anything either. Giselle suspected she made things more complicated by thinking too much, but it was her nature.

They heard the sound of a horse trotting along the road through the village, headed toward the castle. "Who can that be?" Marian asked.

Giselle went to the church door and looked out. The monk from Blyth Abbey, Father Edgar, approached on a small gelding. He swerved when he saw her, guiding the horse toward the church.

"Is Lord Wolfhurst within the castle?" he asked.

"Nay, good Father. He is gone today."

The man's face showed irritation and impatience. "Blast, I need to talk to him. I'm on urgent business for the abbot. I'm not even supposed to be here, but it is on the road to

Nottingham so I thought I'd stop." His eyebrows lowered and he stared at her. He shook his head. "Nay, you're but a woman. What news I have concerns you, but 'tis the baron I should speak with."

The monk seemed agitated and Giselle's curiosity was high. What could he possibly have to tell Alexander that concerned her? "If you would tell your news to me, I promise to convey it to the baron."

He studied her, his head titled to one side. "Nay, I have not the time to linger; I must be on the road. Unless you'd ride with me, a mile or two. That way I'll lose no time." He scowled again."I have your promise, you'll tell the baron what I say to you?"

"Yes."

Behind her, hidden in the darkness of the church, Marian whispered, "I don't like this. Don't leave Wolfhurst without Alexander."

Giselle turned. "He's a priest, I'll be safe with him. I'll ride a mile or two and turn back. I won't be gone more than an hour."

"Take one of the men with you."

"Yes, I will."

"Who are you talking to, woman?" The priest stared past her, trying to see into the church.

"Just a village woman. I'll have my mare saddled and meet you at the road juncture." She did not want him to see Marian, or ask more questions. In fact, the less he saw of Wolfhurst, the safer she'd feel.

"See that you hurry. I don't have time to dawdle." The monk trotted away.

"There's something I mistrust about that man," Marian said.

"You mistrust all men at first sight."

* * *

Father Edgar was waiting for her. He scowled when he saw the young man riding beside her, but said nothing.

Now that they were riding along the main road, toward Nottingham, the monk seemed reluctant to talk.

"Father, I cannot go far with you. Will you not tell me your news?"

"It's most like a lot of nonsense. In truth I feel a bit of a fool now. I've been talking to Father Bernard of late. There are times he makes some sense, but I've noticed even when he appears confused he speaks more truth than others are aware of. He was priest at Wolfhurst and at Guisborne for nigh thirty years."

"I did not know that." Where was all this leading? Father Bernard was a gentle old soul, but his mind was addled as a broken egg.

The monk glanced at her, then away. "I have no proof of this, you understand."

"Of what, Father?"

"You may be the daughter of Lady Giselle of Guisborne and Sir John de Clare of Wolfhurst."

It was as though he'd hit her in the stomach, so unexpected, so astounding was what he'd said. "That's impossible. They had no children. You said their child died."

"Apparently that was not true. There was an older daughter, named Giselle, for her mother. She was given to a cousin of Lady Giselle's. A woman named Maeve."

Giselle could not believe what she was hearing. Did Bernard, somewhere in his confused mind, know the secret of her parents? But why would Maeve take her into the forest? Why hadn't she been raised by relatives? And what proof could the monk provide? Yet he knew about Maeve. Had Giselle mentioned her to Bernard? She didn't think so, but it wasn't impossible, and he could have mixed that up in his addlement and added it to this fantastic tale. "Why would a nobleman's child be taken from her home?"

"Bernard seemed to think the child was in some sort of danger, though he wasn't clear on that point. I think it more like he became confused in his thinking soon after and forgot all about the child. You did know a woman by the name of Maeve?"

"Yes."

"Did she speak to you of your parents?"

"Never. She always claimed she found me, abandoned, when I was an infant."

"That contradicts Bernard. He said the child was four when her mother died." He frowned at that and seemed to settle into deep thought.

She'd been so occupied with their conversation, she only now realized she'd ridden farther from Wolfhurst than she'd intended. She reined her mare to a stop. "This is all the maundering of an old man whose mind is no longer clear. There is no proof of any of this. If you will forgive me, Father, I must return to Wolfhurst."

"But there is proof," the priest said. "Ride with me and I will tell you."

There was no proof. There couldn't be.

"There is a letter, written by Lady Giselle, witnessed by our late abbot and signed with their seals, verifying all of this. There is also the original charters."

She was stunned. It would prove who her parents were. She would be connected to someone, would belong somewhere. "Where is this letter?"

"Poor Bernard cannot seem to remember. Apparently he put it somewhere for safekeeping and has long forgotten where. I thought mayhap you knew where to find it."

"Me?" She stared at him.

"You do not have it?"

"No. Until a moment ago I knew aught of this. Why do you think I would possess this letter?"

"Pity," he said. "But we had to be sure."

She did not understand until after he raised his hand and waved toward the forest growing thick along the road. At his signal a man burst out of cover and galloped toward them. If she had been a better rider she'd have been able to escape, but she had trouble bringing her startled mare under control. The man easily caught the reins of her horse and forced them out of her hands, jerking her small mount roughly up beside him. The boy with her turned his animal and tore back along the road like the devil was on his tail. She prayed he would get free to Wolfhurst, to raise the alarm. Before her sat Guy of Guisborne on a dark horse.

Guy looked beyond her, to the priest. "Does she have it?"

"No," Father Edgar said.

"Are you sure?"

"She knows aught of the letter. I'd swear to it."

An ugly smirk spread over Guisborne's lips. "As though your vow would be trusted. No matter. You've done your duty. The folk at Wolfhurst believe she is headed toward Nottingham?"

"Yes, m'lord. The boy accompanying her will carry the news of her abduction."

"Good. That should bring de Mandeville running, to try to save his whore."

Giselle was not sure she understood all that was being said, but she knew she must escape this man. She'd been naïve to think the priest was trustworthy. Marian was ever telling her she had no sense about people. She'd be sure not to make the same mistake again with Guy.

"What do you want?" she asked.

"Why dear niece, what I've always wanted. Undisputed

title to Guisborne. And to regain Wolfhurst, which is right-fully mine.''

He led her horse into the woods, the priest following, and soon they were far from sight or sound of anyone along the road. She cringed at the thought of this man being her uncle, but if what the priest said were true, it would be so. And if it was true, she was the rightful heir to Guisborne and Wolfhurst. If Guy meant to have them for himself, she feared she knew what he intended to do to her. He would kill her, to preserve his power and wealth. A terrible cold emptiness filled her at the realization. Wher-ever he was taking her, it was not to Nottingham, for they traveled north and east, away from that town. But Alexan-der would waste precious time searching for her in Notting-ham. What did Guy mean to do to Alexander? New fear pierced her until she was shaking with it. She forced herself to crush the panic threatening to unnerve her. If she were to survive, if she were to warn Alexander, she must use her wits to escape, and she must do it soon.

Chapter Twenty-two

From the direction they rode, Giselle guessed they were heading toward Guisborne Castle. She must find a means of eluding them before reaching the stronghold. But how? Guy kept her mare on a short rein. He was close enough to grab her if she tried to slip off her horse, and even if she managed that, he'd be mounted and could run her down easily. The land they rode through was familiar to her. This was her world, the forest and meadows. She knew it intimately, while her uncle was a stranger to it. She sensed the wariness in him, the discomfort most people felt when they traveled in the dense woodlands of Sherwood.

She began to scan her surroundings, her gaze flicking here and there. What she sought, she wasn't sure, but there must be something, somewhere, she could use to her advantage. Then she noticed the conversation between Guy and the priest became heated.

"I've done what you wanted," Edgar said.

"And you'll have what I promised."

"When? I'm tired of waiting."

"When the abbot dies. He's an old man. You'll not be waiting much longer."

"You can have him removed. Declare him incompetent. I want to be abbot *now.*"

Guy looked at the priest and an odd smile slanted across his face. The cold gleam of his eyes sent a shiver through Giselle. Edgar, too hot with his ambition to notice the other man's frozen anger, continued his argument, his voice growing louder, until the baron cut him off.

"Enough! I don't want to hear more of this. I've more important things to take care of just now. You will wait."

"I will not. Do you forget what I know? Do you think the sheriff of Nottingham would look the other way should I tell him?"

Giselle knew what Guy intended before he made a move. She saw it in his eyes.

All color drained from the priest's face when Guy pulled his sword and pressed the point against the other man's chest. "Say your prayers, priest. I'm sending you to hell."

She had never seen so much blood pour out of a person, nor seen a man die so quickly, dead before he fell from his horse.

"Stupid man, threatening me." He looked with disgust at the blood and flesh clinging to his sword, then leaned over and wiped the weapon clean on Giselle's gown. He slipped the blade back into its scabbard.

"You can't leave him here," Giselle said. Her mind was tangled with fear, but she had to find a way to distract Guy. "What if someone finds him?"

"That's unlikely. They'll assume he was killed by outlaws."

"Those men do not use swords."

His cool gaze met hers. "How would you know what weapon such men prefer?"

Her hands were sweaty but she felt cold. She could not completely control the shaking that clawed through her body. "A sword is a knight's weapon. All know that. 'Tis obvious what killed the priest. The boy who rode with me saw you with the man."

Guy slitted his eyes, then with a curse stepped down from his horse, careful to keep the reins of her mare in his hand. "Get down."

She slipped to the ground. The first necessary thing had been accomplished. She was now on foot and so was he. If she could slip away from him she had the advantage, knowing the woods as she did. She was fast on foot. Guy would be hindered by his armor, his sword, his size, and his ignorance. She tried to keep the eagerness out of her voice. "That oak tree looks as though it might be hollow. You could hide the body."

Guy looked where she pointed, then nodded. "None will think to look there."

Giselle prayed he would not question why she would be willing to help him hide his crime. She squatted and lifted the dead man's feet. Guy lifted the man by his arms, and together they staggered toward the tree. She knew what they would find. Part of the trunk near the bottom was hollow, large enough for a person to hide in, as she had often enough in the past. When they reached the opening and laid the body down, she made a great show of checking the space. " 'Tis large enough to hide him well, I think, if we fold his legs and push him to the back." She wiggled back out of the hollow and stood, looking expectantly at Guy. "You cram him into the tree and I'll gather branches to disguise the opening."

Guy laughed. "I think not. You hide the priest. I'll get the branches. I'll have you in sight the entire time, so don't think to do anything."

She tried to look disappointed, as though he'd bested

her, and frowning, flung her cloak to the ground. It would hinder her if she had a chance to run. She was strong for a woman, but the priest was a stout man. Pulling and pushing, she managed to move him into the tree. The last thing she wanted was Guy helping her. He must move away, even if only a few feet. Finally, he did. She could hear him hacking at tree branches with his sword. She pretended to struggle awhile longer, trying not to think what it was she was touching, and praying for forgiveness that she treated the corpse so roughly. She would see the priest properly buried, she promised him.

She glanced over her shoulder to see how far away Guy was. Not more than ten feet, but he was not likely to give her more room. Wiggling from the makeshift tomb, she stood and rolled her shoulders, turning her head slowly from side to side as though stretching her neck. Guy glanced at her, but saw her standing quietly, preoccupied.

"If you're done, come get these branches," he said.

She took a few steps toward him, her heart beating so hard in her chest she was sure he must hear it. When he turned away to resume his damage to the nearest tree, she turned and ran. It did not take him long to realize what she'd done. She heard him cursing, his big body crashing through the underbrush. Praying she remembered the lay of the land correctly, she moved swiftly and hoped she had enough lead to reach the place she remembered.

Reaching the edge of the winterbourne stream she knew a moment of panic. The water was higher than she'd anticipated. Had it washed away the protective overhang she remembered? She did not have time to hesitate, and plunged into the frigid water. Her skirts tangled about her legs and she desperately clawed at them, lifting the sodden wool above her knees, stumbling upstream, searching the left bank. If she did not find it soon, Guy would have her.

She almost missed it. A log had washed up against the

shore and wedged on a rock in the middle of the stream. It nearly blocked the sandy, wet den she'd been searching for. The shelter carved by the stream was half submerged, not the dry, safe place she'd found last summer. She heard Guy behind her. She scrambled into the hole, squirming around the rough log, and crouched motionless. The water came to her chest and the cold of it shocked her. It was March and though the days were milder than before, the water was nearly winter-cold. She would not be able to stay long in her hiding place.

Guy was very close now; she could almost feel his footsteps above her head, and prayed the earth overhang would not give under his weight.

She was shivering violently and clamped her jaws tight to keep her teeth from chattering. She breathed in short, painful gasps. Could he hear her over the noise he made? As he moved away she opened her mouth and took deeper breaths, but the shock of the cold water made everything she did more difficult. She concentrated on listening to him moving about in the woods nearby. She listened as the sound faded, grew distant, then stopped. She waited a few minutes more, her body numbing to the cold.

When she stood, knowing she could not stay longer in the freezing hell she'd been forced to seek, she nearly collapsed. Her legs would not work properly. Half crawling, she clawed her way up the small rise of the streambank. All she wanted to do was lay there, to sleep. She was suddenly so tired. She thought she heard bells, ringing clear and silvery on the spring wind, a happy sound. Her eyes closed.

Alexander was calling to her, but when she reached out she could not touch him. His calls grew desperate, pleading. He was weeping. But the bells seduced her and she turned toward them, toward the glow of golden light that was the music of the bells. Alexander's cry of anguish reached her, tore at her heart, caught her soul, and turned her around. She paused for a long, slow, painful moment, caught between two worlds. Then she reached out to the man and took his hand.

She forced her eyes open. She must not sleep. With a groan she sat up, feeling weak all over, and still so tired. She heard the bells again and frowned. Her brain was muzzy, but those bells were real. Struggling to her feet, she stood, her head cocked to one side, listening. Finally she realized the source. Blyth Abbey lay no more than a mile to the north of where she stood. She moved toward the sound. Not knowing exactly why, not thinking clearly what she was doing, she knew she must find Father Bernard. The old priest would protect her. He would help her.

The day was warm, almost cloudless. The sun began to dry her wet clothes. New life was spreading in the woods, where the tender buds of leaves swollen and ready to burst open shaded pale blades of grass growing upward in the meadows. Bees roamed through the hidden shy flowers blooming so early, birds chattered like old gossips from trees and bushes. Life flowed in renewal all around her. She felt the rhythm and the power of it in her blood, as the sun, which brought life, continued to warm her.

As her legs regained their strength she began to run. Guy could turn at any time, come back this way looking for her. She would be safe in the abbey. Even Guy would not violate the rights of sanctuary to get to her. Then she remembered how easily he'd killed the priest and knew the promise of safety to be illusory. If anything stayed his hand, it would not be the holiness of the place, but the fact that there would be witnesses to his actions. He could not very well kill all the monks.

She stopped at the edge of the forest. Before her lay the fields where the monks grew their crops, and beyond that, the outbuildings, barns, and stables. The abbey itself sprawled on the far side of the acreage. She would have to cross this open space and risk having Guy see her, or keep to the woods, make her way around to the east, where the trees crowded more closely on the enclosure. There was no one in sight. The monks must be at their prayers. It was too risky to be caught in the open when there was no one around to see or hear. She turned back into the woods.

A slow, hot anger centered itself in her brain. Guy would kill her if he could, so that he could keep Guisborne. Had he killed her parents? It suddenly seemed too convenient they had died within a few weeks of each other. Had her mother suspected and sent her away with Maeve? Guy would destroy Alexander as well, to have Wolfhurst. It was the greed as much as the man's cold-bloodedness that angered her. That people had died, that more might die so this one man could cling to land and power, was a sin as great as any she could imagine. It was wicked.

She made it safely to the edge of the woods nearest the abbey gatehouse. Glancing down she realized she looked terrible, her gown caked with blood and still wet, her hair in wild disarray. The gatekeeper would take one look at her and turn her away. A stone wall about eight feet high surrounded the abbey. She saw a tree growing near one corner. Its branches did not quite overhang the wall, but she might be able to get close enough to jump the rest of the way. She could see no other way in. She had climbed more trees in her life than she could remember, and this one gave her no difficulty. She stood on a thick, gnarled branch and stared down at the wall. It was easily within range. The problem would be in landing. The top of the wall was crowned with tiles, peaked to resemble a miniature roof. She could not see what was on the other side of the wall. Whatever it was, she was likely to fall onto it. She hoped it was something soft.

She landed hard and lay with eyes clenched shut as pain arced through her legs and back. She waited until the pain subsided. Nothing was broken or sprained that she could tell, but her entire left side would no doubt be bruised. She opened her eyes and saw that she was atop a woodpile, the huge logs cut to fit an immense hearth. Grateful the careful monks had stacked the pile so it was solid and stable, she slowly climbed down. Pieces of bark clung to her gown and she'd ripped a hole in the front. For some reason the ruined gown made her want to cry. She cursed herself for a fool and refused to give in to despair. Carefully she looked around. She was near the abbey kitchens. A few doves strutted under the cote and a lazy cat raised its head to look at her, then resumed its napping. The door to the kitchen stood open and she heard voices and the clanging of pots. She also heard singing, farther away. Most of the community was in the church. Bernard would most likely be there.

Not wishing to be caught sneaking around, she squared her shoulders, smoothed her tattered gown, and tried to look as though she was out for a stroll. With luck no one in the kitchen would notice her, but if they did, she'd brazen it out and claim to be a guest. She moved quickly past the stone building and breathed more easily when she came around to the other side. The singing was closer now. The cloister walk and garden lay between her and the church. She swallowed hard. No woman was allowed within the cloister, though she never heard exactly what would happen if caught there. Should she go around to the front of the church, enter by the main doors? No. She didn't want her presence known if she could avoid it. Bernard might not be in the church. For all she knew, he was too confused to participate in the Office.

Gritting her teeth, she walked across the garden and onto the covered cloister walk. She'd claim ignorance if caught. She nearly laughed at the absurdity. A man was trying to kill her, and she felt guilty about violating the monks' privacy. The cloister ended at a door and slowly she pushed it open. Before her lay a dimly lighted hallway and a flight of stairs leading up into the church. She stepped into the hallway and closed the door quietly behind her. The entrance at the top of the stairs must be in the monks' choir, near the altar. If she appeared there, no doubt half the brothers would die of shock and indignation. She did not want quite so public an entrance. At least here she could hide and think what to do next. She settled into a corner where the wall angled toward the stairs, hidden by shadows to anyone coming down. The singing went on in a peaceful round, first one side of the choir, then the other. She wondered what they sang, not understanding the Latin.

He was so quiet she didn't hear the monk until he was nearly down the stairs. She must have made a noise because he looked up, seeing her. His eyes rounded with surprise. Grabbing his arm she pulled him closer.

"I beg you, help me. I am desperate."

He pried her fingers from his arm and folded his hands together calmly beneath his scapular. He was young and skinny and there was a precise quality about him that was calming. He did not speak.

"I must see Father Bernard," she whispered.

A dark brow arched, and a faint smile teased his lips, as though what she said did not entirely surprise him. He laid a finger against his lips, signaling her to be quiet, then pointed down the hall, away from the stairs. When she hesitated he moved ahead of her, and signaled her to follow. He led her to a door at the far end, and into a bright little room, with sunshine spilling through the high window. He pointed to a stone bench and she sat. The room was stark, no furniture save the cold bench. There was the single door, no other way in or out.

"Will you send Bernard to me?"

He nodded and then he was gone. He had not spoken to her. She did not know if she could trust him. If he did bring Bernard, what could the old man do to help her? He didn't even know who she was, mistaking her for that other Giselle, her mother. Her parents were buried in the abbey church. Her people, her family. But Guy was her family as well. Her uncle. It was unthinkable. She began to pace, and the longer she strode back and forth, the more nervous she became. What was taking the monk so long? *This is a mistake. I'm trapped here.* She crossed the room and reached for the door handle, just as someone on the other side opened it.

Guy of Guisborne stood in the doorway. A smile spread slowly across his face.

Chapter Twenty-three

"Surely you knew I would find you?"

He advanced into the small room. She could smell him. Sweat, blood, anger, danger. She backed away until her knees hit the marble bench, then she stopped and stood, as straight as fear would allow her.

"Is this the woman?" a black-robed monk asked.

"Aye, Father Abbot. 'Tis the one. I do thank you for your help."

The abbot was a tall man with a sharp nose and dark eyes beneath gray brows. He looked at her now with no sign of sympathy, but without animosity, displaying a careful neutrality.

"You must help me." She took a step toward the abbot. All her hope now rested in what this man would do. "He will kill me."

The abbot glanced sharply at Guisborne at that, then back at her, and there was something new in his expression, a wary interest. "What has the woman done?"

"I caught her poaching game in the king's forest. She was riding a horse stolen from Wolfhurst."

Worse than the lies Guisborne told was the look on the monk's face. He believed every word. "He's lying. Father Edgar asked me to ride with him toward Nottingham, but that was a lie as well. This man," she pointed at her uncle, "was hiding in the brush and met us by arrangement."

"Father Edgar?" The abbot looked puzzled. "You must be mistaken. He has no reason to leave the abbey."

"Edgar is dead. Guy killed him. I can show you where the body is hidden." At last the abbot was listening to her.

"All lies," Guisborne said. He was calm, almost nonchalant.

She knew, from his look, that she would not be able to prove the priest was dead. "You've moved the body." She could not prove she had not been poaching. But she could prove she'd not stolen Alexander's horse. "My lord abbot, I do beg you, send for Alexander de Mandeville. He will swear to you I have the horse with his permission."

"De Mandeville is gone," Guy said.

"Gone where?" the abbot asked.

"To his brother's demesne near Lincoln, to buy grain," she said. "He will return to Wolfhurst soon." She must convince him not to let Guy take her from this place. The monk seemed to be wavering.

"There is still the matter of the poaching," Guy said. "Even if she had the horse with de Mandeville's knowledge, poaching the king's game is a serious offense, do you not agree, Father?"

"Yes, indeed." The monk placed a finger against his mouth and studied her.

He was going to give her to Guy's custody; she could see it in the squaring of his shoulders, the small shake of his head. "I was not poaching."

"So you've said. I say otherwise."

"I cannot very well poach my own game." She was desperate now.

"Your game?" Guy laughed. Moving swiftly, he grabbed her by the upper arm and began to drag her from the room.

"I would hear what she has to say." The abbot waited.

She said the only thing she could think of. "I am Sir Alexander's wife. I was on Wolfhurst land when Guy accosted me."

"His wife!" Guy shouted, his face dark with anger. "You lying whore, I've had all I'm going to take of your games."

The abbot blocked the doorway. "I cannot in good conscience let you leave with her, Lord Guisborne. Not until Lord Wolfhurst has had a chance to speak."

Hope sprang to life in her heart. Alexander would know what to do. They would listen to him.

"Get out of my way," Guy said, his free hand going to the pommel of his sword.

The abbot's gaze was unwavering. "I am offering the woman sanctuary of this place. She will be kept here, do not fear. When Lord Wolfhurst can be found, we will discuss this further. Surely you can have no objection?"

"I damned well do. God's blood, look at the woman. Do you believe she's the wife of a nobleman? She's his whore. She's a liar and a thief and I mean to take her to the king's foresters for punishment."

Giselle tried to pull away from him. Her heart pounded so hard with fear she could scarcely breathe. All knew the forest law was harsh. People hanged for poaching. Guy tightened his grip and pulled her along, pushing the abbot aside.

"If you leave this place with the woman, I shall excommunicate you for violating sanctuary."

The abbot's words were strong and sure. There could

be no doubt he meant to do as he said. Even the worst of men feared so drastic a punishment as that.

Guy angrily stopped and turned to face the old monk. "You wouldn't dare! I've bought and paid for you, my Lord Abbot, or had you forgotten? I can as easily be rid of you."

"Mayhap it is time I do penance for the ambition of my youth. You will be excommunicated if you set foot out of this abbey with the woman. Think on it carefully. Is your immortal soul worth the risk?"

With a foul curse Guy flung her toward the monk. "See you keep her locked up. I'll be back."

Giselle trembled so hard she feared her legs would collapse. The abbot took her by the elbow and guided her back to the small room. She sat on the cold stone bench and tried to breathe normally.

"Do not be afraid, child. If what you say is true, all will be well in the end. If you lie, however, there is naught I can do for you."

It was an odd sort of comfort, she thought. How did a person prove they were not lying when the accusations made against them were false? It was her word against a nobleman's. No one would believe her. She needed Alexander. The abbot stood above her, his face calm, neither smiling nor frowning. She wondered if his thoughts could possibly be as peaceful as his demeanor. "He did kill Edgar."

The monk nodded once. "Yes, he most probably did. That is why I was willing to believe you. I know Lord Guisborne very well, you see. I will send a messenger immediately to Wolfhurst to await Sir Alexander's arrival. Is there aught you need before I leave?"

She was feeling calmer, but did not feel safe. "What if Sir Guy returns in the night?"

"This door can be barred from the inside. You will be quite safe here." He turned to go.

"There is one thing. Could you send Father Bernard to me?"

He glanced back at her, but if he thought her request odd, he did not say so.

Alexander was eager to be home, now they were so close, but he kept his horse to a walk. Ahead of him rode Robyn and beside him, his cousin Geoffrey, whom he'd met unexpectedly at his brother's holding near Lincoln. Tied by a long lead to his saddle was a white mare, dainty and careful, meant for Giselle. It was his wedding gift to her and he smiled at the thought of her bravely mounting the gentle beast. The grain he'd purchased would be delivered within the week. For the first time in months he felt a happy peace. The woman he loved beyond measure waited for him a few miles away. Before the passing of another day he meant to have her to wife.

"Are you sure you want me as a witness to your nuptials?" Geoffrey asked.

"Why wouldn't I?"

"I was less than gracious when you first broached the idea of marrying Giselle."

"If you would rather not . . ."

"Nay, that is not my meaning. I am happy to. I thought it was you who would object, considering how opposed I was. Mayhap I've matured lately. I know better now how unruly and unbidden love can be, even if the person you want so savagely is unattainable."

Alexander glanced at his young cousin at that, hearing the note of near desperation in his voice. "Elizabeth?"

Geoffrey nodded and looked miserable. Alex felt a vast sympathy for him. His cousin could not begin to hope to pay the bride-price the king demanded for Elizabeth's marriage-right until he inherited his fortune. "What do you mean to do about it?"

"What can I do? I'll marry someone suitable and forget about Elizabeth."

Not likely in this life. Alexander could think of nothing but meaningless platitudes to offer as comfort, and so was silent.

Robyn slowed to ride beside them. "You'll not keep Giselle confined to that ugly heap of stone." It was more statement than question. "She'll not be happy, if you don't let her roam about in her forest."

"She'll be free to come and go. I'd be as like to keep a wild thing confined as force her within the walls. I'd have to lock her up to do it and we both know how she'd react to that."

Robyn nodded, as though reassured, and Alexander wondered if the man seriously thought he would even consider locking his wife up. He'd meant what he said as a jest. Apparently Robyn thought noblemen had more control of their wives than other men. He'd have to remember to introduce the man to Julianna someday.

"I would ask a favor of you," Robyn said. "When Marian's time comes, I would have the babe born at Wolfhurst. They'll be safer there than in the wild."

"Of course." It was the least he could do. Robyn had proved an able and reliable man, intelligent and with a mischievous sense of humor that kept him entertained. He also knew Giselle would insist on the same. A baby born at Wolfhurst. He wondered when his own son or daughter would make an appearance there. The thought of fathering those children made him randy and he was sore tempted to urge his horse to a gallop the last miles.

"Do you plan on staying at Wolfhurst long?" Geoffrey tried to sound nonchalant. He was trying very hard to accept Robyn and his men as defenders of Wolfhurst, but Alexander knew the idea was foreign to his cousin. But then, Geoffrey had changed his mind about Giselle. There was hope for the man.

"The agreement was to stay through till spring," Robyn said.

"We'll talk later." Alexander hoped he could get the men to stay awhile longer, until he had time to find knights for his *mesnie*. Knowing Robyn, it would cost him an increase in wages.

The day was bright and green. Birds sang as though their hearts would explode if they could not get the notes out, and small forest creatures, driven to mate, abandoned caution and could be seen doing their part to multiply and replenish the earth. The forest smelled sweet. The fields around Wolfhurst were beginning to grow their crops of wheat and rye. The orchards were beginning to bloom. The air was warm and there had been no rain in a week. If the weather proved mild this year there would be an abundance. He fervently prayed it would be so. The hard work he had planned, to bring Wolfhurst out of her long neglect, called for strong people and goodwill.

Robyn slowed his horse to a stop, his head cocked, listening. Alexander and Geoffrey stopped behind him.

"What's wrong?" Alexander's hand went to his sword.

Robyn turned with a worried look, his bow swiftly lifted from his back and ready in his hand. "I'm not sure."

Alexander felt it now. Something was wrong. Beside him Geoffrey grew wary, glancing behind them.

The attack came from behind. The force of the arrow nearly knocked Alexander from his horse. Pain—intense, red—speared his back near his shoulder. He clung to his mount, fighting the pain that threatened to topple him. There was confusion all around him. Shouting men. Ner-

vous horses. Geoffrey was quickly beside him, a firm hand
on the bridle of Alexander's horse.

"Where's Robyn?" Alexander asked.

"Given chase."

"Alone?"

"I can't leave you here with an arrow sticking out of
your back. Robyn is no fool. He can take care of himself."

Alexander thought of the irony of that statement. Geoffrey had been none too pleased to find him in the company
of the outlaw, but seemed to warm to the man the more
time he spent with him. Robyn had that effect on people.
He charmed them, even as he managed to do exactly as
he pleased. The pain in his back was beginning to throb
as it spread into his arm and around his chest.

"Help me down."

"Shouldn't we ride on to Wolfhurst? You need to have
that tended to."

"God's blood, Geoff. Just do as I say. 'Tis not as bad as
it looks. My mail kept it from going deep." He would be
dead by now without the armor, but he forbore to mention
the fact. Geoffrey would need to keep his nerve to do what
was necessary.

His cousin eyed him skeptically, but dismounted and
helped him to the ground. "Now what?"

"Now you pull the bloody thing out of my back."

"Me? Here?"

Alexander clenched his jaw against pain and annoyance.
"There's no one else. Help me to that tree."

They stumbled to the young maple and Alexander sat
facing the tree. He wrapped his arms around it, clenching
his hands together on the far side. "Tie my hands
together."

Geoffrey did as he asked. Kneeling, he looked steadfastly
into the other man's face. "I don't want to hurt you."

"I know that, lad. It can't be helped. Pull until it's out,

even if I beg you to stop." With luck he'd pass out from the pain.

He was not lucky. He willed himself to silence but could not prevent a low moan to escape his lips as the arrow finally tore free. He slumped forward, gasping, riding the waves of pain. A strange noise drew his attention and he glanced up to see his cousin several feet away, puking in the new spring grasses. No doubt it was the first time the man had been called upon to tend a serious injury. It would not be the last. He'd grow accustomed to it, as Alexander had, though he'd never developed the complete detachment to suffering some men found.

When he was done, Geoffrey unbound his hands. "Now I will take you to Wolfhurst."

"No."

"Damn it, Alex, what do you mean, no?"

"I'm going after Robyn. He'll need help." Alexander struggled to his feet. Anger made his voice hard and cold. "I'm going to stop the bastard who did this to me."

Geoffrey followed after him, a string of imaginative curses flowing from his mouth in a frustrated tirade. He helped Alex onto his horse and mounted his own.

"You can come with me or not, as you please."

A particularly expressive oath detailing Alexander's ancestry and sanity answered him.

"Well, are you with me or nay?"

Geoffrey scowled at him. "You're a de Mandeville. So am I."

It was answer enough, and reason enough. Together they turned off the narrow path, away from Wolfhurst, and into the bright spring forest.

It was Robyn who found them.

"Did you catch him?" Alexander asked.

"No. But it was Guisborne, as you suspected. He rode straight to Blyth Abbey. No doubt he'll ask for sanctuary. There was naught for me to do."

Alexander knew the man was beyond his reach, safe within the church. "He can't stay there forever."

"Why would Guy of Guisborne try to kill you?" Geoffrey asked.

Alexander had been wondering the same. Until now Guy had been content with plundering Wolfhurst. What had changed in the two days he'd been gone? "How far are we from Blyth?"

"Not more than four miles," Robyn said.

"Mayhap I should have a talk with the abbot." Alexander squeezed his eyes shut against a sudden burst of pain in his shoulder. What he wanted was to ride to Wolfhurst, where Giselle waited for him.

"Are you sure it's wise?" Robyn asked. "The abbot is Guisborne's man."

"I'm not launching an attack. I just want some answers."

"You're not going to tell me, are you?" Geoffrey said.

"If I knew what went on in Guisborne's depraved brain I'd tell you. But I don't. That's part of the question I'm hoping to find an answer to."

"You're in no condition to be riding about the country-side. You should be at Wolfhurst, where your woman can tend your wounds."

Alexander knew his cousin was right. He also knew he'd be going to the abbey. Wolfhurst and Giselle would still be there in a few hours.

Chapter Twenty-four

Giselle felt like an animal, caged in the stone-walled room. Only the high, narrow window let her know the passage of the day toward sundown. She paced back and forth, across the small room and back again, growing more nervous with each hour. She hated being locked up. When would Alexander return to Wolfhurst? Where was Guisborne?

"Time will pass no more quickly for your pacing," Father Bernard said. He sat quiet and calm on the stone bench. "Your husband will be here soon, m'lady, and all will be right."

Giselle tried to smile. The old priest was still confused most of the time, thinking she was her mother. But once in a while he had moments that seemed lucid enough. The problem was telling when he made sense and when he didn't. Still, she was glad for his company. It would have been unbearable if she were forced to wait in solitude. How much of what Father Edgar had told her was true?

Were her parents buried here, in this church? If there was proof, only Bernard knew where to find it, and he could not tell. If she could find the letter and the charter, it would prove she was heiress to Wolfhurst and Guisborne. It would be a way of stopping Guy. The king himself would back her claim, if it could be proved. She chewed her lip, thinking. Had anyone played along with Bernard, talking to him as though he made sense? She looked at the old man and wondered if it were fair of her to pretend. Seeing no harm in what she intended, she sat at his feet.

"Father, I need your help. My lord husband has returned from Crusade. It is time we brought our daughter home, little Giselle. Do you remember, we gave her to Maeve to safeguard?"

"You are right, it is time. I'll go to Maeve and bring them both to you."

"There is also the letter I wrote, and the charters. Forgive me, but I cannot remember where you placed them, to keep them from those who should not have them."

The priest chuckled. "Mayhap because I never told you. I've never told a soul, just as we agreed."

"But now 'tis safe and I need the documents."

"I'll retrieve them as well."

"Can you not tell me where they are?"

He frowned at her, confusion clouding his eyes. "Michael has them."

She tried not to sound surprised. "Do you mean the priest at Wolfhurst?"

The monk nodded.

"I thought you told no one."

"And I haven't. Poor Michael doesn't know he has possession of them."

She could pry no more information from him than that. He sat with a beatific smile on his face, humming to himself. Was this all more nonsense? How could Michael have the things and not know it? It was twenty years since the documents, if they existed, had been given to Bernard. Twenty years hidden. If Michael had them twenty years ago, did he have them still? It was then she heard the distant sound of men shouting. Someone ran toward the room. All her fear surged through her heart.

"Open the door, child. I must get you to a safer place."

It was the abbot, on the far side of the door. Bernard rose and raised the iron bar. The abbot stepped into the room. "Guisborne is here and mad with rage. He must not find you."

Giselle did not question him. She followed as he led her deeper into the forbidden cloister, through the monks' frater, away from the church. Bernard followed more slowly, his sandals slapping on the stone floor. They ran through a maze of corridors, up a flight of stairs, always moving away from the church. A scream of pain and terror came hurtling down the halls after them. The abbot faltered, then recovered himself. Behind her Bernard was praying. They came to a large room with windows and a row of beds. It was the monks' infirmary. The three men in the room eyed her with shock and disbelief.

"This way," the abbot said.

It was a small, private chapel at the far end of the sickroom.

"Go to the altar and do not leave it. It is sanctuary. Any man taking you from there against your will risks his immortal soul."

Giselle climbed the stairs to the altar and sat beside it. Would Guisborne care if he added one more sin to his tally?

Guisborne was searching the abbey, she could hear him, cursing and shouting. He would find her within minutes.

The abbot rushed to her side. "There is no time to hear

your confession, child. Do you sincerely repent of all your sins?"

She stared at him, the import of his words chasing the fear that made her tremble. "Yes."

He traced a cross on her forehead. *"Absolve, te . . ."* The familiar Latin words calmed her a little. He was sending her with a clean soul to her death.

"Bernard, absolve me," the abbot said.

The old monk looked startled at the request, but did as he was asked.

A sense of unreality enveloped her. *This is not happening. I am not going to die today. I will live. I will see Alexander again.* Thought of leaving him was most painful of all. It could not be that it would end like this.

The abbey gatehouse was unattended, which was unusual enough to send a shiver of apprehension through Alexander. The churchyard was deserted, none of the monks in sight. "I like this not."

"Nor do I," Geoffrey said.

Robyn was silent, but he was tense with caution. They dismounted, the two knights pulling their swords as they hurried up the stone stairs and into the abbey church, Robyn following, arrow at the ready. Whatever he'd feared, it was not what he found. Monks stood talking loudly, gesticulating wildly. One held an old sword, as though he meant to use it, though he didn't seem to know how to handle it properly. There was an ungodly noise coming from somewhere within the bowels of the abbey.

Geoffrey grabbed the nearest monk. "What is happening?"

The brother looked at them with terror in his eyes, his lips moving in hasty prayer. Geoffrey gave him a hard shake. "I'm the son of the earl of Essex, this is my cousin Lord Wolfhurst. You have nothing to fear from us."

" 'Tis Guisborne, he's gone mad. He's sworn he'll kill your wife."

The man looked at Alexander when he said it. *His wife?* A cold premonition hit him. "Giselle is here?"

The monk nodded. "God help us all."

Alexander did not stay to hear more. He ran toward the shouts coming from the far side of the abbey. He did not turn to see if Geoffrey or Robyn followed. Giselle was here, and so was Guisborne. Rage deadened the pain in his shoulder. If he'd harmed her in any way, Guisborne was a dead man. In the cloister walk he found three brothers standing over the body of a monk. The man had been run through with a sword. Mercifully, he was dead. One of the monks, unarmed save with righteous anger, stepped forward to block his way.

"Where is Guisborne?" Alexander shouted.

"May you and that evil man rot in hell for what you've done."

"What *I've* done? I'm here to stop Guisborne, not help him. Where is he?"

The monk decided to believe him. "The infirmary. This way."

They gathered more dark-robed men on their way, until there was a crowd of a dozen or more, all running toward the infirmary, where they could hear Guisborne ranting. What the unarmed monks thought they'd be able to do, except get in the way, Alexander could not imagine.

Several monks rushed into the chapel, seeking safety at the altar. Close on their heels came Guisborne.

"I want that whore! Now!"

Giselle was pressed back against the stone wall, surrounded by men in scratchy black wool. She could smell their fear and wondered if their hearts pounded as hard as hers did.

"You must kill me first," Bernard said, raising his voice above the din.

The room grew very quiet.

"That will not be difficult," Guisborne growled. He advanced into the room, his bloody sword moving in a deadly arc.

"You'll need to kill me as well," the abbot said. "The lady claims the protection of this sacred place. I will give my life to see she has it."

Guisborne hesitated.

"You must kill me as well."

"And me."

"Also me."

Every monk there vowed to die for her right to sanctuary. Giselle was humbled by the foolish courage of the men. She must not allow so horrible a thing. She pushed her way toward the front of her black wall of protectors. Another voice, low and angry, stayed her.

"You must kill me as well, Guisborne. And I will not be so easy," Alexander said.

"I'm afraid you'll need to go through me, too," Geoffrey said.

She finally managed to work her way to the front of the group. Alexander and his cousin stood behind Guisborne, their swords drawn. Robyn stood with them as well.

Slowly Guisborne turned. Surely he would back down in the face of the three men standing ready to do battle. Robyn raised his bow slightly. But there was something wrong with Alexander. He was a sickly gray color, and his sword trembled in his hand, but the look on his face was deadly.

"Lay your weapon down, Guisborne," Alexander said.

"Do you think you've bested me? I'll see you rot in hell first."

"If that's what it takes to stop you."

"You won't have what is mine!" Guisborne shouted.

"What you've stolen? I'm not taking it from you, fool. You've forfeited it by your actions."

With a roar of outrage, Guisborne raised his weapon. Instead of charging Alexander, he turned and lunged toward the monks gathered around the altar. Someone grabbed Giselle and thrust her back into the phalanx of protective men. She braced herself for what was coming. It seemed time stood still and an eternity passed in the blink of an eye. The impact never came. There was a strange noise, then the sound of something metal falling to the floor. She pushed between two brothers until she could see. Guisborne lay at the foot of the altar, an arrow through his neck, his face a mask of surprise and agony as he died.

"Praise God, 'tis a miracle!"

It looked to her very like one of Robyn's arrows, but if the monks chose to think God used him as an instrument of justice, she was not one to argue the finer points of theology. Gentle hands helped her down from the altar. Alexander met her at the foot of the stairs. He gathered her into his arms and held her until the fearful trembling of her body quieted.

"You are safe, my love."

His voice was low and soft. There was promise in his words. He would keep her safe. When she moved to wrap her arm around his shoulder, he stiffened, as though in pain. She drew back. "You're hurt."

" 'Tis nothing much. It can wait. Let me take you home."

Home. Was Wolfhurst her home? She was not sure. She did know she belonged with this man. The rest she would worry about later.

She stood with Alexander's strong arm around her waist as the abbot approached them. Behind him came Bernard, a look of unearthly calm on his face.

"I've seldom seen men of such courage," Alexander said.

"They did me proud," the abbot said, his voice throbbing with emotion.

"There is no reward large enough to repay you for keeping her safe."

"We want no payment, Lord Wolfhurst."

"I must ask one final favor of you," Giselle said.

The abbot looked at her with a mixture of dread and resignation. "What?"

"Will you bury him here, near others of his family?"

"In consecrated ground?" The abbot scowled, staring at the bloody body lying in his chapel. He sighed. "Who am I to question God's mercy? I'll do as you ask."

Bernard took her hand in his. "Go in God's peace, m'lady. And remember, I am to baptize the babe you carry."

How did Bernard know? She wasn't absolutely sure herself yet. She smiled at the old priest. "Of course, Father. You will baptize all our children, that I promise."

"Why do you care where that bastard is buried?" Alexander asked.

She suddenly felt so weary she feared she would collapse. "He was my uncle."

He closed his eyes tight for a moment, then looked at her with vast sympathy. "Merciful Christ, and I thought it could not get worse."

"It is over now. Take me home, my love."

Chapter Twenty-five

The world was newly green this first day of May, and smelled sweet with the scent of apple blossoms. The villagers had erected a maypole, and long streamers of white skimmed the breezes. There would be dancing and singing and feasting all the day and well into the night. It was said a babe conceived on May Day was especially blessed. All the young folk, and some old enough to have better sense, were up before dawn to go a-Maying, gathering branches of hawthorn thick with white flowers, and bringing them home to decorate their houses. Bright yellow asphodels were gathered by the armful and set in every odd sort of container inside the small church until it looked like nodding sunshine had taken up residence there. Alexander waited at the church door, Geoffrey on one side of him, Robyn on the other. Michael and Father Bernard stood behind them, both smiling so wide one would think their faces ached.

"Are you nervous?" Geoffrey asked.

"I've never been more sure of anything in my life." It was true. Today he would take a wife, and it was the best and truest thing he'd ever done. Nervous? No. He felt alive and joyous and profoundly grateful that real happiness had stumbled into his life in the guise of a maiden more at home in the wildwood than confined within the walls of a castle. No doubt life with Giselle would not be boring.

Villagers gathered in the churchyard to witness their lord's wedding, happy for the excuse to celebrate a bride-ale. They were in an expansive mood. The weather had been mild, with gentle rain now and then, and the fields were green with young grain and beans and peas. They believed the bounty of the land was tied to the generosity and good stewardship of their lord. If he prospered, so would the fields. More than one ribald voice called supplications to be fruitful, for it was well known if the lord and his lady were fertile, the land would be as well.

"There she is." Robyn pointed toward the castle gate.

She rode the white palfrey he'd given her as a wedding gift. The women of the village trailed behind her, the children ran ahead, singing and shouting and waving branches of white or yellow or pink blossoms. They had crowned her Queen of the May with a garland of violets and lady's bells. Like a beacon, the gold gown she wore reflected sunlight and drew all eyes to her. Odin trotted beside her, a collar of flowers hanging from his neck, though he didn't seem to mind the frivolity. Of course, he never had been a dog possessed of an abundance of dignity. Alexander knew she was apprehensive about becoming Lady of Wolfhurst and so he'd suggested including the villagers in their wedding. She had picked the day, though having to wait two weeks after returning from the abbey had nearly driven him mad.

"When will you marry me?" he'd asked.

"Soon."

"How soon?"

"I am working on a gift for you."

"I need no gift but you. When?"

She had smiled. "Soon, Alexander."

The day had come and he watched as she rode down the long slope of green hill from the castle to the village. When she stopped the mare he walked over to help her down.

"When will you marry me, love?" he asked.

"Very soon."

She was more beautiful than he thought possible, with her brilliant hair streaming down her back, fired copper and red in the sun. She looked at him without shyness, with joy full on her face and love in her touch. Together they walked to the church porch and knelt. The crowd gathered closer and grew quiet. They said their vows, with the priests nodding and smiling, and when they rose to their feet they were man and wife. They followed the priests into the church to hear Mass.

Giselle whispered to him as they walked through the sweet-scented church. "I have my wedding gift for you. I'm sorry I made you wait, but I needed the extra time to be sure. I have the one thing only I can give. An heir."

He stopped and stared at her.

"Are you unhappy . . ."

He picked her up and twirled her around and around, there in the middle of the church, with all the villagers watching. He knew he was grinning like an idiot, but he could not help it.

" 'Tis good to see a wedded couple so happy," Michael said.

Bernard nodded, doing a little dance as he went to the altar.

*   *   *

The day moved past noon. Giselle sat at the head of the long table, set up beneath an oak tree, the remains of the wedding feast scattered before her. The villagers had brought gifts, simple but heartfelt. A group of boys had proudly laid a cloth-covered basket in her lap. When she pulled the cloth back she found five kittens and looked up to see that the boys, in their innocence, meant it not as a jest but as a true gift. She'd managed to thank them without laughing. Odin had pushed his nose into her lap only to be greeted by a chorus of hissing feline indignation. "You're outnumbered, old boy." He'd grunted and settled on the edge of her gold silk gown, keeping a watchful eye on the basket.

People still sang, but there was less dancing as the day wore on. Some napped, replete with food and ale. Children shrieked and chased each other, fell down, cried, recovered, went back to their play. Women gossiped and laughed. A few hearty souls still managed to put more food in their mouths and eat. Robyn was one of them, Marian beside him.

"Does he always eat like that?" Geoffrey asked.

Marian rolled her eyes and nodded. "Especially now that I'm pregnant. It gives *him* cravings."

Michael and Bernard had deserted them a while ago, but Giselle spied them now, hurrying toward the table. Bernard had something tucked up under one arm.

"Now what?" Alexander asked.

"Whatever it is, indulge him. We can leave soon."

"How soon?"

"Very soon." She'd promised to take him back to the hot spring in the forest for their wedding night. Thought of him naked, loving her, made her more eager by the moment to be gone.

"I have a gift for you," Bernard said. He sat on the bench beside her and plopped his bundle down on the table. It was a book.

She touched the plain leather binding. It really was sweet of him to give her so precious a thing, except that she could not read. "Thank you, Father."

"Eh? That's not it."

Michael stood behind Bernard and circled his finger beside his head in warning. " 'Tis the book of Aurelius's *Consolations* Bernard gave me when I took over his duties here."

Bernard was probing the book cover with his gnarled fingers. He drew his eating knife from his girdle and before anyone could stop him he sliced open the leather cover on the front of the book. From under the leather he withdrew a cloth bag and handed it to Giselle. "This belongs to you, m'lady."

She knew what was in the pouch before she opened it. With shaking hands she withdrew the letter written all those years ago by her mother, and the vellum charter with the faded ribbon and seal of a long-dead king. "Read them, please, Father."

Bernard spread the king's charter flat on the table, his old hands surprisingly sure in their task. He cleared his throat and squinted at the document. *"Dei Gratia, Henrici, Rex Angliae et Dominus Hiberniae—"*

"In English, please," Giselle said.

"Of course, silly of me, my dear." He snaked one finger quickly over the Latin words. "The preamble is greeting, King Henry declaring the charter is his will."

"Which King Henry?" Alexander asked.

"Why, the Conqueror's son. I thought you knew that, lad."

"Then 'tis older than you thought," Michael said to Alex.

"Have pity, both of you," Giselle said. "Let him read it."

Once more Bernard cleared his throat.

"I Henry, King of England, and Lord of Ireland, do hereby declare Sir Lionel de Guisborne, Lord of Guisborne Castle, having no Sons of his loins, is Granted the Privilege and Right to pass all he holds, by the Benevolence of his Sovereign King, to his daughters in Fee Simple; the same Right granted to his Descendants in Perpetuity should any generation fail of male heirs. Only in the case of no surviving children of any Generation may the Estates and Chattel of Guisborne pass to Cadet branches of Guisborne's family, a Bastard Son taking Precedent over Uncles or Nephews.

"And then of course the usual tedious ending for such charters. The king's signature and seal, and that of Sir Lionel. Signed 'The year of our Lord, 1103.' "

"I don't understand," Geoffrey said. "What has this to do with Alexander?"

"The letter will make it clear, if it contains what I believe it does," Alexander said. "Read, Father."

Giselle moved closer, until she felt Alexander's warmth the whole length of her body. He wrapped his arm around her shoulder, his gesture gentle and caring. He understood how much this letter, this one scrap left to her from her mother, meant to her. She was grateful for his nearness, knowing she did not have to explain her feelings of joy and sadness, mixed all together in a confusing swirl. She was shaking with emotion by the time Bernard picked up the parchment and broke the seal. Never before had the words written by her mother been spoken aloud.

The priest recited in a gentle tone, his voice full of remembrance and love.

"*My dearest child, my heart and all my love, my sweet Giselle. If you are reading this it is because I cannot be with you, but know this to be true, for I swear it on all I hold holy. Your father and I loved you with all our love and grieve that we will not be there to see you grow into the beautiful woman you are destined to be. It is in desperation that I pen this, and have little time left to see you safe. My cousin, Maeve, has sworn to me to keep you safe until I can send for you. If, as I fear, that day never comes, she is to take you and this letter, and the original charter granting ownership of Guisborne Castle and all its land and chattels to you as my rightful heir, to Father Bernard at Wolfhurst. He will know what to do and will be expecting you. You are your father's heir as well to Wolfhurst, but this I cannot prove. The charters have been stolen. 'Tis more than I can bear, losing you even if it be for a short time. But I fear for your life should I die now. My half brother, Guy, I do not trust. I fear he has had a hand in your father's death. God send him to hell if it be true. My only comfort, if this fever does take me from you, is that I shall be reunited with my beloved John. I am sending dear Bernard a stipend to say Masses for our souls. Trust him, my child, as I trust him with your life. May God keep you always in His hands. Be happy, my sweet, and remember me.*

Giselle,
Lady Guisborne."

"It's true, then," Alexander said. "You are heiress to Guisborne."

The others were staring at her as though she'd suddenly sprouted another head.

She tried to ignore them and placed a hand on Bernard's arm. "I do thank you for giving my parents back to me. I thought I had no family. Someday, will you tell me all you remember of them?"

"Of course, child. Come for a visit anytime. I've always need of another pair of hands in the garden."

"There is one thing that confuses me," she said.

"What is that?" Bernard asked.

"I don't remember Maeve bringing me to you. Why didn't she do that?"

"She did not feel it safe to leave you alone, nor to bring you with her to Wolfhurst. She sent a messenger."

"Who?"

Bernard pointed.

"Robyn?" She turned her attention fully on the man, who looked a bit surprised to be singled out by the priest. "You knew about this and never told me?"

"I knew very little. Maeve had me bring a message to Father, but I don't know what it was. She wrote it. In Latin. Bernard refused to read it to me, but he told me to look to your safety. When Maeve grew ill, Father Bernard was . . . ah . . . ill himself by then and back at his abbey, but I knew he'd not want you abandoned in the woods. That is when I approached Maeve, and when she brought you to us."

"I always wondered, those years I was alone with Maeve, where the sides of venison or freshly killed hares came from. You have been my loyal protector far longer than I ever realized. I don't know how to repay you."

"There is no need, I assure you. But if you insist, you can persuade that arrogant husband of yours to look the other way on occasion."

"As if I haven't already," Alexander said.

Michael laughed until tears filled his eyes.

"What is so amusing?" Geoffrey asked.

The priest wiped his eyes on his sleeve. "All these years Bernard's been telling me to search *The Consolations,* that I would find the truth hidden there. I thought he meant what Aurelius had written. I'm sorry, Giselle. Had I known they were in my possession I would have given them to you."

Giselle and Alexander left soon after. They rode quietly for a while through the sun-splashed woods. She'd lied and told him she was not yet comfortable with the little mare he'd given her, and so sat before him on his horse. The feel of his broad chest against her back made her feel safe. He nuzzled her ear and planted a kiss on her neck. She wiggled closer until he growled and told her to be still or they'd never make it as far as the secret pond.

Her thoughts turned to her parents. She could not truly know them—that had been taken from her—but the assurance that she belonged, that she had been loved by them, filled an empty place in her heart she had not known was there. Or rather, she had suspected its existence and been unwilling to probe too deeply, fearful of the pain it might cause. The grievous longing was gone, though sadness lingered. Did she have her father's eyes? Her mother's hair? Had they loved each other with the surprising, humbling love she had for Alexander, and he for her? She hoped they had. She hoped she was the fruit of such a union, as her children would be. Alexander's children. "If we have a son I want to name him John," she said. "After my father."

"And if 'tis a girl?"

"What was your mother's name?"

"Marie," he said.

"There are others we should honor by naming our children after them. There is your brother, and Julianna, and your father. His name was William?"

"Aye. And then there is Geoffrey and Elizabeth."

"And Robyn and Marian."

"We'll need a dozen children at least," he said.

"That will keep us quite busy for several years, making all those children."

"Indeed."

He pulled his horse to a halt and dismounted. She slid down into his arms.

"Why are we stopping?" she asked.

"That damned pond will need to wait."

Dear Reader:

This book presents a challenge to me different from that of my previous books. Instead of weaving the stories of historical persons with fictional characters, in *Queen of the May*, I used entirely fictional characters. While the background is historically accurate for the time and place, most of the rest is a product of my imagination. In this book I wanted to concentrate less on historical events and people, and more on the love story between two characters.

I was also intrigued by the legendary characters of Robyn Hood and Maid Marian. The stories we all grew up with, while old in our eyes because they originated in the Middle Ages, are actually fairly new additions to an older belief system. The ancient religion of the British Isles appears to have centered around an Earth Mother, as was common throughout the world in many agrarian cultures. Since humans were ultimately dependent on the earth to provide their needs, it was natural to personify Earth and all her elements and mysteries.

Robyn Hood is an amalgam of older legends, a strange transformation of the Stag King who, each spring at May, would plant his seed in Mother Earth, providing the bounty man depended on. I won't go into the phallic worship involved, except to say that the Maypole was originally much more "earthy" than we now think of it. The British tales of the Green Man, a manlike creature associated with the green earth of summer and the mysteries of the uninhabited woods, is also mixed up in Robyn Hood's history.

That there were undoubtedly men like the Robyn Hood

we are familiar with from the fairy tales of our childhood, men who escaped the hardships of feudal life by seeking refuge on the outskirts of civilization, perhaps even men who fought for justice, helping the poor at the expense of the rich, is where the medieval tales are added on to the older beliefs. Since there apparently was no one man known as Robyn Hood, I felt free to make him what I wanted. Maid Marian, by the way, is the medieval embodiment of the Earth Mother. Together, Robyn and Marian travel through the ages, potent symbols of a sexual love that gives life and bounty, and is a cause for celebration.

I've thrown my characters, Giselle and Alexander, into this mix of legend and imagination. The worlds they know are vastly different, but once love changes their hearts they begin to see that their differences are insignificant. In a story as ancient as life, a man and a woman discover the transforming power of love. I hope you have enjoyed the love story of Alexander and Giselle.

My next book, *Lady of Rosmar*, will be published by Zebra in March 1998.

Denée Cody lives in Colorado with her husband and cats, who insist upon sleeping in her lap and on her computer while she works (the cats, not the husband). She is a member of Mensa, which means she almost always knows when she's just done something dumb.

Denée Cody
P.O. Box 261066
Highlands Ranch, CO
80163-1066

or

DeneeMCody@aol.com

ROMANCE FROM FERN MICHAELS

DEAR EMILY   (0-8217-4952-8, $5.99)

WISH LIST   (0-8217-5228-6, $6.99)

AND IN HARDCOVER:

VEGAS RICH   (1-57566-057-1, $25.00)

DANGEROUS GAMES   (0-7860-0270-0, $4.99)
by Amanda Scott

When Nicholas Barrington, eldest son of the Earl of Ul-
combe, first met Melissa Seacort, the desperation he
sensed beneath her well-bred beauty haunted him. He
didn't realize how desperate Melissa really was . . . until
he found her again at a Newmarket gambling club—being auctioned off by her father to the highest bidder. So,
Nick bought himself a wife. With a villain hot on their
heels, and a fortune and their lives at stake, they would
gamble everything on the most dangerous game of all:
love.

A TOUCH OF PARADISE   (0-7860-0271-9, $4.99)
by Alexa Smart

As a confidence man and scam runner in 1880s America,
Malcolm Northrup has amassed a fortune. Now, posing
as the eminent Sir John Abbot—scholar, and possible
discoverer of the lost continent of Atlantis—he's taking
his act on the road with a lecture tour, seeking funds for
a scientific experiment he has no intention of making.
But scholar Halia Davenport is determined to accompany
Malcolm on his "expedition" . . . even if she must kidnap
him!

ROMANCE FROM JO BEVERLY

DANGEROUS JOY   (0-8217-5129-8, $5.99)

FORBIDDEN   (0-8217-4488-7, $4.99)

THE SHATTERED ROSE   (0-8217-5310-X, $5.99)

TEMPTING FORTUNE   (0-8217-4858-0, $4.99)